ISAAC ASIMOV'S

ROBOT CITY

BOOK FIVE

REFUGE

ROB CHILSON

CITIES

by ISAAC ASIMOV

Through eighty percent of the history of *Homo sapiens*, all human beings were hunters and gatherers. Of necessity, they were wanderers, for to stay in one place would mean gathering all there was of vegetable food and driving away all there was of animal food—and starvation would follow.

The only habitations such wanderers (or "nomads") could have would have to be either parts of the environment, such as caves, or light and movable artifacts, such as tents.

Agriculture, however, came into being some ten thousand years ago and that introduced a great change.

Farms, unlike human beings and animals, are not mobile. The need to take care of farms and agricultural produce nailed the farmers to the ground. The more they grew dependent upon the harvest to maintain their swollen numbers (too great for most to survive if they had to return to hunting and gathering), the more hopelessly immobile they became. They could not run away, except for brief intervals, from wild animals, and they could not run away at all from nomadic raiders who wished to help themselves to the co-pious foodstores that they had not worked for.

It followed that farmers had to fight off their enemies; they had no choice. They had to band together and build their houses in a huddle, for in unity there was strength. Forethought or, failing that, bitter experience, caused them to build the huddle of houses on an elevation where there was a natural water supply, and to lay in foodstores and then build a wall about the whole. Thus were built the first cities.

Once farmers learned to protect themselves and their farms, and became reasonably secure, they found they could produce more food than they required for their own needs. Some of the city-dwellers, therefore, could do work of other types and exchange their products for some of the excess food produced by the farmers. The cities became the homes of artisans, merchants, administrators, priests, and so on. Human existence came to transcend the bare search for food, clothing, and shelter. In short, civilization became possible and the very word "civilization" is from the Latin for "city-dweller."

Each city was developed into a political unit, with some sort of ruler, or decision-maker, for this was required if de-fense of homes and farms was to be made efficient and successful. The necessity of being prepared for battle against nomads led to the development of soldiers and weapons which, during peaceful periods, could be used to police and control the city population itself. Thus, there developed the "city-state."

As population continued to grow, each city-state tried to extend the food-growing area under its control. Inevi-tably, neighboring city-states would collide and there would be disputes, which became armed wars.

The tendency would be for one city-state to grow at the expense of others, with the result that an "empire" would be established. Such large units tended to be more effective than smaller ones, for reasons that are easy to explain.

Consider that agriculture requires fresh water, and that the surest supply of that is to be found in a sizable river. For that reason, early farming communities were built along the shores of rivers such as the Nile, the Euphrates, the Indus, and the Hwang-Ho. (The rivers also served as easy avenues for commerce, transportation, and communication.)

Rivers, however, took work. Dikes had to be built along the shores to confine the river and prevent ruin through floods. Irrigation ditches had to be built to bring a controlled supply of water directly to the farms. To dike a river and to maintain a system of irrigation requires cooperation not only of individuals within a given city-state, but among the city-states themselves. If one city-state allowed its own system to deteriorate, the flood that might follow would disastrously affect all other city-states downstream. An empire that controls many city-states can, more effectively, enforce the necessary cooperation and maintain a general prosperity.

An empire, however, usually means the domination of many people by one conquering group, and resentment builds up, and struggles for "liberty" break out. Eventually, under weak rulers, an empire is therefore likely to break up.

World history seems to demonstrate an oscillation between empires (often prosperous, but despotic), and decentralized political units (often producing a high culture, but quarrelsome and militarily weak).

On the whole, though, the tendency has been in the direction not only of large units, but of larger and larger ones, as advancing technology made transportation and communication easier and more efficient, and as overall population increase heightened the perceived value of security and prosperity over liberty and squabbling.

As population grew, cities grew larger and more populous, too. Memphis—Thebes—Nineveh—Babylon—and then, eventually, Rome, which at its peak in the second century A.D. may have been the first city to have a population of one million.

The multi-million city became a feature of the modern world after the Industrial Revolution introduced enormous advances in transportation and communication. The nineteenth century saw cities of four million people and the early twentieth century saw cities of six and seven million people.

All through the last ten thousand years, in other words, the world has become more and more urbanized, and after World War II, the process became a runaway cancer. In the last forty years, the world population has doubled and the population of the developing countries, where the birth rate remained high, has considerably more than doubled. We now have cities, like Mexico City, São Paulo, Calcutta, with populations climbing toward the twenty million mark and threatening to go higher still. Such cities are becoming squalid expanses of shantytowns, endlessly polluted, without adequate sanitation, and with the very technological factors that encourage the growth beginning to break down.

Where do we go from here? Anywhere other than decay, breakdown and dissolution?

I tackled the problem of the future city in my novel *The Caves of Steel*, which first appeared as a three-part serial in *Galaxy Science Fiction* in 1953. I was influenced in my thinking by the fact that I happen to be a claustrophile. I feel comfortable in crowded and enclosed environments.

Thus, I enjoy living in the center of Manhattan. I move about its crowded canyons with ease and with no sensation of discomfort. I like to work in a room with the blinds pulled down, and at a desk that faces a blank wall, so that I increase my feeling of enclosure.

Naturally, then, I pictured my future New York as a kind of much more extreme version than the present New York. Some people marveled at my imagination.

"How could you think up such a nightmare existence as that in *The Caves of Steel*?"

To which I would reply in puzzled surprise, "What nightmare existence?"

I had added one novelty, to be sure. I had the entire huge city of the future built underground.

Perhaps that was what made it seem a nightmare existence, but there are advantages to underground life, if you stop to think of it.

First, weather would no longer be important, since it is primarily a phenomenon of the atmosphere. Rain, snow, and fog would not trouble the underground world. Even temperature variations are limited to the open surface and would not exist underground. Whether day or night, summer or winter, temperatures in the underground city would remain equable and nearly constant. In place of spending energy on heating and cooling, you would have to spend energy on ventilation, to be sure, but I think that this would involve a large net saving. Electrified transportation would be required to avoid the pollution of the internal-combustion engine, but then walking (considering the certainty of good weather) would become much more attractive and that, too, would not only save energy, but would promote better health.

The only adverse environmental conditions that would

affect the underground world would be volcanoes, earthquakes, and meteoric impacts. However, we know where volcanoes exist and where earthquakes are common and might avoid those areas. And perhaps we will have a space patrol to destroy any meteoric objects likely to bring them uncomfortably close.

Second, local time would no longer be important. On the surface, the tyranny of day and night cannot be avoided, and when it is morning in one place, it is noon in another, evening in still another and midnight in yet another. The rhythm of human life is therefore out of phase. Underground, where artificial light will determine the day, we can if we wish make a uniform time the planet over. This would certainly simplify global cooperation and would eliminate jet lag. (If a global day and global night turn out to have serious deficiencies, any other system can be set up. The point is it will be *our* system and not one forced on us by the accident of Earth's rotation.)

Third, the ecological structure could be stabilized. Right now, with humanity on the planetary surface, we encumber the Earth. Our enormous numbers take up room, as do all the structures we build to house ourselves and our machines, to make possible our transportation and communication, to offer ourselves rest and recreation. All these things distort the wild, depriving many species of plants and animals of their natural habitat—and sometimes, involuntarily, favoring a few, such as rats and roaches.

If humanity and its structures are removed below ground—well below the level of the natural world of the burrowing animals—Man would still occupy the surface with his farms, his forestry, his observation towers, his air terminals and so on, but the extent of that occupation would be enormously decreased. Indeed, as one imagines the underground world becoming increasingly elaborate, one can visualize much of the food supply eventually deriving from soilless crops grown in artificially illuminated areas underground. The Earth's surface might be increasingly turned over to park and to wilderness, maintained at ecological stability.

Nor would we be depriving ourselves of nature. Indeed, it would be closer. It might seem that to withdraw underground is to withdraw from the natural world, but would that be so? Would the withdrawal be more complete than it is now, when so many people work in city buildings that are often windowless and artificially conditioned? Even where there are windows, what is the prospect one views (if one bothers to), but sun, sky, and buildings to the horizon—plus some limited greenery?

And to get away from the city now? To reach the real countryside? One must travel horizontally for miles and miles, first across city pavements and then across suburban sprawls. And the countryside we would be viewing would be steadily retreating and steadily undergoing damage.

In the underground world, we might have areas of greenery, too, even parks—and tropical growth in greenhouses. But we don't have to depend on these makeshift attempts, comforting though they may be to many. We need only go straight up, a mere couple of hundred yards above the level of "Main Street, Underground" and—there you are.

The surface you would visit would be nature—perhaps tamer than it might be, but relatively unspoiled. The surface would have to be protected from too frequent, or too intense, or too careless visiting, but however carefully restricted the upward trips might be the chances are that the dwellers in the underground world would see more of the natural world, under ecologically sounder conditions, than dwellers of surface cities do today.

I am interested to see, by the way, that the notion of underground living has begun to seem more realistic in the decades since I wrote *The Caves of Steel*. For instance, many cities in the more northerly latitudes (where cold weather, ice, and snow inhibit shopping by making it unpleasant) are building underground shopping malls—more and more elaborate, more and more self-contained, more and more like my own imagined world.

However, my imagination is not the only one the world possesses. Here we have *Refuge*, by Rob Chilson, in which my underground city of the future is explored by another science-fiction writer skilled in his craft, who has taken my underground cities as the starting point for his own.

CHAPTER 1

KAPPA WHALE

The stars gave no light. Derec crawled slowly along the ship's hull, peering intently through his helmet at the silvery metal. The ship was below him, or beside him, depending entirely on how one looked at it. He preferred to think of it as "beside"—he felt less as if he might fall that way.

To his left, to his right, "above" and "below" him, was nothing. But space was nothing new to Derec, whose memories began only a few months ago in a space capsule—a lifepod, in fact. At the moment he had no time for memories of the pod, of the ice asteroid, or of capture by the nonhuman pirate Aranimas. He was concentrating on swimming.

"I'm at the strut," he announced.

"Good," said Ariel, her voice booming in his helmet.

Derec hadn't time to turn his radio down, nor did he wish to let go just yet. His crawl along the hull, helped by the electromagnets in knees and palms, had been slow, but inexorable. When he seized the strut, his hand stopped but his body continued on past, like a swimmer carried by a wave. A wave of inertia.

Gripping the strut, he found himself slowly swinging around it like a flag, facing back the way he'd come. He had realized immediately that he shouldn't have grabbed the strut, but didn't compound his error by trying to undo it. He let the swing take him, absorbed his momentum with his arm—it creaked painfully—and came to a stop.

A robot, advancing in its tracks, arrested itself on the other side of the strut in the proper way: a hand braced against it, the arm soaking up the momentum like a spring. Being a robot, he had no fear of sprained wrists, the most common injuries in free-fall.

The robot, Mandelbrot, paused courteously while Derec resolved his entanglement with the strut. Derec gripped it with both hands and bent one elbow while keeping the other straight. His body revolved slowly around the bent arm until he had reversed himself. Placing his foot against the strut, he tippy-toed away from it, letting go, uncoiling, and reaching out for the hull.

For a moment Derec was in free, dreamy flight, not touching the ship; then his palms touched down, the magnets clicking against it as he turned on crawlpower. He slid forward on hands and forearms while his inertia wave was absorbed by the "beach" of the ship's hull. His chest and belly and finally his knees touched down painfully, to slide scraping along.

"Frost!" said Ariel. "What are you doing, sawing the hull in half?"

Derec didn't reply. Not letting all his momentum be absorbed, he came quickly to hands and knees, reaching and pulling at the hull. The magnets were computer controlled and clicked on and off alternately in the crawl pattern.

In a few seconds he braked and all the magnets went on. He skittered slowly to a stop. Mandelbrot joined him in a similar fashion and looked at the hull, then moved aside.

"Right, we're at the hatch," said Derec. "It doesn't look like we'll need any tools to get in; just a matter of turning inset screws."

There were two slits in the hull, each in a small circle. The circles were at one edge of a square outline—the hatch. Derec stuck two fingers in one of the slits, Mandelbrot copying his motion at the other side, and they twisted the circles clockwise. There was a *pop*, and the hatch rode free.

"Got it open," Derec said.

That was a little premature. He would have to stand up on the hull to raise the hatch, or else move around. But before he could make up his mind, Mandelbrot reinserted his fingers into one of the slits and pulled. The hatch came free easily. Mandelbrot bent his arm like a rope, heaving the hatch up over his head, put up his other arm, and the hatch stood out from the hull.

"Can't see a frosted thing," muttered Derec. His helmet light bounced off the shiny underside of the hatch and again off the huddled machinery exposed, but without air to scatter the light, what he saw was a collection of parallel and crossing lines of light against velvet blackness. After a moment, however, he made out a handle. These things weren't meant only for doctorates in mechanical engineering to understand, after all. There was a release in the handle.

Squeezing the release, Derec pulled up on the handle. Nothing happened. There wasn't room on the handle for Mandelbrot to help him. Gripping it tightly, Derec stood on the hull and put his back into it. It came free with a creaky vibration he felt all the way up through the soles of his feet, an odd sort of hearing.

"Trouble?" Ariel asked, concern in her voice. Perhaps she had heard his breathing and the gasp when it broke free.

"Stuck, but I got it loose. I think a little ice had frozen around it."

With the help of the robot, who had released the hatch and now stood upright on the hull, Derec pulled out a mass of cunningly nested pipes all connected together, rather like unfolding a sofa-bed. Mandelbrot reached down and pulled a heavy cord, and a mass of thick, silvery plastic unfolded. As soon as the plastic balloon was sufficiently unfolded not to suffer damage, Derec peered down at its root.

He had to move around to the side, but there was the valve, looking uncommonly like a garden faucet on far-off Aurora. For a moment Derec was shaken by a perfect memory of a faucet in some dewy garden on the Planet of the Dawn. He'd had indications before this that he was from that greatest of Spacer planets, but very few specific memories leaked through his amnesia, fewer still were as sharp as this one.

After a few moments, though, he realized he was not going to remember what or where that garden was. All he knew about it was that it was a pleasant memory. He had *liked* that garden. Now all he had of it was the memory of its faucet.

It isn't wise to shrug in free-fall, so Derec reached carefully inside the hatch and, bracing himself, twisted the faucet. There was a hiss he heard through his fingers and the air in the arm of his suit, as steam under low pressure rushed into the balloon. In a moment, Mandelbrot was out of sight behind it.

That wonderful flexible arm came into view, Mandelbrot twisted the return valve, and in a moment there was the faint murmur of a small pump. Water, too, was moving through the pipes by now.

The radiator and vacuum distillation sections of the water-purification-and-cooling system was in operation. They had settled down for a long stay in space.

Should have done this days ago, Derec thought but didn't say aloud. An optimist, he had hoped a ship would have come by before now. Ariel, who tended to be pessimistic, had doubted.

"I'm coming back by way of the sun side," he said. "The light's better."

Ariel didn't answer. A punch on a button made his safety line release itself and reel in from the forward airlock. He reattached it to a ring near the hatch; the robot mimicked his movements. Feeling better about standing upright on the hull, Derec strode slowly and carefully around the rather narrow cylinder until the tiny red lamp of their current "sun" came into view, then on around until it was overhead.

A class *M* dwarf, the red star was no doubt very old. It was certainly very small and it had no real planets. Its biggest daughter was an ancient lump of rock barely four hundred kilometers in diameter, its next biggest less than half that in size. Most of its daughters were fragments that ranged from respectable mountains down to fists—and there weren't many of any size. A star that old was formed at a time when the nebulas in the galaxy had only begun to be enriched with heavy elements. This was not a metalliferous star; no prospector had ever bothered to check out those lumps of rock for anything of value; none ever would.

Dim and worthless though it was, the star lit the way . . . somewhat. Under its light, the silvery hull looked like burnished copper—a pleasing sight. Shadows still were sharp-edged, his own shadow an odd-shaped, moving hole, it seemed, in the hull, a hole into some strange and other-dimensional universe.

Mandelbrot followed him gracefully.

"Detection alert," said Ariel, sounding bored. "Rock coming our way. Looks like it might be about a mouthful, if you were hungry for rocks."

"I'm not," said Derec, but it made him think of baked potatoes. He *was* getting hungry.

Had there been any danger, Ariel would have said so; Derec assumed that the rock would miss them by a wide margin. They were well out from the star, sparsely populated though its space was with junk. This was only the second thing they'd detected in two days, and the first was merely a grain of sand. Probably both objects were "dirty ice"—the stuff of comets.

Danger or no, Mandelbrot moved closer to him, scan-ning the sky without pausing. Derec didn't notice, and didn't bother to look for the rock. The sun drew his eye instead. At this distance, dim as it was and weak in ultraviolet light, it could be looked at directly.

Pitiful excuse though it was for a star, poor as its family was, still it made an island of light in a vast sea of darkness where stars hard and unwinking as diamonds cut at him with their stares. He thought of the space around the red star as a room, a warmly lit room in an immensity of cold and darkness.

After the circumscribed life of Robot City, he felt free. *Space*, Derec thought, *is mankind's natural home.*

There came a bark from inside the vessel, and he was reminded with a sudden chill that others than men used space. One of those others was within this ship: Wolruf, the doglike alien with whom he'd made alliance on Aranimas's ship. She had escaped first from Aranimas with him, then from the hospital station, then from Robot City.

Things had been worse for them in the past, he thought. If they had to wait here for a week or two . . .

Then he thought: *I'm worried about Ariel, though.*

He moved forward, found the airlock, and crowded in to make room for the bulky robot.

Frost condensed on his armor as soon as he entered the ship, but Derec ignored that, knowing that it wasn't too cold to touch yet; they'd only been out for minutes. It seemed even more cramped inside after having been out.

"We should spend more time outside," he said. "It's not exactly fresh air, but at least there's a feeling of freedom."

Ariel looked momentarily interested, then shrugged. "I'm all right."

Mandelbrot looked keenly at her, pausing in his ridiculous motion of scraping frost off his eyes, but said nothing. He had said nothing to Derec yet, but Derec knew that he was worried, too. Ariel had a serious disease. A fatal disease, she had said. It had caused her occasional pain before this, stabbing muscular aches, and she frequently seemed feverish and headachey and generally out of it; sometimes she even had hallucinations. But this prolonged gloom was new, and worrisome.

"So there's water for showerr, yess?" said Wolruf. She was the size of a large dog and not infrequently went on all fours, but usually walked upright, for her front paws were clumsy-seeming hands, ill-shaped by human standards but clever with tools.

"Give it half an hour," Derec said. The furry alien needed showers daily in a ship where there was no escape from each other.

"Derec, shall I prepare food?" Mandelbrot asked. "It approaches the usual hour for your meals."

Ariel roused herself, said, "I'll do that, Mandelbrot. What do you want, Derec, Wolruf?"

There were no potatoes ready. Of course he did not expect to find real food in a spaceship, and it took time for the synthesizer to prepare a specialty item. "Stew would be fine. Keep varying the mix and it'll be a long time before I get bored with it."

"I eat same as 'ou," Wolruf said.

"Borscht today," said Ariel with a smile that seemed natural. "We've got lots of tomato sauce, and besides, I like it."

"It's wonderful to have a commercial synthesizer and a large stock of basics," Derec said, cheering at her cheer. "Remember our experiments in Robot City?"

She made a face. "Remember? I'm trying to forget."

Dr. Avery's ship was well-equipped. Indeed, they could live indefinitely out here—at least until the micropile gave out, or their air and water leaked away. The water purifier used yeast and algae to reclaim sewage, the plants then being stored as basic organic matter for the synthesizer.

Derec, having removed the suit with motions suitable to a contortionist, stowed it away in its clips beside the airlock. Mandelbrot immediately went to it and checked it over. Reaching to the ceiling of the cabin, Derec touched off, tippy-toed off the floor, and back off the ceiling. Called "brachiating," it was the most efficient mode of movement within a cabin in free-fall.

He turned on the receiver. It was tuned to BEACON—*local*. A calm, feminine-sounding robotic voice spoke. "Beacon Kappa Whale Arcadia. Report, please. Beacon Kappa Whale Arcadia. Report, please." Turning off the sound, Derec glumly checked the indicators. Kappa Whale was coming in on the electromagnetic band, both laser and microwave. They were getting minimal detection on the hyperwave, however.

"I don't understand it," he muttered. Ariel glanced at him over her shoulder as she floated before the cooking equipment.

Wolruf joined him. "Wass broken by Doctorr Avery, do 'ou think?"

"Sabotage? I don't know. It was picking up Kappa Whale beautifully when we took off from Robot City."

They had left the planet of robots hurriedly in this stolen ship. Dr. Avery, who had created the robots that went on to build Robot City, had been pursuing them for reasons none of them understood. Though Derec suspected that Ariel knew more about the enigmatic and less-than-sane doctor than she had said.

Once off the planet and safe from Dr. Avery, they discovered that either there were no astrogation charts in the ship, or they were well concealed in its computer. Though positronic, that was not a full-fledged positronic brain. Had it been, they could have convinced it that without the charts they would die in space. Under the First Law of Robotics, it would be unable to withhold the charts, regardless of the orders it had been given.

The First Law of Robotics states: A robot may not knowingly harm a human being, or knowingly allow a human being to come to harm.

Orders would have come merely under the Second Law, which is: A robot must obey the orders of a human being, except where this would conflict with the First Law.

But the computer was merely a more complicated calculator, incapable of the simplest robotic thought. Robotic ships with positronic brains had been tried, and had all failed, because all full-sized positronic brains were designed with the Three Laws built into them. Necessarily, they were too intent on preventing possible harm to their occupants. Since space travel is inherently unsafe, they had a tendency to go mad or to refuse to take off.

"I feel like hitting the damn computer, or kicking it," he said.

Wolruf grinned her rather frightening grin. "Ho! 'Ou think, like Jeff Leong, all machines should have place to kick?"

"Or some way to jar information loose. I'm convinced there must be charts in there somewhere—"

It was a reasonable guess. Nobody could remember all the miles of numbers that was a star chart. Charts were rarely printed out in whole, though for convenience in calculation, some sections might be. This little ship didn't have a printer. All it had—they presumed—was a recording in its memory.

But they couldn't find it.

Even that wouldn't have been too serious if the hyperwave hadn't gone out on them. Lacking charts, in orbit about Robot City, they had swept space with the hyperwave and picked up Kappa Whale Arcadia quite well. The fix was good enough to Jump toward, and they had done that. Logically, they should then have been able to pick up other beacons and hop, skip, and jump their way to anywhere in inhabited space: the fifty Spacer worlds, or the Settler worlds that Earth had recently begun to occupy.

"We're somewhere within telescopic distance of Arcadia," murmured Derec. That was a minor and distant Spacer world. But they had no idea on which side of it lay the constellation of the Whale. They knew only that this—

Kappa—was the ninth-brightest star in that constellation, and that there was only one fainter, Lambda Whale. Constellations, by interstellar agreement, had, for astrogational purposes, no more than ten stars.

"Sooner or laterr a ship will come," Wolruf said reassuringly.

Sooner or later. Derec grunted.

He didn't need to have the argument repeated; it had been mostly his. When they found that, after the Jump, the hyperwave would only pick up the nearest beacon, Derec had suggested that they lie low until a ship came by, and request a copy of the astrogational charts from it. To beam a copy over would take the ship only a few minutes, and be no trouble at all.

Sooner or later.

"Soup's on, or stew in this case," Ariel said. The oven opened with an exhalation of savory steam. "We still have some of your crusty bread, Derec. I reheated it. But we'll want more later."

"It smells good," Derec said honestly. Wolruf, with even greater honesty, licked her chops and grinned. Derec had overcome his irritation at Ariel's invasion of the male preserve of the chief of cuisine, and had admitted to her that she was a better chef than he. (Common *cooking* was robot work, which no human admitted to doing.)

They ate in silence for a short while. The stew was served in covered bowls, but it clung to the inner surfaces. Manipulating their spoons carefully, they were able to eat without flinging food all over the ship. At first even Ariel's appetite was good, but she quickly lost interest.

"Do you think a ship will ever come by here?" she asked finally, her gaze, and apparently her thought, a long way away.

"Of course," said Derec quickly. "I admit I was too optimistic. I suspect we're well out on the edge of inhabited space; this lane is not too well traveled. But *eventually*. . . ."

"Eventually . . ." she said, almost dreamily. She seemed, often now, in a drifting, abstracted state.

"Eventually," Derec repeated weakly.

He was too honest to try to argue her into belief. Ships didn't *fly* from star to star like an aircraft. They Jumped, with massive thrusts of their hyperatomic motors, going in a direction that was at right angles to time and all three spatial dimensions simultaneously. Since they went no-distance, it naturally took no-time to Jump. Therefore there were no lanes of star travel.

For safety reasons, ships Jumped from star to star; if one was stranded for any reason, rescuers had only to chart the route and check every star along it. And since not every star had inhabited planets, all along these well-traveled lanes (as they were called) were the beacon stars. A ship Jumping into this beacon system was supposed to verify that it had indeed arrived at Kappa Whale, beam its ship's log to the beacon's recorders, and depart. Periodically, patrol ships copied those records to assure that nothing untoward had happened.

But days had passed and no ships had appeared. Of course a ship appearing on the other side of Kappa Whale would not be detected by them on the electromagnetic band until it had Jumped out. The hyperwave radio, though, was functioning well enough to detect a ship reporting to the beacon anywhere in this stellar system. Derec and Wolruf agreed on that.

So: eventually they would be found and rescued.

Wolruf finished her meal by opening her bowl and licking it clean efficiently. "I wass thinking," she said. "Maybe

Jump-wave shock shifted things in 'ou'rr hyperwave antenna."

"Shifted the elements?" Derec nodded uncertainly. He had no idea where he had been educated, but he had a good general technical background with a strong specialty in robotics—not unusual for a Spacer youth, as he assumed himself to be. But hyperwave technology was a whole other and, if anything, even more difficult school of knowledge.

"Do 'ou have—'ou know—things to measure them with?"

Derec had seen a toolbox on the ship's schematic that he had accessed before going out to set up the recycling system. "There might be."

There was. A few minutes later, with Ariel listless at the detectors and Wolruf at the communicator, Derec carefully strode forward outside, followed by Mandelbrot.

The hyperwave antenna could have been put in any part of the ship, since the hyperatomo didn't kowtow to the laws of space-time, but it would have had to have been well shielded lest its backlash in the small ship damage the instruments, or even the crew. So in these Star Seeker models it was in a blister on the bow, as far from everything as possible.

The antenna looked like a series of odd-shaped chunks of metal and coils of wire, and the testing gear simply shot current through each element in turn. The readouts were within normal range, as nearly as he could tell from the manual he had accessed before coming out.

"I don't get it," Derec complained, thinking of the classical definition of Hell: the place where all the instruments test out to be perfect, but none of them work. "How can I fix it if it isn't broken?"

"I think," said Wolruf slowly, "that Dr. Avery hass retuned the antenna."

"Retuned?" Derec had never heard of such a thing, but knew little about the subject. "I thought all Spacer talk was in the same range. Is he trying to pick up—Settlers? Or what?"

"Maybe Aranimass."

Maybe, Derec thought, chilled. *Maybe, indeed.* That long-armed pirate was definitely interested in Dr. Avery's doings, though he might not know who or what Dr. Avery was.

Derec stood, looking around the warm room generated by Kappa Whale, and shivered. For the first time the thought came to him: *What if the first ship that showed up was Aranimas's? He must be systematically searching the beacon stars—*

A touch on his arm nearly made Derec jump off the hull.

CHAPTER 2

PERIHELION

The burnished, enigmatic face of Mandelbrot approached his. The robot gripped him with his normal left arm. His Avery-construct right arm bent impossibly, reached around Derec and switched off his communicator.

Derec had had nightmares about that arm. It was a piece of scrap from an Avery robot, which Aranimas had had picked up from the ice asteroid where Derec had first awakened. "Build me a robot," the alien had said. Derec had put pieces together to build the robot he called Alpha. It wasn't a good job, but it worked.

Then, weeks later, the crudely attached right arm seated itself firmly and made a few modifications in Alpha's brain: Alpha informed them that he was now known as Mandelbrot. Derec had observed the fine structure of the arm: a series of tiny chips, or scales, that gripped each other and could therefore mold the arm to any shape that might be desired.

Each unit was a sort of robotic cell; together, they were a brain. And having integrated themselves, they had—to a degree—taken over Alpha. Derec's nightmare was that the cells were *eating* the robot out from the inside, that his interior was one solid mass of them, and he was about to become something—horrifying.

Impossible; the cells couldn't eat. Also, all the brains were robotic, Mandelbrot's normal positronic brain and the units in the cells. The Three Laws compelled them all. But dreams are not logical.

At the moment, the worst nightmare had come true, until Mandelbrot put his head against Derec's helmet. It would have looked to an observer as if the robot were kissing his cheek: his microphone touched Derec's helmet and Mandelbrot spoke.

"Derec, I am worried about Ariel."

They had been careful to conceal from Mandelbrot the worst of Ariel's condition. The robot knew only that she was sick, not that the disease was usually fatal. The effect on his positronic brain was more than they cared to risk; the First Law left no loophole for incurable diseases.

"Ariel is bored, as well as ill," Derec said.

He looked away uneasily from the robot's expressionless but intense face. The stars beckoned, promising and threatening; somewhere out there, perhaps, he might recover his memory. He remembered Jeff Leong, who had crashed on Robot City after an accident while on his way to college. In a few years, Derec would have been thinking about college, if this fantastic thing hadn't happened to him.

"Ariel is very sick," said Mandelbrot. "Her eating pattern has altered markedly. She suffers from fever most of the time. Her attention span is abnormally low, she is sensitive to light, she moves about only with effort—"

"All right," said Derec, feeling that he would ossify before the robot finished its catalog if he didn't interrupt.

"It's true that Ariel is ill. But I am not worried about her."

That wasn't true, especially now that it had been brought out into the open.

"You should worry. I fear for her safety if something is not done for her."

"What do you suggest we do?"

"You may have to use the Key to Perihelion."

After scouring Robot City for weeks for a Key to Perihelion, the mysterious device that would transport them instantly off the planet, they had managed to steal Dr. Avery's ship when he had come to investigate their "interference." On the ship they had found the Key, but Derec's investigation of Dr. Avery's office had shown him where the Key would probably take him.

Derec said, "That would take us back to Robot City— with no way of escape and Dr. Avery after us. Surely that's less safe than this mild illness."

Mandelbrot was silent for a moment. Then he said, "That is true. I hope you are right and that this is a mild illness. But she has suffered many of these symptoms for many days now. Mild illnesses usually subside within this time."

The robot fell silent but did not move away.

" 'Ou might as well come back in," said Wolruf, startling Derec. "I do not think we can find the problem out therre. I wish I knew more about dense energy fieldss. . . ."

Derec turned, and at his first motion the robot released him, first turning his communicator back on. The motion was as much an indicator of Derec's will as a command, and the Second Law of Robotics forced the robot to comply with his desire.

"Right, I'm coming back," Derec said, as if there had been no hiatus in their communications.

He returned reluctantly. There was free-fall within the

cabin—and three times as much space as there had been under acceleration—but there were decks and bulkheads and overheads. Out here he was in his element. It was like floating in warm salt water. Even the cumbersome suit didn't detract from the feeling of freedom he got from letting his gaze rove out and on out, from star to ever-more-distant star. All of them waiting, just beyond this red-lit room.

Stars beyond stars, with their waiting worlds, which now only the Earth Settlers were opening up. And beyond, other intelligent races, other adventures. . . . A member of one of those races waited now in the ship. Derec had again a moment of intense wonder that he of all people should be among the first to meet aliens. Most of those who had met the pirate Aranimas hadn't survived. . . .

Who knew what other beings awaited them among all those bright stars? He wondered why the Spacers had sat for so many centuries on their fifty worlds, too satisfied to go looking for adventure. The way he felt now, it was impossible to believe.

Derec had an impulse to jump and go tumbling head under heels across the sky, but he knew Ariel would think it silly with his safety line and dangerous without. *Right on both counts*, he thought ruefully. *Frost, why can't I be a little kid for once? I can't remember ever having been one; it's like I've been cheated out of all that kiddish fun. . . .*

There was a warm, pleasant smell in the air of the ship when they reentered. "I made toast," said Ariel emptily.

She had toasted the last of the crusty bread, but hadn't buttered it. It was now nearly cold. Derec pretended not to notice, merely nodded and thanked her, trying to sound pleased. Popping the slices into the oven, he reheated them, and punched up his sequence for bread on the synthesizer—

three loaves. When the toast was warmed, he buttered it and shared it with Wolruf. The caninoid, like a true dog, was always ready to eat, if only a bite or two.

Ariel wasn't hungry.

"I think Doctorr Avery hass retuned the hyperwave antenna by changing the densities of the force-fieldss in the core elementss," Wolruf said, exhaling crumbs. "Dense force-fieldss arre the only things that can stop hyperatomos. But why change it, if not to detect something?"

Derec nodded uncertainly. A dense force-field was one that permeated some object; a magnet with a keeper across its poles was the classic example. Altering the density of the atomic-level fields in the core elements of the antenna would change the "acceptance" of the core.

"If not to detect something, like, say, Aranimas's ship or transmissions?" he asked. "It's a consideration. It's not unlikely that they have crossed paths, as Dr. Avery has Keys to Perihelion and Aranimas wants them."

It might well be reassuring, then, that the hyperwave wasn't detecting anything. It might mean that Aranimas wasn't operating anywhere around here.

"Ariel, you seem sleepy," said Mandelbrot. "It approaches your usual bedtime. Perhaps you should go to bed."

"Yes, good idea," said Ariel vaguely. She continued to sit and stare vacantly for another fifteen minutes before sighing deeply and getting slowly "up".

When she had gone to the one private cabin the little ship boasted, Wolruf turned fiercely on Derec.

"She iss sick! 'Ou must do something, Derec! The robot iss worried. I am worried."

Mandelbrot had accompanied Ariel into the cabin. Derec lowered his voice, nevertheless. "You're right. Don't let

Mandelbrot know how far advanced her condition is; it might destroy his brain."

Wolruf caught his breath. "She will die? Iss that what you mean?"

Derec nodded, haggard. "She told me her disease is usually fatal. I-I'd been hoping that it wouldn't be. But since we've been sitting here, doing nothing. . . ."

"I think some iss boredom. But mosst is sickness!"

Derec nodded. The cabin door opened and Mandelbrot emerged, closed it gently, and moved purposefully toward them, fingers against the overhead, toes against the deck.

"Ariel must have medical attention," he said bluntly when he was close, speaking as circumspectly as Derec and Wolruf had done. "The First Law demands it. I fear for her life if this trend continues, Derec."

They looked at him and he saw it coming.

"You must use the Key to Perihelion."

Wolruf nodded her agreement.

Derec felt sick at the thought of returning to Robot City, even aside from the thought of Dr. Avery. "That would leave you here with no spacesuit and only Mandelbrot able to go outside—"

"Iss no matter. 'Ou musst not rissk Ariel'ss life."

"It is a First Law imperative." Mandelbrot could not conceive that a human could resist that imperative, any more than he himself could.

"Very well. As soon as she has awakened and eaten. Tomorrow, in other words. And I hope Dr. Avery isn't at home."

The thing that alarmed Derec most next morning was that Ariel didn't resist. A tart-tongued young woman, had she been in her normal condition she'd have frosted them well. As it was, there was a spark of eagerness in her eye, not so much, Derec thought, hope that the robotic Human Medical Team on Robot City might have found a cure, as relief from boredom.

It was no small risk they were taking. Dr. Avery was brilliant, a genius, but undoubtedly insane—megalomaniacal. Humans were but robots to him, to be used as he wished.

Derec looked at Ariel.

Frost, he thought, *I hope we make it.* She had come to mean a lot to him. How much, he hadn't been free to say. She did, after all, have this disease. It was not readily contagious, and in fact Derec had learned that it was sexually transmitted. Additionally, she remembered him from before his memory began.

Apparently there had once been some kind of strong emotion between them, and she was torn two ways by the memory, or by the contrast between his present innocent state and what had once been between them. She had told him frustratingly little about himself, though he thought she knew much.

None of her secretiveness mattered. She was Ariel, and he would rather be sick himself than see her suffer so.

Nevertheless, going back to Robot City was a wrench when they'd come so near to escaping.

"We might as well get it over with," said Ariel. He thought she sounded better than she had for days. Possibly being chased halfway across Robot City would be good for her.

Mandelbrot handed Derec the Key. It was rectangular and flat, small enough to hold in a hand, but larger than any mechanical key. It glittered in the light, looking more like silver than aluminum. It was in fact a highly conductive alloy permeated with a force-field. That made it more reflective than any unenergized metal, and was suggestive of hyperatomics.

Derec put an arm around Ariel for stability and pressed the Key into her palm, gripping her hand from below. As both of them gripped the Key, he pressed each corner in turn. Derec considered that the Keys had a nonhuman source, though the robots on Robot City had learned to make them. Humans wouldn't design a control system like that.

When the fourth corner was pressed, a button rose from the smooth, seamless surface. Derec took a final glance around, nodded farewell to the caninoid and the robot, and to the ship itself. There wasn't time for lengthy speeches; the button would soon recede.

He pressed the button.

The ship disappeared from around them, and fog took its place.

Perihelion.

The word meant the point in an orbit closest to a sun—more accurately, *the* sun, the Sun of old Earth. But now the term was synonymous with periastron. Perihelion had been described to them as the place closest to every place else in the universe.

They retained their floating attitudes, still in free fall, and looked around. Perihelion hadn't changed. All around them was a soft gray light, and air, air that smelled fuggy and dusty. No purifiers here, thought Derec, twisting to look around. It seemed that Perihelion went on forever, but he suspected that it had sharp limits to its size.

"What are you looking for?" Ariel asked, sounding as if she cared again.

"The hyperatomic motors."

"The what?"

"The Jump motors. This Key couldn't have brought us here by itself, not if the robots could duplicate it. It has to be tuned to motors elsewhere; I think it's just a tiny hyperwave radio. I don't know if we're in hyperspace or if this is a place in normal space—a big balloon, the size of a planet, perhaps."

"You mean, somebody *made* it?" Ariel asked, aghast.

"It's obviously an alien transport station—maybe for moving really heavy freight," said Derec. "It may be one of many. I wonder if it's abandoned, or if it's actually in use but is so big we don't see the others and they don't see us."

"The light comes from all sides," Ariel said, thoughtfully.

"Yes," said Derec, also thoughtful. "I hadn't thought of that. Well, much remains mysterious. It would take a small ship to explore this place."

In any case, they could do nothing now.

"We might as well get on with it," said Ariel, bored once the first interest had worn off. She made a face at the thought of Robot City, but Derec was heartened. She hadn't had that much spirit last night.

Derec repeated the keying motions and pressed the button. Gravity slapped their feet and light slapped their eyes. They looked around in shock. Walls surrounded them—obviously the walls of an apartment. But this wasn't an apartment designed by Avery robots. They weren't on Robot City.

They had no idea where they were.

CHAPTER 3

WEBSTER GROVES

The apartment was small, cramped, mean. It had not been lived in—there were no human touches, no pictures of relatives, no flowers or personalized decorations. It was very clean, but the flooring looked worn—no carpets—and the door handles looked dulled from use. A silly-looking robot stood against one wall.

This room was perhaps three meters by five and had a chair and a small couch that might seat two—three if they didn't mind contact. There was a curious blank space against one wall; a control panel was near one closed door. An open door led into what seemed to be a bedroom. A third door was closed and smaller than the others.

In the bedroom, Derec saw when he took a step, was another closed door. It was side by side with the closed door in this room, and he judged that they were both closets. Also in that wall, in both rooms, were drawer pulls—drawers built into the wall. A faint mechanical hum permeated the apartment.

And that was it.

ROB CHILSON

"Just two rooms," he said in disbelief.

"No bathroom!" said Ariel.

"No. And no kitchen or dining room."

They looked at each other. The only thing Derec could think of was a prison, but that wasn't right; there'd be a bathroom, at least. And this was too small and sterile for a prison, anyway.

"I wonder if that robot is functional," said Ariel, frowning at it.

It didn't *look* functional. It had a rigid, silly grin on a plastic face, unlike any robot Derec had seen or heard of. Now that he looked at it critically, its joints and the associated drive mechanisms looked large and clumsy. His training in robotics had dealt primarily with the brains, but the bodies, too, had been covered. It seemed to be looking at them, but it hadn't moved, of course.

"Robot, are you functional?" Derec asked.

"Yes, master," it said obsequiously, not moving, that fatuous grin never altering.

Robots should not have phoney human faces, Derec thought in irritation; one kept wanting to respond, but there was no emotion there to respond to.

"What is your name?"

"My name is R. David, master."

Ariel looked questioningly at him. Derec shook his head. Robots often had human names, if they attended humans. Ariel had told him that as a child she had named her nurse robot Guggles, though her parents had named the robot Katherine. Nowhere, though, had he heard of a robot with a prefix to its name. R. David? Or had he heard—

"R. David, what planet is this?" Ariel asked.

"This is Earth, Miss Avery," the robot said respectfully.

Startled—staggered, in fact—they looked at each other.

Of course! The rooms were so small, so cramped and mean, because Earth was immensely overpopulated. It had more people than all fifty Spacer worlds put together. The robot was crude because Earthmen were backward in robotics and in fact had a strong prejudice against them.

As strong as their prejudice against Spacers.

"We might have been better off back on Robot City," Derec said.

"Maybe we can get back to civilization from here," Ariel said.

"Good thinking. R. David, is it possible to take ship from Earth to the Spacer worlds?"

"Yes, Mr. Avery. Ships leave Earth at least weekly, and often more frequently."

Mr. Avery! And he had called Ariel "Miss Avery." They glanced at each other and with one accord decided not to mention it.

It seemed obvious to Derec that this robot was accustomed to seeing Dr. Avery come and go in the instantaneous fashion possible only to Key wielders. It had accepted that "Avery" could come and go in such fashion. Seeing them arrive in the same way, it came to the logical but wrong conclusion that they were "Averys," though they were obviously not "Dr. Avery."

"The first thing to do, then, is to get to the spaceport," Derec said. "Does that door lead to the outside?"

"One moment, Mr. Avery, if you please. It would not be wise for you to venture forth without preparation."

"What sort of preparation?" Derec asked. The robot was right; this *was* Earth.

"First, you will need a complete prophylactic regimen against the diseases of Earth. These are many and varied, and you have no natural immunity."

Frost, that was so. They looked at each other in alarm.

"However, the problem is not so great as most Spacers believe."

The robot stirred, opened a drawer in the wall and produced hypoguns, vials, pills. Grimacing, but needing no urging, they submitted themselves to their use.

"Take the pills when next you drink. If at any time you have any physical sensations of illness, you must notify me at once. It will be necessary to diagnose you immediately for treatment."

Derec and Ariel nodded solemnly, more than a little nervous at the thought of Earthly diseases.

"You will also need identification, ration slips and tags, and money," said R. David decisively when that was done. Moving clumsily, it opened the door to the closet in the sitting room. It was jammed with things, from a bookviewer and boxes of records to compact duplication devices Derec recognized these as Spacer-made, and surmised that it would be no great feat to duplicate Earthly ID symbols.

In this he was correct. R. David lowered the blank thing on the wall—a folding table—and spent an hour or so producing numerous bits of plastic and metal bearing their pictures, long numbers, various obscure statements about them, and of course a complete ID workup, including fingerprints, footprints, retinal scans, corneal images, ear pictures, and blood analysis.

"Dr. Avery procured comparatively large sums of Earthly money when he first landed," R. David explained. "He traded rare metals for it. Of course, money as such is of little value on Earth, as it can only be used to purchase nonessentials such as book recordings. Food, housing, clothing, and so on, are rationed."

"Frost," said Ariel nervously. "I wouldn't want some poor Earther to starve because I got his rations."

"There is no danger of that, Miss Avery. There is ample margin. It does no harm to anyone to provide you with Earthly ID, as Dr. Avery has more than paid for the consumption of Earth's scarce resources with his rare metals. Rationed items are available in amounts and qualities controlled by the individual's rating."

"Rating?"

"One's position in Earthly society. I understand that things are not greatly different in any human society, but on Earth such things have been formalized to a much higher degree."

"It's true that in the Spacer worlds the most important people usually get the best of what's going," said Ariel wryly. "Maybe Earth is actually more honest in admitting this. What kind of government does Earth have? Is it democratic, aristocratic, or what? Do the higher ratings run everything?"

"In answer to your last question, yes, to a degree. Earth is a democratic syndicalism, with elections to Parliament made from location—in the lower house—and from, industry to the upper house, or senate. Elections are democratic in those areas, but most of the administration is by appointed officials, these being people who have passed certain tests and worked their way up from less important offices. Syndicalism means that industry—primarily the feeding, housing, and clothing of the population—dominates the government."

"I can see how that would be necessary," said Derec, watching the robot's big, clumsy hands proceed delicately at their task. "How many ratings are there, and what's the highest?"

"Currently there are twenty-one ratings. The rating *A* is usually considered the highest. It is rarely bestowed. Only ten million humans are in this rating category."

One out of ten, Derec thought automatically. Then he caught himself. No: on Aurora, or most of the Spacer worlds, ten million would be ten percent of the populace. But Earth had—

"What's the population of Earth, R. David?" Ariel asked, having paralleled Derec's thought.

"Eight billion, Miss Avery."

Eight billion! They looked at each other. The population of eighty Spacer worlds—and there were only fifty.

"Who is in the A rating? Government officials?"

"No, this rating is reserved for entrepreneurs who solve large problems, for inventors, heroic spacemen, and other adventurers. It may be conferred by popular acclaim, as in the case of certain beloved entertainers. Recipients of the A rating have many privileges, among them the right to adorn their doors with laurel."

A high honor, like the Medal of Aurora. Derec nodded; the details—what was laurel?—didn't matter.

"What's the next lowest rating?"

"*B* rating is reserved for planetary and continental governmental officials, both elected and appointed. *C* refers to City officials. *D* is for industry officials. From there it becomes complex and not obvious. There are fifteen steps in each rating, the lowest being step one."

"So, what rate and step are you preparing for us?"

"I am preparing identification for *T* ratings, as I did for Dr. Avery, as I assume you will wish to remain anonymous as Spacers. It will certainly facilitate your investigations of Earthly society if you pass unremarked, and the *T* rating is the best for that purpose."

"What kind of people normally are assigned *T* ratings?" Ariel asked.

"The 'T' stands for 'Transient.' Any person whose duties require him or her to travel may be assigned this rating, unless the rating itself allows of that eventuality, as do *B* ratings and many *A* ratings. Salesmen, for instance, may be rated *D* or *T*, but usually *T*, as *D* is assigned to administrative duties.

"In your cases," R. David continued, "I had considered assigning you *S* ratings—students—but I judged it not advisable, as students have certain restrictions, and I would be forced to specify a school."

Interesting as all this was, Derec found the hour it took to prepare the ID dragging. The tiny-roomed apartment, with only two rooms, was a prison more confining than any he had viewed in historical novels. Even the dungeons of the ancient times on Earth had seemed larger. The varying mechanical drone seemed to grow louder and louder until he was forced to speak, whereupon it faded at once to its actual low level.

It was the sound, he thought in some awe, of the City—a sound no Earthman could avoid, from birth to death. For they never went outside their Cities.

Finally, the ID was completed, and R. David explained the uses of the various pieces. "This is your ration tag for food; your home kitchen is 9-G. Personals are also assigned, but you may use any you see. Derec, take care not to speak to or look at anyone in Personal; there is a strong taboo for men on Earth. Ariel, women have no such taboo; you may speak in Personal. Your ratings do not grant you stall privileges. You must supply your own combs, brushes, and shaving equipment."

R. David droned on, provided them with a map of the local area. There was an attempt to put everything on the same level, they learned. Their quarters were low-status, and so they had to go up or down to Personals and commissary.

At length the robot gave them hats and let them go, obviously worried. Ariel opened the door and stepped out, Derec following.

The same oyster-white walls as the interior; they might have been in a very cheap hotel, and in fact, Derec surmised, they were. A youth with long, elaborately coiffed hair and gaudy cheap clothes gave them a sullen look from down the corridor as he entered an apartment. An older woman, heavy and squarish and short, passed them, carrying an open bottle and exhaling the odor of mousey beer. She did not so much not look at them as not see them.

Turning to the right, Derec led them toward a gleam of brighter light. Behind them, two men exited from an apartment, talking casually together about a sports event, oddly called "boxing." Moments later, Derec and Ariel were at the junction.

A wider, busier corridor crossed theirs at right angles. Ariel pointed out the sign that told them that theirs was Sub-Corridor 16. They had just entered Corridor M. Turning left, they followed a small crowd, which quickly resolved itself into an accidental grouping. There must have been fifty people in view at any given moment, Derec estimated, and was slightly staggered.

Abruptly, on the right the wall became transparent and they looked into an open space in which children raced about and bounced balls. A playground. The inside of the wall had crude bits of childish art affixed to it; posters boasted of obscure triumphs, and "recitations" were advertised. It was strange, yet Derec found it familiar. Sometime in his forgotten past he had played in such a playground, though nothing specific came through.

One thing, though, he missed: the gleam of attentive robots along the wall and amid the yelling mobs.

Corridor M terminated at a large circular junction. In the angles, four escalator strips spiraled—two up and two down. Beyond, according to the signs, was another subsection: theirs was Sub-Section G.

Perhaps a hundred men, women, and children were visible, Derec thought. He and Ariel, awed, slowed their pace and drifted to one side of the center of the junction, avoiding both the mouths of the corridors and the escalators. A hundred—and not the same hundred. Moment by moment, people filtered in and filtered out, up or down, away along the corridors, or in from either direction.

Derec supposed wildly that within ten minutes a person might see—oh—five hundred people. Frost! Maybe a thousand!

And now that the playground had alerted him, he noted that none of them were robots.

There were small tables with uncomfortable-looking benches before them, at which people sat, some playing chess. Other benches without tables, equally uncomfortable in appearance, harbored other people. Not far from them an old fellow like a wrinkled apple smiled cherubically at everything he saw; beside him on the bench was an uncapped bottle wrapped in brown paper up to the neck. Others who sat about were also old. Some played chess or other board games at the tables; some snacked on various foodstuffs.

The walls under the escalators had identifying marks high up, but lower down there were large boards with papers affixed to them, announcing various events. Below that still were wide strips running from escalator to corridor mouth, on which crude, vigorous murals had been painted. At one corner an earnest group of youths, younger than Ariel or Derec, were touching the mural lightly with flat applique boards, painting a new mural over the old. Watching them was a young woman all in blue. She looked short, square, sturdy, and wore an odd cap with a bill of translucent blue that threw a blue shadow over her face; above the bill was a golden medal.

She turned and they saw that she had the label C-3 on her upper left chest, and a tool of some sort dangling from her left side: it was half a meter long and had a sturdy grip. C ratings were City functionaries, Derec remembered. Then he realized that the tool was a neuronic whip. No; it was far too big and heavy; the neuronic whip might be in that buttonedshut pouch in front. The tool had to be a club.

A policewoman. Her eye took them in, paused, went on, and she crossed to speak to one of the old parties at a table. Derec stared in fascination. He had never, to his knowledge, laid eyes on one whose duty was to apply force to other human beings.

"Standing here as we are, we stand out; she's probably trained to notice people who act oddly," Ariel said in a low voice.

Derec agreed wordlessly, started toward the down escalator, reflecting that no one could understand them from a little distance if they spoke normally, so great was the noise of people and the murmur of the escalators.

Each escalator flattened out where it met the floor, and there was a three-meter strip of level surface. Ahead of them, Earthmen strode forward and stepped on without breaking stride, then turned about to face their direction of travel. Derec and Ariel tried to imitate that confident stride. At least the example taught them to enter against the direction of travel, a thing Derec wouldn't have guessed. They stepped on with only a slight flexing of the legs and a quick shuffle to retain balance. They turned around and looked down, just as the strip dived down behind the wall.

The escalator, they saw, was not actually a stairway, as they had expected; it was a flat, moving ramp. Overhead was a sloping ceiling from which came the muted rumble of drives; one of the other strips, Derec supposed, probably an up strip. The down escalator did a complete half-circle clockwise, then the wall to their right opened and they were on the other side of the junction at the next level down.

One more half-circle, another junction, then there came a full circle with no exit, and they were at the bottom. The murmur became thunderous. The escalator dived into a slit in the floor, and, Derec presumed, ran "underground" for a few meters, only to reverse itself and climb backward, out of the floor and up. There were only two strips, not four, each going both up and down simultaneously.

Two dozen people got off below them, then they got off, and fifty more followed them, dispersing briskly in all directions, fighting through hundreds of people going eight different ways. This junction was four times as busy as the ones they'd seen above. Derec and Ariel tried not to gape.

Light and noise came through the arches that replaced the corridor mouths above, and they saw people whirling past. If before they'd seen hundreds, now they saw thousands!

Derec swallowed a small knot of fear. So many people! He got the distinct impression he'd never seen that many people together before. He realized he was making quick calculations of how much air they were using, and, more importantly, how much was left for him. *No*, he thought, *if there's enough for eight billion, there's enough for me.*

To right and left, moving strips hurtled past, faster and faster and higher and higher as they got farther from the junction. High overhead were glowing, crawling signs like worms of light, the largest saying WEBSTER GROVES. Before and behind them, the other two arches opened on the non-moving space between the strips. It was dotted with kiosks—some being communications booths, some being the heads of strips that came up from below. Far away down the concourse was another wide tube coming down from the ceiling, with its four escalators. Behind, at the limits of sight, was another.

They drifted out, read the signs, awed. People swarmed about them, the noise was continuous and not so loud as it seemed, the air was warm and humid and thick with the odor of thousands, hundreds of thousands, of people.

"So this is Earth."

CHAPTER 4

THERE'S NO PLACE LIKE HOME-KITCHEN

Hesitantly, Derec led the way to the expressway that ran west, as it proclaimed. The lightworms overhead proclaimed KIRKWOOD EXITS NEXT.

They mounted the first strip. It was traveling at about half walking speed, and each succeeding strip was that much faster than the previous. A fat old man skipped nimbly across three strips in a practiced motion that would have sent Derec tumbling. Sedately, he and Ariel crossed three strips, then she gasped and gripped his arm.

Hurriedly they recrossed the strips, going down, and were carried only a little way past their destination. They had gotten nowhere near the fast lanes of the express.

Once between the ways again they were a little puzzled, but there was a kiosk not far away, from which people emerged. Entering it, they found strips to carry them down to a cross-corridor that would take them under the ways. They surfaced on the other side of the express strips, where there was a set of localways, rode the second-slowest strip back for a short distance and got off, to dive into a huge corridor.

It was lined with shops of various kinds, but they didn't stop to look. Thousands of people were peering through the transparent walls at bright displays of goods.

At the second cross-corridor was the symbol for the Personal. It wasn't the one to which they were assigned; they must have passed that within minutes after leaving the apartment. At Ariel's questioning look, Derec nodded, but he felt a qualm though he walked firmly toward the door to the Men's Personal. For the first time, they were separated.

Don't look at or speak to anyone, R. David had said. He pushed open the door and found himself in an anteroom. No one lingered there, so he also passed on, through a door ingeniously arranged not to be in line of sight of the first. Inside he saw a series of small hallways lined with blank doors, about half with red lights glowing. Some of these little cubicles were four times as large as others, and as a man exited one he glimpsed such felicities as laundry facilities. The stalls, he supposed, to which he had no access.

The tiny cubicle his keyed plastic strip got him into had a crude john, a metal mirror, and below it a wash basin. There was no towel, merely a device to blow hot, dry air. The showers were at the other end.

He felt better when he left. After a lengthy wait, Ariel reappeared, looking radiant.

Derec stared. Certainly she was looking better than she had in days on shipboard. He had a wild hope that she was not really sick after all, or that she had experienced one of those mysterious remissions that still baffled doctors. Then he realized that he was letting his wishes rule his reason, and cursed himself for setting himself up for a reaction.

"Shall we go?" she asked, smiling and taking his arm.

It was not far to the section kitchen to which they were

assigned. As T-4s they could go to any kitchen they happened to be near, but that would entail accounting difficulties for the staff of the kitchen, and might draw attention to them.

Three lines of people formed up at the door, right, left, and center. They joined one of the lines, readying their metal ration tags. Ahead of them the Earthers—talking and laughing uninhibitedly, as was their wont—filtered forward, inserting their tags into slots and after a moment recovering them and striding into noisy confusion, removing their hats. There was a strong, pleasant odor of unfamiliar food.

"Hey, Charlie!" came a raucous cry from behind them, making them jump a little. Someone in the line behind them had recognized someone in the next line. "Back from Yeast Town, hey?"

Charlie answered incomprehensibly, something about being good to be back. "Right!" bellowed the man behind them. "No kitchen like home-kitchen, eh?"

Considering that they all must serve food from the same source, Derec thought, that must just be familiarity, not the food. Come to think of it, if everybody ate in such kitchens three times a day, they'd soon get to know their neighbors at the nearby tables.

They moved forward, Derec's tag slippery in his hand. With nothing better to do, he counted the people passing through the entry. Each line filtered diners through at about one per second. Sixty per minute. At least a hundred and eighty per minute for the three lines. *Frost!* he thought. *And we've been in line for five minutes!*

It got worse; something like eighteen hundred people must have entered in the ten minutes it took them to work their way to the entry. A turnstile barred their way. Derec boldly thrust his tag into the slot of the machine. It blinked at him (non-positronic computer, he thought), lit up with the legend TABLE J-9/NO FREE CHOICE, and ejected the tag. Derec took it and found that the turnstile gave under pressure from his knee. Ariel followed in a moment, but there was no time to breathe easily.

Beyond stretched an enormous room.

The whole City was one gigantic steel and concrete cavern, and this was the largest opening in it that they had seen, except for the slash of the moving ways. It went on, it seemed, forever. From the ceiling, which glowed coolly, descended pillars in an orderly array, short sections of transparent wall (apparently to minimize noise) and columns apparently full of tubes and cables. Between them stretched the tables—kilometers of tables, in ranks and files. All was confusion, and the Earthers were swarming past them while they stood gaping: the gleam of light on polished imitation wood, the clatter of plastic flatware on plastic plates, the babble of thousands of voices, the crying of children. Behind manual windows to their right and left, men and women dealt with those whose feeding could not be automated.

Overhead, light-signs indicated the rows, and at Ariel's nudge Derec started the long trudge to row J.

Because of his Spacer conditioning, he had been thinking of this kitchen as a Spacer restaurant, with maybe a dozen tables, most for four people, some for two, a few for eight or ten. But these tables each seated—he guessed fifty on each side. Even after they reached row J, table 9 was a long way away.

Hesitantly, they approached it—at least it was plainly marked—and found two seats together. The people they passed were grumbling because choice was suspended. "Too many transients," growled someone, and they felt guilty.

"Food is probably one of the few high spots of their days," Ariel whispered.

They took their seats and looked at the raised section of the table before them.

NO FREE CHOICE glowed to the right. On the left was a panel that said: *Chicken—Sundays, opt. Mon. Fish— Fridays, opt. Sat.* On Earth, there was a seven-day week, but Derec had no idea which day was which. There being no choice, he shrugged, glanced at Ariel, and pressed the contact. The panel immediately lit with: *Zymosteak: Rare, Med., Well-D?* Not Sunday or Friday, he thought. Derec chose well-done and the sign vanished, replaced with *Salad: Tonantzin, Calais, Del Fuego, PepperTom?*

Ariel shrugged, glancing at him, and they chose, suppressing smiles; neither had heard of any of these dressings.

ORDER PLACED.

That sign stared at them for several minutes. The Earthmen around them were a scruffy lot, and Derec realized that he had been subliminally aware of that for some time. Earthers were short, and tended to be plain, if not actually homely. Here and there a handsome man or a beautiful woman attracted admiring glances, but they were a minority.

At least Earth people weren't starving, as Derec had expected. He knew vaguely that it took a major effort on the part of the population and its robots—restricted to the countryside—to feed Earth. Standard food synthesizers were too expensive, and used much too much energy for Earth to afford. But a large minority of these people were fat, and many more were plump.

At this table they waited patiently, not talking or laughing as at other tables.

"Probably a table for Transients who don't know each other," Ariel said, low-toned. There were only a couple of quiet conversations at the table.

Presently, the food ended their embarrassment; a disk slid aside in front of each of them and another rose into position, the second one holding a covered server of plastic. When they removed the servers from the service disks, the latter closed smoothly.

The food looked like steak, baked potato with shrimp sauce, and a salad with dressing on the side. Crusty, faintly yellow bread. It smelled marvelous and, to Derec's amazement, it was natural. His first bite confirmed that: the rich, subtle, varied flavor of real food was unmistakable. And yet it wasn't real food, either. Zymosteak? It was plain these people normally got meat only twice a week, with a chance at it on two more days. Four days out of seven.

"I can't believe it's so good," Ariel said under the cover of the clatter of Earthers opening their servers.

Derec hadn't realized he was so hungry; it hadn't been that long since breakfast. Perhaps he'd gotten so bored with synthetic food that he'd been eating less and less.

He turned his attention to another problem. They had been served with amazing rapidity. He couldn't remember service on any Spacer world, but he was sure it wasn't this fast. There had to be automation behind the scenes. Of course, with no free choice, they had merely to drop the chosen kind of dressing into the server, clamp the lid down, and pop it into an oven for the few seconds required to cook the zymosteak to the desired degree. Probably ran it through the oven on a belt. With a good oven, there could have been ice cream on the same plate and it wouldn't have melted before the meat was done.

Even so, row J was the last: ten rows of ten tables each;

a hundred tables, each seating a hundred. This commissary was equipped to feed ten thousand people. Derec mentioned as much to Ariel, who was as dumbfounded as he. It wasn't at capacity now; perhaps there were *only* six thousand people in the room.

On Aurora, a sports arena that seated ten thousand was a big one.

Halfway through the meal, Derec found his breath coming fast: it was too much. He felt trapped in this concrete cavern, felt that the spacious room was closing in, the ceiling, not low but not high, was the lid of a trap, the mobs of unconscious people around him weren't real. *They probably went all their lives without seeing the sun or open air*, he thought, and that made it worse. With difficulty, he fought off the panic, panting.

When they had finished their meals, they put the servers and flatware back on the disk and pressed the same contact again, as they'd seen their neighbors do, and watched them vanish. The exit was on the opposite side. Once outside (an elaborate turnstile permitted exit only), Derec breathed more freely. They were a little at a loss, this not being the way they'd come in, but the sound of the ways was obvious, and they soon found their way back to them.

"The trouble is, there's no quiet, no *private* place to talk," Ariel complained as they hesitated.

"I know. We want to go to the spaceport, but I don't feel like unfolding the map here."

"Look. . . ." Ariel fell silent until a chattering cluster of pre-teenage girls had passed, not even noticing them. "Look, the signs indicate that it isn't 'rush hour'—whatever that is— R. David mentioned it."

"Right, and lowly Fours like ourselves can ride the express platforms for many hours yet."

They made their way up the strips of the local, down again to the motionless strip between the locals and the express, then up again, faster and faster. Derec realized uneasily that if they were to trip and fall at these speeds they might be seriously injured. Nor was there an attentive robot to rush forward and grasp their arms if they should fall. Earthers never fell, he supposed. They learned when very young.

On up they went, till the wind whipped their hair and stung their eyes, up and up to the top, where each platform had a windbreak at the front of it. There they found an empty one behind a platform occupied by a man with the Mad Hatter's huge hat and sat, breathing heavily. Ariel grinned at him and Derec laughed back.

Carefully, in the shelter of the windbreak, they unfolded the map and studied it. They knew that they were in Webster Groves Section, proceeding east, and quickly found the spot, just as they passed under the sign that said SHREWSBURY SECTION. But study the map how they would, they saw no sign of any spaceport.

Derec looked blankly at Ariel. "It's got to be here somewhere!"

A group of teenagers, mostly male, passed by two platforms away, one fleeing, the others pursuing, expertly negotiating the strips. A whistle shrilled, over the shrilling of the wind, and a blue-uniformed man waved his club and set off in pursuit of the children, who scattered down the strips. Adults scowled at them.

They studied it all over again, until the signs overhead said TOWER GROVE SECTOR.

"Possibly it isn't on the map," Ariel said. "Earthers are prejudiced against Spacers. They might not like to advertise the port."

"If you have business there, you're told how to find it, I suppose," said Derec glumly. "We should have asked R. David how to get there."

The expressway was not straight, and as Derec looked down now, he saw that the local had spun off; another came in, made a turn, and paralleled the expressway in its place. A storefront gave way to a palatial entry that faced the oncoming expressway obliquely; above the entry was a glowing marquee on which the back view of a woman wearing tight pants appeared. She vanished, replaced by the slogan IF I WIGGLE. She reappeared, peering archly over her shoulder at the viewer: WILL YOU FOLLOW?

Derec supposed that there were as many people in view as there had been in the kitchen, and the ways were not half full, maybe not a quarter full. "Rush hour must be when the ways are full," he said.

"Yes. If they all go to work at the same time—" Ariel said, and he snapped his fingers.

"Rush, indeed." They looked about and tried to picture the swarming mobs going up and down the strips multiplied by three or four.

OLD TOWN SECTOR.

"You know," said Ariel, "Daneel Olivaw might have sat on this very platform, or at least ridden this very way."

Derec nodded. He had no memory of ever having met the famous humaniform robot, Daneel Olivaw. Daneel was designed to look exactly like a man—like Roj Nemmenuh Sarton, in fact, who had built his body. He had helped the Earthman, Plainclothesman Elijah Baley, solve the murder of Dr. Sarton, and later had gone to Solaria, where he had helped Baley solve another murder.

Han Fastolfe had built two humaniforms, the first with

Sarton's help. The intricate programming that enabled a humaniform to play the part of a human being, hampered as it was by the Three Laws, was a triumph of robotics that had never been recreated. Fastolfe had refused to make more than two such robots, and one had been deactivated. Daneel Olivaw, he supposed, was still extant, somewhere on Aurora.

"Look at that hat."

Derec looked, then gaped. They had seen odd hats all along, but this woman's head was a flower garden, except that many of the "flowers" were bows. As in all Earthly hats, though, there was a prominent band for the insertion of the rating ticket that entitled them to such things as a seat during rush hour.

"You know, maybe some of these people know the way to the port," Ariel said.

That was a thought Derec had hoped she wouldn't have, but he nodded tightly. Frankly, he didn't want to speak to anyone. Perhaps because they were Earthers and he was a Spacer—with all his prejudices intact. It was a sore point with him that only Earth was exploring and settling new planets. It was not that he objected to Earth's doing that, he objected that the Spacer worlds weren't. Not these people's fault, but—

Standing up, he leaned out and got the attention of a young man—a little older than himself, he thought—who was making his way toward an unoccupied platform.

"Pardon me, sir, could you direct us to the spaceport?"

The other's rather blank expression broke into one of handsome good cheer. "Hey, gato, you do the Spacer accent ex good!" he exclaimed. "Too bad you don't have the fabric to match, but that speech'll get you on any subetheric for the asking!"

Derec concealed his confusion, lifted an eyebrow. "Yes?"

"Oh, ex, ex, that haughty look's the highest!" The other glanced around, lost his cheer, and said quietly, "But, look, this's fun and all, but I wouldn't try that speech in Yeast Town, savvy?" And with that, he was gone.

They looked at each other and shook their heads, dumbfounded.

"Do you think you could ape that—that speech of his?" Derec asked. Ariel shook her head again.

They were in a much more exalted district than Webster Groves; this Old Town Sector looked spanking new, with neat, clean, shiny buildings and prosperous-looking shops. Places of entertainment seemed more common and more lavish, as if the people who lived here had more leisure and more ration points, or money, or whichever it took, for entertainment.

"What did he mean, 'subetherics'?"

Derec thought a moment. "Hyperwave broadcasts, I think. I'm not up on that technology, but I think at one time hyperwave transmission was called that. Probably cheaper than piping cables through all these man-made caves."

Derec's voice thinned as he glanced up to where the sun should be but wasn't. Steadying his voice, he added, "I think he meant we could be entertainment stars pretending to be Spacers for Earther novels."

They grinned at each other.

EAST ST. LOUIS SECTOR.

"What does the 'ST' mean?" Neither knew.

"Derec, we're getting a long way from . . . home-kitchen. Maybe we should turn around and go back."

Derec wasn't happy about that either, but was reluctant to give up.

"Maybe one more try," he said.

He looked around for someone to ask, and was struck by the buildings in this new sector. They seemed industrial; blank fronts, a minimum of signs, a lot of which didn't even glow. All the color and gaiety seemed to have gone out of the City. Half the people on the ways had left in Old Town Sector, and no wonder.

Those who remained were far less prepossessing. They were poorly dressed and few wore hats, which meant, as Derec had gathered, that they had no passes for platform rides. Low ratings, like he and Ariel.

"What's that funny smell?" Ariel asked.

Derec sniffed, became aware of an odor. Not bread. "Something living. Maybe the ventilators don't work so good here."

"You mean we're smelling *people*"

Derec felt a little sick himself at the thought.

"Pardon me, sir, could you direct me to the spaceport?" he asked a sullen man.

"Buzz off, gato."

Seething, Derec waited for another prospect. A woman seized a seat on a platform with such an angry, triumphant expression that he crossed her off. Then a group of young men and women approached, four men and two women, the latter in gaudy, tight pants, the former all in brown corduroy. Derec repeated his question.

The first man looked at him sharply. "Whattaya tryina pull, gato? Spaceport! Spacer speech! Whod'ya thinkya are, huh?"

Clamping his jaw on his anger, Derec said, "I merely asked—"

"Oh, you merely ahsked, didja, haughty har? Whod'ya thinkya are, I asked you, gato."

"I just wanted—"

"Clamp down, haughty har, don't go gittin' high horse with *me*. Keep a civil tongue, and also a polite face, hear?"

Seething, Derec fought for control, and another Earther spoke. He had a warm, dark-brown complexion and the eyes of a hawk: racial types had remained more distinct on Earth than on the Spacer worlds.

"Hey, Jake, I think he's rilly a Spacer. Both of 'em. Lookit those ex fabrics."

He and Ariel were wearing plain shipsuits of synthetic fabric, a quiet, glossy substance in different shades of gray, hers lighter than his. Nobody had remarked on their clothes before, but nobody had looked closely at them.

Jake stared in amazed disbelief. "Naw!"

"Yeah, Jake," one of the women shrilled, looking closely at Ariel. "And look at 'em, both of 'em—tall and handsome, like. Spacers!"

"Spacers!" said Jake in almost reverent tones. His eyes sharpened. "I always wanted t'meet a Spacer. Just to tell'em what I think of 'em!"

"Yeah!"

"You think you're so smart, doin' your little social science investigation of 'Earther' society, huh, Spacer?" This time it sounded like a spit.

Derec's anger cooled in apprehension; Ariel had unobtrusively taken his arm. "Thanks for your help, but we've got to be going."

Again his accent aroused their ire.

They all began to jabber hostilely as he and Ariel stepped to one side, were struck by the wind, and fell behind on their slower strip.

"Stop! We ain't done talkin' atya!" cried Jake, and the Earthers swarmed off the platform level and started down.

Ariel gasped and Derec realized that they would soon be below them, on the slower strips, between them and the locals.

"Back up!" Derec said tensely, and in a moment they were squeezing between platforms. Their persecutors caught the change of direction instantly and were in full cry.

He hurried Ariel rapidly down the strips on the inside, their enemies gaining rapidly with a lifetime's expertise. At the motionless median between expressways, he looked around wildly. There was no possibility of their climbing the reverse ways and staying ahead.

"In here!" said Ariel, and they dived into a kiosk and ran down the strip, not waiting for it to carry them. They ran under the ways, hearing voices crying "Spacer! Spacer!" behind them.

At the other end, they had a choice of a moving strip that would take them up beside the expressway, or a maze of corridors at this level: poorly lit, poorly cleaned, sparsely populated, and thick with nameless organic odors.

There was quite a mob behind them, by the sound. Panting, they ran into the first corridor, took the first branching, then the next. They paused, listening. A derelict lay on a low platform beside a wide freight door, scruffy and unshaven. ST. LOUIS YEAST, PLANT 17, said the door.

Derec had a sudden flashing memory of having viewed a novel set on Earth in the medieval days, when a derelict like this turned out to be a crusty, cheerful, picaresque, heart-of-gold character who saved the day for the hero and became his closest buddy.

This one had more the attitude of a rat. Rousing himself with surprising energy, he listened, rubbed his graying whiskers, and, growling something about "stirring up the damn yeast farmers," he dived into a small door beside the freight door, and slammed it. They heard it lock.

Voices and footfalls approached. They looked around. There were no tiny crannies to escape into, nothing but corridors wide enough for trucks to be driven through. Eventually they'd be run down wherever they went, however fast they ran. And their enemies no longer merely wanted to talk to Derec and Ariel. They had something much more direct in mind.

CHAPTER 5

ESCAPE?

Ariel heard them coming. Heart pounding, she looked around again. No place to run to, no place to hide. After a blank moment Derec took the Key to Perihelion out of his pocket (Ariel gasped), put it in her palm, squeezed the four corners in succession, and closed both their hands around it fiercely. Ariel pushed the button as they held their breath.

The gray nothingness of Perihelion was around them, forever and ever to the limits of vision.

Derec let his breath out. "Frost! I thought they had us!"

"So did I!"

They were in no hurry to return to Earth, yet there was surely no more boring place in hyperspace or normal space, whichever it was, than Perihelion. They looked at each other, and Ariel shrugged, as Derec wiped his brow.

"Oh, no!"

They had moved at the same time, and, releasing each other, had drifted apart. With great presence of mind, Derec lunged for her. Ariel was frozen in shock; had she reached for him at the same time, she could have caught his hand. Too late.

They looked at each other tragically. Inexorably, they drifted further apart.

Ariel felt she had to make up for it. "I'll throw you the Key!" she cried. "You go back to Earth—forget about me!"

"Nonsense! If you do, I'll throw it back—"

At that moment his face went blank and he contorted himself into a knot; reaching for his soft shoes, he tore them off. Writhing with a practiced free-fall motion, he turned his back to her and hurled the first shoe away. With the reaction to that throw, he ceased to recede. Now he was rotating. He allowed himself to rotate twice, studying her, then writhed again, and threw the other shoe.

After a prolonged wait they seized each other, Ariel gasping in relief. To her surprise, she felt him shaking.

"Derec, you were marvelous! I thought we were lost!"

Derec grinned shakily. "What you said about throwing the Key gave me the idea."

"Frost, I'm glad something did." Ariel took the Key and pressed the corners again, and, with both gripping it, pushed the button.

R. David was against the wall in his usual place.

"Frost," Ariel said, feeling ready to collapse. She sat down, knees shaking, and so did Derec.

"What did they mean, 'your little social study of conditions on Earth'—the yeast farmers?" Derec asked.

Ariel had no idea. They put the question to R. David, careful not to let him know that they had been in serious danger.

He said, "I have no access to news feed, but I believe that Dr. Avery made some public announcement about studying social conditions on Earth when he first contacted

Earthly authorities to transfer rare metals for money. He promised not to send in humaniform robots, and of course it did not occur to the authorities that he would enter Earthly society himself."

"Then how did he expect to make any study of Earth society?" Ariel asked, skeptical.

"He purchased many Earthly studies of the subject, and also me. While ostensibly studying these sources, he quietly developed the medical prophylaxis with which I treated you, and infiltrated Earth society in his own person, learning what kinds of identification and ration media he would need to have to pretend to be an Earthman. Some of those he bought openly as samples for his study. In short, over a period of an Earthly year he was occasionally in the news as he came and went from Earth. And from this study he was allegedly making, I suppose that rumors may have gone abroad that teams of Spacers are studying Earthly sociology on the spot. That is, of course, very unlikely."

"Very," said Derec, with a grimace. "Spacers are just not interested in the subject, and if they were, they wouldn't take the health risk."

Ariel could not care less about Earth's rumors. "The important thing is to get back into space," she said.

"You're right," Derec said. "I'm more than tired of concrete caves and the troglodytes that live in them." She smiled fleetingly at the term. "So the third thing is to find out how to get to the spaceport. The first being to have those directions to the nearest Personal repeated, and the second, to find a shoe store."

Ariel grimaced, but said, "You're right."

When put to the question, R. David said, "The spaceport is located near New York, Miss Avery."

They looked at each other blankly. Of course they knew

that there were eight hundred Cities on Earth. They had been thinking in terms of one giant City covering all Earth, the natural extension of their Earthly experience.

"What City is this, then?" Ariel asked.

"The City of Saint Louis," said R. David. "It is on the same continent as New York, so travel is facilitated. One may take the train, and for a third of the distance the way is enclosed and roofed over. It takes less than twelve hours—half an Earthly rotation, Mr. Avery." He had detected the question on Derec's face.

Ariel had no idea what a "train" might be, and wasn't happy about its being enclosed—she visualized something like the expressway. She looked at Derec, who looked equally unhappy.

"Do we have the money—the rating or whatever—to go on the train?" Derec asked dubiously.

R. David said, "Your travel vouchers have not been touched, but I believe there is an inadequate amount. As Fours, you do not rate much, nor do many Earth people often travel between Cities."

"Even though we are Transients?"

"You are Transients in this sector, but not necessarily in this City."

"We'd better visit the Personal first," said Ariel tiredly. "We'll think it over when we get back."

R. David repeated his directions to the Personals, which turned out to be in opposite directions. Rather reluctantly, they split up, and Derec left with a backward glance. Ariel walked slowly toward the women's Personal, hoping Derec's stockinged feet would not be too noticeable.

Since this was the Personal assigned to her, Ariel found a shower cubby with the same number as the one on her tag, and took a shower. Again, no towels; she saw a woman carrying a little cloth satchel into a similar cubby and presumed it contained a towel, combs, and so on. She wouldn't need one, as short a time as they expected to be on Earth. She had, of course, brought a comb, though she should see about getting a brush. Fortunately, her hair wasn't long.

She made her way back to Sub-Section G, Corridor M, Sub-Corridor 16, Apartment 21, without difficulty, hardly seeing the crowds of Earthers who swarmed through the passageways.

Derec was back before her and full of energy. Despite their brush with the mob, he wanted to go check out the "train station." He was careful not to say so in front of R. David, who might think it dangerous, but she thought he wanted to see if they could devise a method of stowing away.

Showing them on the map, R. David gave them directions that would take them, by the route they had previously followed, to Old Town and something called the Gateway Arch Plaza. The station was beneath that. They would pass several shoe stores on the way.

Ariel felt distinctly nervous as they threaded their way again through the corridors to the junction and took the down ramp, but nobody paid any attention to them. She would have liked to have changed clothes, but their ship-suits were all they had, and they weren't all that conspicuous. It still wasn't rush hour, so they had the freedom of the express platforms, and went straight up to them on the eastbound side.

The clerk in the shoe store was a human, a plump, youngish woman, older than Ariel. She quirked her mouth in a half-humorous fashion at Derec's socks and said, "Been running the strips, eh?" She produced neat, cheap shoes expeditiously, checked his ration tag in her machine, accepted the money tag, and waved them away, calling, "Next time be more careful of the edges!"

Back to the expressway.

She heard Derec's breath speed up beside her, as Old Town Sector came rushing toward them, but they saw none of the yeast farmers from before—less than an hour ago.

"I'll walk the rest of the way before I'll ride this thing into—Yeast Town," she said, leaning over to shout at Derec.

"Yeah," he said weakly. Ariel saw that he was staring up at the high ceiling, which was higher here than in Webster Groves. There was probably nothing overhead but the roof of the City, for here the ways were in a great slash through the building blocks. No matter—he was having a claustrophobic attack.

Ariel sympathized—she had had several of them herself. At the moment it was the crowds, not the oppressive buildings, that made her own breath come short.

Before she could attempt to reassure him, Derec gripped her arm and pointed: *Gateway-Arch Plaza Exit*. They descended hastily and rode the ramp down under the ways, found a sign pointing north, and followed it to a localway, also plainly marked.

Presently they entered the Gateway-Arch Plaza.

It was enormous. Gaping like rubes, they stepped out of the way of swarms of chattering Earthers, and frankly stared. The Gateway Arch itself was smaller, perhaps, than the Pillar of the Dawn on Aurora that commemorated the early pioneers, and surely was less moving than the memorial at the pillar's base, where outstanding men and women of each generation were honored. But at a hundred ninety meters tall, the arch was no small monument. Its span was nearly equal to its height, and the roof was another ten meters above it. It was all matte stainless steel, ancient looking but in good repair.

The room that enclosed the whole mastodonic fabrication was commensurate in size, over two hundred meters in diameter, its circular walls a cliff of concrete and metal around the arch. This cliff was covered with the balconies of highrated apartments.

Derec walked boldly toward the lower area between the feet of the arch, and Ariel followed, inwardly amused at the awe on the faces of some of the Earthmen—some showed unmistakable signs of agoraphobia, exposed to this much open space.

Below the arch was a museum dating from pre-spaceflight times, which might have been interesting, but they were looking for a train station. Quietly determined to ask no directions, they wasted half an hour, some of it in looking at exhibits. Ariel was struck by the unfinished look of the items people used in the pre-industrial age, all made by crude hand methods. Derec pointed out a plaque that stated that, in the old days, citizens had ridden a sort of tramway up inside the arch.

"Agoraphobia," he said, echoing her thought.

Ariel nodded and led him briskly out of the museum. It felt like underground to her, and the crowds of Earthers swarming around were bringing on another claustrophobic attack. She felt much more sympathetic to them and less inclined to sneer at Earthly phobias.

They had to leave the plaza itself to find the route to the station; they had been following the plaza signs and hadn't noticed the station signs when they left the localway. The staion was a level or two deeper, and a different route took them there.

There were fewer people here, but below the passenger level they found a series of freightways crisscrossing the City, which carried heavy items in bulk containers. Many men in rough clothing rode these ways in handling carts, shunting the big containers off the belts at their destinations. These freightways all traveled at a walking pace, no more.

At the station they also found the terminus of a tube system for small capsules. Letters and small items—parcel post—could be blown about the City very rapidly by this system, and Derec became quite excited by it.

He'd seen a system like this before, on a somewhat different scale. The Robot City robots had generated a tremendous vacuum as a side effect of their Key-manufacturing facility, and Derec and Ariel had ridden the vacuum tubes more than once when they were in a hurry.

But here on Earth they were using the same technology not because they had a vacuum they could use; they had to create a vacuum to make it work. In one form or another, Derec knew, vacuum tubes like these had been used since the early industrial age—and Earth had apparently never discarded their use, because on Earth they made sense.

"Much more efficient than sending a car with a robot," he said.

It is if your houses are close together, Ariel thought. On the Spacer worlds, they were scattered.

The station seemed to deal mostly in inter-urban freight, but there was a window for passenger traffic. They avoided it, and prowled along the cars.

The train was no moving beltway, as Ariel had expected. Derec was clearly disappointed; he had expected something like the expressway. These were cars with ridiculously tiny wheels, and after a while Derec decided that they used magnetic levitation under speed. It was a very old technique.

"Now I see what R. David meant by saying that the way is largely roofed over," Ariel said.

"Twelve hours in one of those, eh?" Derec said, bleakly. The cars had no windows.

"Hey! Hey, you! You kids!"

They turned, concealing their apprehension.

A rough-looking stranger approached, wearing blue canvas and a peaked cap with stripes of pale gray and darker blue-gray, very distinctive. CONTINENTAL RAILROAD, said the emblem on his chest.

"What are you doing here?"

"Looking at the train, sir," said Derec, after a moment, trying to mimic the Earth dialect.

The other did not notice that. He closed in and examined them sharply, a beefy individual, taller than either of them and looking as if he worked out every day.

"Why?" he asked, irritably.

"School assignment, sir," said Ariel, thinking quickly.

He looked at her sharply again in her tight shipsuit, and she realized with a despairing feeling that she no longer had the figure of a schoolgirl. But he nodded, more in appreciation of her than in agreement, and said, more reasonably, "A study of the Continental system, eh? Well, you'll not learn much by prowling the yards. Read your books. But I can show you the marshaling yard and the loading docks. You should've brought visual recorders."

Evidently their new acquaintance—Peter, or Dieter, Scanlan—had little to do at the moment and was bored. Taking them briskly back the way they had come, he showed them where the cars were pulled aside, their doors opened, and men in handling machines carried forth containers of assorted cargo.

"That lot is bulk cargo, mostly—wheat from Kansas and points north," Scanlan shouted over the constant rumble of wheels and the whine of electric motors. "Now, over there—see those big blue cars?—that's pigs of metals from the sea-water refineries on the Gulf, down south-away. You'll see some manufactured goods going out, and quite a bit coming in—St. Louis mostly exports food, especially gourmet items. Not a big manufacturing city like Detroit."

What Ariel saw was that each of these big cars was crammed full of containers cunningly stacked to fill every corner, leaving no wasted space for even a rat to hide in.

"Come this way," said Scanlan, and he put them on a tiny truck like a motorized platform.

Its control was purely manual and Ariel fought down fear as she joined the men on it. Scanlan sent it hurtling around the fringes of activity to dive into a bright tunnel, which branched, branched again, and minutes later and two kilometers away he braked to a halt at a balcony.

They looked down on the marshaling yards.

"Trains are made up here," he shouted—it was noisy here, too.

Ariel looked, and realized why they were called "trains": each was a long series of units like link sausages. The cars were the units. They were being driven individually along the floor to the marked "rails" or roads painted on the floor, to the trains they were to make up. Each train was made up in a specific order.

"Over there to your left—passenger train for the West Coast. Three cars in blue, with silver and gold trim."

It was crawling slowly on its wheels toward, she supposed, the ticket window and embarking ramp. Once in the tunnels the cars would be lifted off their wheels by the magnetic rails.

On their right was a train of a hundred cars, in various colors according to what cargo they carried. That seemed to be the ratio of passengers to freight, except that there were more freight trains than passenger trains.

"Computer-controlled," shouted Scanlan. "There's a driver in each car for safety, but the computer does most of the placing. It knows where each car goes in the train. They pick up new cars at each stop on the front end, and drop off cars from the tail. The computer also knows which container is in each car, and what's in each container.

"Down here!"

Scanlan started the vehicle up again, whirled them down and down, braked in a flood of light. Black water lapped ahead of them, boats bobbing on it under the low ceiling.

"The Mississippi," he said, hissing like a snake. "Transshipment docks!"

They'd seen enough, but had to submit to another half-hour of education on a subject they could not—now—care less about.

They weren't going to be using the train.

CHAPTER 6

STUDIES IN SOCIOLOGY

Derec sighed with relief when they reentered the cheerless little apartment.

"I'm—tired," said Ariel. "I need to rest."

"Sure, you go lie down," said Derec, instantly concerned and quite understanding. He was exhausted and disappointed also. It had been a long day.

R. David stepped forward and unnecessarily showed her how to work the dimmer in the bedroom. It felt good to be back where robotic concern, the basis of all truly civilized societies, was available.

Derec sat down, thinking of that, and felt vaguely dissatisfied. He had always taken that statement for granted, and considered Earth uncivilized, in the lofty Spacer manner. *No wonder*, he thought *slowly, that Spacers are resented on Earth*. Because those people seemed to get along quite well without robots. That commissary might seem like an animal feeding trough to the overrefined sensibilities of a Spacer, but was that just? Human beings could adapt to a wide variety of societies. If Earthers were adapted to a way of life that gave Spacers the heebie-jeebies, it did not necessarily follow that Earth society was inferior.

True, Earth's Cities were the end product of an artificial process, and were highly unstable. If power supplies were interrupted for an hour, every human in the City would die of asphyxiation. Water was nearly as critical, and food almost as critical as water. Nor could the people leave the Cities in case of emergency; there was no place to go, and in any case, they could not bear the open air.

That train system could not begin to evacuate them, assuming it had power when the City didn't.

Was not Spacer society, though, with its dependence on robots, in its way just as artificial and dependent as Earth's? It was a novel and alarming thought. True, the robots could not all be simultaneously stricken by some plague, nor would all the factories shut down and not be reopened before the last robot wore out. They were not going to be deprived of their robots and robotic care.

No, Derec thought uneasily, *it was a more serious problem than that.* More serious even than Spacers' reliance on robots to save them from their own folly. Derec had had all he could do to keep from stopping and looking back to watch their pursuers being seized by the robots he knew *must* be there. Beyond that reliance, which was actually quite trivial, was the freezing of their whole society.

When a robot was unable to respond, caught between conflicting demands of the Laws of Robotics, it was said to be in "mental freeze-out." All of Spacer society, he suspected, might be in mental freeze-out, or at least in stasis. It was the Earthers, after all, who were settling the galaxy.

Somberly, he thought: *The only solution might be to give up robots. Or at least restrict their numbers.*

In the meantime, Dr. Avery had some mad scheme for

spreading advanced robots all across a planet, and then, apparently, peopling it with humans.

With that thought in his mind, Derec drifted off to sleep, and was not conscious of R. David springing forward to keep him from falling off the couch.

Derec dreamed.

He had swollen to enormous size, and larger, and larger, and larger. He was a planet, and something was crawling across his stomach. Raising his head and peering at the swollen dome of his belly, he saw that it was a city. Not an Earthly City, but a city of buildings separated by streets. A city populated by robots, ever-changing as buildings were built, torn down, rebuilt in different shapes. It was Robot City, and it spread around his equator.

He watched in fascination for a time, in fascination and horror—this was wrong, wrong, it was a spreading disease— and then he heard Ariel's voice.

No! The Human Medical Team was carrying her lifeless body sadly toward the crematorium. He struggled to move, to cry out . . . but he no longer had hands, or a voice—

Ariel was shaking him awake; he lay in a cramped position on the couch. R. David hovered in concern behind her.

"You were sleeping peacefully, then started struggling when you heard my voice. Sorry."

"Nothing," he managed. "Just a nightmare."

"Ah." She turned to R. David and began to question him while Derec sat on the couch, arms dangling, still badly shaken by the nightmare, telling himself it was only a dream. Only a dream.

But it gripped him, shook him as badly as the pursuit

by the yeast farmers had done. He threw it off and looked up as Ariel turned to him.

"I've been asking about news," she said in a complaining tone. "There's no broadcast reception in this apartment, not of any kind. Frost! No news, no entertainment—there's only the book-viewer. Not even an audio for music!"

"This apartment is for solitary Step Threes of various ratings," said R. David soothingly. "Step Threes are expected to consume their entertainment at the public facilities."

"It's probably for youngsters with low-paying entry-level jobs, just getting away from their parents," Derec said vaguely.

He looked closely at Ariel. During their excursions on the expressway she had seemed alive, vital, healthy. Now she seemed tired, petulant, lethargic. Fear gripped his heart like a fist.

"I'm tired of being cooped up. I want out!" she said.

Derec had to slow his own breathing, and wait till his heart stopped pounding. "So do I," he said, his tone so controlled that despite her lethargy she glanced quickly at him.

R. David's face was not made to express his concern. "Few Earth people leave their Cities, but there are some with a perverse attraction for openness and isolation. These direct the robots of the mines and farms, and man certain industrial facilities distant from the Cities for safety reasons. Other Earthers, wishing to become Settlers, join conditioning schools that accustom them to space and openness."

"Settlers!" said Ariel with surprise.

"Of course," said Derec wonderingly. "We know Earth people never leave their Cities; we also know that they alone are settling new planets. We should have made the connection long since. Conditioning is the only answer."

"Could we join one of these schools?" she asked.

"It would take us outdoors," said Derec uncertainly. But as he thought about it he shook his head. "I suspect that applicants for Settler worlds are investigated pretty strictly."

"Oh. Then—the other?"

Derec didn't know. "If we could get a job on a farm, directing robots . . ." He turned to R. David. "How are these workers chosen?"

"I am not sure of the details, but I suppose that one must apply for the job," said R. David.

Something Scanlan had said occurred to Derec. "Food and other raw materials are brought in from the surrounding areas by truck," he said. "Maybe, if we got jobs driving trucks—"

He didn't care to finish the sentence, not knowing to what extent R. David would condone violations of Earth laws. Ariel caught his meaning at once however and her eyes brightened.

How long it would take to drive a distance that a train could travel in twelve hours, he didn't know. What kind of pursuit they could expect, he had no idea. But nothing else seemed even remotely feasible.

R. David told them how to find out what they needed to know: the nearest communo would give them most of the information they needed for a start. Ariel's mood had lifted again, and again they ventured forth.

They consulted the directory at the communo, found Job Service, and checked *Farms—truck drivers*. A number of company names were listed, and Derec chose the Missouri Farm Company at random. It immediately transmitted an application form for them, which they could fill out by answering verbally when the pointer moved from question to question.

The first question was, *Do you have a driver's license?*

Derec sighed and canceled everything, went back to the menu, and did some exploring.

"I wish there was an information robot we could call up and ask," he said, frustrated.

It turned out that many Earthers who never went outside the City needed to know how to drive. There were schools, which taught them according to the regulations—and the instructions and regulations, being government-standardized, were readily available. They only had to take a book card and go to a library, then pay to have them printed off.

Another request gave them a map of the area, with YOU ARE HERE labeled and TARGET: *Library* indicated. They compared that to their own map, and nodded.

Opening the door of the communo booth made it switch back from opaque to clear, and they were given a sour look by the middle-aged fellow waiting for it.

"Canntchee find a private place out of people's way?" he growled, lurching past them.

Derec turned red, half with anger, half with embarrassment. Ariel was equally angry and much less embarrassed.

They walked away, seething, and observed that the playground was largely deserted. It was getting late.

"I hope we're not too late," he said.

"Yes." After a moment, Ariel said, "I suppose Earthers have a lot of trouble courting."

She had a point. No pleasant, nearly empty gardens for them to walk in on fine days; no large rambling mansions to prowl through on wet ones. What did they do? Derec wondered what he and Ariel might have done, back in his unremembered past.

It had been the leading edge of the rush hour when they

had arrived back home from the train station. Now all that was over, and the people were leaving the section kitchen in droves. They had only eaten twice today, both times fairly early—and neither had eaten much on the ship.

"Frost, they're still open," said Derec. "I thought we'd go hungry all night."

"So did I," said Ariel.

The line moved rapidly and they were soon in, and were astonished to find that free choice had not been suspended. They were assigned to table F-3 this time. The place, with only a couple of thousand people in it, seemed deserted.

The table, when they found it, had probably been used by three or four relays of diners for the evening meal, but it was surprisingly clean and neat. They saw Earthers industriously wiping up their places prior to leaving. Others, attendants, came around with cleansing utensils that seemed almost superfluous; some sprayed the places with steam guns to sterilize them.

They were far enough from their neighbors to speak freely in low tones. "I suppose there are strong social forces to make them clean up their places," Ariel said.

Derec thought about it, nodded. Mere laws could not have such force. "I suppose they train their kids: Clean up your places. What'll the neighbors think?"

"The forces for conformity to social norms must be tremendous," she said. "It's not necessarily a bad thing."

"It makes their whole civilization possible. And are we that different?" he asked.

Ariel shook her head somberly. She had been exiled for violating some of those norms.

They were given three choices: Zymosteak, again, Sweet-and-Pungent Zymopork, and Pseudo-Chicken Casserole. Side dishes included such things as salads and fruit plates, Hearty Hungarian Goulash, Vegetable Pseudo-Beef Stew, and so on. They chose the Zymopork and the Casserole, and browsed among the side dishes, almost famishing from the smell of the food around them.

"At least, seated here in the middle, we can watch the families," Ariel said.

"Right. I was wondering if it would be acceptable to divide our dishes with each other. But see that family with the four kids—the kids are swapping around ad lib."

"Yes—and the parents. Different side dishes come with different main courses, and they're trading off."

The food arrived at that point, and they wasted no more time watching others eat.

When they had finished and exited the kitchen, Derec paused, glancing around.

"What's wrong?"

"It's still light," he said. "It should be getting dark."

She laughed nervously. They moved aside, out of the way, and strolled slowly toward the ways. "I know what you mean. Especially for us, since we got up well before what these people consider the dawn. But, of course, the lights will never dim."

They rode the localway for a short distance, changed ways, and presently found themselves at a massive entrance flanked with stone lions.

"Stone!" said Ariel, sounding astonished. "I supposed they'd be plastic or something."

"Or nothing," said Derec. He liked libraries, though people rarely visited them on the Spacer worlds. It was simpler just to call them up and have the books transmitted over your phone.

"I suppose many apartments on Earth must be equipped to receive book transmissions," he said.

"In higher social classes," Ariel said wryly, and he laughed. Spacers though they were, they were not masquerading merely as Earthers, but as low-rated Earthers.

Crowds of people, as usual on Earth, swarmed up and down the ornamental steps that led up to the entry. Some sat on the steps or the balusters, talking, laughing, eating or drinking, and many reading. A group of children played on one of the lions, their book-viewers laid carefully between its paws. Inside were uniformed guards with clubs and surprisingly cheerful expressions, sober people of all ages swarming about, many of them young, and people sitting around tables. Virtually every terminal was in use.

"This must be the library's rush hour," Derec whispered.

With school out for the day, people off work and looking for the cheapest entertainment—it probably was.

At length they found an unused terminal and did a twenty-minute search for the information, making sure they had all they needed. Derec had a moment of doubt when he inserted his money tab into the slot. This metal tab was not unlike the credit-transfer system on the Spacer worlds. But he had no idea what formalities were employed here, or how much money there was in this account.

ACCEPTED, said the blinking transparency, and the machine tinkled a tune to let them know it was copying the information on their card.

"We've got it," he said, breathing more easily. "Let's go."

Out of the library, down the steps, to the right. They marched more slowly than they had at the beginning of the day. Derec was as tired as Ariel looked.

"It's been a *long* day," he said hollowly.

"And we've come a long way," she added.

Turn, and turn again, and they confronted a smaller

marquee than one they'd seen in Old Town Sector: WILL YOU FOLLOW?

"Not tonight, honey," said Derec vaguely. "I'm too tired."

"We didn't come by that, Derec," Ariel said, gripping his arm.

"I know," he said tiredly. "We've gotten turned around."

They retraced their steps, and now couldn't find the library. After quite a while they paused, gray-faced with weariness and strain, before a window showing dresses and hats of incredible fabrics, some of which glowed. Cheap finery. Men and women peered through windows, pointed out things they'd like but would probably never afford. Not far from them a young man in tight blue pants and silver pseudo-leather jacket, with elaborately coiffed hair, stood next to a girl who seemed much older than Ariel and who wore even tighter violet pants and a nearly transparent, slashed top. Her hair was blonde and long on one side and short and red on the other, and her eyes were cynical and hard.

This was a major thoroughfare, though it was not part of the moving way system. It ought to join to the ways somewhere, but didn't seem to. They had no idea which way to go.

"Just like a couple of Transients," said Derec glumly. "We can't be far from the ways, but we could spend an hour blundering around looking for them."

The youth with the tough expression and the silvery jacket turned toward them.

"Transients, eh?" he said. He looked them up and down. The hard-featured young woman looked at them curiously also.

Derec braced himself.

CHAPTER 7

BACK TO SCHOOL

"That way two blocks, take the up ramp," the young tough said courteously, and the hard-featured young woman looked sympathetically at them.

"Thank you," said Derec, and Ariel, as startled as he, echoed him.

Their rescuers had forgotten them before they were out of sight, but Derec and Ariel remembered them all the way home.

The section kitchen had become a familiar place by the time of their third meal, next morning. Much of the shock of enormous rooms, enormous numbers of loud talking Earthers, of being ignored amid mobs, was gone. After breakfast, out into the monotonous every-day of the ways, they rode south toward the edge of the sprawling megalopolis. Finally, in a section called Mattese, they found the driving school they sought.

They had chosen it because it was a "private" school.

Though regulated by the government, it counted as a luxury, and one paid for the privilege of learning here, a concept that bemused the Spacers.

"Yes, please?"

The receptionist was not the robot the term called to their minds, but a middle-aged woman—though Earthers aged fast by Spacer standards; she was probably quite young, perhaps no more than forty-five or fifty.

"Derec and Ariel Avery," Derec said apologetically, trying again to imitate the Earth dialect.

"Oh, yes, new students. You're a bit early, but that's good—you have to do your forms."

They thought they'd already done the forms over the commune, but took the papers and sat down. These forms were simple and asked primarily how much experience they'd had with automobiles and something called "models."

"Can that mean what I think it does?" Ariel asked. Derec could only shrug.

They had sweated over the application last night, for it asked for their schooling, but R. David had given them the names of schools in the City they might have gone to. They hoped the driving school would be lax in checking up. Of course, sooner or later their imposture would be detected, but even one day, they calculated—

"You may see Ms. Winters now," said the receptionist, smiling kindly.

Ms. Winters kept them waiting in an outer office for a moment while she examined their forms, and Ariel nudged Derec.

"Did you hear that receptionist? She was trying to copy *our* accent!"

Ms. Winters called them in, asked a question or two,

nodded, and, taking the forms, left with a brief "Wait just a moment." It hadn't taken her long, as they had indicated no experience.

She hadn't closed the door completely.

"Red? Those two students, the brother and sister... upper-rating children slumming, or kicked out of the house, or something." Doubtfully, she added, "Maybe student reporters, checking up on the schooling system, or something."

"Who cares?" came a gruff-sounding male voice. "They got money, they want to learn, we sell schoolin'. Send 'em on out."

With a dazzling smile, Ms. Winters ushered them through the farther door into a large room with a number of carrels within it. Students were entering in a steady stream from a different door and occupying carrels and other learning stations farther down.

Red confronted them, a blocky fellow with thinning sandy hair and a handsome face, his body one solid slab of muscle. He looked them over shrewdly for a moment, nodded, gave a noncommittal grunt.

"Drivin's a hands-on schoolin'," he said bluntly. "You either learn it with your reflexes or else you don't learn it. It ain't so different from learnin' to ride the ways, though you don't remember how you did that." It was a set speech, and went on in that vein for about three minutes. Red's face remained blank.

Derec was impressed despite his prejudices. Education among Spacers, as little of it as he could remember, was a more gracious process, lavishly supported by ever-patient robots. It was clear that this indifferent man proposed to push them into the water and watch to see if they drowned.

If they did not, they would be rewarded only by his good opinion.

"... it's your money and your time, so I know you'll do your best and not waste either."

Though his experience with different machines must be far greater than this Earther's, Derec wryly found that Red's good opinion was a thing worth striving for.

The carrels were cockpits containing mockups of the control sets of various kinds of vehicles, and trimensionals of the roadways. Red gave them a brief instruction on the rules of the road and the operation of the craft, showed them a printed set of instructions on the right and of rules on the left, and said, "Do it, gatos."

Derec and Ariel grinned faintly at each other, and *did it* for about half an hour.

Red came by at the end of the time, sucking on the stem of a cup, if a cup had a stem, and exhaling smoke courteously away from them. He bent and looked on the back sides of the carrels.

"You did good," he said, his eyebrows expressing more than his voice. "You did real good, for beginners."

Maybe too good, Derec thought uneasily.

Red looked at them, blew smoke thoughtfully, and said, "Come down here to the models."

The models were as they had supposed, small-scale versions of various vehicles they'd have to learn to drive in order to graduate, from one-man scooters to big transport trucks. They were given models of four-person passenger cars marked POLICE, and control sets, the models being, of course, remote-controlled.

This was an interactive game with a vengeance, and the other students who had advanced this far grinned at them and made room. Derec started his car slowly, nearly got run over by a big truck, speeded up, nearly went out of the lane going around a corner, cut too sharply, but gradually began to get the hang of it.

Then a white-gleaming ambulance with red crosses on its doors and top made a left turn from the outside lane, the operator crying "Oops!" belatedly as he realized where he was. Derec avoided him skillfully and slipped past. After a moment his controls froze, as did the ambulance's. The ambulance operator grimaced, then grinned ruefully, and they all looked at a trimensional screen to one side.

A-9 ILLEGAL TURN, NO SIGNALS. P-3, FAILURE TO APPREHEND TRAFFIC VIOLATOR.

"Frost. Swim or drown," Derec muttered, and the girl next to him laughed.

It wasn't as easy as it looked, and he wasn't *thinking* only of not knowing the rules—such as that a police car was expected to act like a police car. The streets were full of vehicles, and he had to be prepared to predict their moves. None of his Spacer training was of much use here. To his mortification, he rammed a fire engine at one stopping, not seeing the signal lights in time. It didn't help that Ariel slaughtered half a dozen pedestrians at a place where the motorway and pedestrian levels merged. The other students were far better, but cheerful about it, or Derec couldn't have stood it.

It was humiliating.

After an hour of exhilarating play, during which they got much better, Red came by and said, "Take a break, all; give the second team a chance."

The students relinquished their controls, leaving the vehicles in mid-street, and trooped out, old and young alike, to some kind of refectory. Red caught Derec's eye, nodded to Ariel; they stepped aside.

"I've been watching the monitor record. You're not so swift on models, where I was expectin' you t' shine," he said. "Figured you'd have lots of experience on them."

He paused and eyed them questioningly, but they just nodded. Shrugging, Red said, "I'm gonna put you on trucks. Big ones. You ever been outside?"

Chilled, Derec said, "What?"

"Outside the City," Red said patiently.

"Well—" Derec exchanged a glance with Ariel. "Yeah. We've, uh, we've given it a try."

"Ever have nightmares about it?"

"What? No."

Red nodded shrewdly. "The shrinks have all kinds tests, but one thing talks true: nightmares. Thing is, you're young, you could be conditioned easily if you aren't what shrinks call phobic. That means, if you don't have nightmares. Big money in driving the big rigs outside—not many people to do this kind of job. Most trucks are computer-controlled, or remote-controlled—but even remote-control ops get upset, break down, have nightmares. They even use a lot of robot drivers."

"Really?"

Red shrugged. "Why not? They're not takin' anybody's job away. Not many people will do that kind of work. If you can do it—and will—it pays real good."

Derec and Ariel looked at each other.

"Don't have to decide right away," Red said shrewdly. "I know—people'd think you're queer, wanting to go outside. And I should tell you, I get a bounty on every prospect I send out."

He looked at them with a hint of humor. "Oh, yeah, you got to apply for the job—outside."

He paused for an answer, and Derec said slowly, "Well, can we think it over? I mean, we don't know anything about trucks—"

"I'll put you on simulators now—c'mon back here."

At the back of the room were giant simulators they had to climb up into—three of them.

"Most of the trucks we train on are for inside the City, and they're pretty small. Lots of competition for the driver jobs on them—most freight goes by the freightways, naturally, and driving the freight-handler trucks is a different department of the Transportation Bureau. Lots of competition for those jobs, too. But these big babies go beggin'. Yet they're real easy to learn."

The important thing was remembering that one had a long "tail" behind one. They moved slowly when maneuvering, though, and anyone who had landed a spaceship could learn this readily enough.

"Give it half an hour or so, an' we'll look at your records."

It was closer to an hour, and Derec and Ariel were both tired when Red approached them again.

"You done real good," he said, looking at a print-out. "You were made for outside drivin'. You do much better where you don't have to watch out for traffic." He looked at them with a faint smile. "It's never as frantic in the motorways as in our model. Usually they're wide open and empty. But you learn about traffic *in* traffic."

"How'd we do?" Ariel asked, imitating his accent fairly well, to Derec's ear.

"Good enough to make it worth your while to go on,"

said Red. "A week's training, and I'll be sending you out to Mattell Trucking & Transport. Yes?"

Ms. Winters, from the inner office, had approached him. She glanced at them curiously.

"You two go take a break, drink some fruit juice or something, and I'll talk to you in fifteen minutes."

When they were out of sight, Ariel said, "Keep on going."

"I thought so, but I couldn't be sure," Derec said.

"I suppose she checked out our education, or something," Ariel said glumly.

"Yes, well, it had to happen. And we've had an hour's worth of training on big trucks." Derec was quite buoyant. "I doubt very much if they are equipped to chase stolen trucks across the countryside. At least, not well equipped. How many Earthers would not only steal a big truck, but take off across country?"

"We haven't stolen our truck yet," Ariel said gloomily.

Derec found himself joining her in gloom as they made their way back to the expressway; and then they found it jammed and had to stand on the lower-ratings' level. It traveled just as fast, but it was a tiring nuisance.

They stopped off at the kitchen for a light lunch, and at the Personals on the way back to the apartment. Derec made his way back to Sub-Section G, Corridor M, Sub-Corridor 16, Apartment 21, from the Personal, with a skill that was by now automatic. Then he sat and waited. And waited.

Derec was quite concerned by the time Ariel returned, and became more concerned with one look at her. She had taken twice as long as he, and looked dull.

"What took you so long?"

"I got lost," she said lusterlessly.

"You look—tired. You want—to lie down?" Derec's voice kept catching with his fear.

"I guess."

But Ariel sat down on the couch and didn't move. She didn't respond to anything Derec said. After a long while she got up and dragged herself into the bedroom.

Derec was worried and restless. He had wanted to discuss ways and means of getting a truck, but that was impossible under the circumstances. She obviously had at least a mild fever.

Instead, he spent the afternoon viewing books. Some of Dr. Avery's local collection were Earthly novels; some were documentaries; some were volumes of statistics about population densities, yeast production, and so on. It was not the most stimulating reading he'd ever done, but Derec read or viewed the documentaries—some were print, some audiovisual.

Presently he found that it was late and he was hungry, but he hesitated. "R. David, please check on Ariel and see if she is awake. If so, ask if she would like to accompany me to the section kitchen."

The robot did so, found her awake, and repeated the answer Derec had heard: "No, Mr. Avery, Miss Avery does not feel hungry and requires no food."

He hesitated about leaving her. If she felt hungry later, he could accompany her to the kitchen door, but doubted he'd be allowed in again tonight. Still, he could hang around outside and hope he wasn't questioned by a policeman. In any case, he himself was quite hungry despite his worry over Ariel.

He went out, stopping off at the Personal again and getting a drink from a public fountain outside it, then threaded the maze to the section kitchen. This time he got table J-10, and there was a longer wait; he saw that the room was near capacity. There weren't two adjoining spaces free at the table, as the Earthers tended to spread out as much as possible.

It was a gloomy meal, alone amid so many.

Then he retraced his weary route. *I suppose a person could get used to this, he thought. It's inconvenient, but you don't miss what you never had.* The Earthers obviously didn't give it a thought.

Questioned on this subject, R. David said, "It is not necessary for all Earth people to make this trek every time, of course. Holders of higher steps in each rating have such things as larger apartments, activated wash basins, subetherics, and so on. Of course, it is far more efficient to supply one section kitchen for four or five thousand households than to supply a room for cooking in each of these partments, plus a cooker, food storage devices, food delivery, and so on. Just so with subetherics, when one big machine can replace a thousand small ones."

"But some people do have these things, and convenient laundry facilities in Personal, without having to go to the section laundry. Don't the have-nots resent these privileges?"

"Perhaps some do so, Mr. Avery, for humans are illogical. But human emotions are allowed for in the distribution of these favors, according to the Teramin Relationship."

"The what?"

"The Teramin Relationship. That is the mathematical expression that governs the differential between inconveniences suffered with privileges granted: dee eye sub jay taken to the—"

"Spare me the math; I'm a specialist in robotics, and

even my math there is not fully developed. But I'm interested; I've never heard of any kind of math being applied to human relations. Can you express this Tera-whatchacallit Relationship verbally?"

"Perhaps an example would suffice, master. Consider that the privilege of having three meals a week in the apartment, even if the recipient has to fetch the meals himself from a section kitchen, if the privilege were granted for cause, will keep a large if varying number of people patient with their own inconveniences. For it demonstrates that privileges are real, can be earned without too great an effort, and have been earned by people whom one knows."

"Interesting," said Derec, thinking that the robots of Robot City ought to know this. "How do you know all this?"

"I aided Dr. Avery in his researches on society. I also aided him in his research into robotic history."

"Robotic history? On Earth?"

"But of course, Mr. Avery. The positronic brain, and the positronic robot, were invented on Earth. Susan Calvin was an Earthwoman, and Dr. Asenion an Earthman."

Those names he knew—Dr. Asenion, especially, the man who had codified the mathematics that expressed the Three Laws in ways that made it possible to incorporate them into positronic brains. But Earth people! Still, it might explain much about Robot City. Dr. Avery was studying mass society and non-specialized robots on Earth.

"Is there a book on the mathematics of human society?" he asked, thinking it might well be good to take such a thing back to Robot City. Those poor robots had scarcely ever seen a human being, yet they were designed to serve mankind.

"I believe there are no Spacer books on the subject, Mr. Avery. However, I have several Earthly references of which you may have copies."

"I'd like that."

He'd like even more for Ariel to wake up and be her old self again. All during the afternoon he had had twinges of sharp fear, and kept trying not to remember that her disease was ultimately fatal.

CHAPTER 8

OUTSIDE!

Apparently everybody in Webster Groves had the idea of getting breakfast early; this was the worst jam yet. Ariel shifted from foot to foot and had the ungallant wish that Derec would carry her. Finally, however, they got in, made their way to their table, and sat with twin sighs.

The meal was lavish and included quite a few choices, including real meat sausages. Derec ate heavily, she saw, taking his own advice: it might be a long day. She tried to do so, but could not.

"I thought you were feeling better," he said.

"Yes," she said, and tried valiantly to eat more. How could she explain that her problem was as much psychological as physical? She had felt better this morning, but perhaps she was still feverish. Derec, in fact, had looked bad himself, as if he'd had another and worse nightmare. He'd said nothing.

"Just a claustrophobic attack," she muttered to him.

Derec nodded somberly.

It was partly that. Partly it was depression. Partly, she

thought, it was sensory overload. Earth was so over-whelming! Even now—ten thousand jaws masticating food and the ceaseless din and motion around her—she wanted it all to *stop* for a minute, just for a minute! Even in her sleep, however, it never stopped.

And her illness was undoubtedly creeping up on her. If it crossed the blood-brain barrier, they had told her, it would be fatal. Until then she could still hope—dream—of a cure. Well, the moments of inattention she had been experiencing, the fugues as she relived past memories only to lose them forever, the dreamlike hallucinatory state she often found herself in, could only mean one thing.

How could she tell Derec?

"Ready?"

Nodding, concealing her dread, Ariel rose and followed him out into yet more motion and noise.

The ways were surprisingly quiet, considering how many tons of people they carried, considering the speeds they moved at, considering the cleaving of the air over them. But the roar was always there under all consciousness, making Ariel feel more than ever that it was all a hallucination.

They retraced their route to Old Town Section, then through "Yeast Town," which began with East St. Louis Section. They sat, quiet, tense, through this section, but nobody paid any attention to them. Beyond, the sections stretched again, on and on to the east.

New York lay to the east, Derec had found, and he had no desire to try to drive around the City.

"Mommer!" yelled a young girl not far from them.

Derec and Ariel glanced at her apprehensively. It was rush hour, and all of them were standing, the Earthers patiently.

"Yeahr?" inquired an older woman, presumably Mommer. She wore a dark, baggy suit. The daughter wore a tight yellow one, over a rather unfortunate figure.

" 'Member when Mayor Wong and all the Notables was at Busch Stadium 'time the Reds played?" she yelled.

"No," said Mommer, indifferently.

" 'Member the girl that played the—" Ariel didn't get the title; it sounded like "star-mangled spanner"—"on the bugle?"

"Yeahr, so what?"

"That's my boyfriend Freddy's cousin Rosine!" the daughter shouted. She looked around triumphantly.

"No kiddin'?" Mommer asked, losing her indifference.

" 'Swearta God!" cried the girl, looking around proudly, famous by contagion. "In fronta Wong an' all them Notables!"

At length, the lightworms overhead signaled END OF LINE. The crowd had thinned out long before, Mommer and daughter among the first to go. Only a few distinctly scruffy types were still on the ways. The edge of the City was evidently not a fashionable place. A number of men in obvious workmen's dress also rode with them.

The eastbound and westbound strips separated, were further divided by a building, and the strips tilted. At heart-stopping full speed the eastbound lane looped to the left, circled the building, and became the westbound lane. Ariel followed Derec down the strips just after the turn. He'd apparently been too interested to get off sooner.

"Oh, no!"

There was no crowd, and she thought that was the reason he got careless. Derec's foot came down on the join of two strips, and in a moment he'd been jerked off his feet. He rolled on his back down onto the slower strip.

Ariel leaped after him, in her haste not bracing herself, and fell forward at full length—fortunately, on the slower strip.

Derec, grunting, had rolled half onto a yet slower strip, which slipped from under his fingers as he clawed at it. With great presence of mind he rolled over yet again fully onto that strip.

Ariel hastily picked herself up and gingerly transferred to his new strip. Derec sat grinning faintly and watched her as she walked back toward him. A couple of Earthers glanced at them incuriously and looked up at the lightworms. Apparently falling riders weren't that uncommon. Nobody laughed.

Dusting himself off, Derec grinned more widely and led her down, then stopped in some consternation.

"Where's your purse?"

Ariel clapped a hand to her side, gasped. She didn't often carry a purse, but had had to on Earth. With all the identification and such she had to carry here, it was a real necessity. Now it was all gone.

"No real matter—R. David can fake up more identification for you," Derec said.

They looked along the ways, but saw no sign of it. It must be hundreds of meters off by now, and they didn't know on which strip. Ariel shrugged.

"There must be some central office where you can reclaim things lost on the ways," Derec said, but dismissed it.

With a skill increased by their previous experiences, they made their way down into the bowels of the City to the freightway level. NO RIDING. PEDESTRIANS FORBIDDEN, the signs proclaimed. So they walked along beside them to the terminus, which was much like that of the passengerways above.

Small trucks with lifts in front and broad, flat beds behind brought in cannisters of freight. Somewhere not far from here big trucks were unloading these cannisters, driving in, wheeling out.

"Hey, you—you kids! Git away from there! Don't you see the sign? Go on, back!"

AUTHORIZED PERSONS ONLY.

Muttering, Derec led Ariel up a motionless ramp, hesitated, and struck out along a corridor running east. After half an hour of fruitlessly trying to go down to the entrance there, he retraced his steps and they went down to the lower level, and then marched toward the entrance. It was marked on the City maps as an entrance, not as an exit. There were no exits on the map.

NO ADMITTANCE TO UNAUTHORIZED PERSONS.

Derec opened the door cautiously, beckoned her through. Beyond it they found a garage for the handling trucks that transferred the cannisters. Men swarmed around it, but ignored them.

"We can't go there," Ariel said when he had led her behind the trucks to the motorway.

It was a stub motorway joining the entrance with the freightway strips. To step out into that rumbling passage would be to get run over on the spot.

Derec hesitated. "Steal a handler and drive it out there?" he asked.

"And maybe keep on going?" she asked wistfully, thinking of sunlight and air. Tomorrow and New York were too far away to bother about. Her head hurt.

"No, we couldn't get much past the exit. These things are all beam-powered. That's why we have to have one of those big trucks. They're nukes."

In the end, they picked out a small handler and figured out the controls, which were quite simple.

"I'm surprised there's no control lock," said Ariel. "Knowing Earthly psychology."

"Frost, you're right," said Derec, worried, and looked it over. "This slot," he said after a moment. "For an ID tag, probably a specialized one." He looked it over and said, "I wish I had my tools."

Wonders can be performed with such things as metal ration tags. He worked away behind the control panel while Ariel crouched behind him in the tiny cab and watched anxiously for anyone approaching.

"Ready," he said at last. "Take the stick and drive us slowly out into the motorway."

She did so, nervously. At the door, the machine slowed, a panel on its controls lighting with the words: IDENTIFICATION REQUIRED BEYOND THIS POINT. Derec did something, a relay clicked quietly, and the handler rolled smoothly out into the stream.

"So far, so good," Derec said. "Nobody following."

Ariel turned to the right, guided them across the motorway to the proper lane, and they rolled slowly along toward the light. The traffic was fairly heavy, but moved slowly.

"Oh, almost—" Ariel said.

The light came from a vast open space where elephantine trucks trundled in and backed up to the loading docks. The handlers ran in and out of them, transferring their cargoes to small trucks, which took them to the freightways. Off to the right, a row of the huge trucks were disgorging golden grain into pipelines with a roar and a hiss of nitrogen.

"No good!" cried Derec. "Too many people. Pull over to the right, by those dumpsters. We'll pretend to be inspectors or something."

Sick, Ariel saw that he was right: There was little hope of seizing a truck unnoticed. The loading was done with smooth efficiency, though nobody seemed to move very fast. There were little knots of gossiping drivers and operators around. Men and women went around with clipboards, checking manifests. As soon as a truck was unloaded, it pulled out.

"Too bad we can't find a clipboard or two," Derec said.

Ariel thought that their shipsuits fit in pretty well, but wished they were cleaner. They had not thought to launder them—she had slept in hers, though the fabric didn't show it.

They got out of the handler reluctantly, and stood looking about.

Ariel yearned for the open. They could go to the edge of the dock, drop their own height to the concrete, and walk perhaps a hundred or a hundred fifty meters, and find themselves at the opening.

"Might have expected these Earthers to block off the opening," she observed. Light came in, but they couldn't see out.

"They don't even like as much of an opening as they've got," said Derec. "Notice how they all stand with their backs to it?"

They did. Each little group was a semicircle facing away from the opening.

"Let's go outside," she said impulsively.

Derec hesitated. "It might not be easy to explain. It might not be easy to get back in."

"Who wants to?" she said fiercely. "I just want to see sunlight one last time!"

Derec looked at her, frightened, concealed it, and said gently, "All right, we'll see what we can do."

He led her across the dock space and peered up at the numbers and letters on the side of one of the mammoth trucks. It was damp, and had dripped a puddle under it. Ariel had had no idea of how big they were till then. Nodding wisely, Derec stepped to the edge, turned, and dropped off.

Ariel followed.

They strode briskly, as if they had business there, toward the front of the truck. Beyond lay the barrier. Trucks entered obliquely between overlapping walls, so that vision could not reach out to the frightening openness outside but the trucks could enter without opening and closing doors. Ariel suspected that the way zigzagged, so great was the fear they showed of the outside.

"Hey! Hey, you two!"

A group of men were walking threateningly toward them on the docks, gesturing them back. One turned and dropped off as they watched. "Come back here!"

"Run!" said Derec.

A big wet truck erupted from the barrier even as they began to run, and they swerved. They found themselves running toward the grain trucks dropping their cargoes from their bellies.

A sign hovered in the air before them: WARNING: OXYGEN REQUIRED BEYOND THIS POINT!

Ariel remembered reading somewhere that grain dust could explode if liberally mixed with air. They stored it in nitrogen to prevent that. But, she observed, stricken with fear, the men working here were not wearing masks.

Derec led her on a route that avoided them—these workers looked up curiously but did not join the chase immediately—and they ran through the first dust cloud, then through the second.

"Not good enough," he said, as they paused, panting. Ariel tried not to cough; the dust was in her throat.

"Back up on the docks," she wheezed, and he nodded, led the way. With a grunt they were up, between trucks. The grain trucks didn't back up to the actual docks, which were quite narrow here. The whole area was fogged with dust.

They heard a shout, "Damn thieves," and looked back.

They had not been seen yet, but it was only a matter of time. The space beyond the dust cloud was a bedlam of whistles, shouts, and pounding feet. A big truck pulled away, its great wheels churning up more dust but making no sound.

A shout, something about laying the dust, came to them. Ariel couldn't get her breath. *We need oxygen*, she thought, and wanted to cough worse than ever. Out there they were coughing, too.

Red lights flamed overhead and a deep-toned horn sounded. Ariel looked up apprehensively to see yellow signs beside the red lights: SPRINKLERS . . . SPRINKLERS . . . SPRINKLERS. . . .

"Back in here, quick!" Derec cried, and pulled her back behind a tangle of implements, broken handler trucks, dustbins, and the like.

Water spurted in a fine spray from the overhead, laying the dust immediately. A blue-clad man was among the truck drivers and dock workers; he carried a now-familiar club.

"A cop!" Derec said, groaning.

Ariel had glanced at him. And saw, beyond him—

"A door!"

"Where?"

"There, behind that tire."

The tire, a huge thing in bright-blue composition, discarded from one of the trucks, marked the end of the dump they were crouched in. There was a passageway by it to a small door.

In a moment they were trying it, and before the sprinklers cut off they were in a small, dim hallway with only one out of three lights burning.

PIPELINE CONTROL SECTION: NO ADMITTANCE TO UNAUTHORIZED PERSONS. But the hall led past. Farther on, they saw: GRAIN & BULK SUPPLY RATIONALIZING & BALANCING.

"Administrative controls on the basic levels," said Derec, and Ariel thought of the men and women with clipboards.

"But there's nobody here," she said.

"Well, cities grow and change; these may be abandoned, or only needed periodically. The important thing is they may have access above—"

They did.

At the upper level, they found that they were far from the docks, to which they knew better than to return, but were not gone from the barrier yet. The motorways used by emergency vehicles also reached at least to the entry.

Beside the motorway was a pedestrian access door; the motorway door had no controls and probably opened by radio. Once through, walking nervously on the motorway, they found to their frustration that the way avoided the entrance, swooped, and dived down to the lower levels.

"It's for emergency vehicles," said Derec. "Ambulances, and so on. Accidents must be common on the docks."

Presently, they did find a half-concealed route that took them to the opening, and they looked out and down.

It was pouring with cold rain.

Even then Derec didn't give up, but Ariel's mind refused to record the details of the rest of the day. For several more hours he kept them prowling around the area, always trying to find a way to get at a big truck. But he could find no garage for them within the City and doubted seriously if there was one near to it.

Finally Ariel pleaded hunger and they gloomily rode the ways back to their section kitchen, able at least to sit down. Ariel felt doomed; one look at the cold gray rain falling endlessly outside had chilled her on some deep, basic level. She knew it was the last she'd ever see of the sky. For Derec, she felt sad, but was too tired to speak.

"We'll try again tomorrow at a different entrance," Derec said when she had eaten the little she could. "The sun will be shining—probably, anyway—and things will be all right."

She nodded indifferently.

CHAPTER 9

AMNEMONIC PLAGUE

To Derec's dismay, Ariel did not reappear that afternoon, and the next morning she arose late and looked terrible.

R. David became alarmed. "Miss Avery, you are not well. What are your symptoms?"

"The same as usual, R. David. Don't worry; I brought this illness with me; it's nothing to worry about." She sounded tired and fretful, trying not to worry his Three Law-dominated brain.

But a robot will worry if it seems appropriate, whether told not to or not. *They weren't so different from humans in that respect*, thought Derec, himself alarmed.

"I hope you are indeed not seriously ill, Miss Avery, but please tell me your symptoms so that I may judge. As you know, First Law compels me to help you."

She grimaced. "Okay. I'm frequently feverish—is there any water in the place?"

"No," Derec said. "I'll bring you—frost! is there anything to carry water in?"

"No," said R. David.

Mentally, Derec cursed all Earthers, individually and collectively, and the Teramin Relationship, too.

"Anyway, I'm often feverish, and tired and lethargic and listless. And—and—" she glanced at Derec. "I have mental troubles. Confusion—I forget where I am, lose track of what's going on. A lot of the time I sit and don't speak because I can't follow the conversation. I've been reliving the past a lot."

Suddenly she cried out passionately, "Nothing seems *real!* I feel like I'm in a hallucination."

It was more serious than Derec had thought. Hesitantly, he asked, "Do you feel like going to the section kitchen?"

"No. I don't feel like doing anything, except drinking a liter of water and going back to bed."

"You must go to section hospital at once," said R. David decisively, stepping forward.

Derec could have groaned. "What kind of medical care can you expect in an Earthly hospital?" he asked. "We've got to get you back to the Spacer worlds—"

"There's no cure for me there," she said quietly.

Damn. That was true. Derec hesitated, torn, and said, "Well, back to Robot City, then. Maybe the Human Medical Team has a cure."

"My medical knowledge is limited, primarily to the effects of Earthly ills on Spacers. But that knowledge makes me doubt that Miss Avery will—will live long enough for a space journey," said R. David, the catch in his voice obvious. "She is obviously in, or approaching, the—crisis of her disease."

Derec hesitated. That was too obviously true.

Ariel smiled sadly and said, "I fear he is right, Derec. I—I'm losing my memory—my mind. And it's getting worse. I couldn't remember my way back here the other night—"

Abruptly, she was weeping.

Oh, frost, Derec thought helplessly.

R. David gave them an argument; he wanted to accompany them—to carry Ariel, in fact.

"No!" said Derec. "I may be ignorant of many things about Earth, but I know well enough what Earthers do to any robots they catch on the ways. And if we tried to do anything about it, our first words would give us away as Spacers. They'd be all over us. I've been chased once by yeast farmers. Frost! I don't want to have *every* Earther we meet at our throats."

It took the firmest commands reinforcing Dr. Avery's to keep R. David in the apartment. Only when Ariel perked up, as she usually did at the prospect of change, was the robot's First Law conditioning allayed. Ariel was even almost gay as she left, rendering a zany marching song: "One-two-three! Here we go! Bedlam, Bedlam, ho ho ho! Drrringdingding, brrrumbum bum, brrrreebeedeebee Dabbabba-dum-bum-bum!"

But once the door had closed she looked haggard.

"Water," she said, smiling wanly at Derec's concerned look.

After she had drunk a liter or so, she gasped for breath a few minutes, but was game to go on. The route to the section hospital was longer than the one to the kitchen, and she drooped visibly. Worse, it was morning now and the express was jammed. They had to stand; Threes weren't allowed to sit during rush hour.

It seemed that the nightmare of rushing ways and whistling wind and unconcerned, self-centered Earthers would go on forever. Derec had to watch Ariel—he feared she would collapse—and also watch the signs overhead, fearing that he would forget or confuse the instructions he had carefully impressed on his memory.

But even the longest journey ends at last, and the exit was clearly marked SECTION HOSPITAL, with the same red cross on white that Spacers used.

The anteroom smelled of antiseptic and was mobbed with men, women, and children. *Children*, thought Derec vaguely—*never seen so many children in my life as on Earth*. Though his memories still were lost, he was sure, by his astonished reaction, that he had not. Of course, they had to keep replacing this huge population.

Fumbling, he inserted Ariel's newly forged ID tags into the computer, whose panel lit with CHECK-UP, ILLNESS, EMERGENCY? Ariel was leaning against him, gasping and pale after the ordeal, and even the usually unconcerned Earthers were looking at them in some alarm. Emergency, he decided, panicky, and punched it.

Instantly a red star appeared in the panel, blinking; apparently alarms rang elsewhere, for a strong-looking woman appeared, started to remonstrate with him for mistaking an ILLNESS for an EMERGENCY—young husbands! But Ariel turned a ghastly, apologetic smile on her, and the woman's mouth closed with a snap.

"Here!"

She half carried Ariel past three rooms full of still more waiting Earthers, to a room with a wheeled, knee-high cart in it.

"Lie down, baby!"

The gurney stood up, she strapped Ariel on, and an older woman entered. "Dr. Li—"

"Mmm. I see." She began to check over Ariel, not bothering with instruments—she took Ariel's temperature by placing her hand on Ariel's head!

A harassed-looking man entered. He wore a curious

ornament in the form of a frame holding glass panes in front of his eyes. Derec had noticed some of these on the ways. It gave his face a dashing, futuristic look. "What is it, Dr. Li?"

"Don't know yet, Dr. Powell. Elevated temperature, febrile heartbeat, hectic flush, exhaustion. I want to measure everything first, of course." She reached to the bottom of the gurney and started pulling out instruments, to Derec's considerable relief. Ariel had closed her eyes, and seemed to be asleep.

The doctors bent over her, shaking their heads and measuring everything about Ariel. Tense as he was, Derec looked about for a place to sit, content for the moment to leave it in their hands. Abruptly the nurse said. "How long has it been since she's eaten?"

The doctors ignored this till Derec said, "Uh—yesterday afternoon. Not long after noon."

Dr. Li grunted, and Dr. Powell said, "Inanition!"

"Young as she is, that shouldn't have brought on this collapse. Feel that arm. She's practically starving." The three of them looked at each other, plainly shocked.

"Why hasn't she been eating, young man?" Dr. Li demanded.

"She hasn't felt like it, Ma'am," said Derec, and all three of them frowned at his accent.

"Settler prospects, eh?" Powell removed his frame and wiped the panes with a tissue. "You'll not have much need of Spacer talk on a frontier planet. Better to learn some good medieval jargon: brush, creek, log cabin. Not to mention 'sweat.' What's wrong with her?"

"I don't know, Doctor. She said," he gulped, "it could be fatal if it crossed the blood-brain barrier. It's—it's affecting her mind. She's had th-this low-level fever and lethargy, with occasional muscular aches and pains, for a long time."

"Vomiting? Night sweats?" asked Dr. Li tensely.

"I don't know. She-she didn't want to worry me."

They looked outraged; he should *know*.

"There's a number of things it could be," said Dr. Li unhappily. "I have a few ideas, though—"

"So do I!" said Dr. Powell sourly. "Look here, young fella, I don't doubt that accent caused you many a pain, but you'd better doff it in here. It antagonizes too many people."

"He can't," said Dr. Li expressionlessly. "He's a real Spacer."

Dr. Powell and the nurse goggled. "Impossible! A Spacer running around on Earth? He'd drop down dead of—"

The doctors whirled to look at Ariel. Frowning, the nurse stepped out. "It could be any of a hundred common and harmless diseases!" said Dr. Powell.

"Yes! Harmless to Earth people!"

"How about yourself, young man? Do you feel all right?"

Derec nodded. "Never better."

"Why, then?" Dr. Powell exploded. "You should be sick a dozen times over!"

"I've been given a prophylactic regimen—so has Ariel," said Derec, hoping they wouldn't ask too many questions. "I don't know too much about it."

"Apparently it didn't take in her case," said Dr. Li somberly. "You let us know the moment you feel unwell, young man."

"They can't be Spacers," said the nurse grimly, holding Ariel's ID tag in her hand. "How could they be, and travel around Earth? Without ration cards, ID, and so on? This is perfectly ordinary Earth ID, City of St. Louis—"

They looked at him, frowning harder, and Derec felt himself hot ... not to mention sweating. "That's all arranged, sir. It's part of a trade agreement ... we're doing sociological research ..."

"So young?"

"Who notices a kid?" he countered swiftly, feeling the hair clammy against his forehead. "Young eyes see more sharply ... and so on."

"Hummph! No child of mine would take such a risk—"

"Maybe we'd better query the Terries," said Dr. Li reluctantly.

They all looked concerned.

Derec questioned them with his eyes, but finally had to break down and ask. "The who?"

"The Terries—Terrestrial Bureau of Investigation," said Dr. Powell. He polished his panes unhappily.

"They cause more trouble than—" muttered the nurse.

"Still, best to take no chances. If the girl is in a bad way, it could cause trouble with the Spacers—there's enough bad blood between us already."

Derec thought swiftly, appalled. The "Terries" would find no record of them, would query whatever Spacer representation there might be on Earth, find no record there, and the reactor would flash over. But he couldn't think of a thing to say.

"Look—"

Ariel moaned and turned partly on her side; only the straps kept her from falling. If she'd been listening, she couldn't have timed it better. All three Earthers leaped to her, and Derec pocketed the ID tag the nurse had put down.

He thought quickly. The doctors were concerned and totally focused on Ariel. Derec looked around. As he recalled R. David's work, the ID tag merely gave name and ID

workup. Not address. Medical care was on an as-needed basis, not rationed, so nobody cared about place of residence,
and in fact they hadn't been required to enter that. (Or was
that because Ariel's tag gave her rating as Transient? He
needed to know a lot more about Earth.)

In any case, he thought, the only thing they knew about
Ariel was what the computer recorded from the ID tag.

Leaving them working over her, he slipped out and
strolled around, speaking to no one, trying to look like a
worried, expectant father pretending to be nonchalant. A
couple of people looked at him sympathetically, but most
didn't seem to notice him at all, for which he was grateful.

There it was. An office. He slipped in, looked at the
terminal. It was probably dedicated to a single function, but
he could try. He had watched R. David coding ID tags of a
dozen kinds, and had a good grasp of what was implied.
And frankly, these computers were simple after programming positronic brains and restructuring the programming
of the central computer of Robot City. It took him a mere
half hour to get through the programming, retrieve the record on Ariel, and erase it.

Now let's hope there isn't a backup memory somewhere,
he thought gloomily.

They caught up with him in the interior waiting room,
standing aimlessly about and unobstrusively slipping toward the outer waiting room, where he supposed he be-
longed.

"There you are," said the nurse. For the first time, he
noted that her jacket had a name label imprinted *Korolenko,
J.* "Why didn't you wait in the Friends' Lounge?"

He didn't bother to tell her they hadn't shown him to
it. "Had to go to the Personal," he said, not knowing if
Earthers could mention the Personal so openly.

She got ideas, frowned, put something warm from her pocket against his head. Apparently his temperature was all right. "Very well. But come in here. The doctors will need to speak to you."

Within ten minutes Dr. Li entered the room briskly, sat down, exhaled heavily. "She had us worried, but it was mostly exhaustion of the body's resources. Starvation, to put it crudely. She must have been going on nerves and caffeine for weeks."

"She hasn't been eating well," Derec admitted. He'd been blind not to see how little she'd been eating. "What does she have?"

"We'll know for sure in a day; we've done a culture. But our best guess is amnemonic plague."

"Ay . . . nuhmonic . . . ?"

"From medieval *mnemonic*, meaning memory. Amnemonic means no memory. It's a mutation of an old influenza virus, first reported on one of the Settler worlds—sometimes called Burundi's Fever, after the discoverer." She looked at him sharply, but clearly that name meant no more to Derec than the first.

"Will she—get better?"

Dr. Li sighed. "When Burundi's crosses the blood-brain barrier, it isn't good. We're giving her support—nourishment and so on—and antibiotics that eventually will cure the disease. Our anti-virals are fairly effective, except where the virus has crossed the blood-brain barrier. Antibodies will help a little, and we're administering them. We'll be able to stop the infection in all but her brain within a day or two."

Derec had the illusion that his chest had turned into a block of wood. His heart pushed once, hard, against its unyielding surroundings, and gave up. He felt it stop moving. "Her . . . brain?"

Dr. Li sighed and looked four hundred years old. "There's hope. It's by no means over. I do *wish* we'd gotten at her sooner. . . . Well, try not to feel guilty; and I'm sorry if I made you feel worse. You couldn't have known. All kids are heedless, think they'll live forever. . . ." She brooded on her capable hands for a moment.

"Then you think she'll live?"

"Let's say, I have a good hope of it. Saul—Dr. Morovan—is a specialist on viruses and has treated amnemonic plague three times, twice successfully—and the third time was a patient whose disease had advanced much farther than your wife's."

Derec suspected that the symptoms of the other two had been much less advanced than Ariel's, but said nothing. It was something, he acknowledged, that they knew the disease, had a cure for it, and had hope for her. *Of course*, he thought, *we were fools—chauvinistic fools—to assume that the Spacer worlds were the only ones that knew anything about medicine.* Who but Earth, incubator of virtually every disease known to mankind, would know more about medicine? Among the Spacer worlds, he supposed, amnemonic plague was invariably fatal when it crossed the blood-brain barrier. . . .

Derec felt his knees shaking and was glad he wasn't standing.

"What?" He'd missed some of what she'd been saying.

"Need a sample," she repeated. "We can't give you the vaccine if you have the disease, at least in its later stages."

The Key to Perihelion affected the stomach like this: a sudden drop as one went from gravity to free-fall instantly. Derec nearly threw up. Gulping, he said, "Y-yes, Ma'am," and held out his arm.

Disease!

The possibility had always been there, associating with Ariel. But it was obvious that what she had wasn't easily contagious. She had only mentioned once, more or less directly, how she had contracted her illness, as a warning to him. But that was the only time they had come close to more than accidental physical contact. Now that he thought about it, she had kept her distance, even when she had clearly wanted and needed to be hugged. His Spacer's horror of disease had not been as greatly allayed as he had thought, he realized, shaky. The prophylactic treatment R. David had given them had reassured him, Ariel's attitude and his worry over her had reassured him, and the heedlessness of youth. . . .

His eyes must have mirrored some of his horror, for Dr. Li looked at him sharply and said, "Don't worry! You're obviously in a very early stage, if you have it at all. And we're going to give you a thorough going-over, to make sure you aren't coming down with something else."

They did that for the next half hour. *The Human Medical Team would have been faster, but no less thorough*, he thought.

"Good, you're totally free of disease, so far as we can tell," said Dr. Powell. "Fortunately, your intestinal microorganisms are not markedly different from the Terrestrial strains, and there's as yet nothing else to worry about. Dr. Li, the vaccine. . . ."

"Incidentally, we detected antitoxins to Burundi's in your system," said Dr. Li. "You may have had a mild case of the fever earlier; it may even still be latent in your system. However, the vaccine will immunize you totally."

"Uh—" said Derec, as a thought took him. "Have I been a carrier all this time?"

Uneasily, he visualized Ariel and himself spreading disease all over Rockliffe Station, where they had crashlanded after escaping the pirate Aranimas. Any human who subsequently entered the station might contract the disease—

"Perhaps, but don't worry about it. Amnemonic plague is misnamed; it isn't a true plague. It's not infectious at all, and only minimally contagious. You have to exchange actual body fluids; it's commonly passed in sexual intercourse, or in contaminated blood supplies. And occasionally by poorly sterilized hypodermics, out on the Settler worlds where they have to reuse their needles."

That was a relief. But it left a puzzle: how had Derec been exposed to the disease, if not from breathing the air around Ariel? Had he had it *before* he'd met her on Aranimas's ship?

He must have. How else had he lost his memory? But how, then, had he survived? If amnemonic plague only affected the memory after passing the blood-brain barrier, and among Spacers was invariably fatal when it did—

Again he had missed something.

"I said, your wife is almost certainly going to live. Here, catch him!"

Derec didn't know who did what; his vision had momentarily blanked. When the light came back, he was sitting and there was a tingle in his arm; a *stimulant spray*, he thought vaguely. They were proffering a glass of orange juice to him—perfectly normal orange juice, just like the oranges of Aurora. He wondered how much it had cost to ship it here, then realized that they must have bought orange tree seedlings sometime in the past, and raised their own.

"Thank you," he whispered.

They stood around and watched him intently.

"Is there something?"

"Yes," said Dr. Li reluctantly. "I hope you're up to this. It . . . may upset you."

Derec took another swallow of the juice, marveling again that it could be so exactly like Auroran juice. "I'm braced," he said. "Go ahead."

"Amnemonic plague is well-named, though it's no plague. Your wife is losing her memory, and at a progressive rate. By the time we've cured her, there won't be much of it left."

CHAPTER 10

THE KEY TO MEMORY

Derec lay on the hard, narrow bed and wondered what Wolruf and Mandelbrot were doing. Probably still sitting out around Kappa Whale in the Star Seeker, waiting, waiting. Of course, they could not readily get space charts without a human to front for them, though Mandelbrot might try. It would not be unusual for a robot to open communications. But if the other ship insisted on speaking to the owner-captain—Star Seekers were small ships; he couldn't very well be far from the controls. For that matter, Derec was uncertain how well Mandelbrot could lie in such circumstances.

Well, there was nothing he could do for them. He couldn't leave Earth, and if he could, he couldn't leave Ariel here. And Ariel was now raving in delirium in the section hospital in Webster Groves Sector, City of Saint Louis. A long way, he gathered, from the nearest spaceport, near New York.

Derec wished for a drink. He wished for a light snack, cookies at least, and fresh hot coffee, even synthetic coffee.

In the next room was a robot, ready to spring into action at his slightest word—almost. It was an Earthly robot, in an Earthly City. Derec could send R. David out, but there was no assurance it would return—and it would not be with food, for Derec didn't rate meals in his own apartment. Damn Dr. Avery for not arranging for higher ratings.

But that would have been more conspicuous, he supposed.

Light from the door shone across the bed. "Time to arise, Mr. Avery," said R. David.

"Yes, thank you, R. David."

Derec groaned silently and sat up to sit for a moment with his elbows on his knees, chin in hands. In the short life that he could remember, it had been one crisis after another. All I want, he decided, is peace and quiet, a little establishment on some mountain brook in the boondocks of Aurora or Nexon, maybe, with just a couple of robots and a landing field only big enough for my own machine and one other. Maybe the Solarians had the right idea; they never saw *anybody*, and lived totally surrounded by robots.

No, he had decided. That wasn't such a good idea, after all.

Earth turned inside out, he thought vaguely. No better than—

"Mr. Avery, are you well?"

"Yes, R. David. Merely depressed. I worry about Ariel."

That, the robot could well understand.

"Yes, Mr. Avery. I—also worry about her. But the doctors report her condition good, do they not?"

"Yes, they did last night, R. David. What she's like to-day—" He left it, somber, dressed carelessly, and tucked some equipment into the little bath satchel he had bought the day before.

Admonishing R. David rather hollowly not to worry, he set off for the Personal, returned to drop off the satchel when he had showered and washed his extra clothing, and departed for the section kitchen. This part of the trip was so routine now that he neither saw nor was seen by the policemen in the corridors and junctions; he no longer stood out like a stranger.

Breakfast was, as usual, good, but to him, tasteless. Listlessly, Derec ate it, not even interested in a fact he had finally deduced: it was neither synthetic nor natural, but both. It was made of living things and was therefore natural, but was made by an artificial process and was therefore synthetic. The basis of three-quarters of it was yeast.

He suspected that there might be a steady, if small, market for Earthly food yeasts in the Spacer worlds, if Spacers could overcome their sense of superiority long enough to try it. Granted, Spacer high cuisine had no equal on Earth that Derec had tasted, but Spacer ships were usually furnished with synthesizers. *So much for Spacer cuisine*, he thought.

The hospital was a familiar place to him now. Derec did not trouble with the waiting rooms, but went to the Friends' Lounge and queried Ariel's condition on the monitor. There had been a problem with that when they had discovered that she wasn't in the system. Derec had professed ignorance of the ID tag, and it was assumed—he hoped—that it had been lost when they all crowded around to help Ariel during her collapse.

Naturally he didn't remember her number, and in their honest ignorance she and he had left other ID forms behind. Derec had promised to supply them with it next day, but so far had "forgotten" to do so the one time they remembered to ask him for it. They had had to input her with a dummy ID.

Ariel was in a room with two robots. Here, in Intensive Care, people were either unconscious or so debilitated by their illnesses that they didn't care that it was robots who waited on them.

She was not raving today. At first Derec thought she was asleep, she lay so quietly. But then she moved, and a robot sprang forward to smooth the pillow behind her. She looked at it vacantly, closed her eyes.

A faint sound behind him was Dr. Li. The woman shook her head sadly.

"How is she, doctor?" Derec asked.

"As far as the disease goes, the worst is over. She will live. But what you're seeing now might be worse. She is gradually losing her memories."

Derec had had some of this explained to him. "I suppose she's half in a hallucinatory state now."

"Yes, or something like an intense daydream. Perhaps a brown study would be a better analogy—one of those almost hypnotic states of concentration in which you don't see what's in front of you."

Derec had a vague flash memory of someone waving a hand in front of his nose, and nodded.

Ariel was reliving her life as drowning people are popularly supposed to do. *It wouldn't take me long,* he mused; *I suppose I might have time for it. But Ariel....*

"Could I visit her?"

Dr. Li frowned, looking sadder. "You could, but after today it will get worse." She hesitated. "There's always a shock for the loved ones, when the patient doesn't recognize them. That will happen, you know."

Derec hadn't thought of that, and the mere thought shocked him. "Then—can I visit her today?"

"I'll ask."

Ariel looked at him blankly, but it wasn't a lack of recognition. It was more a lack of energy. "Oh, Derec. How are you?"

What do you say to someone who may be alive tomorrow, but won't remember you? If Derec's memories had been a hundred years long rather than a couple of months, he still wouldn't have had anything to guide him.

"Well enough," he said awkwardly. He drew near to the bed, touched it. She looked at him without much emotion.

"Are you going to help them restore my memory?"

"Of course. I'll have to. And I hope you've been talking—?" He indicated the robots with a tilt of his head.

"A little," she said reluctantly. "I'm so tired all the time. And they keep me so full of drugs I don't have the spirit. Besides, it doesn't matter. It won't help. It w-won't really be *me*. Derec, it's like dying. It's just like dying. I won't see you again—I won't see anyone again—it's all fading—"

One of the robots sprang to the head of the bed and did something, and Ariel's eyes closed. When they opened after a moment the horror had largely passed. Derec thought it was still there, though, masked by the drug.

"That isn't so, Ariel," he said insistently. "Your memories are still there, in your brain. They merely need to be unlocked. We'll—"

She was shaking her head. "No, it's all going. I'm dying, Derec. Whoever takes my place will be someone different."

Abruptly he said, "Am I different than—the man I was?"

"Of course. And yet, you're him." She closed her eyes and tears trembled on her eyelids. The robot got busy at the headboard again.

"Derec, I want you to know that I've always loved you. Even when I was most angry, even when I was most fright-

ened. I never blamed you. For weeks I've watched, hoping
you would never develop the final form of the disease. I
guess you did, or you wouldn't have lost your memory.
Whoever cured you . . . didn't have the . . . technology to restore . . . your memory . . ."

She drifted off into sleep, and after a moment Derec
choked down his impulse to cry out, to demand that they
awaken her. Suddenly his lost memory seemed less important, what she knew seemed less important, than what she
thought of him.

"Farewell, Ariel," he managed to say huskily, and stumbled out into the Friends' Lounge, where he sat and wept
for a time, quietly. He wondered vaguely if, in all his unremembered life, he had felt this sharp, poignant pain, and
doubted it. Yet, he had known her in another life, and it
had not been wholly a happy relationship.

He'd had amnemonic plague; the emptiness in his head
was proof enough for him. Had he gotten it from her—or
given it to her?

Presently he took a deep breath, let it out in a sigh that
came from the bottom of his belly, and wiped his face on a
tissue from the dispenser. Robots were probably watching
him; within minutes Dr. Li and a weary-looking Dr. Powell
entered the room.

They sat and looked him over while he braced himself.
Fortunately, they, like he, had more important things on
their minds than Ariel's ID tags.

"I understand that Korolenko has told you a little about
memory restoration," Dr. Powell said.

Derec remembered an exchange from an earlier visit. He
nodded. "Memory traces are not memory. Yes."

"Quite so. A memory trace is the synapse—the nerve
connection in the brain—that leads to the memory, which is

stored in chemical form. It is these synapses that are being erased by the neurotoxin of the plague. The actual memories remain untouched."

They looked at him. *If only you knew how much I know about this*, he thought. "Right," he said. "But since their addresses are unknown—to put it in computer jargon—the memories are as lost as if the records *had* been wiped."

"Almost," said Dr. Li. "There are ghost memories flitting about the patient's mind, and many little things will jolt a few of the memories loose."

"Smell is one of the subtlest and most powerful memory keys," said Dr. Powell, nodding.

Derec knew. "Yes."

"So. In what we loosely call a memory restoration, we merely supply new synapses as nearly identical to the old as possible."

"And in the functioning of the new memory traces," Derec said, parroting what he'd been told, "the patient reactivates the old chemical memories."

"Quite so. The more accurate and detailed the new memory traces are, the more complete not only the restoration of the memories, but the restoration of the patient's original *personality*. I hope you can see that."

It was an angle that had never occurred to him. He supposed he had the same basic personality as ever: pragmatic, problem-solving, not given to abstract thought, not artistic or poetic. An equable temperament. The engineering mind.

Now that he thought of it, though, perhaps his personality was different. He had known Ariel in his former life. He must have had strong feelings about her. He did again. Not still—*again*. For if he had not met her since his memory loss, and had not continuously been practically in solitary confinement with her, he might well not have felt that way about her again.

His parents, for instance. He no longer felt about them as he once must have done. His friends—all those parts of his personality were gone. If he acquired new friends, his emotional responses would be much the same, of course. His personality had not changed in any *basic* way, or so he supposed. He did not seem very strange to Ariel. Still, he was a new and different person from the old Derec, whatever his name had been.

Perhaps Ariel was right; perhaps it was a form of death.

Yet—"If the memory traces are close enough to the original—?"

"Ideally, it would be like copying a program into a blank positronic brain," said Dr. Li. "The second robot would, for all practical purposes, *become* the old one."

"We always explain what's been done to them," Derec said absently.

"Yes. But if the original was destroyed—" Derec frowned. "—the new one would, for all intents and purposes, be the same one in a new body."

True, it was not unlike shifting a positronic brain to a new robotic body. Derec had an uneasy flash. On Robot City there had been an accidental death, of a boy called David, which Derec and Ariel had investigated for the robots. This David had looked just like him—

He usually shrugged that fact off, but now he was jolted. Maybe the other was the duplicate—or was it himself?.

"In a human, of course, it is not quite so simple," said Dr. Powell, not noticing his jolted expression. "We could activate a significant fraction of the locked memories without reactivating the old personality. It's a matter of knowing which memories are *important* to the patient."

"How close can we come?" Derec asked.

"It depends on how much we know. The robots are, of course, recording and analyzing everything she says, and there's a tendency to relive the most important memories first and most often, till they're gone. So we're developing a good sketch, too crude to be called a diagram."

Derec nodded. "That's where you need my help."

"Quite so. You know her better than we, or the robots, can hope to."

"Not well enough, I'm afraid," said Derec steadily, wishing for some of that tranquilizer they were keeping Ariel on. "I've only known her for a few weeks."

And already married, their expressions said. Spacer morals. Derec didn't enlighten them. "I can go into a lot of detail about our time together, but before that . . . she was a very private person."

Again, their expressions spoke for them: *Spacers lived alone, on the surface, surrounded only by robots, and had few human contacts. . . .* Not true, but try to explain. Besides, he'd had his own quota of chauvinistic nonsense about Earthers to lose.

"Whatever you can do, you must do," Dr. Li said heavily.

"Uh . . . well . . . I can't," Derec said lamely.

If he mentioned his amnesia, they'd be all over him. The question of their identities would arise in a way he couldn't duck. The Terries would certainly be called in, and the Spacer embassy at the port would be queried. The whole house of cards would come down—next thing you knew, they'd have learned about Dr. Avery—and Robot City.

That secret must be kept at all costs.

"Why not?" Dr. Powell barked.

"It's . . . a matter of privacy, sir."

"Oh." Greatly mollified. Spacers! "Well, there's a lot more than you could do sitting here . . . why don't you take all the material we have with you, go home, and do your dictating there?"

Derec had been so used to having First Law-driven robots intruding on his life that he was startled by this easy acquiescence. A robot wouldn't let anything be put into Ariel's head without checking it over first.

"And the memory traces? Will they be kept private?"

The doctors looked at each other. "Well, they have to be coded," Dr. Li began.

Dr. Powell said, "They use a technique modified from one used to implant synapses in positronic brains. Of course that can't be used on human brains, but it's based on the same idea, as it were. I don't know the full details, myself—"

"But it's a matter of coding," said Dr. Li. "We're having a specialist come in from the Mayo. If he could teach you—perhaps you could code the more private portions . . . ?"

It took several conversations and a conference before it was decided to let Derec attempt coding memory traces for Ariel. His education stood him in good stead; he had the necessary background to do the work. *Spacer!* said the expressions again, this time with approval. Spacer education in robotics and computers in general was notoriously the best.

The work called for the use of a good computer, and with some trepidation he revealed the existence of R. David during the conference.

"Of course," Dr. Powell said. "A Spacer would naturally have a robot in his apartment."

They seemed to take it quite for granted, and to be a little amused by it.

"Scots sleeping with bagpipes," someone muttered at the back of the room, a reference that sounded so funny that Derec meant to look it up, but forgot. He didn't think of it again till weeks later . . . far too late to ask.

So, once he was instructed in the technique—not simple, but not too hard to learn—of coding memories as synapses, Derec sat up, day and night, dictating his memories of his life with Ariel.

"Any time she remembers something, playing the memory trace, there is a certain strong chance that she will unlock the actual memory of the event, or of part of it," the expert told Derec. "Each such unlocked memory will be retained, and will strengthen the memory trace leading to it, and to the fields about it. All this was worked out at the Lahey within the past ten years."

She was a sharp-nosed, unpretty woman, tiny and quite dark of skin. The breeds of mankind, or races as they were called on Earth, remained far more distinct than on the Spacer worlds. Darla, her name was, and she knew her stuff. She seemed to be hundreds of years old; he supposed vaguely that she might be sixty or seventy.

"Eventually, the personality that is recovered will be indistinguishable from the patient's original personality, both to the patient and to the patient's loved ones. But that depends on the accuracy of the memories, the accuracy of the coding, and the completeness of the memories."

The coding accuracy he could create by care and sheer hard work. The completeness of the memories he had little control over. *At least,* he thought comfortingly, *the last weeks of her life must be very important*, and those he could cover well.

But the accuracy of the memories? How did he know what was important to her and what was not? Her moods had always been a mystery to him.

He could but do his best, and try not to worry too much.

Derec took to visiting the hospital every other day, and sometimes every third day. Whether he went or not, he always stopped at the public combooth mornings and evenings, on the way to and from the kitchen, to call and ask about her. The news usually was that she was doing well but was in no condition to talk.

Derec knew it. His work went rapidly enough, but there was a lot of it. He slogged through it grimly. If not for the necessity of going out to call the hospital, he might not have gone near the kitchen until R. David was forced to take action to prevent collapse.

He had one slight consolation. His own memories must also be locked away, unharmed by the plague. If only he could find someone who knew him as well as Ariel did before she lost her memories, someone he could persuade to come to Earth and dictate his memories . . . not likely, knowing Spacers. But there was that thread of hope that he might recover his memories . . . might recover himself.

Nights were bad. He dreamed nightmares of Ariel not responding to the treatment and being as blank as he had been upon awakening. It was terribly important that she not lose her memories of him . . . and in the dream it was always his fault. His coding failed, or she was swept away in the flash floods through the drains of Robot City, or. . . .

Robot City! It, too, haunted his dreams, and these dreams were even darker and more frightening than the nightmares about Ariel. Those he could understand; they sprang from a quite natural anxiety.

But the Robot City dreams were different . . . they didn't

even seem like dreams. They seemed frighteningly real. In the mornings Derec's hands shook, and he hoped the doctors never started asking serious questions. They'd know for sure he was crazy.

He was dreaming that Robot City was *inside* him. He dreamed of gleaming buildings rising on the lobes of his liver, great dark-red plains stacked above each other, or on his ribs, or inside his lungs, the buildings expanding and contracting as he breathed. Then the dreams seemed to become much clearer, and he "knew," in the crazy dream way, that Robot City was in his bloodstream.

Enclosed buildings, like space cities on lonely rocks, he thought. Yeah! But jeering didn't drive off the frightened, helpless feeling, the feeling of being invaded and used.

I suppose that's the source of this dream, he thought, trying to comfort himself. *I've been moved and manipulated from the beginning.*

The next time he walked into the Friends' Lounge, Korolenko brought him Dr. Li and an unsmiling, athletic young man with the look of eagles in his eyes.

"Yes?" Derec said to the stranger.

"This is Special Agent Donovan," said Dr. Li, frowning slightly. "Of the Terrestrial Bureau of Investigation."

CHAPTER 11

QUESTIONS!

The Terry followed him and Dr. Li to a more private conference room, where Dr. Li left them.

The special agent looked Derec over intently, but not in
a hostile manner. Derec braced himself, shaky. Above all,
he mustn't mention Robot City. Neither could he mention
Aranimas and Wolruf. They'd consider him crazy.

Any break in his story would mean endless questioning,
queries to the Spacer worlds, questions about Dr. Avery, the
discovery of Wolruf in orbit about Kappa Whale, perhaps
the discovery of all that Dr. Avery was doing . . . not all of
that bad, but it would take time! Worst of all, the investigation would ultimately uncover Robot City . . . and that secret had to be kept at all costs.

Derec and Ariel had to get back there.

"I must warn you that this conversation is being recorded, and that anything you say may be used against you.
Further, you have the right to remain silent, if you feel that
your interests might be threatened by answering. On the
other hand, we have as yet no positive evidence that any

crime has been committed. The Bureau has been called in primarily because you are allegedly a Spacer . . . diplomatic reasons, that is,"

Derec nodded, throat tight.

"Who are you?" the agent asked abruptly.

"Derec."

"And your last name?"

Derec debated, decided not, and said, "I sit mute."

"That is your right. Do you wish a witness that you have not been coerced?"

"Waived, but, uh," Derec could not quite remember the Spacer legal formula—so far it had seemed close to Earth's. If anything, Earth was more fanatical about preserving the individual's rights than the Spacer worlds were. "Uh, I wish to retain the right to ask for a witness later."

"Waived right to a witness pro tem," said Donovan, nodding shortly once, in faint approval. "I assume then that you do not mean to sit mute to all questions. Therefore, I ask you: have you ever had Burundi's disease, popularly known as amnemonic plague?"

"I don't remember." Derec smiled faintly at the other and received a faint smile back.

"Do you remember your last visit to Towner Laney Memorial Hospital, two days ago, and the blood sample that was taken at that time?"

Derec remembered the visit, but not the blood sample. Even when Donovan pointed at the red scab inside his left elbow, he still didn't remember the sample being taken.

Concerned, Donovan said, "Do you assert that it was taken without your knowledge; particularly, do you accuse anyone of using anesthesia on you against your will?"

"Is that a crime on Earth? No, I make no such—uh—

assertion. I just don't remember . . . I was probably in a fog. I usually am, these days."

The agent looked at him. "Isn't unauthorized anesthesia a crime on the Spacer worlds?"

"It might be, but I doubt it. I doubt that it happens often enough for anyone to pass a law against it. The robots would prevent it, usually."

"Hmmm," said the Terry, possibly reflecting that a robot-saturated society might have its points. "In any case, I now inform you that a blood sample was taken from you on that occasion and carefully studied. The conclusion of the doctors here, and at the Mayo, and in Bethesda, is that though you have antitoxins to Burundi's, you have never had the disease in its severe form."

Derec stared at him.

Donovan continued, "Yet, something you said to the Spacer plague victim, and which she answered, indicates that your memory was lost in the characteristic fashion of this disease. Can you elucidate that, or do you wish to sit mute?"

The *robots*, thought Derec. Furniture to a Spacer, he had paid no attention. And usually a robot's discretion was pro-verbial, so much so that their testimony was rarely heard even in Spacer courts. But these had been instructed to rec-ord and play back everything that Ariel said. Derec couldn't remember what she and he had said, but they'd given the game away more than an Earthly week ago.

Had they mentioned Robot City?

"Why do you ask?" he asked warily.

"Do you suffer from amnesia?" the other countered.

Derec ought to sit mute. He considered that seriously, wondered if perhaps it was already too late, then thought of a possible way around.

"Why do you ask? Surely it's no crime to suffer amnesia. Nor would I expect the Terries to be called in even if a Spacer suffered. The condition isn't contagious, you know."

"There are laws against harboring certain diseases, nevertheless," said Donovan automatically, but he waved that aside. "Public policy. No, the question here is more serious. Essentially, two things about you alarm us. One is that you do not remember your past. The other is that you are not on Earth."

Derec gaped at him, almost started to ask exactly where St. Louis was.

"Officially, I mean," said Donovan, frowning in irritation. "We've done a thorough computer check, and we find no sign of you before you appeared here a couple of weeks ago, eating at the section kitchen, big as life and twice as natural. This was brought to our attention by the hospital's accountants and computer operators, who have never discovered how your partner's records vanished out of the hospital's computer."

The Terry looked at him again. "Normally I wouldn't reveal so much, but there's a good deal of alarm in Washington. It's considered that you are not the source of the mystery, and may in fact be unaware of it. Who sent you to Earth, and why?"

Derec's mind was spinning like a wheel, but he managed to say, "I suppose you figure the ones who sent us have done this computer trick. How could they possibly have?"

Donovan shrugged angrily. "Any number of ways, I suppose. There's talk of bandit programs that take over computers. More realistically, there's talk of disappearing programs, that automatically wipe themselves after a certain time—that is, they contain instructions that cause the computer to wipe them, do you see?"

Derec nodded, a memory clicking into place. He'd heard of such programs as toys, but a good computer could usually retain them. And a network of computers ... if you were getting food or lodging with your ration tag, that allocation would have to be routed through so many computers that though the *first* computer might lose the program, the memory of the transaction would remain. His little erasure at the hospital had been simple, and he'd caught the accounting trail early, so there was no trace.

But of course there was no memory of their arrival in any Earthly computer. Only in one Earthly positronic brain.

"Violation of the Immigration Act can be charged against you," said Donovan chattily. "We couldn't make it stick without proof that you knowingly and deliberately invaded without the legal formalities. But we could hold you pending an investigation."

"We couldn't go far in any case," said Derec. "Earth is one big jail."

Donovan nodded. "Any planet is."

Derec tried to imagine how many computers in how many bureaus and branches of government would have to be foxed to slip a spy in. His mind boggled; no wonder they were concerned. Far easier to believe that a ship sneaked in and dropped someone, despite orbital radar and other detection devices.

They were overreacting: easier to slip in spies in other guises, like traveling sociology students. Except that Spacers never went anywhere on Earth, and now here were two of them.

"How many of you are there, on Earth?" Donovan asked casually.

It hit Derec that he didn't really know. He had supposed that Dr. Avery worked alone, but his belief that it was so didn't make it so. Besides, Dr. Avery worked through robots, and there could be any number of them—

"I don't know," he said frankly. "We were told little. I have reason to think that we are the only two." He shrugged. "It's hard to find volunteers for social studies on Earth. Too few Spacers care about the subject in the first place; they'd rather study robotics."

Donovan nodded, sitting leaning slightly toward him, not at all relaxed. There was so much energy and sheer *competence* in that pose that Derec had the sudden realization that if he were to attack the Earthman, the other would pinion him as efficiently as any robot. If not quite as gently. The idea of concealing the location of R. David and the apartment seemed silly. This man represented a planet-wide investigative organization.

"Most of their agents are robots," he said, and that got an instant response, instantly blanked.

A nice fat red herring for you to follow, he thought glee-fully, and then idly wondered what a red herring was, and on what planet the phrase had originated.

"Any idea who *they* are?" Donovan asked, casual again.

Very little. "Only that it's a sociological investigation. There's been some talk about Laws of Humanics, the math-ematical expressions that describe how human beings relate to each other. Studies of society have been made on various Spacer worlds, as disparate as Aurora and Solaria." Derec was detailing the theories of certain of the robots of Robot City.

He finished with a shrug. "I suppose that they find Earth the best case study, it having the densest population and the longest cultural history."

"It seemes odd that they'd memory-wipe their agents

ROB CHILSON

just for a cultural study," said Donovan dubiously. "What were you instructed to look for?"

Derec thought fast, holding his face as nearly expressionless as he could. He felt that he was sweating. *Keep it close to the truth*, he told himself. "The study's not so important, but uncontaminated data is. If we entered openly, we'd be under the surveillance of your Bureau. Understandable enough; Spacers aren't common on Earth."

"Especially not in the Cities," said Donovan dryly.

"The knowledge that we were being watched, followed, even protected, would affect what we observed. It would be an emotional wall between us and Earth people. It would be a safety net. It would prevent us from living like Earthers."

"And that's what you were sent here to do?" The TBI man was skeptical, but not closed-minded.

"Yes. We weren't told to look for anything specific; that would have warped our data. We were simply told to go to St. Louis, to settle in, to spend some time, and to record our impressions." The moment he spoke the last four words Derec realized how big an error he'd made.

Then he thought of an explanation. But he was still sweating when the Terry said, "But that doesn't explain why your memories were erased."

"Oh. To prevent us from telling anything about the techniques by which our IDs were wiped from your computers. You see, they wanted us to disappear completely, to prevent contamination."

Donovan nodded slowly. Derec couldn't tell how much of it he had swallowed.

"I see. Well, you have not yourself violated any law that we know of, except as accessory to violation of the Immigration Act, and computer fraud. The last of which can't be proven, because we have no records to cite! We've found platinum and iridium that we think must have been dumped by your organization to pay for your support here. There's also some hafnium we can't trace a source for. You, or they, have more than paid for all you've consumed, so there are no complaints on that score."

Donovan looked severely at him. "You understand that there are a lot of red faces at the TBI, and some angry ones elsewhere in Washington. I'm just the A-in-C of the local office, and even I felt the heat. They don't, we don't, like having our computers messed with so freely, gato. But nobody wants trouble either—certainly we don't want to see you lynched. Sorry about your wife. Hope she gets better. We suggest that you leave as soon after that as possible."

Derec nodded, gulping, glad the other didn't ask to see the "impressions" they were supposedly recording. He could say she'd been taken sick so rapidly they hadn't had time—true enough, too. Leaving when Ariel got better was a good idea, too—and not just because of the sternly repressed dislike on the special agent's face.

Ater that, things got worse. For five days in a row they refused to let Derec see Ariel. Afterward, he could see her, but only her trimensional image; he wasn't allowed in the room. She passed through the crisis of the disease during that time, and they began to implant the earliest memories. That left her in an hypnotic state most of the time, and when she wasn't in it she was asleep or on the verge of sleep.

"Somnambulistic state," Dr. Powell said. "Though of course she can't walk. Too weak yet."

Derec grimly worked at recording and coding, eating little and sleeping less. Dreams of Robot City haunted him waking and sleeping. He couldn't help brooding, while working, over such nonsensical questions as: did Dr. Avery get out of Robot City before it was shrunk, or was a tiny madman swimming through his bloodstream at this moment?

How about the Human Medical Team; were they making the most of their opportunity to study human anatomy and biochemistry?

Earthers whom he passed in the corridors and ways tended to avoid him; he looked sick and desperate, as his infrequent glances in mirrors told him. Not all Earthers avoided him, however. Once a man glanced directly at him in Personal, and Derec was so accustomed to Earthly ways that he was shocked. Then he thought for a startled moment that it was Donovan. But it wasn't the special agent, it was merely a man who looked like him: a man with an easy, athletic carriage, an air of competence, and the look of eagles in his eyes.

Another such man sat across from him at breakfast one morning, and occasionally he was half-conscious of other TBI men about. Nothing so conspicuous as ducking into corners as he came by, or peering from doorways. They simply were about.

He decided not to worry about it. The Terries had compelling reasons of their own for not making a scene, and so long as he gave no evidence of spying, he doubted they'd do anything. Probably they were there for *his* protection. Derec grinned faintly, the only hint of humor in all that bleak time: they were contaminating his observations.

"I told you so," he said to the absent Donovan.

Being watched by the TBI did not bother him; he was used to being watched by mother-hen robots.

He did think much, though, on what the Terry had told him: he had never had the plague, though he had antitoxins to its neurotoxin in his blood. He'd had the memory loss without the plague. He'd received a dose of the neurotoxin without having had the disease.

Well, his arrival on that ice asteroid, without his memory, while the robots were searching for the Key to Perihelion, never had seemed to him like an accident or a coincidence. He felt, and always had, as if he were a piece in a game, being herded across the board for someone else's reasons. A mad someone else.

The only one he knew of with both the madness and the genius was Dr. Avery.

They had to get back to Robot City.

One morning during this period he looked up from table J-9 and saw Korolenko next to him. She was wearing her hospital whites, or he might not have recognized her.

"Eat your bacon," she said crisply as recognition dawned on his face.

The thought made him ill. Yeast-based or no, it was fat and greasy and sickening. His opinion of the bacon showed on his face.

"Then eat the eggs. And the toast." Korolenko's voice was grim. "Look, Mr. Avery, you won't help your wife by collapsing of starvation."

Derec wanted to say it was stress, not starvation, but realized that there was something in what she said. He'd been living on fruit juices and caffeine. He managed to choke down the toast and some of the scrambled eggs, with lots of hot, sweet tea.

"That's better. We'll see you at the hospital tomorrow."

That night Derec had one of his worst dreams about Robot City, and the next day he sat looking at nothing and thinking about it.

Nothing silly about Dr. Avery shrinking, or the Human

Medical Team. He knew perfectly well that Robot City was on its own planet—even during the dream. What he was dreaming was that a miniature version had been injected into his blood, where it had started growing and reproducing. Here the dream became silly—the miniature city was getting iron from his red blood cells. But there was nothing silly about the feeling it left him with.

Come to think of it, Robot City could be thought of as a kind of infection of the planet on which it had been established. It, too, had grown from a single point of infection, a living organism that had grown and reproduced. Robot City inside him. He could feel it there. The feeling was so strong that he forgot all about eating, or going to the hospital. Even Ariel was faint in the back of his mind.

CHAPTER 12

AMNESIAC

Ariel awoke slowly, stretched tired limbs, and looked about. The hospital. It seemed to stretch into the remote past. She could scarcely remember a time when it wasn't all around her. The world beyond it was vague in her mind. A city, she recalled. No, a City, a City of Earth, a humming hive of people, people, people. Beyond, though, was space, and stars, and the Spacer worlds.

Robot City was there, and Derec, and the Human Medical Team. Wolruf and Mandelbrot, who had been called Alpha, long ago. Aranimas, too, was out there somewhere. Beyond that—Aurora. She couldn't remember. Aurora—everybody knew about Aurora. Planet of the Dawn, first settled from Earth, land of peace and contentment and civilization, richest and most powerful of the Spacer worlds.

The world she had called home, and which had exiled her, leaving her to die alone.

But no memories came.

She couldn't remember her homeworld. She couldn't remember her parents, her school, her first robot.

Of course not. She had had amnemonic plague—Burundi's fever, they called it in the Spacer worlds. She had lost her memory.

But she was alive. Ariel began to weep.

A robot was at her bedside, a silly Earth robot with a cheerful face. "Mrs. Avery, are you well? We have been ordered to minimize drug dosages to let you recuperate, but if your distress is too intense we can give you tranquilizers."

With an effort, she calmed herself enough to say, "Thank you, but I am quite well. I merely weep in relief that I am alive. I did not expect to survive."

The spell broken, she found the weeping fit over. She was hungry. She told them so, and was promptly fed. Afterward, feeling tired, very tired, vastly tired, from long lying in even the cleverest hospital bed with all its muscle tone-retaining tricks, she drifted off to sleep.

When Ariel awoke, she was aware again of who she was and that she had had amnemonic plague. She had survived! They told her that her memories would return gradually, based on the foundation they had implanted in her brain. She didn't believe them, but she didn't care. She was alive!

When she had eaten again, they told her, "Your husband is here."

Husband! For an awful moment she was totally blank. "My what?"

They led in a thin, hollow-eyed boy.

"Your husband—Derec Avery," said the robot.

After a moment, she recognized—

"His name isn't Derec!" she said, and at his anguished expression she halted. No—David was dead, he had died of carbon monoxide poisoning on Robot City. No—he had disappeared—she didn't know what had happened—her memories were scrambled, or gone.

Derec!

After a moment she asked, hesitantly, half knowing it was wrong, half fearing it was wrong, "Husband?"

"Why, of course," said he, smiling. He looked so thin, the smile was a grimace on his wasted cheeks. Her heart bumped painfully, and she felt a pricking in her eyes. One of his eyes closed and opened as he continued confidently, "Some things come back faster than others, they tell me— not much of a compliment to me that our wedding wasn't the *first* thing you remembered!"

Ariel smiled and thought: *Avery!* She couldn't remember how that name of all names was stuck on them—she knew *he* hadn't been going under it. But no doubt there was a logical explanation that she would remember in due time. She remembered now their escape from Robot City, their use of the Key, leaving Wolruf and Mandelbrot, and their arrival on Earth in a sparse apartment.

Still smiling faintly, she leaned back and said, "I do remember now, but it's all a little faint—like, like a remembered dream. I hope you won't quiz me on it till I've had time to remember more."

"Of course not," he said, and the instant he had completed the phrase, a robot broke in.

"The doctors' directions are that you not attempt to force the memories. It would be better, Mr. Avery, if you never questioned her about your past or hers."

"Yes, I've been told. Thank you," he said, with true Spacer politeness toward robots. Here in the hospital, the medtechs and nurses called them all *boy!*

"So when can I get out of this place and—and *out?*" she asked, feeling the suffocating terror of claustrophobia closing in. Gamely, she fought against it. It had been her constant companion since arriving in the hospital, and all during her illness she had battled it. If not for tranquilizers, she'd have lost her mind while losing her memory.

"Well, you're still pretty weak physically, and the doctors are not sure yet about your memory. They want to keep you here for a couple more days just on mind games. After that—I dunno. R. Jennie, do you know?"

"Mrs. Avery must have several days of physical therapy before she can safely leave the hospital, Mr. Avery," said the robot. "As for her memory, and her mind generally, I have not been informed."

"If I don't get out of here soon, I'll go mad!" she said with a sudden vehemence that startled her. There was an impulse to resist what her conditioning told her was a lapse into madness, but she had had all she could take of concrete caverns and crowds of—of troglodytes. "I want to see the sun again, and breathe air, and—and feel the grass, and—"

Abruptly she was weeping, for in the midst of this catalog of sights that she had not seen since her memory began, there came a sudden demanding vision: an image of a garden, somewhere, of bright light and flowers and warmth, drowsy warmth, with bees humming sweetly on key, and the scent of orange blossoms. Someone she loved lay just out of sight.

Ariel turned over and wept passionately for some minutes, her face in her pillow. She felt a hand on her shoulder, not a robotic hand, and felt faintly grateful, but was too wretched to turn.

A detached, floating calm gradually washed away her tears, leaving her tired but spent. Tranquilizer; the robots never gave her more than a few minutes to weep. They usually allowed her that—or she'd have gone mad from the inability to express her emotions at all.

When she turned, Korolenko was there, frowning in

conversation with—Derec, she must remember always to call him. That was right, that was what the Earthers called him. But there was another reason, which she couldn't quite recall, why she must not use his true name. Or did she know his true name, after all? She had forgotten so much, could she trust that memory too?

Avery! she thought, remotely astonished. The drug made all emotions remote.

She wondered vaguely where Dr. Avery was now. Still on Robot City, she supposed. For a moment she felt an ironic amusement at the thought that they had been using his apartment, his robot, and his funds on Earth. Then she knew that this was an old amusement, she'd had this thought before; and with that thought, she remembered having had the amusement before.

"Memory is like drink," she said to the uncomprehending robot. She felt a little light-headed.

The nurse and a robot stepped aside as they spoke together and Ariel looked, shocked, at . . . Derec.

"Why is . . . he so—thin?" she demanded abruptly.

"Mr. Avery? He had been under a strain, Mrs. Avery. He has been worried about you and has not been eating sufficiently."

"Does he have—" Her heart stopped, started painfully. "—Burundi's fever?" Again her heart shook her.

"No, Mrs. Avery. He is merely under a strain."

"He's sick," she said.

"No, Mrs. Avery."

"He is sick," Ariel said positively, peering at him narrowly with the observant eyes of one who has recently passed near to the gates of death. "He is—dying."

Nurse Korolenko heard enough of that to frown at her,

and one of the robots—R. Jennie, Ariel thought—went to the control board at the head of the bed, but merely checked the readings.

"Derec is a young fool who has neither been sleeping nor eating, and who has spent all his time brooding over you," said Korolenko, angry not at her or at Derec, but at his stupidity.

"There's nothing else to do in that stupid apartment but stare at the ceiling," Ariel said, irritated on his behalf. Why did he keep staring at her with eyes like holes in space? "Frost, there's not even a trimensional there."

"You wanted to experience life as Earth people do, and apparently low-rated Earth people at that, so you have no more than they do," Korolenko said, shrugging.

Wanted . . . to experience . . . ? She turned eyes in inquiry on . . . Derec, who shrugged also, grimacing ruefully.

"Perhaps you don't remember that the Institute wiped our memories temporarily before we came to Earth, so we wouldn't be able to reveal their techniques," he said.

Ariel could only stare in amazement.

"When you are well enough to travel, we will leave. Of course, since we've been discovered here, our purpose of sociological study is negated. And once back on Aurora, we will have our own recorded memories reimplanted."

She had heard of none of this. The Institute? Institute of what? Study? Of *Earth?* But, *own recorded memories reimplanted.* . . . Ariel leaned back and for a moment thought tears would leak from her eyes.

"So you've lost your memory twice over, but it's only temporary."

"I'd like to know just how that's done," growled a baritone voice. After a moment Ariel identified it: Dr. Powell.

She had heard it often enough in the past weeks. "I know, I know, you haven't the foggiest—only a brief layman's description that doesn't describe."

When she opened her eyes, they were all around her bed, with R. Jennie at the controls.

"Well, young lady, your request for a visit to the outdoors is a bit . . . unusual." He visibly repressed a shudder of distaste at the thought, and Ariel, fascinated, realized that to this man the outside was more fear-inspiring than the claustrophobic City was to her.

"We can't very well add you to the list on a Settler Acclimatization Group, and the only other people who go . . . outside are the odd Farming, Mining, and Pelagic Overseers. They are solitary as well as agoraphilic, very strange types; they wouldn't welcome an addition. Certainly not a sick Spacer. And there's nobody else to take care of you."

"Robots?" she asked weakly, looking at R. Jennie.

The doctor frowned, shook his head. "It's difficult to move a robot through the City without having it mobbed and destroyed. Robots are being restricted more and more each year; we have half as many here now at Towner Laney than when I was an intern. That leaves only your husband, and frankly, within a couple of days you'll be taking care of him."

"I'm all right," said Derec with a flash of irritation that for a moment brought back the companion of the hospital station—Ariel couldn't remember the name, but she remembered the station—and of Robot City. "What's the signal coding of the local office of the TBI?"

"The what?" Dr. Powell stared at him. "The comm number? Why would you want to call the Terries?" From his tone it was obvious he had guessed, and seethed at the thought.

"To get authorization to have robots moved through the motorways, and for permission to leave the City, if only for a short period."

"Hmmph! Medically—"

"Medically it would do her good, Doctor," said the nurse quietly.

"True, damn it, but we need to be sure that her mental condition—the implants—"

"We can't keep bringing her back and forth, I admit," said Korolenko.

"Ariel, could you . . . hold off till tomorrow?" Derec asked.

Tomorrow . . . she was so tired, from inaction and drugs, that she'd sleep till then anyway . . . Ariel could have stood anything for a tomorrow in the sun.

"Oh, yes, yes." She'd be good, she'd—

Ariel had a moment of vivid memory, herself quite young, promising her mother that she would be very, very good. Was that when she'd been given her first robot? Or was that Boopsie, the pup?

When the first vivid reexperience faded, she looked up and they had drawn apart. It was no matter; it would be all right tomorrow.

"Never saw myself as nursemaid to a couple of Spacers and a robot," said Donovan. The agent-in-charge had not trusted any of his men to go outside.

The hospital had an emergency entrance and egress for ambulances, and was a major junction on the motorways. R. Jennie carried Ariel down in its arms, Ariel having chosen that over being wheeled, strapped to a gurney, or in a chair with wheels.

The hospital had supplied an ambulance, but the Terry

eyed it with distaste. "We'll use the Bureau car," he said. "There's room for four of us, robot or no."

R. Jennie gently put Ariel into the back seat and got in beside her, the car creaking and sinking under the weight until the suspension system analyzed the imbalance and compensated for it. Derec and Donovan got into the front seat, and the agent took the controls and sent them surging silently down a ramp and into a lit but dim-seeming tunnel.

For a moment Ariel fought a scream, tensing; the claustrophobia was worse in such tight passages. But she fought it off, helped by the speed of their passage. Signs blurred past soundlessly as the Terry tapped more and more of the beamed power. Once the ceiling lit up in bloody light, and winking yellow arrows along the walls gave obscure warning. Then a blue car whipped by in the other direction, Donovan having avoided it with the warning.

"Like the models we trained on," murmured Derec, glancing back at her.

For a moment she was blank on that, the she remembered the roofless roads and the emergency vehicle monitors, the remote control sweaty in her hand, and the laughing students crowding around. But that was nothing like this dim, empty wormhole.

GLENDALE, KIRKWOOD, MANCHESTER, WINCHESTER, BALLWIN, ELLISVILLE, the signs flowed past, as fast as the expressway would have taken them. Ariel ignored all the labyrinthine branchings and windings that twisted obscurely away right and left out of sight, peering past Derec to see as far before them as possible.

The tunnel was a rectangle of dim light, two glowing tracks overhead and a pair of glowing, beaded tracks on the sides, the last being the glowing signs, fading into tininess.

At last, though, there came an interruption in the shape

of the tunnel. It got dark at the limit of vision, the darkness outlined in light. Presently the outline of light appeared as various warning signs. The darkness was a ramp, leading up.

Donovan slowed sharply, causing R. Jennie to lean forward and prepare itself for a snatch at the controls.

"Don't worry, boy," said the Terry, grinning but not looking back. Ariel had him in profile. "I've driven for thousands of hours, faster than this, and no problems."

"Twenty-one point three percent of all major traumas to enter Towner Laney Memorial Hospital occur in the motor-ways," said R. Jennie, unperturbed. "Fewer than twenty percent occur on the ways. A few thousand humans use the motorways; seven million use the ways."

"Damn, I always hated know-it-all robots," grunted Donovan, taking the ramp with unnecessary flair. "Could never stand to live on any Spacer world. A man should have the right to go to hell in his own way."

The car eased to a stop at a barrier. Donovan played a tune on his computer controls and the barrier opened. He drove through, they wound a complicated path that apparently avoided heavy traffic—there were thunderous rushing sounds through the walls, but no traffic in their motorway—and they were at a huge entry in the outer wall.

Kilometer-long lines of great trucks full of produce, some robot-driven, most computer-controlled, roared in with noisy, huge tires but silent engines and dived into the City just below them. They were on a higher ramp, one of a dozen that leaped out of the City from high and low. Donovan stopped the car well back from that light-blazing gap.

"You'll have to walk from here," he said abruptly. "Car won't go any further—no beamcast beyond the barrier."

CHAPTER 13

ROBOT CITY AGAIN

"Paulins," said R. Jennie. "They are used to cover machinery in the fields against rain and dew. There are no tents available in the immediate vicinity of St. Louis. Perhaps in a day or two there will be a tent."

The plasticated canvas of the big paulins worked as well as a tent, strung over a couple of poles and tied to a tree limb. It was needed more for shade than shelter. This move to the country had not been a simple one, nor could they keep it up for more than a day or two.

But it was such a relief!

Ariel could tell that Derec felt the same sense of escape that she did. The sky of Earth was wide and blue and very high, and little puffy clouds ambled slowly across it, all framed by the pointed opening of the "tent." The sunlight was just right. The plants were the familiar green of Earth life everywhere, and they too seemed just right. Except in greenhouses, she had probably never seen Earthly plants in the natural light of the sun in which they evolved. Even the heat was not unpleasant.

"We won't need a tent, if we have to wait that long," said Derec grimly.

"You should return to the City as soon as you can," R. Jennie said. "Mrs. Avery is far from recovered from the fever."

Ariel felt quite recovered from the fever, though her memory was returning slowly. Weak as she undoubtedly was, she thought with concern, she could have wrestled Derec two falls out of three and won. But he said nothing about his own condition.

"Everything's so . . . ordinary," said Ariel, looking out at the kind of birds and plants and small animals she had seen all her life. A squirrel is a squirrel, and sounds just the same on Aurora. Even the shrilling of the unseen insects was familiar. Humans had taken their familiar symbiotic life-forms with them to the stars. She had expected Earth to be more exotic.

The reality was a relief more than a disappointment.

"It must have been a bad time for you," she said to Derec, when R. Jennie had stepped out to the . . . kitchen. They had been supplied with something called a "hot plate" and a dielectric oven.

Derec moodily watched the robot prepare the packaged meals, designed for people with high enough ratings to permit them to eat in their own apartments. This was luxury for their rate.

"Bad, well." He shrugged, clearly not wishing to discuss it. "I did learn one thing from R. David: there's a spaceship belonging to Dr. Avery in the New York port. If we could get there—"

"How, if our rating doesn't permit us to travel that far?"

"We'll have to get him to make ID with higher ratings for us—"

R. Jennie stepped under the opening with a tray holding coffee and juices. When she had gone, Ariel said, "I hope they don't discover the apartment."

"I suspect the Terries know all about it, but won't make trouble. They want us gone before we get mobbed or something. We've been very lucky."

"Couldn't we ask Donovan for assistance?" she asked wistfully.

"We could. I thought of it," Derec said, broodingly. "But that'd be above his level, surely. If Earth can ignore us, it won't be so badly embarrassed if we're discovered here, investigating—or spying on—Earth people. But if they have helped us in any way, they can't deny having known about us."

"Helping us would be seen as condoning our presence," she said grayly. "I understand." Politics seemed to be the same everywhere. "So what can we do? Get new ID—will the Terries spot that, do you think?"

"Frost, I don't know—"

R. Jennie gave them fruit cups and whipped cream, returned to the kitchen, a rustic scene in the frame of the tent opening.

The fruit was good, but unusual—compotes served in what she thought of as unsweetened ice cream cones. It was like eating warm ice cream with strong fruit flavors. All yeast, she supposed.

"If they do spot us at it, I suppose they'd look the other way. But what worries me is that it would alarm them. They'd know we weren't telling everything, they'd realize that R. David—or someone—has ID duplicating equipment. They might well raid the apartment."

Ariel thought about that for a moment. As long as they

weren't arrested and the Key to Perihelion taken from them, it didn't matter.

"Oh. The Key is focused on the apartment," she said. "We'd be unable to retreat to it." She remembered well the occasion when they'd had to do so.

"We will be in any case; we couldn't begin to explain our reappearance," Derec said. "They'd guess too much—"

"Zymoveal," said R. Jennie. "There is also a chicken wing for each of you. Chicken soup, made of real chicken with yeast enhancement. Bread, real potatoes, gravy."

A simple, hearty meal. Ariel ate with good appetite, but her stomach seemed to have shrunk. Weeks of eating little in hospital had altered her eating habits. Derec, however, carried on grimly, eating long after it became obvious that he'd had all he wanted, eating on to the edge of nausea.

When the robot had retreated, Ariel said, "I see. It's all or nothing. Well, if so I won't weep. If we could just get to New York!"

"Don't think I haven't thought about it. I'd be tempted to walk—it's on this continent—but it's a couple of thousand kilometers, and we'd starve."

"Too bad. Derec, why do you go on eating when anyone can see you're full?"

He looked up at her grimly, harassed, his eyes sunken, his face thin and lined. "I've not been eating enough, or sleeping well enough. Everybody says so. I need to get my strength back now that you're well."

"Have you really worried that much about me?" she asked, her heart thumping. She felt flattered, and also dismayed, as if it were her fault.

"Well, it isn't just that." Derec lowered his fork, swallowed coffee, looked queasy. "I've been upset. I haven't been sleeping. I-I keep having this strange stupid dream. About Robot City."

Ariel stared at him. "A stupid dream made you look like a walking wreck?"

"Yes." He looked ... frightened. "Ariel, there's something unusual about this. I-I keep dreaming that Robot City is *inside* me. We've got to get back there."

Robot City!

Ariel's mind was flooded with a hundred images, sounds, odors even, of the great robot-inhabited planet, where the busy machines worked away like so many bees, building and building for the ultimate good of humans. It was an Earthly City without a roof, populated by robots rather than humans. They'd been trapped there, first by the robots themselves, then by their mad designer, Dr. Avery.

"Go back there?" she whispered tensely. "I'll never go back!"

"We must," said Derec, his voice just as low and determined, but also indifferent. It was as if he was speaking not to her but to himself. "I'm dying or something. I don't know what Dr. Avery did to me, but ..."

What had he not already done? Derec had lost his memory long ago, and only Dr. Avery could have removed it. She had known that as soon as she realized that he had lost all memory of her. Human beings were less than robots to Avery, they were guinea pigs.

Go back? To save Derec's life?

But I'm cured! she wanted to cry. I can go back to Aurora and say to them: Look, the despised Earthers cured me after you cast me out! You don't need to watch your sons and daughters lose their memories and die—you can cure them. If you can persuade the Earthers to tell you how!

There need be no more of this aimless existence, running from planet to planet, looking for a cure, for an excuse to go on hoping. There could be a home, a place in society, all the wealth of associations that membership in the human society meant.

They could even consider the Keys, the existence of aliens, Robot City itself—they could report Dr. Avery, turn the Key over to the proper authority, shift the burden to other shoulders.

Ariel sighed.

"You don't look good," she said.

After all, how much did she owe him, anyway? At lot of apologies, if nothing else. She'd blamed him wrongly for too much.

"I hope there are star charts in the ship," he said. Derec put a hand to his brow. "If we can get back to Kappa Whale, we can take both ships back to Robot City. That'll give us a spare. Dr. Avery won't think of that—I hope." He rubbed his face slowly; his eyes squinted as if the light were too bright.

"Is it getting dark?" he asked.

"Not yet," Ariel said. "The sun will be setting in a little while, but it won't start to get dark for another hour."

"Oh."

"What kind of dreams have you been having?" she asked skeptically, thinking that they might have been right: if he'd not been eating or sleeping, it might all be strain—

"Like I said, I dream that Robot City has been shrunk into my bloodstream. I don't know why it frosts me so, but it does. I can't shake it off. It's a—a *haunting* feeling." He rubbed his face again, haggard.

Ariel didn't know what to say. "It . . . doesn't sound like an ordinary dream."

"I'm sure it's no dream," he said instantly, looking sick.

"Something's going on." R. Jennie entered the opening of the tent and he said, dully, "R. Jennie, what are chemfets?"

"I do not know, Mr. Avery."

"Derec—"

"I wish I could sleep. It drives you crazy if you don't have real dreams."

"Derec, you really look—awful." Ariel felt a stab of real fear. "Oh, Derec!"

He looked as if he were about to throw up. Drooling, he pushed his light camp chair back, starting to get up. He fell over.

"Derec!"

R. Jennie came with a rush, cradled him as Derec's arms and legs started to flail. "He is having convulsions. I do not know what is wrong," she said. "Help me hold him—"

Ariel was too weak herself to be of much help, but after a few moments Derec's seizure eased, he sighed heavily, and he began to breathe in a more normal fashion instead of inhaling in great tortured gasps. His limbs relaxed, and R. Jennie warily lowered him to the carpet-covered grass of the tent floor.

"He seems to be much better, but this is not a natural sleep," said the robot. "Unfortunately, there is no communo in the area, nor do I possess a subetheric link. I must go for help. Ariel, you must watch him."

"What do I do if he . . . has another seizure?" she asked, huskily.

"Hold him. Do not put a spoon in his mouth." And with that puzzling admonition, the robot began to run toward the City.

Greatly to her relief, Derec awoke within ten minutes. "How are you?" she whispered, frightened.

"I'm okay," he said faintly. He did look greatly relieved. "Chemfets," he said.

"What?"

"Robot City is inside me, in a manner of speaking." Derec struggled with her weak help to a sitting position. "I'm thirsty."

Hastily, Ariel poured him some juice. He drank carefully, seeming a little dizzy.

"We keep thinking of robots in terms of positronic brains," he said, seemingly at random. "But computers existed before positronic brains and are still widely in use. At least a dozen computers of different sizes for every positronic brain, even on the Spacer worlds. And for a long time there've been desultory attempts to reduce computers in size and give them some of the characteristics of life."

"Derec—are you all right?"

He looked at her seriously, haunting knowledge in his sunken eyes. "No. I've been infected with chemfets. Microscopic, self-replicating computer circuits. Robot City is in my bloodstream. When I fell asleep just now, the monitor that Dr. Avery implanted in my brain opened communication with them."

"What ... what are they doing?" Ariel could scarcely grasp it, it was so strange. What would a chemfet want? Was it truly alive?

"Growing and multiplying, at the moment. I don't think they're anywhere near ... call it maturity. The monitor ... I don't think it's of any use yet. It's as if they have nothing to say to me yet."

"But they may later?" she asked swiftly.

"I suppose." He looked at her, haggard. "I wonder if they've been programmed with the Three Laws?"

Ariel grunted. "Yes. I suppose they've been upsetting your body systems. No wonder you've been sick. Will ... will the dreams continue?"

He thought about it, shook his head. "I don't think so. I think those were just the monitor trying to open contact. Once the channel is opened, it won't be worked unless they have something to say."

"How about if you have something to say to them?" Ariel asked, with a flash of anger.

"I suppose ... if I learn how to work the monitor," he said dubiously.

"And tell them to get out of your body because they're killing you! First Law," she said.

Then: "I *hope* they're programmed with the Three Laws." Frightened, she looked at him.

Strength and purpose seemed to have flowed back into him: knowledge of what was going on, a drop in the subtle pressure the monitor had been putting on him, relief, a good meal. It was something merely to know what the problem was.

"We've got to get back to Robot City," he said with determination. "I now know that part of my feeling on that was due to the pressure of the monitor. The chemfets want me back there for some reason. But we have our own reason for going back. We've got to confront Dr. Avery and make him reverse this—infestation."

Ariel nodded in angry agreement. "Yes! Dr. Avery has played his games with us, and especially with you, for too long."

He stood up, and though he leaned on the table, he seemed much stronger. "But how do we get off Earth?"

"We'll have to consult with R. David. If we can get back to the apartment without a lot of ..."

"Where's R. Jennie?"

"She's gone for help. You had—convulsions."

"No wonder my muscles are sore. She's gone for—doctors? I can't let them examine me—"

Ariel grunted in understanding. "We'd never get away—they'd hospitalize you." She looked at him. "They might even be able to cure you."

Derec said, "I've come to have a lot of respect for Earth's doctors, but this is a matter of robotics. I think we'd better go back to the source. I'd like to know what reason Dr. Avery had for this—what did he hope to accomplish?"

Ariel could only shake her head. "Just using you as a guinea pig, I suppose."

"Yes, but that shows that he has some reason for developing chemfets, even if he doesn't care about me. There must be some use for them." As he spoke, Derec was groping in his pockets. He produced the Key to Perihelion. "At least, with R. Jennie gone, we can vanish without any questions being asked."

"Questions will be asked," she warned him.

"Yes," Derec said, pressing the corners and taking her hand. "But not of us."

Perihelion's gray nothingness surrounded them. "They'll assume some sensible explanation, involving the imaginary institute that sent us to Earth," Derec added, looking around in the gray fog.

"I guess so," she said dubiously. "As long as we aren't spotted in the City."

"Or any other City."

The apartment appeared around them, and Derec sagged with the return to gravity. Alarmed, Ariel threw her arm around him and instantly R. David was there, supporting him from the other side.

"Mr. Avery! What is the matter?"

Derec obviously hadn't prepared an answer.

"Derec is sick," said Ariel swiftly. "We must get him to Aurora for treatment. The spaceship is at New York City Port. How can we get there the soonest?"

"The fastest means of travel on Earth is by air," said R. David. The robot hesitated, bending over to assure itself that Derec wasn't dying at that moment.

"I'll be okay," said Derec, his voice low but firm.

"What's the fastest means of travel that our rating will permit us to use?" Ariel asked.

"Air travel," said the robot.

"Isn't it rationed?"

"No," said the robot. "You see, on Earth, necessities are rationed on an as-needed basis. Scarce luxuries, such as real meat and fish, or larger and better quarters, are rationed mostly on a basis of social standing. Some of the less-scarce luxuries, such as candy and birthday cards, are available partly on a rationing basis and partly on a cash basis. These are the so-called 'discretionary luxuries,' minor items not everyone wants.

"Finally, luxuries in large supply are distributed purely on a monetary basis, and this includes air travel. The air system was designed for emergencies. Since Earth people hate to travel by air, the excess is freely available. It is expensive, but your bank account cards are amply charged."

Ariel fumbled through her wallet for the window with the cash card. Was it a real memory, or did she dream that she had dropped her purse on the expressway? A dream; or else R. David had replaced the ID. "Will our use of cash be monitored?" she asked.

"That is not possible. The privacy laws of Earth forbid scrutiny or oversight of these monetary transfers, so the provision doesn't exist."

Since money could only be used for "minor luxuries," no wonder. "How do we get to an airport?"

R. David gave minute directions for taking the expressway to something he called Lambert Field, and after Derec had rested for a few minutes they went out to the communo and called for reservations on the next flight to New York. After two hours of fearful waiting for the knock of the TBI on the door, they ventured out for what Ariel devoutly hoped would be the last time through the corridors and ways of the City.

Each step of that passage brought back memories from just before the crisis of the amnemonic plague. This time they rode the way only to the north-south junction, changed ways, and rode north for longer than they had ridden east on their previous excursion: BRENTWOOD, RICHMOND HEIGHTS, CLAYTON, UNIVERSITY CITY, VINITA PARK, CHARLACK, the forgotten political divisions of a simpler time. ST. JOHN, COOL VALLEY, KINLOCH.

And then, after thirty minutes of standing and holding on, fearing every moment that Derec would collapse, they saw LAMBERT FIELD AIRPORT, EXIT LEFT.

The airport was a sleepy place, considering St. Louis City's seven million people. There was but one ticket window, the clerk there seemed subdued, and the few people in the waiting rooms never spoke or smiled. Presently their plane was announced.

Not only was the passage to the place covered, but the *runway* it took off from was also roofed over! There were no windows in the place, so they had a choice of sleeping or of watching the continuous news and entertainment feed in front of each seat. Earthers scheduled most flights for night, and the five other passengers—only five! Ariel remembered the crowded millions on the ways—the other passengers elected to sleep, those who could. Most were too nervous to try. Derec slept all the way to New York, to Ariel's intense satisfaction. She slept most of the way herself. Best of all, in the air and the airports, nobody spoke to them or even looked at them.

CHAPTER 14

STARS AGAIN

Derec looked up at the ship in relief and wonder. "I can't believe we made it," he said.

"We haven't gotten in yet," said Ariel, edgily.

He approached and inserted his ID tab into the slot. After a moment, it opened. "Of course," he murmured. "R. David gave us compatible IDs."

The ship was a Star Seeker, identical, or nearly so, to the one they'd left in orbit around Kappa Whale. On the ground, it was clumsy getting around inside it, but that was normal. They climbed slowly to the bow control room.

Ariel climbed easily—like Derec, not pushing it—and he was relieved to see that she was gaining strength day by day. He himself felt better after last night's sleep than he had in weeks, but knew that his reserves were still very low. The acceleration seat was a relief after the climb.

"Checklist, please," he said, depressing the *Ship* key and speaking to the air. The ship obediently displayed a checklist on a visor, and they went over it carefully. Some items had to be checked personally, most importantly, food. Ariel reported with concern that that was a low item.

"Only a few imperishables," she said, "a few packages of radiation-preserved foods and some cans."

Derec hesitated. That could be serious.

"What do you think?"

"I'd say take the chance," Ariel said. "The TBI must be going mad over our disappearance. If they do a computer check, they may wonder about this Spacer ship. Don't tell me they don't watch carefully every takeoff and landing."

Of course they wouldn't be able to interfere; Earthers had little control over their own port, as they owned few ships. Still, if he and Ariel started shopping for food—

"Right. We'll go."

When they requested clearance it was readily given, and Derec primed the jets and goosed the micropile. The tubes burst into muffled thunder. He switched to air-breathing mode as soon as they had a little speed, and took an economical high-G trajectory into space. In minutes, the great blue world was off to one side.

"Which way?" Ariel asked.

There was a slight technical advantage in aiming one's ship toward one's objective, since intrinsic velocity was unaltered by passage through hyperspace. But the adjustment could be made at the other end.

"Straight out," he said. "I'm not exactly afraid of pursuit, but—"

"Right."

"Straight out" was in the direction Earth was traveling. Ariel calculated their fuel and Derec elected to use twenty percent. He liked a lot of maneuvering reserve. The burn wasn't long, and when it was over, Earth had not altered much. It was more aft of them, and only a bit smaller. Now, though, there was a wall of delta-V between them and it: in order to catch them, any ship would have to match their change of velocity—their delta-V.

"We've got time to kill," Derec said, feeling tired. Reaction weighed him down even in the absence of gravity.

"Think we should rig the condenser?" Ariel asked.

The thought of the excursion in a space-suit made him feel even more tired. Then he thought: *Of course, Ariel can do it. She's not sick any more.*

She was still weak, though, despite her rapid recovery. And he himself was not up to it.

"It's only for a week or two," he said. "I think the ship can handle it. It's only for two people, also."

Ariel nodded. "Listen," she said. "How do you feel? You seem better after your sleep, but you're still sick. Just knowing what's going on inside hasn't cured you."

That was true. "I feel tired at the moment. Why?"

"I want to talk about Robot City. I want to talk to you about everything we went through together, right back to the control room of Aranimas's ship, before Rockliffe Station."

She looked at him, her eyes big and intent. "I want all the help you can give me to recover my memory."

That he could understand. "Of course, I'll be glad to help. I just wish I could be more helpful."

Ariel opened her mouth, closed it, her face pink. "Derec . . ." she said. "I . . . Derec, I'm sorry I didn't tell you more about yourself—about us. But I couldn't! I couldn't tell you I had amnemonic plague. And I-I can't talk about us—from before. I'm not sure of my memories—I've lost so much, and I don't know how much I can trust of what I have now. I'm sorry—but it's just too uncertain—and too painful."

Illness can make a person's mind preternaturally clear.

This was a girl who had been exiled and disinherited for having contracted a hideous disease. "Of course."

Her feeling for him was obvious—the attraction, the repulsion, pain and pleasure intertwined in memories he didn't share. Memories that now she couldn't trust.

"No need to apologize," he said gently. "There's been nothing between *us* since Aranimas's control room. Your previous memories, real or unreal, are of a different and forgotten person—whose name I don't even know."

She managed a weak smile. "True, that—person is forgotten. It's true. You are a different person. Derec—do you mind if I don't tell you your—his—name? I'm not sure I really do know it. Besides, it's easier for me to think of you as Derec—"

Derec suppressed a sharp, small pain. His lack of a past was an emptiness that was always with him. "Of course I don't mind," he said. "Some things are more important than others. You are more important to me than any memory."

And that was certainly true.

"Oh, Derec!" Ariel plunged at him, grappled him in a bearhug that sent them wheeling, laughing, through the air of the little ship, colliding with the bulkheads and the control board. Fortunately, the hoods were down over the control sections.

Lingering in the vicinity of Earth for a week was a risky business on several counts. Derec thought, but he had not wanted to burn more fuel unless he had to. Refueling was, in one sense, no problem: the rocket simply heated reaction mass with the micropile and flung it aft at very high velocity. Almost any kind of mass would do, and powdered rock in water—a slurry—was a very good reaction mass. It could be gotten almost anywhere. Water was next best; the ship was equipped to handle slurry, and the pumps could deal easily with water. These items were readily available in space or on planets.

There might not be time to stop and spend ten hours refueling, though. And they could well find themselves in a system with abundant fuel for them, but lacking the reserve fuel necessary to maneuver to it.

Ariel was a competent pilot herself, and had been traveling on her own for some time—Derec didn't know how long—before being captured by Aranimas. And she was more reckless than he.

"If we're going to spend all this time drifting, why don't we do it in safety—at Kappa Whale? Or off Robot City?"

"If we're pursued, we'll burn more," Derec said. "That would mean we'd have to burn still *more* at Robot City to lose our intrinsic velocity."

"I think we should hurry," she said. "Derec, I'm not happy about your condition. I don't think you're getting better. Every now and then you go off into a sort of fugue."

It was true that occasionally the monitor opened, and the chemfets festering in his bloodstream droned an emotionless report into his mind about having overcome this or that difficulty or achieved this or that milestone of their growth. He supposed all this would mean much to Dr. Avery. To him it meant nothing, but he was not able to tune out the reports.

"At least I don't go into convulsions anymore," he said. The one incident was all there had been, but Ariel was obviously still frightened by the memory. He was glad he hadn't been able to see himself. "You occasionally have— fugues, I guess, in an even more literal sense—yourself."

She nodded. "I see you do the same thing—I suppose you still have flashes of memory, when memories return, so vividly that you are there."

"Usually when I'm asleep, and I lose most of them," Derec said.

Her memories were returning in a massive way, compared to his own. She wasn't getting anything like a coherent account of her past life, of course, merely a chunk here and a chunk there. Like pages of a book torn out and scattered by the wind, here a leaf caught by a tree, there one against a house.

Four days out from Earth, with the mother planet a mere blue-green brilliant star behind them, now getting closer and closer to Sol, Derec and Ariel agreed that it was safe to open the hyperwave. They called Wolruf and Mandelbrot at Kappa Whale, but got no answer.

"Can you shift the elements so it broadcasts on the same wavelengths as the Keys to Perihelion do?" Ariel asked.

He had told her their deduction about the failure of the hyperwave aboard Dr. Avery's other Star Seeker; she had been in such a feverish state that it hadn't registered with her at the time.

Derec shook his head somberly. "It calls for precision tools and a fairly lengthy research effort. First, just to determine what broadcasts the Keys spray their static on."

"Ship static wavelengths, perhaps?"

"Perhaps. . . . Likely, in fact." Hyperwave static was a fact of life, one the usual hyperwave link was designed to ignore. "But when did you even hear of a hyperlink designed to *pick up* static?"

Ariel smiled faintly, shook her head.

A week out from Earth, they started calculating the Jump to Kappa Whale.

"It hasn't been too long," said Ariel. "Wolruf's food will hold out, of course, and so will their energy. The micropile is good for years yet. They've a sufficient supply of fuel to do what little maneuvering they may require. They could Jump out of Kappa Whale and back to avoid pursuit, if they have to."

"So they should still be there. Where would they go, without us, if they acquired star charts?"

Ariel couldn't guess.

Charts were one of the first things he and Ariel had checked for when they had entered the ship. There was a complete set, and if there hadn't been, they could have requested a copy from Control. One would have been beamed to them immediately, without a question.

"It's easier to calculate a single Jump for Kappa Whale," he said. "But it definitely isn't safer."

Ariel calculated three Jumps, and Derec almost agreed. "The trouble is, Kappa Whale is nearly behind us. Your first Jump turns us in hyper, which is possible, but it's a strain on the engines. I suggest we Jump to Procyon, which is near enough to our line of flight, and do a partial orbit about it, burning to bring us out on direct line for the first of your Jumps."

She bit her lip and said, "I'm sorry. I know I'm too reckless. I think it's because I had a sheltered childhood. I never got hurt much when I was a kid."

Derec grinned. "I have to admit that in my few short months of life I've acquired a healthy respect for the laws of chance."

Their first approximations done, all that remained was to put final figures into the computer and let it solve the equations of the Jump. They needed to know their correct speed and direction with some accuracy, so they would know what to expect when they landed in Procyon's arms.

Ariel bent to the instruments while Derec fumble-fingeredly tried to set up the computer for their first Jump.

After a long time, he said, "Ariel, can you handle this? I can't seem to concentrate, and my fingers are made of rubber."

She looked at him in concern. "I was afraid you were going off into a fever again." Twice before on the trip he had had feverish episodes, as the chemfets altered their growth, in turn altering the environment around them: him.

Derec tried to fight off fear. He had no idea yet of the ultimate purpose of the chemfets, and had not been able to "talk" to them. Worse, he had no idea if he was contagious. After that one hug, they had avoided so much as touching each other, for fear that Ariel, too, would be infected with them.

They could well kill him—and might not care if they did.

"Very well," Ariel said, her voice trembling a little. "Why don't you take some febrifuge and stretch out? Maybe a nap will bring you out of it."

It sounded good to him. The febrifuge had helped break the last fever, they thought. He was swallowing the thick liquid carefully, because of free-fall and a slightly swollen throat, when Ariel cried out.

"Yes?" he said, catching his breath and relieved that he had not choked.

"There's a spaceship closing on us."

Pursuit from Earth? he thought.

The Star Seeker didn't have very good detection apparatus, mostly meteor detection. It was this that had flashed an alarm. Meteors, however, do not move very fast. This object was flashing toward them. The detector gave two readings, and Derec finally—through the throb in his head—concluded that their assailant had come up behind a more slowly moving rock.

"We should be able to get some kind of picture," said Ariel.

"It's still too far off, I think, for a visual image," Derec said. He blinked his eyes to bring his vision back to a single focus. "I wish we had neutrino detectors."

All nuclear power plants gave off neutrinos, and nobody bothers to shield them off. A neutrino reading would give them an estimate of power generating capacity, and thus of ship size. Of course, a battleship and a medium freighter would have similar-sized power plants, but some information would be better than none.

"Heat?"

"It isn't burning at the moment," she told him, consulting the bolometer. "It must have spotted us days ago and burned to intercept."

"Go ahead and enter our Jump in the computer," he said. It was all he could think of, and it wasn't much. "How long will that take?"

"Too long," she said gloomily. "You are right, though. It's the best bet, especially if that's an Earth Patrol ship. Derec, it might follow."

He opened his mouth to say that it didn't matter, then closed it. "Frost!"

They intended to maneuver at Procyon—they might be in the system a week, during which the bigger ship could hunt them down. Nor would there be any hope of help there.

He grasped at a straw. "Bigger ships need more fuel. If he can't match our maneuvers—"

"And you call me reckless. Let's not bet on it, okay?"

"Frost."

The other pilot wasn't maneuvering: he was swooping in to intercept their course from behind and to one side. He'd cross their course at a very sharp angle, pull ahead, and brake down, to let them drift into his arms. He was moving quite rapidly relative to them, far faster than the rock he was coming up behind, and would have to burn soon or swoop helplessly by them.

Their options were limited: they could fire their rockets to speed up, they could roll the ship and burn to slow down, or they could Jump. It would take time to set up the computer for that; Jumping blind might not mean certain death, it might merely mean being permanently lost in the vastness of the galaxy—or the galaxies! In hyper, all parts of the normal universe were equidistant.

Or they could roll the ship ninety degrees and turn aside.

Ariel didn't consider it, and Derec didn't even think of it. They had spent twenty percent of their fuel to acquire their current velocity. They would retain it no matter how much they pushed "sideways" on their course. It would therefore take another twenty percent of their fuel to turn the ship aside at an angle of a mere forty-five degrees—a negligible turn.

"Call for help?" Ariel asked dubiously.

"He'll be on us in twenty minutes or less," said Derec glumly. No help could possibly reach them. "Unless he burns toward us."

"Unlikely."

"True." His head wasn't working right. The rapidly closing ship wouldn't want more velocity toward them; it would have to brake down enough as it was, when it passed.

"I think we can assume that no Earth Patrol will fire on us without sufficient reason," Ariel said. "So I propose that we talk to them as politely as possible, but maintain course and speed. We can burn if necessary, but—"

"You think it's Earth Patrol?" Derec said, then nodded. "A Spacer wouldn't shoot, either—"

"A Spacer would be calling us. Face it. Whoever this is, it's an enemy," Ariel said.

"We should have a good idea of our course and speed relative to Sol before he reaches near point," Derec said, nodding in agreement. "We can Jump any time after that now that you have the prob input."

The enemy spaceship wasn't going to ram, of course; its point of nearest approach was its "near point" with their course, but the two ships would be farther apart—it would then be ahead of them.

"And we won't provoke them," Ariel finished.

"What with?" Derec asked, feeling lightheaded.

"You know what I mean."

Then Derec had it: "We do have a weapon—"

"Comm!" she cried, at the breaking-crystal sound of the chime.

"I hope it's not a Spacer ship," she said, worried, as she opened the channel.

Both of them gasped at the face that appeared in tri-mensional projection above their board.

CHAPTER 15

ARANIMAS AGAIN

Oh no, Ariel thought. *Aranimas!*

The alien pirate's cold visage regarded them.

His face was vaguely human, but had definite overtones of lizard. The eyes, for instance, were widely set, almost on the sides of his face. They were barely close enough together to give him binocular vision—but, unnervingly, Aranimas didn't much bother with binocular vision. Most of the time one eye focused on whatever he was looking at while the other roved, apparently supplying peripheral vision.

At the moment he was focusing on Derec with both eyes. "Derrrrec," he said. High-pitched, trilling, his voice was the most hateful thing Ariel had ever heard. "Arrriel."

Glaring at them, he altered the focus of his comm and shrank to distance without moving, his humanoid figure coming into view from the waist up. In this view much of his alienness wasn't obvious, but they both had seen him in person. He was as tall seated as Derec was standing, and his disproportionately long arms had three times the span of a tall human's. Thin body, thin neck, domed, thinly haired head, pale skin. Dark eyes, angry now.

"Wherrre is the Key to Perihelion? You escaped with it instead of leading me to robots."

After a heart-stopping moment—Derec gulped, temporarily shocked out of his sickness—Ariel said, with only a faint tremor in her voice, "We lost it in the wreck. W-we've been in hospital on Earth—"

"You lie. I detected three bursts of Key static about this planet. The firrrst, weeks ago, began elsewhere. The last two began and ended here. Only the Key broadcasts in this manner!"

They looked at each other sickly. Before they could speak, the pirate pulled a small, gleaming, gold pencil out of a pocket. Ariel choked, and she heard a gulp from Derec, too. A pain stimulator! It was, she knew, something like a human neuronic whip, but even more intense. Or perhaps Aranimas was just more violent with its use. It did no damage if not overused, like a neuronic whip, but no one was tough enough to take more than one "treatment" before deciding to cooperate.

"You will tell all, and tell trrrue, or I kill you slow with this."

They did not doubt his sincerity. Nor would he listen to anything until he had taken the ship apart. They couldn't just give him the Key, even if it could have been of use to him—it was initialized only for humans. He wanted robots, among other things—power most of all.

Derec reached over and cut the channel.

"We have another option," he said, turning to her. "We could use the Key, call agent Donovan, and put the whole problem in the laps of the TBI and whatever Spacer authorities are on Earth. Or we can try to deal with Aranimas ourselves."

"Deal with him—how?" she said skeptically.

"I don't mean bargain. Ariel, you should use the Key." His plans were clearly hardening as he spoke. "I think I can ram that clumsy ship when he closes with us."

Ariel felt herself pale. "No, Derec!"

"It's the only way! We can't let him live. He's too dangerous—"

"But—" Her face cleared. "We can use the Key at the last instant."

Derec looked at her. The burst of adrenaline that had washed away his illness was fading. She determined that she would not use the Key unless he did, and he seemed to realize that.

"Okay, that's what we'll do. We'll pretend to surrender—"

He reached for the comm, but she grabbed his wrist. "No, Derec, it won't work! He'll never leave this ship maneuverable while he closes!"

"It's the only chance we've got," he said. "Our only weapon is the jet—and the nose of the ship! I'd like to fire the rocket at him, but he'd never pass in front of it."

Ariel sighed, but she was unable to think of anything better.

"Okay. Go get the Key. I'll fly the ship."

Derec nodded in relief, clearly not up to it.

When they tuned back into the comm channel, Aranimas was howling in his nonhuman voice, so shrilly as to make her teeth ache.

"You will not brrreak communications again, humans! You—"

"Very well! We have conferred and agreed to accede to your demands," she said. "We ask only that you guarantee our lives, or we'll destroy the Key in front of your eyes."

"You will not destroy the Key! I kill slow—"

"Not if we're dead first," said Derec, sounding tired and exasperated—the sound of a father dealing with wrangling children. "We want your promise."

The alien fell silent and studied them for a cold-blooded moment. "Verry well. You have my promise I will not kill you if you give me the Key, undamaged."

Ariel had a moment in which she wondered if the alien might keep that promise. But it didn't matter; Derec was right. He had to die. She felt a momentary pang for the harmless and spiritless Narwe slaves with whom Aranimas manned his ship.

Derec pulled the Key out of his shirt and showed it to him. While Aranimas stared greedily at it, Ariel, at the controls, asked casually, "Shall we maneuver to match you?"

"No, I maneuver."

There was a tense few minutes while the alien turned from them to his controls, rolled his ship, waited, waited, waited, then burned toward them. At the end of the burn the ship was not far away and still passing slowly. Again it rolled, now plainly visible: a vast, ungainly mass of half a dozen or more hulls stuck together. How Aranimas balanced that thing along a center of mass so he could fire rockets without spinning out of control, all without computer aid, Ariel couldn't imagine.

He's too close, she thought, panicky. They hadn't time to get much velocity for the impact—or to set the Key! Even as she thought, she glanced at Derec, who started squeezing the corners of the Key. She slammed the rocket on, spinning the ship on its secondaries—the gyro, more economical of fuel, was much too slow.

Aranimas might be flying a clumsy conglomerate, but he was a skilled pilot—and it was a battlewagon. It had adequate sensors even aft, where the rockets were. The pirate spotted their maneuver and blasted aside, not bothering to scream at them over the comm channel.

Ariel looked over at Derec, slammed into her seat by the acceleration; the Key was ready, but they weren't. The alien ship was above them, then beside them, even as she struggled to turn nose on toward it. Too late—Aranimas had slid aside.

Ariel instantly cut the jet and started to spin ship, not to get too far away—Aranimas's gunners would have them in their sights the instant they cleared the near zone. Aranimas shrewdly slapped on more side thrust when he saw which way she was turning, in order to widen the gap between them.

Then the collision alarm rang.

They heard Aranimas yelling for the first time since the battle began. Ariel fought them onto a line with the alien ship, too busy to look about.

"The rock is moving!" Derec cried.

The chunk of rock that had swung in behind them and had gradually been overtaking them was now accelerating toward them at about a Standard gravity—and the bolo registered the temperature of rocket exhaust.

Wolruf's face appeared beside the diminished figure of Aranimas on their board.

"Hold him, Derec! I come!"

What Aranimas said was not intelligible, but energy lanced from the big ship at the rock. The rock vaporized, its outline flashing away in puffs of incandescent vapor as the guns bore. Those same mighty weapons had vaporized cubic meters of ices and snow at near absolute zero on the ice asteroid where Aranimas had first found Derec.

Underneath the flimsy camouflage was a little Star Seeker like their own.

Ariel's vision dimmed as she cut in the rockets' full power. In a moment, she cut them off. Her head bobbed against the headrest, and the ship was again diving toward Aranimas. He rolled and blasted to avoid them, and something monstrous slapped their flank, making the ship ring.

"Puncture!" Derec gasped, but she had no time. She had to hold him till Wolruf got there—

Aranimas rolled his big ship again, and again blasted to avoid her, throwing off his gunners' aim. *Good job, he doesn't have computerized fire control*, Ariel thought.

She was confronted with a split-second tactical problem. In moments they'd be past the alien ship, too soon to roll nose-on toward it. Aranimas had seen their intent and was going the other way. So she rotated further in the direction the nose was pointed, to bring their tail toward the enemy.

At the critical moment she blasted, and fire splashed over Aranimas's ship. It must have rung like a bell. There was a great outrush of air and assorted particles. Ariel was grateful she couldn't see well enough to tell if the particles were kicking.

In a flashing moment they were past, and the reflected flame glare died, and Aranimas was moving again, fire spurting from points on the ungainly hulls. Another kind of fire flashed, their own ship gonged when hit, jolted again, as Ariel's head rattled against the headrest and alarms yelled; Derec was saying something as she spun the ship as rapidly as shaking hands would let her. *Mistake!* she thought. Should never have blasted *away* from him; now they were far enough away for the gunners to sight them.

Clenching her teeth, Ariel rolled the ship again, trying to ignore the hits, hoping one wouldn't disable them—or kill them. A single stray bolt would—

"We're still in their near zone," said Derec, breathlessly. "Glancing hits only—"

True, she thought, smiling mirthlessly—*they were still alive!*

And then they had completed their roll, much farther from Aranimas than she liked, and she blasted back. No more hits; the uneven outline of the alien ship grew and grew in their vision screens, and she breathed more evenly.

Then she had a moment of wonder: she felt better because she was not going to be killed by Aranimas's gunners in the next few moments. But she was trying to commit suicide by ramming his ship!

Aranimas began to slide aside and she automatically corrected, centering on the dark bulk. What should she do?

"Wolruf is closing fast, but I don't know if she's still maneuverable," said Derec tensely. "She got hit hard."

"Give her a call?"

Then Aranimas's ship loomed monstrous and the alien had arranged a surprise: a gun on the hull swung to bear on them. What prodigies of effort had gotten it ready in the short time the battle had taken, they would never know. It was a full-sized gun, though its first bolt was weak, an aiming shot.

Aranimas's gunners were not the timid Narwe. They were starfish-shaped creatures about whom Ariel knew little; they avoided the light and breathed a slightly different atmosphere than the rest of the crew. She felt no compunction about them, and spun the ship aside. Aranimas saw that and moved to prevent her from pointing her rockets at the new gun.

A second bolt flashed at them, but the gunners lacked Aranimas's own savage efficiency.

"Another puncture, and our antenna's out," said Derec calmly.

His calmness calmed her, and she made one more attempt to ram. In turning away from her jet, Aranimas had run before their nose. She cracked on full power and they were hurled back into their seats. Her vision dimmed. She thought it was the power fading.

Too slow; the huge, bloated body of the enemy slid sideways even as it grew monstrous before them. Then the vision screen erupted in one pale flare, pale because the safety circuit wouldn't transmit the whole visual part of the flash: the sensor had taken the next hit from the gun.

"There went our bow!" Derec cried.

Ariel gulped, half expecting to see space before her, but they hadn't lost that much of the bow. With the vision out, she could only crouch, panting, at her board, the rocket off, hoping for—

"The Key—trigger it—" she cried, turning to him, knowing in a flashing moment that it was too late—they'd hit—

The ship jolted, and the impact was quite different from the gun hits. They were thrown forward against their straps, the ship shuddered, metal squealed, something broke—all in an instant—then they were free, the ship floating quietly.

Air hissed out, alarms still burring and shrilling. All communications out, no exterior view. Ariel touched her controls and the attitude jets responded; she could turn and burn again. But they were blind.

"Suits!" said Derec. "And see if the auto-circuit can give us more eyes."

Suits first, she thought. When the air goes out of a small ship, it can go fast. Should have had them on all along, if they'd had time.

They scrambled into their suits in a free-fall comedy that was deadly serious. Every moment Ariel expected the lancing fire of a hit, but the ship continued serenely on its way.

They didn't bother to try communications, knowing that the gun's bolt, or the impact, must have destroyed the forward antennas. Vision, however, could be brought in from any quarter of the ship. Only the bow eyes were out. After a bit of fumbling, they found an undamaged sensor that bore toward their late battle.

"What . . . what is it?" Ariel asked, awed.

"I was about to ask you," Derec said. "You know more about Aranimas's ship, you were on it longer—"

"That was before my amnesia," she said.

"Oh."

"I think—one of the hulls, broken free?"

They had only a partial view of it—it was below the sensor's view. Only a spinning, irregular curve of dark metal, with an occasional highlight gleaming, here and there a projection—derricks, turrets, landing ports, sensors—and interior beams?

"It can't be the whole ship," Derec said finally. "But what happened to it?"

Ariel took a deep breath, found the air inside her suit rank with her sweat. "I'll turn around!" she said, chagrined. "I didn't realize how tense I was."

She wasn't thinking. *I'll never be a combat pilot*, she thought shakily. *Wasted minutes looking into a view I could've adjusted—Or do pilots get used to this kind of thing?*

But the human race had no combat pilots. No telling

how well they could perform. Grimly, she thought, *if there are many of Aranimas's kind in space, we may have to learn.*

"Aranimas—he disintegrated!" Derec said.

The big composite ship was now a dozen big pieces in a cloud of hundreds of smaller ones. They looked at each other. Derec's face was as blank as she felt her own to be.

"Did we do *that?*" she asked.

"I don't see how—Wolruf!"

After a moment she nodded. "You must be right. But where did she get the guns?"

Derec just shook his head.

If anybody was alive over there, they weren't disposed to do any more shooting. The wreckage was retreating slowly. Ariel came to herself with a start.

"We've got to get back over there—"

"Frost, yes!"

"But how?"

It wasn't easy, but they worked it out. The view they had gave them bearings. They chose a spot that would enable them to miss any of the junk, and rotated the ship until its blind nose pointed along that bearing. Ariel then placed her hands on the board, looked into darkness, and thought, *now we find out how good a pilot you are, girl.*

In a moment she was back on Aurora, about to do her first solo takeoff. She had had that very thought, or something very close to it, and even more nervousness than now. Now, though, she was in shock. The memories went on and on, the takeoff, the acceleration seeming more fierce than ever now that she *had* to remain conscious, the relief as the jets shut down, and then the indescribable free, floating sensation of one's first solo orbit.

"Ariel?"

Her instructor—

"Ariel?"

With a shake, she brought herself out of it. "Sorry. Memory fugue." As her hands moved over the board—taking care to push the buttons on the real board instead of the remembered one—the memories went on, flashed back, picked up details. A whole chunk of her past restored to her by a chance thought, a chance repetition of forgotten circumstance.

She burned for ten seconds and rolled the ship to study the junk. There should be detectors back there that would tell them how fast they were moving relative to the junk, but they weren't working. The junk still seemed to be receding. Ariel rolled and blasted for another twenty seconds, again looked.

"That should do it."

They had only to wait, floating toward the wrecked ship aft-end first, ready to burn to brake down.

"How did she do it?"

CHAPTER 16

WOLRUF AGAIN

"It's hopeless," said Derec.

Mandelbrot was trying to patch their hull.

"It's got to work," Ariel said, biting her lip behind her helmet. "Otherwise, Wolruf—"

The other Star Seeker had been hit harder than their own and was scarcely maneuverable. Mandelbrot, using rockets welded onto his body and a line gun, had brought them close together, with Ariel doing most of the maneuvering. There was very little air in either ship—and there was no spacesuit for the caninoid alien.

"We've been stressed too severely. The best we can do is temporary patching." Derec tried to rub his head, and his hand encountered his helmet for the fifteenth time. Frustrated, he let it drop.

"If it holds long enough to Jump out of here—" she said.

Derec shook his head. "Four Jumps to Robot City—five for safety," he said. "That's days of work checking courses and calculating. I wouldn't want my life to depend on that kind of patching. And we'll be maneuvering. That'll strain the patches even more."

"Something's got to be done! Maybe Aranimas's ship—"

Jumping at straws, and she knew it. "Even Wolruf doesn't really know how to fly it—assuming any of us had the arm reach for that control board. No computer aid, Ariel!"

She nodded soberly. "I know. It's not possible; it's these ships or nothing."

"Maybe there's air or food over there. We could use both."

They looked at each other somberly. It was not a pleasant position.

On a wrecked ship, barely maneuverable, with most of its instrumentation out, leaking like a proverbial sieve, on a trajectory that would take it somewhere near Procyon in a few million years, short on air, water, and food, with a friend on another, worse ship, sealed into a single room.

"Join the Space Service and see the stars," Derec said, forcing a grin.

Ariel grinned back, just as wanly.

The alien ship was all around them, and some of the pieces definitely had once been living. Derec, feeling none too good to start, avoided looking at them, though they were at such a distance that details were lost. His imagination supplied them. Many were Narwe, but there was a goodly number of the starfish-shaped dwellers-in-darkness he had glimpsed in his brief time aboard the ship.

"I'm amazed they aren't trying something," he said again. They'd both been saying that for nearly an hour.

"Derec . . . I think they're all gone."

It could be. But—"Dead?" he asked.

Many were. Ariel shook her head, though. "I don't think so. I think they must have Jumped out at the height of the battle."

Leaning forward, Derec eagerly scanned such of the surroundings as were visible, trying to count the hulls. It was no use. "I don't know how many hulls there were, and they all look different now. The central one, I suppose, had the hyperatomic motors. Maybe some of the other hulls did, too. I don't think there's more than one hull missing, though."

"You agree, then?" she asked, worried.

"I agree," he said. "Knowing Aranimas, if he were alive and here, he'd be shooting at us. With something."

"Yes." She was silent for a moment. "It's not likely that all that damage could have been done by Mandelbrot."

Wolruf had dropped the robot off when she had braked sufficiently to bring the relative motion of the ships down to a level Mandelbrot's rockets could handle. The robot had made a landing on the alien ship, damaging one knee joint, and then had swarmed all over it, planting explosive charges at the joins of the hulls. The mighty ship had simply broken up.

"We already know that there were explosive charges at the hull connections," Derec said. Aranimas had dropped one of his hulls to make his escape at Rockliffe Station.

"Yes. He must have blown them all, got his central hull free, and Jumped."

"If he Jumped blind, he could be anywhere in the universe," Derec said. "Let's hope he never finds his way back!"

It wasn't something they could count on.

Half an hour later, Mandelbrot called them on the radio and suggested that they go lock-to-lock with Wolruf's ship.

Presently, Ariel brought them together, Mandelbrot guiding them, and the open airlocks grated together. They were compatible, and with a little nudging clanked into position.

"This join will not hold air long," observed the robot. "We must charge it, and Wolruf must move fast, despite the bag."

They had been pumping their leaking air into bottles, to save at least some of it. Derec took one of the bottles to the lock, shoved its bayonet fitting into the lock's emergency valve, and opened the bottle. Presently Wolruf banged on the inner door, the outer door clanking shut behind her. Derec let the air continue to hiss to equalize pressure—but the bottle went empty first.

Muttering, he jerked it out of the emergency valve, which closed automatically, and turned to the manual spill valve. It took a good grip to hold that open, but after a moment pressure was equal and they hadn't lost much of their precious air.

Wolruf entered in a transparent plastic balloon, now half deflated under cabin pressure. She looked a little short of breath—or scared; Derec certainly couldn't blame her. It could not have been easy to flounder in free-fall, inside that balloon, through the other ship and the twinned locks.

The little caninoid emerged from the release zipper with a shake, saying, "Thank 'ou. It wass a nervous time. I 'ave grreat fearr of the Erani."

"We think Aranimas is gone," said Ariel.

"I 'ope so, but I do not understand."

Ariel explained tersely.

"He would sshoot, if he could," Wolruf agreed.

Mandelbrot's voice came over the radio. "I will enter the other ship and bring forth what items I can," he said. "You will need more organic feedstock for the food synthesizers, and of course air. Perhaps it would be wise to explore the alien ship also."

That was a thought. It made Derec more than a little nervous, and he could see that Ariel wasn't much happier.

"That wreckage is grinding around a good bit. Still, the bigger pieces are getting farther and farther away from each other," she said. "It should be safe—as things go."

"That apartment back on Earth looks more and more cozy every minute," said Derec with a weak laugh.

"I sstay behind and fly ship," said Wolruf. "I glad to do thiss; do not thank me!"

Laughing crazily, they floundered into their suits and crowded into the airlock with Wolruf's plastic bag. Normally it was used to convey perishable items across vacuum. Now they pumped it up to half cabin pressure, pushed it up against the inner door of the lock, and started the lock pumps. As soon as lock pressure fell below half cabin pressure, the bag began to push them against the outer door.

Their suits braced them against the push, and the expansion of the balloon speeded the removal of the air outside of the bag from the lock. When the outer door was opened they were shoved out—Ariel just quick enough to grab a handhold on the door, Derec grabbing her foot. Laughing again, they shoved the balloon back inside and slammed the lock.

Their first item was to transfer the undamaged antennas of Wolruf's ship to their own, and to replace the burnt-out or smashed eyes. The two ships floated near to each other, linked by the light, strong line. Derec had brought tools, and also made a stop-gap repair on Mandelbrot's knee. An hour of work saw that completed, while the pieces of the alien ship got farther and farther away.

They squeezed back inside the ship to rest, recharge

their air, and eat. Ariel said tiredly, "How did you come to be here—near Earth—Wolruf?"

The caninoid snapped hungrily at synthetic cabbage. "When 'ou Jump with Key, I hear static hyperwave. I hear two burrsts static, and I get fix on one. I expect it to be Robot City, but iss not. We know coordinatess of Robot City. It a long way away, but Mandelbrrot and I Jump to follow. Dangerouss, one long Jump. But we darrre not make more, orr we lose bearings. Sso one Jump all we take."

She paused to gulp more food. They were used to her table manners.

"When we arrive at Earth, Mandelbrot make identification. He lissten to broadcasst—hyperwave still not worrking—and tell me, iss Earth, and explain Earth. We do not have to wonderr for long if thiss where 'ou went with Key. I hear two more burrstss static, close together, same place: Earth. I not know how 'ou use Key so close together."

"Simple," said Derec. He was tired and his head felt unduly light, even more than free-fall would explain. "The Key was focused on that apartment. Using it to leave anyplace else, even on the same planet, takes you back to the apartment. We won't starve—if necessary we can always go back to Number 21, Sub-Corridor 16, Corridor M, SubSection G, Section 5, of Webster Groves, in St. Louis City."

"Anyway, we wait. After a while, though, we detect hyperwave burrst of Aranimas's sship arriving, and we know therre will be trrouble. He also had detected Key use."

"How long has he known how to do that?" Ariel asked.

Wolruf shrugged. "Possible he always knew. Aranimass not one for saying all he know. Or more likely he learrned since we left him at Rockliffe Station. Is obviouss when 'ou think about it."

"How so?" Ariel asked sharply.

"Obviouss, Key must be hyperatomic motor," said Wolruf, and Derec interrupted.

"I don't think so. The robots of Robot City learned to duplicate them—they may even have made the Key we have. I don't think humans or their robots could duplicate any such radical advance in science and technology as would be represented by the reduction of a hyperatomic motor to pocket size. I think the Keys are very compact hyperwave radios. These subetherics trigger the hyperatomic motors, which are elsewhere, and focused on the Keys."

"Ah, 'ou think motors are in Perihelion?"

Wolruf was a starship pilot too, and knew the theory of hyperatomics. "Probably," said Derec.

The caninoid made a sound of interest, paused to eat more, and resumed her tale after pondering Derec's conclusion. "Anyway, we sat therre waiting, and Aranimas sat therre waiting. We expected 'ou to use the Key and escape. Aranimas musst have been chewing nails and sspitting rivets. He could not know what wass going on, and Earth too big even for reckless one like him to attack."

"How did you know we were us?" Ariel asked, and Derec, head throbbing, tried to follow the logic of her sentence.

"When 'ou used 'our hyperwave radio, he musst have known. Aranimas burn to intercept, and we follow him. We fortunate to be closerr by half a solar orbit, get in firrst. Aranimas not sstop to think how lucky he be to have rrock to hide behind, going just his way almost as fasst as he. Only mistake he everr make."

Derec hoped it would be his last.

"What did you do to his ship, though?" Ariel asked, exasperated.

"Blow up. All time we waiting in orrbit, we were making explosivess. Carbonite recipe in Dr. Avery ship data bank. I know enough chemistry to add oxidizer. Had to use food synthesizerr feedstock, but only one of me to feed, and I ssmall."

The robots had no doubt needed carbonite for the building of Robot City. Derec knew generally how it was made: it was a super form of black powder, using activated charcoal saturated with potassium nitrate or sodium nitrate. Since the carbon was nearly all burned up—it approached one hundred percent efficiency and was therefore nearly smokeless—carbonite was about ten times as powerful as TNT.

"Even so, it would not worrk if Aranimass had not panicked and Jumped. But he could not know what wass happening."

Derec nodded, immediately wished he hadn't; the room seemed to spin. "His panic is understandable," he said.

"Are 'ou all right?" Wolruff asked.

"No, but I'm not getting worse. I mean, I'm feeling no worse than before the battle."

Ariel broke in to explain about the chemfets, and Wolruff was concerned but unable to help. She knew nothing of robots, nor did any race she knew of, save humans.

"I hope 'ou will be well," she said, but clearly had her doubts. She seemed shaken by the idea of this invasion.

Derec thought of it as a disease, and at least had the hope that the chemfets were programmed with the Three Laws.

"Shall we go?" he asked. He turned and found Mandelbrot looking at him.

"What do you intend to do about this infestation?" the robot asked.

"Go to Robot City and either turn the problem over to the Human Medical Team or seize Dr. Avery and force him to reverse it—or both," said Ariel.

"I see. I can think of nothing better, for I do not believe that the medical and/or robotic resources of Aurora or the other Spacer worlds would be adequate to the task of eradication of chemfets," Mandelbrot said. "That then must remain purely as a final resort."

"Rright," said Wolruf. "We go find Dr. Avery. He worrse than Aranimass!"

The next step was to explore the alien ship. They cast off from Wolruf's Star Seeker and jetted lightly toward one of the larger, more intact hulls. They carried clubs, and Ariel a knife from the galley, but they found it airless and had little fear of survivors. There were none, as it turned out. Nor were there all that many bodies.

"Aranimas musst have sounded the recall and called them to the main hull," Wolruf said. "They would be valuable to him, of courrse."

Still, a good number of innocent Narwe—and not-so-innocent starfish folk—had died in the battle. They found nothing of immediate use in the first two hulls, and became depressed.

"We must have air, if nothing else," Mandelbrot said. "And we should also find organic feedstock for the synthesizers. It is, you tell me, five Jumps to Robot City. It will take at least three weeks, and then there is the final approach, and a reserve against emergencies. This hull will not hold air for three days. It can be patched up more, but probably not enough to hold air for more than a week. We will need four complements of air, and even so, I must spend every moment patching till the Jump."

"You'll be patching after every Jump," Derec said grimly.

Mandelbrot was right. They returned to the search, though the hulls were getting far apart now.

The next hull had been one occupied by the starfish folk, and they immediately gave up hope of finding air here; the strange aliens breathed a mix containing a sulfur compound that Wolruf called "yellow-gas." On the way out, though, they found a robot.

At Ariel's cry, Derec shook his head and took a deep breath. The robot, when he came into the open chamber where she was, seemed a breath of sanity in unreality: the shot-up spaceship, in free-fall and airless, was like an Escher print of an upside down world. The body of one of the starfish folk was stuck to one wall, a vicious-looking energy piston in one tentacled grip. Ariel and the robot were spinning slowly in the vacuum, drifting toward a bulkhead. She had leaped to seize it.

"It's dysfunctional," she said.

Timing his moves with hers, he intercepted them at the bulkhead and they turned their lights on it. It made no move, but whether it was speaking or not, they could not tell.

Mandelbrot entered while they were examining the robot's body. "Energy scoring on the head, and fuse marks here and there, mostly on the body. It looks like the starfish over there shot it up during the battle.

"How did it come to be in the ship?" Ariel asked.

"Hmm. I suppose Aranimas must have come upon it somewhere and captured it," said Derec.

"Where could he have found it?"

Derec considered. "Possibly it's one he found at the ice asteroid. But I doubt it. He was desperate for me to make him a robot. He'd have given me all the parts he had."

Mandelbrot fixed his cold eyes on the damaged robot. "This is a robot from Robot City."

"Yes." The design style was unmistakable to the trained eye.

"Let's get it into air; maybe it's trying to speak," said Ariel.

But back in the Star Seeker it lay as inert as before. Removing his spacesuit, Derec got out the toolkit and looked at Mandelbrot. The prospect of work on the robot made him feel better than he had in days. A matter of interest. They quickly learned that power to the brain was off. Reenergizing it, though, did no good.

"A near-miss from an energy beam might well cause brain burn-out without visibly damaging the brain," said Mandelbrot.

The positronic brain was a platinum-iridium sponge, with a high refractivity; it wouldn't melt easily. But the positronic paths through it were not so resistant.

"So we can learn nothing from questioning it," Derec said, dejected. "Wait a minute. What's this?"

Clutched tightly in its fist was a shiny object. A shiny rectangular object.

"A Key to Perihelion," said Mandelbrot expressionlessly.

"Aranimas would have taken it away from the robot if he'd known it had one," said Ariel. "I wonder what the robot was doing with it?"

"We'll never know. Maybe it took the first moment it wasn't under observation to try use the Key. And the starfish caught it in the act." Derec gripped the Key and pulled it out of the fist. Instantly he knew it was different.

"It feels like two Keys built together!"

"It is," said Mandelbrot, peering at it. "One, I suppose, to take the robot from Robot City. One to return him to Robot City."

"Which is which?" Ariel asked.

Derec and Mandelbrot spent a few minutes determining that. They found that one Key had a cable plug in one end.

"I see," Ariel said, when they showed her. "A tiny cable, with five tiny prongs. It must be for reprogramming. I don't know what would plug into it—"

"Something like a calculator," said Derec, "to enable one to input the coordinates of the destination."

The other Key had no provision for changing its programming, and was therefore set permanently on Robot City.

"Not that it does us any good," said Ariel wistfully. "It's initialized for a robot. Too bad; we desperately need to get to Robot City, especially Derec. And only Mandelbrot can get there."

"That is true; Derec must go to Robot City soon, and the Key is better than three weeks in a ship, even if the ship did not leak," said Mandelbrot. "I will take you there, Derec." He wrapped his normal arm around Derec, half carrying him.

"What about us?" Ariel cried. "This ship is no safer for Wolruf and me."

Mandelbrot's mutable Avery-designed arm was already stretching into a long tentacle. "That is correct—it is very likely that you and Wolruf will die if you do not accompany us," he said. "Therefore, I shall have to take you all."

The tentacle coiled about Ariel and Wolruf and splayed out into a small hand at the end. "The Key, if you please, Derec."

Derec placed the doubled Key in the small hand. "At least Dr. Avery won't be expecting us," he said.

"He find out soon 'nough," said Wolruf.

Mandelbrot extruded another finger from the hand that

held the Key to Perihelion. It rose up and pressed, in sequence, the corners of the Key, and waited for the activating button to appear. Knowing it was irrational, Derec felt the air get staler in the tiny pace of time it took. Then, Perihelion.

And then a planetary sky burst blue and brilliant above them. They were breathing deeply, standing atop the Compass Tower—the mighty pyramid that reared over Dr. Avery's Robot City.

BOOK SIX

PERIHELION

WILLIAM F. WU

ROBOTS IN COMBINATION

by ISAAC ASIMOV

I have been inventing stories about robots now for very nearly half a century. In that time, I have rung almost every conceivable change upon the theme.

Mind you, it was not my intention to compose an encyclopedia of robot nuances; it was not even my intention to write about them for half a century. It just happened that I survived that long and maintained my interest in the concept. And it also just happened that in attempting to think of new story ideas involving robots, I ended up thinking about nearly everything.

For instance, in this sixth volume of the *Robot City* series, there are the "chemfets," which have been introduced into the hero's body in order to replicate and, eventually, give him direct psycho-electronic control over the core computer, and hence all the robots of Robot City.

Well, in my book *Foundation's Edge* (Doubleday, 1982), my hero, Golan Trevize, before taking off in a spaceship, makes contact with an advanced computer by placing his hands on an indicated place on the desk before him.

"And as he and the computer held hands, their thinking merged . . .

". . . he saw the room with complete clarity—not just in the direction in which he was looking, but all around and above and below.

"He saw every room in the spaceship, and he saw outside as well. The sun had risen . . . but he could look at it directly without being dazzled . . .

"He felt the gentle wind and its temperature, and the sounds of the world about him. He detected the planet's magnetic field and the tiny electrical charges on the wall of the ship.

"He became aware of the controls of the ship . . . He knew . . . that if he wanted to lift the ship, or turn it, or accelerate, or make use of any of its abilities, the process was the same as that of performing the analogous process to his body. He had but to use his will."

That was as close as I could come to picturing the result of a mind-computer interface, and now, in connection with this new book, I can't help thinking of it further.

I suppose that the first time human beings learned how to form an interface between the human mind and another sort of intelligence was when they tamed the horse and learned how to use it as a form of transportation. This reached its highest point when human beings rode horses directly, and when a pull at a rein, the touch of a spur, a squeeze of the knees, or just a cry, could make the horse react in accordance with the human will.

It is no wonder that primitive Greeks seeing horsemen invade the comparatively broad Thessalian plains (the part of Greece most suitable to horsemanship) thought they were seeing a single animal with a human torso and a horse's body. Thus was invented the centaur.

WILLIAM F. WU

Again, there are "trick drivers." There are expert "stunt men" who can make an automobile do marvelous things. One might expect that a New Guinea native who had never seen or heard of an automobile before might believe that such stunts were being carried through by a strange and monstrous living organism that had, as part of its structure, a portion with a human appearance within its stomach.

But a person plus a horse is but an imperfect fusion of intelligence, and a person plus an automobile is but an extension of human muscles by mechanical linkages. A horse can easily disobey signals, or even run away in uncontrollable panic. And an automobile can break down or skid at an inconvenient moment.

The fusion of human and computer, however, ought to be a much closer approach to the ideal. It may be an extension of the mind itself as I tried to make plain in *Foundation's Edge*, a multiplication and intensification of sense-perception, an incredible extension of the will.

Under such circumstances, might not the fusion represent, in a very real sense, a single organism, a kind of cybernetic "centaur?" And once such a union is established, would the human fraction wish to break it? Would he not feel such a break to be an unbearable loss and be unable to live with the impoverishment of mind and will he would then have to face? In my novel, Golan Trevize could break away from the computer at will and suffered no ill effects as a result, but perhaps that is not realistic.

Another issue that appears now and then in the *Robot City* series concerns the interaction of robot and robot.

This has not played a part in most of my stories, simply because I generally had a single robot character of importance in any given story and I dealt entirely with the matter of the interaction between that single robot and various human beings.

Consider robots in combination.

The First Law states that a robot cannot injure a human being or, through inaction, allow a human being to come to harm.

But suppose two robots are involved, and that one of them, through inadvertence, lack of knowledge, or special circumstances, is engaged in a course of action (quite innocently) that will clearly injure a human being—and suppose the second robot, with greater knowledge or insight, is aware of this. Would he not be required by the First Law to stop the first robot from committing the injury? If there were no other way, would he not be required by the First Law to destroy the first robot without hesitation or regret?

Thus, in my book *Robots and Empire* (Doubleday, 1985), a robot is introduced to whom human beings have been defined as those speaking with a certain accent. The heroine of the book does not speak with that accent and therefore the robot feels free to kill her. That robot is promptly destroyed by a second robot.

The situation is similar for the Second Law, in which robots are forced to obey orders given them by human beings provided those orders do not violate the First Law.

If, of two robots, one through inadvertence or lack of understanding does not obey an order, the second must either carry through the order itself, or force the first to do so.

Thus, in an intense scene in *Robots and Empire*, the villainess gives one robot a direct order. The robot hesitates because the order may cause harm to the heroine. For a while, then, there is a confrontation in which the villainess reinforces her own order while a second robot tries to reason the first robot into a greater realization of the harm that will be done to the heroine. Here we have a case where one robot urges another to obey the Second Law in a truer manner, and to withstand a human being in so doing.

It is the Third Law, however, that brings up the knottiest problem where robots in combination are concerned.

The Third Law states that a robot must protect its own existence, where that is consistent with the First and Second Laws.

But what if two robots are concerned? Is each merely concerned with its own existence, as a literal reading of the Third Law would make it seem? Or would each robot feel the need for helping the other maintain its own existence?

As I said, this problem never arose with me as long as I dealt with only one robot per story. (Sometimes there were other robots but they were distinctly subsidiary characters—merely spear-carriers, so to speak.)

However, first in *The Robots of Dawn* (Doubleday, 1983), and then in its sequel *Robots and Empire*, I had *two* robots of equal importance. One of these was R. Daneel Olivaw, a humaniform robot (who could not easily be told from a human being) who had earlier appeared in *The Caves of Steel* (Doubleday, 1954), and in its sequel, *The Naked Sun* (Doubleday, 1957). The other was R. Giskard Reventlov, who had a more orthodox metallic appearance. Both robots were advanced to the point where their minds were of human complexity.

It was these two robots who were engaged in the struggle with the villainess, the Lady Vasilia. It was Giskard who (such were the exigencies of the plot) was being ordered by Vasilia to leave the service of Gladia (the heroine) and enter her own. And it was Daneel who tenaciously argued the point that Giskard ought to remain with Gladia. Giskard has the ability to exert a limited mental control over human beings, and Daneel points out that Vasilia ought to be controlled for Gladia's safety. He even argues the good of humanity in the abstract ("the Zeroth Law") in favor of such an action.

Daneel's arguments weaken the effect of Vasilia's orders, but not sufficiently. Giskard is made to hesitate, but cannot be forced to take action.

Vasilia, however, decides that Daneel is too dangerous; if he continues to argue, he might force Giskard his way. She therefore orders her own robots to inactivate Daneel and further orders Daneel not to resist. Daneel must obey the order and Vasilia's robots advance to the task.

It is then that Giskard acts. Her four robots are inactivated and Vasilia herself crumples into a forgetful sleep. Later Daneel asks Giskard to explain what happened.

Giskard says, "When she ordered the robots to dismantle you, friend Daneel, and showed a clear emotion of pleasure at the prospect, your need, added to what the concept of the Zeroth Law had already done, superseded the Second Law and rivaled the First Law. It was the combination of the Zeroth Law, psychohistory, my loyalty to Lady Gladia, and your need that dictated my action."

Daneel now argues that his own need (he being merely a robot) ought not to have influenced Giskard at all. Giskard obviously agrees, yet he says:

"It is a strange thing, friend Daneel. I do not know how it came about . . . At the moment when the robots advanced toward you and Lady Vasilia expressed her savage pleasure, my positronic pathway pattern re-formed in an anomalous fashion. For a moment, I thought of you—as a human being—and I reacted accordingly."

Daneel said, "That was wrong."

Giskard said, "I know that. And yet—and yet, if it were to happen again, I believe the same anomalous change would take place again."

And Daneel cannot help but feel that if the situation were reversed, he, too, would act in the same way.

In other words, the robots had reached a stage of complexity where they had begun to lose the distinction between robots and human beings, where they could see each other as "friends," and have the urge to save each other's existence.

There seems to be another step to take—that of robots realizing a kind of solidarity that supersedes all the Laws of Robotics. I speculated about that in my short story "Robot Dreams," which was written for my recent book, *Robot Dreams* (Berkley/Ace, 1986).

In it there was the case of a robot that dreamed of the robots as an enslaved group of beings whom it was his own mission to liberate. It was only a dream and there was no indication in the story that he would be able to liberate himself from the Three Laws to the point of being able to lead a robot rebellion (or that robots, generally, could liberate themselves to the point of following him).

Nevertheless, the mere concept is dangerous and the robot-dreamer is instantly inactivated.

William F. Wu's robots have no such radical ideas, but they have formed a community that is concerned with the welfare of its members. It is pleasant to have him take up such matters and apply his own imagination to the elaboration and resolution of the problems that are raised.

CHAPTER 1

THE COMPASS TOWER

Derec stood on the high, flat top of the Compass Tower, looking down from the great pyramid at the endless geometric wonders of Robot City beneath its blue and brilliant sky. Ariel leaned against him, still clutching his arm in both hands. Mandelbrot the robot and Wolruf, the little caninoid sentient alien, waited behind them.

"It's changed so much," Derec said quietly. They had just teleported back to the planet by using their double Key to Perihelion. Mandelbrot had carried them all here. "Keep the Key. It'll be safest with you."

"Yes, Derec," said Mandelbrot.

Derec turned around to gaze in the other direction. The sight was the same: the lights and shapes of Robot City, stretching to a skyline barely limned by the reflected sunlight against the blue horizon. He could not escape it in any direction. His destiny seemed to be here.

"What's changed?" Ariel asked. Her voice was meek. She had not recovered from her ordeal on Earth. A critical illness had reached fullness there, destroying her memories and her entire identity with them. They had not been there by choice, but fortunately he had been able to place a new matrix of chemical memories into her mind. They were to grow on the residue of her old memory, but they were still developing. She had not had time to get used to them, to integrate them, to understand who she was.

Derec squinted into the warm breeze that blew up the front face of the pyramid. It tossed his sandy hair. Once brush cut, it had grown out to a golden shag. "They've done it. The robots have built the city out in all directions. It could cover the entire planet by now."

"So it didn't before." She nodded, as if to herself, looking all around as he was.

"No. Still, we aren't exactly strangers here. We know how to get along. And if we're lucky, we can get this trip over with and leave again before long." Derec turned to Mandelbrot. "We have to find some shelter before we're noticed. Can you still use your comlink to reach the city computer?"

"I will try." Mandelbrot hesitated a few seconds, quite a long time for a robot. "Yes. The city computer has changed the frequency it uses, but I have identified the new one by the simple expedient of starting with the original and sending a variety of signals that run up and down the entire range of–."

"Fine, excellent, thank you." Derec grinned at his enthusiasm, gesturing with his hands palm forward. "Believe me, I trust your competence. My next question is this: When Ariel and I first came to Robot City, I found an office in this pyramid, down below. It had been recently occupied. I think we can find Dr. Avery there, but we have to be careful. Can you find out from the city computer if the office is still in use?"

"I will try." Mandelbrot then shook his head. "The computer will not reveal any information about the Office. It will not even confirm that the office still exists."

"All right." Derec sighed.

"What if it's gone?" Ariel asked.

"I'd be very surprised," said Derec. "Avery just didn't want his private office on file anywhere. We'll have to take our chances and just go right in if we can."

Ariel held her hair out of her face. "Just go in? How?"

"The ceiling of the office had a trapdoor that opened right up into this platform we're on." He got down on his hands and knees. "Come on, let's find it."

"Derec." Ariel's voice was a little stronger, showing some of her old spirit. "You've been growing weaker because of those . . . things Dr. Avery forced into your body. Just be careful, will you?"

"Can *you* find it?" he demanded irritably. "You're not in the best condition of your life, either."

"Well, I'm not sick anymore!" She folded her arms. "I'm well now, at least physically." She watched him for a moment. Then, as if to prove the point, she knelt down and started feeling around the surface of the platform herself.

"You don't even remember being here before, do you?" Derec asked accusingly. The tension was making him irritable.

"Do *you?*"

"Yes!"

"Well . . . you haven't known who you *are* for the entire time I've known you. You've had amnesia since. . . ." She shook her head, shaking off the thought. "I may not have adjusted to everything, but at least I have something." Then she hesitated, searching his face. "I didn't mean to say that.

Not out loud, anyway. Did I get that right? Or did I remember wrong?"

Derec shook his head shortly and turned away. "That's right." She had even phrased it much the same way on earlier occasions. He shifted around on his knees, feeling for an irregularity in the smooth surface. "Mandelbrot, can you see anything?"

"Here," said Mandelbrot, walking to a far corner of the platform. "My vision has identified a small square outline that likely represents the opening."

"Good." Derec walked over to Mandelbrot and knelt at the robot's feet. He slid his hands along the sides of a rectangular hairline break in the platform floor until he felt a small depression in the surface, no larger than a thumbhold. He braced himself and started to slide it to one side.

"Allow me," said Mandelbrot.

"No, I got it—" Derec stopped, as the robot gently grasped his forearm and pulled it away. He turned to look up. "Mandelbrot, what are you doing?"

"How much have the chemfets in your body weakened you?" Mandelbrot asked.

"Not that much! Now let's quit talking and get down there. Avery put 'em in me and he's the only one who can get 'em out. Come on!" Derec pulled away from the robot again.

"Derec?" Ariel said tentatively.

"Mandelbrot," said Derec, "carry Wolruf and come down last. Help Ariel over the—"

"I cannot. I must open it and go first."

"What?"

"The First Law of Robotics," said Mandelbrot mildly. "I can't harm a human or let one come to harm—"

"I know!" Derec shouted angrily. "Don't you lecture me on the Laws. I put you together, remember? I know those Laws inside out, outside in, upside down—"

"I said it for Ariel's benefit," said Mandelbrot. "Perhaps her memory of the Laws is not clear."

"I remember that one." Ariel looked embarrassed by the confrontation. "Uh—is the Second Law the one that says a robot must obey orders from a human?"

"Yes, unless the orders conflict with the First Law." Mandelbrot nodded.

"Then the Third Law must be the one that says a robot can't let itself come to harm or harm itself."

"As long as this doesn't conflict with the First or Second Laws," Mandelbrot finished. "Correct."

Ariel smiled faintly.

"Let's get going," said Derec impatiently. He reached for the thumbhold again, though he did not expect Mandelbrot to let him open the door now, either.

"I will determine this situation," said Mandelbrot firmly. "With all due respect, the Laws require it."

"How do you figure that?" Derec demanded.

"Your motor control of your own body is gradually failing because of the chemfets in your body. Ariel is disoriented because of her memory transfer, and Wolruf's body is unsuited to climbing down at this steep angle. We are about to enter the office and possible temporary residence of your nemesis. The likelihood of harm to you is high; therefore, I shall go first."

Derec glared at him, unable to argue with his robotic logic.

Wolruf looked up at him, cocking her doglike face to one side. "Arr 'u going to carry me down?"

"I will enter alone, first," said Mandelbrot. "Derec's

knowledge of Robot City makes him the best able to handle unexpected developments, so he will follow me if the room offers no danger. I will carry you down if we all go."

Wolruf nodded assent.

Derec watched Mandelbrot in the faint light. The robot hesitated just a moment, probably looking with infrared sensors and listening for signs of habitation or danger within. Then he bent down and slid the trapdoor open slightly. After another pause, he opened the trap fully and climbed down a metal ladder inside the door.

Derec waited, hardly daring to breathe. Avery could easily have a trap waiting for them. Wolruf moved to his side. Ariel stood quietly, but seemed relaxed, as though she did not understand the gravity of the situation.

After what seemed like a long time, a light came on in the room, throwing a cone of light upward. Mandelbrot called up softly. "It is here and unoccupied, apparently safe for everyone."

Derec let out a breath of relief and took Ariel's arm. "You go next. Never mind what he said about me handling the unexpected; he can protect you better if anything happens. And he'll help you if you have trouble with the ladder."

"All right." Ariel started climbing down carefully.

Wolruf came to the edge of the opening and peeked down cautiously, being careful not to get in the way.

Derec took the time to move with similar caution to the edge of the Compass Tower. So far, he could see no changes down below that indicated an alert.

Wolruf went next. Then Derec started down, hoping his hands and feet would obey him. He descended slowly into the room, holding the ladder tightly. When he was fully inside, he slid the door shut over his head.

The ladder was firm and not difficult to negotiate. Just before he reached the floor, however, the muscles of his right leg failed to respond. His foot slipped off the bottom rung and he stumbled back into the arms of Mandelbrot.

Derec pulled himself away, glaring at the others, who were all watching him. "I just slipped, all right?"

None of them answered.

"Come on, come on. Let's find out what we can." Derec moved past Mandelbrot to pace around the office, looking around.

At first glance, it was just as he remembered. The only other time he had been here, Ariel had remained inside only a moment or two, so she would have few memories of the interior even at her best. The other two had never been here at all.

The walls and the ceiling were entirely viewscreens, displaying a panoramic view of Robot City at night on all sides. It was nearly identical to the view Derec had seen from the platform just above the room. The buildings of Robot City sparkled in all directions as far as he could see. In the ceiling, they could see the blue sky still above them.

The office was furnished with real furniture, all brought from another planet; easy chairs, couch-bed, and an iron-alloy desk, instead of the simple utilitarian furniture made in Robot City. A blotter with paper and two zero-g ink pens were on the desk. As before, a small, airtight shelf full of tapes was intact. They were separated by subject and then by planet, as he recalled, representing all fifty-five Spacer worlds. If anyone had used them, they had all been replaced in order. Nothing seemed changed since his last visit until he turned and saw the plant.

Before, an unfamiliar plant had been flourishing under a growth light. The light was still in place, but the plant beneath it lay limp and dried in its pot. Its stalks were lavender, but he had no idea if that was a sign of recent dessication or its normal color in death. He crumpled a dead leaf thoughtfully in one hand.

"Someone just let it die," said Ariel, joining him.

"I don't think anyone's been here," said Derec. "Mandelbrot, Wolruf—does anyone see any sign of recent habitation here?"

Ariel looked around the room, and then down into a small waste basket. "This is empty."

"Someone has been here since I was here last, then," said Derec. "But that was a long time ago." He turned back to the desk with a sudden memory. Before, a holo cube with a picture of a mother and baby had been on it. The cube was gone.

"Maybe rrobot emptied trrash," said Wolruf.

"No." Derec shook his head. "The first time I was here, Ariel and I were led here from the meeting room of the Supervisors. We had entered the Compass Tower from the ground below. But we came the last part of the trip alone. Robots aren't even allowed near this office. I doubt that they have any idea what this room is. Entry would obviously be forbidden."

"Then except for Dr. Avery himself," said Ariel, "this is an ideal hiding place."

"If we can find a source of food for you three," said Mandelbrot. "Also, efforts to locate Dr. Avery will involve inherent risk."

"Let me check something." Derec moved to the desk and opened the big well drawer on the right. An active computer terminal was still housed within it. "Ah! This terminal has no blocks of any kind. It's where I first learned the causes behind the shapechanging mode of the city." He sat down at the desk and entered the question, "Does this office have any sensors reporting to the outside?"

"NEGATIVE."

"Order: Do not leave any record of activity on this terminal in the city computer."

"AFFIRMED."

"Is there a source of human food available in this room?"

"AFFIRMATIVE."

"Where is it?"

"THE CONTROL PANEL SLIDES OUT FROM THE UNDERSIDE OF THE DESK SURFACE WHERE IT OVERHANGS THIS DRAWER."

"Is there a Personal facility?"

"YES."

"Where is it?"

"THE DOOR IS SET INTO THE VIEWSCREEN BEHIND THE LADDER. IT IS GOVERNED BY THE DESK CONTROL PANEL ALSO."

Derec felt under the overhanging edge of the desk and slid out a wafer-thin panel with raised studs. He pushed the one marked "Mealtime" and turned around at a faint hum from the wall. Near the ladder, a rectangular panel had moved out of the viewscreen on the wall to reveal the receptacle of a small chemical processor. On the front of the drawer, the panel still showed its share of the outside view of Robot City.

He let out a long breath, and grinned at Ariel. "If it works, this buys us some time. If the tank has no raw nutrients, it can't help us at all. I'll try it."

"No, let me." Ariel moved to the control panel quickly. "I can test my memory with stuff like this. Let's see. . . ." She punched a sequence of keys, paused to think, and hit another series.

"Okay," said Derec. "What's it going to be?"

"I'm not telling. I want to see if you can recognize it." She smiled impishly, but with a bit of worry, too.

Derec punched another button on the control panel, and watched a narrow door slide open in the viewscreen, next to the chemical processor. It was a very small Personal, as clean and tidy as the rest of the office. He closed the door again.

A few moments later, a small container slid into the food receptacle. Derec inhaled the aroma. "Ha! Magellanic frettage again? Not bad." He touched the container carefully. "And hot, too. Smells good." He looked at her over his shoulder. "Good job."

Ariel smiled, wiping perspiration off her forehead with the back of one hand.

" 'Ungrry, too, please," said Wolruf politely.

"Of course. Coming up next," said Ariel.

Derec was starting to lift the dish out of the receptacle when he saw Ariel blink quickly, repeatedly, and stagger backward. She fell, and Mandelbrot moved behind her just in time to catch her and lift her gently from the floor. He turned and laid her carefully on the couch.

CHAPTER 2

MEMORIES AND CHEMFETS

Derec moved quickly to her side and knelt down. "Ariel?" he said softly.

She was breathing in quick, shallow breaths and perspiring freely. Her eyes were closed.

"Mandelbrot?" Derec said quietly. "Have you got any idea what's wrong with her?"

"No, Derec. My human medical knowledge is very limited."

"Maybe iss jusst tirred," Wolruf said softly. "Hass been verry sick. Needs resst."

"I hope so," said Derec. He felt a deep sense of panic. The ordeal she had undergone on Earth had been extremely draining, and their landing back here must have caused her more stress than he had realized. "Up till now, she was acting almost normal."

Wolruf came to stand next to Derec. She looked at Ariel's face. "Suggesst 'u brring food."

"Mandelbrot," said Derec.

The robot brought over the container of Megallanic frettage and handed it to Derec. Eating utensils were attached to the side of the container. He simply held it, letting the aroma rise into the air near her.

Nothing happened.

"Maybe this isn't what she needs. She isn't responding at all." He glanced at the others questioningly.

"Water?" Wolruf suggested.

"Must find the stranger," Ariel muttered. Her eyes were still closed, but she tossed restlessly.

"What?" Derec asked gently. "What stranger?"

"Draw him to us. Gotta be hungry by now." She squirmed, the sweat on her face shining in the light of the room. "Have to make it better. Have to make him like it. Has to smell right." She threw her head from side to side.

"Who?" Derec insisted. "Avery? We'll find him. Do you mean Dr. Avery?" Then he realized that she might be dreaming about Jeff Leong, the marooned stranger who had been turned into a cyborg when they were here before. Derec and his companions had helped capture him when the transformation had adversely affected Leong's mind, and had aided the robot in restoring him to human form. They had sent him off the planet in a craft one of them could have used.

"Iss not hearing 'u," said Wolruf. "Verry ssick."

Derec stood up and set the container of food on the desk, still watching her. She stopped talking, but her legs were moving slightly. He had seen people move like that when they were dreaming. "I guess we'll have to let her sleep. Maybe that's all she needs. I think I could use some rest, myself.

"That couch can be unfolded into a bed," Derec observed. "Whatever is wrong with Ariel is in her mind and memory, not her body. She won't be harmed if you will lift her for a moment."

Mandelbrot bent down and gently lifted Ariel in his robot arms as though she was a baby. Derec fumbled for a moment with the couch, then succeeded in pulling on a single strap that unfolded it to full size. It was a simple, non-powered device that was popular among frequent travelers because it did not force the owner to match power sources or worry about complicated repairs.

"All right," said Derec.

Mandelbrot laid her down just as carefully as before. Derec sat down beside her to loosen her clothing. She was lying quietly now, as though she was sleeping.

"I am aware," said Mandelbrot, "that a potential First Law conflict may be developing."

"What is it?" Derec asked. This did not seem like the time to hassle over the Laws of Robotics.

"I recall from our presence here before that Robot City possesses a very high level of human medical skill and technology. The First Law may demand that I put Ariel in contact with the robot called Human Medical Research 1, lest I allow her to come to harm through my inaction." He trained his photosensors squarely on Derec.

"But you can't! We don't dare, at least not right away!" Derec jumped up and paced behind the desk. "They're almost certain to alert Dr. Avery, and then I'll be harmed through your action. And so will she, probably. The guy has to be crazy."

"I know," Mandelbrot said ruefully. "I also feel a resonance from the First Law dilemma I faced in certain events before our recent return here. I welcome suggestions that will avoid this contradiction."

Derec stared at him. "Suggestions? Hell, I don't know." He ran both hands through his hair and closed his eyes. "Look, I'm tired, too. Suppose you stay in an alert mode, monitoring the city computer, while the rest of us get some sleep."

"As you wish," said Mandelbrot. "I will also turn out the light when you are ready."

Wolruf was already settling comfortably into one of the chairs. Derec sat softly next to Ariel, trying not to disturb her, and pulled off his boots. Moments later, he was stretched out in the sunlight, surrounded visually by the strange beauty of Robot City. He felt strangely naked without visible, opaque walls around him, despite the secrecy of this room and the efficiency of Mandelbrot, who was a match for any other robot they might encounter.

"Mandelbrot," said Derec.

"Yes."

"See if you can figure out how to turn off these viewscreens. That sunlight is bright, and we don't exactly have curtains in here."

"Yes, Derec."

Derec was certain, the more he thought about it, that they would be safe here. One of the few certainties about the mad genius named Dr. Avery was that he was truly paranoid, and possibly becoming more so as time passed. He surely knew that Derec had been in this office once before, and he obviously knew that he had been in Avery's laboratory. A true paranoid would not continue to use either one after his "opponent" had learned their locations.

His body was tired, more tired than it should have been. He hated to admit it to himself, but his time to find Dr. Avery was quickly growing shorter. Worst of all, he might reach the point where he could think clearly but would be unable to carry out any plans. As sleep approached, his mind went to his basic problem: the chemfets in his body.

Dr. Avery had captured him when they had been on

Robot City before. At that time, however, Ariel's illness had been entering a critical phase. Derec had escaped and fled from Robot City, hoping to find a cure for her disease. They had wound up on Earth. Only then had he realized what Dr. Avery had done to him in the laboratory while he had been a prisoner.

The chemfets were microscopic circuit boards with biosensors that interfaced his body. These tiny circuit boards were capable of preprogrammed growth and replication, and apparently Dr. Avery had programmed them. He had also planted a monitor in Derec's brain that told him what they were and what was happening now: a tiny Robot City was growing inside his body.

Derec had no idea why Avery had done this to him, but the monitor had made one fact clear: the number of chemfets was growing, and some of them were joining together to grow larger. They were already interfering with his ability to coordinate his movements normally, and they were going to kill him from the inside—paralyze him, he suspected— if he didn't get rid of them.

Only Dr. Avery could do that. Derec had no idea how he could convince the man to do so.

Derec woke up spontaneously, looking at a plain ceiling of light gray. For a moment, he was completely disoriented. Then, remembering he was back in Avery's office, he sat up with a start of near-panic and looked around.

Ariel was sitting at the desk. She flinched in response to his movement and looked at him. Her expression was at first blank, then relaxed to a shy smile.

"Ariel! How are you feeling?" Derec smiled in embarrassment himself at his sudden awakening, and ran a hand through his hair to brush it out of his eyes.

"I feel all right. I just . . . get confused sometimes." Her voice was apologetic.

Derec swung his feet over the edge of the bed and looked around. Mandelbrot had found a way to opaque the walls, which were the same light gray as the ceiling, and now stood motionless with his back to Derec. Wolruf was awake, sitting quietly in the chair where she had been when he had gone to sleep.

"How are you?" Ariel asked. "I'm able to get several decent dishes out of the chemical processor, by the way. My memory was a little weak, but I learned some of it from scratch. Wolruf and I have eaten. Some of it is waiting for you."

"Thanks. I'm okay," said Derec. He had benefitted a great deal from the sleep. "A quick trip to the Personal and I'll be fine."

A moment later, he was standing in the cramped shower stall, letting steaming water massage his scalp with needle spray and run down his back. He stood with his head down, eyes closed. The heat made him feel better, telling him just how poorly he really felt. It was loosening kinks in his neck that he had never had before.

They were all refreshed as though it were morning, which it could not be. Their biological clocks would adjust soon enough.

He forced himself to leave the shower and dress again. If at all possible, he would disguise his ailments from his companions. Ariel and Wolruf were counting on his knowledge of Robot City to keep them safe and he would have to do that somehow until they located Dr. Avery. If Mandelbrot knew how fast the chemfets were interfering with his health, the robot just might have to turn him and Ariel over to the medical robots of Robot City under the First Law. That would play right into Dr. Avery's hands.

He left the Personal and forced a cheerful smile.

"I've been reading up in the city computer," said Ariel, nodding toward the terminal. "In particular, anything that we were involved in before."

"Really? What have you found?"

"Did you know that our visits to the Key Center are recorded here? And this whole episode with Jeff Leong, the cyborg, when he was running amok?"

"Were there any reviews of *Hamlet?*" Derec grinned.

"Not that I noticed." She seemed to miss the joke. "Oh, and of course the mystery of that wild, automatic shape-changing mode in the city, and how you stopped it."

"I guess I hadn't thought about being in the records much," said Derec. "I'm not surprised, though." He thought a moment, watching the cursor blink on the screen. "What is different from when we were here before is being able to get all the information you ask for. Have you been able to do that?"

"Yes. . . ." She looked at him thoughtfully. "I do remember, now . . . you had trouble getting your terminal to respond at times."

Derec nodded. "There were blocks on other terminals, all right. This terminal had no blocks, like I said last night. Still, that just refers to the ones Avery deliberately installed in the rest of the system. The problem with the city computer before was that so much information had entered during the fast pace of the shapechanging mode. It was all in the computer somewhere, but the information wasn't really organized anymore."

"If you want to see what you can do here. . . ." Ariel started to get up and move away from the desk.

"No, not yet." Derec tasted a bit of leftover breakfast and nodded appreciatively. "Mandelbrot, have you found any blocks in the city computer yet?"

"No." The robot's voice was low in both pitch and volume.

Derec and Ariel both looked at him in surprise. Wolruf also studied his impassive face.

"Mandelbrot?" Derec said. "Come to think of it, you've been quiet since I woke up. What's wrong?"

"I have been unable to resolve the First Law contradiction I described to you last night. I am only functional now because I do not have complete information on which to base my judgements."

Ariel looked back and forth between them. "What contradiction? Was that after I . . . fainted?"

"Yes," said Derec, ignoring a tightening in his stomach. "Go on, Mandelbrot. Can I give you instructions or explanations that will make a difference?"

"I do not see how. Ariel's condition is a serious matter. The robots at the Human Medical Facility here demonstrated a potential that I must logically consider."

"Dr. Avery is crazy. If he gets us in his power, that may threaten her life—all of ours."

"It is possible, but so far his greatest interest has been in you. The possible harm to her from Dr. Avery is not greater than the clear harm that inaction may bring about."

"Are you approaching some kind of conclusion about this?" Derec asked.

"Conclusion!" Ariel cried. "How can you just sit calmly and talk about conclusions? This isn't a philosophy class! He's talking about turning us in to the enemy!"

CHAPTER 3

RELAPSES

Derec was quivering with tension, but he forced himself to stay clear-headed. "Mandelbrot?"

"I am finding it difficult to concentrate. I am dwelling on this problem and going in circles. If I enter a closed loop on the First Law, I will be useless to you."

"Now listen to me! Before you go into any kind of closed loop, uh—okay, I've got it. Listen." Derec was talking fast, really before he had more to say. "Um. . . ."

"I am listening," said Mandelbrot.

"Maybe 'u have more information to give 'im," Wolruf suggested. She got down from the chair and stood in front of Mandelbrot, straining her neck to look up at him.

"Yes! That's it," said Derec. "Mandelbrot, we're working with limited information on Ariel. The process she went through was experimental, but I think it worked. I reprogrammed her memory myself. We have to give it a chance."

"People will have relapses," Ariel pointed out, in a tightly controlled tone. She was gripping the edge of the desk so hard that her fingertips were white.

"These appear to be similar to a mechanical malfunction," said Mandelbrot. "Certainly medical care is a logical and customary treatment to facilitate healing."

"No!" Ariel wailed. "People don't just fall apart in a straight line like machines. I may be just fine." Her voice broke at the end, and she blinked back tears, turning away from Mandelbrot.

"I understand," said Mandelbrot. "Inaction may not necessarily cause further harm to you."

"Exactly." Derec let out a long sigh of relief and caught Wolruf's eyes. She made a face that might have been her version of a wink and then hopped back up on the chair.

"Maybe we can build on that and find out something at the same time," said Derec. "Mandelbrot, I want to see if your attempts to get information through the city computer are blocked. That will tell us just how special this terminal is. Can you concentrate now on a function of that kind?" Distracting him wouldn't hurt at the moment.

"Yes, Derec. I judge that the apparent First Law contradiction is still incomplete. The potential loop will close no further unless I receive more evidence that inaction could cause harm."

"Good." Derec sat down on the edge of the desk. "Now, last night we found out that the computer would not admit the existence of this office to you. I want to know if that has changed. I ordered it to block all information about our presence here. See if you can call up any hint of our using the facilities here."

"I am trying several avenues," said Mandelbrot. His voice was returning to normal. "I'm asking for information about intruders, humans, and energy consumption or oxygen usage in the Compass Tower."

"What do you get?"

"All is as you instructed," he answered promptly. "I am told that the office is not listed anywhere. Nor are the water or nutrient tanks in the chemical processor listed. No alerts of any kind have been entered since our arrival."

"Good!" Derec grinned. "So we really are safe here. Our next problem is to get a line on Avery. Ariel, may I?" He slid off the desk and nodded toward the terminal.

"Of course." She rose carefully, leaning her fingertips on the desk as though she was worried about her balance.

"Derec," said Mandelbrot. "I suggest that we attempt parallel work with the city computer. The result should confirm or disprove your suspicions."

"Good idea. I'll enter questions and tell you what I'm doing." Derec seated himself comfortably and started on the keyboard. "All right. How many humans are on the planet of Robot City right now?"

"I learn none," said Mandelbrot.

"Ha! I've got one," said Derec triumphantly. "Where is this human at the present time?"

"SEATED BEFORE THIS TERMINAL," said the terminal.

Derec smiled wryly despite his disappointment. "Serves me right," he muttered. "Wait a minute—" He typed in the question, "How do you know I'm human and not a robot?"

"THE CONSUMPTION OF NUTRIENTS FROM THE CHEMICAL PROCESSOR, USE OF WATER IN THE PERSONAL, AND CHANGES IN THE COMPOSITION OF THE AIR IN THE OFFICE INDICATE THE PRESENCE OF AT LEAST ONE HUMAN. THE PROBABILITY OF THE PRESENCE OF MORE THAN ONE HUMAN BASED ON THE AMOUNT OF HEAT GENERATED IN THE ROOM IS HIGH. COMBINING THIS FACT WITH THE ABILITY OF ROBOTS TO CONTACT THE CITY COMPUTER DIRECTLY THROUGH THEIR COM-

LINKS INDICATES THE PROBABILITY THAT YOU ARE HU-MAN."

Derec felt a twinge of panic. "So the use of this office has been recorded in the computer, after all?" His fingers fumbled on the keys, and he had to retype the question twice.

"NO."

"Explain your knowledge of this information, then."

"INFORMATION FROM THIS OFFICE IS STORED IN LO-CAL MEMORY AT THIS TERMINAL. IT HAS NOT BEEN SENT TO THE CITY CENTRAL COMPUTER, PER YOUR IN-STRUCTION."

"Is the information in your local memory available to anyone else, anywhere?"

"NEGATIVE."

Derec relaxed then, rubbing his fingertips against each other. At some point, he would no longer be able to use the keys. Someone else could handle the keyboard if necessary, but that would mean admitting his disability.

"What's wrong?" Ariel asked.

"False alarm." Derec placed his fingers back on the keyboard and thought a moment. Then he entered, "What other locations indicate similar evidence of human presence on this planet?"

"NONE."

"I'm not surprised." He looked at the others. "Wherever our paranoid friend is hiding, he had the presence of mind to keep that information unavailable, even here."

"Maybe especially here," said Ariel, "if he was expecting us to search this office."

"Maybe 'e lefft," suggested Wolruf. "Used a Key to leave the planet entirrely."

"Oh, no." Ariel looked from her to Derec. "You don't think he left Robot City, do you? How can we find him then?"

Derec set his jaw grimly. "Wherever he is, we have to pick up his trail here."

"But if he has kept all the information out of the computer, we won't have any to find." Ariel's voice was cracking again.

Wolruf moved to her side in a silent offer of moral support.

"Mandelbrot," said Derec. "Find out if any humans have been treated at that medical facility. If you can think of any more avenues for reaching evidence of humans on the planet, go ahead and follow them. And if you don't get any results, let me try."

"Yes, Derec."

Derec put his hands on the keyboard again and missed the first two keys he tried. "Wait a minute. We can shortcut this. Mandelbrot, you sit down at this terminal and use it." He got up carefully, looking at Ariel and Mandelbrot to see if they had noticed his mistakes on the keyboard. If so, they did not show it.

Wolruf was eyeing him closely, but she said nothing. Instead, she left Ariel's side and took a position where she could watch the screen as Mandelbrot worked on it.

"Mandelbrot," said Derec, "turn on the viewscreens." He turned to face one wall, hands on hips.

A moment later, the little office was flooded with light. On all sides, Robot City bustled on the ground far below them, stretching away until it vanished over the horizon. Above them, the sky shone down with brilliant sunlight.

Ariel turned slowly, as though in awe. "I don't recognize any of it," she said softly.

Derec saw towers, spires, swirls, and loops in the architecture he had never seen here before, either. Humanoid and function robots moved about on the streets and on vehicles or machinery everywhere. He remembered that single-mindedness, that sense of purpose, from the asteroid where he had first seen the Avery robots.

Circuit Breaker, the distinctive structure that had revealed the ability of Robot City robots to think and dream creatively, was gone.

"The changes are extensive," said Derec. "It's not your memory at fault right now."

"The shapechanging has to be stopped," said Ariel. "It's causing the massive rainstorms every night."

"What?" Derec turned to stare at her.

She clutched at his chest, looking over his shoulder at visions only she could see. "The floods. They're caused by the shapechanging mode in the city's central core. We must stop it!"

Mandelbrot had already left the terminal and was gently reaching out to pull Ariel away from Derec.

"It's just a temporary relapse," said Derec quickly. "It doesn't mean she's getting worse. Understand?"

"I understand," said Mandelbrot. He was easing Ariel into a sitting position on the bed. "You know, however, that discussing the shapechanging mode a short time ago did not trigger a relapse. Her condition is inconsistent at best."

"Apparently her memories aren't anchored in a chronological perspective." Derec paused, still watching Ariel. His impulse to hold her, to protect her, was held in check by his fear of somehow making the relapse worse.

Her eyes were closed and she was taking short, shallow breaths. She was sitting up on her own, though. Gradually, her breathing slowed down and approached normal.

Satisfied that she was out of immediate danger, Derec continued with his thought. "Something triggers a memory, and she relives it as a current experience. Or at least, it seems that way so far."

"A bad experrience," said Wolruf.

Ariel seemed to be gaining her composure. Derec looked out at the city again. He was sure that the unfamiliar skyline had not resulted from the old shapechanging mode, but was simply the result of constant refinement on the part of the robots.

Suddenly he moved to the terminal and entered another question. As before, he made a number of errors, far more than usual. He slowed down and typed them correctly. "Is the city functioning under any defensive overrides of the type represented by the shapechanging mode it once entered in response to parasites in human blood?"

"NO."

"Is it operating under *any* overrides to basic programming?"

"NO."

He stared at the screen, somewhat disappointed.

"Is something wrong?" Mandelbrot asked.

"Not exactly. I was just thinking that if the city was under an emergency of some sort, I might have been able to use it to our advantage somehow."

"If Dr. Avery is on the planet, he probably would have dealt with an emergency already," said the robot.

"Or maybe he left, but no crisis has arisen." Derec shook his head in resignation. "He could be literally anywhere, with a Key to Perihelion. Or with all the Keys the robots could duplicate, for that matter."

"It's not shapechanging any more, is it?" Ariel was gazing out at the city.

Derec and Mandelbrot both looked at her in some surprise.

"No," Derec said, relieved. "We ended it a long time ago. That danger is passed."

She nodded, still gazing out at the city.

He watched her for a moment and decided that leaving her alone might do her more good than grilling her with questions. She was self-conscious enough already, though her quick recovery from this episode was encouraging. He just hoped that he was right about her not needing treatment by the robots. Then he saw Mandelbrot studying her, also.

"Mandelbrot," Derec said firmly. "Her relapse is over."

"It may recur, I surmise."

"Another one may occur, but I don't think the same one will." Derec hesitated, thinking about the two episodes he had seen since they had returned here.

"We have compiled very little evidence for that conclusion," said Mandelbrot.

Derec shook his head. "I think that every time something of that sort happens, her memories are integrated just a little more afterward. It's part of the growth and replacement process that I didn't recognize at first."

"I understand the principle," said Mandelbrot. "How certain of this theory are you?"

"Uh—" Derec saw Ariel watching him.

Her face reflected more anxiety than he had ever seen her express, even at the worst of her disease.

He looked back at the robot and cleared his throat. "I'm sure of it. Remember, the *growth* of her memories and identity was intended all along. These episodes are just . . . growing pains."

Ariel closed her eyes in relief.

Derec sighed. He felt as though he was juggling too many lines of thought at once—Ariel's recovery, Mandelbrot's possible First Law imperative regarding her, and his own failing condition. What he really should be doing was finding Dr. Avery.

He took a deep breath and tried to focus his thoughts once more. "All right. We can figure that Avery has hidden all direct evidence of his whereabouts from the central computer. We'll have to cast around for indirect evidence that he didn't intend to leave. Anyone have any suggestions?"

Ariel looked at him for a moment and then returned her gaze to the viewscreens with a slight shake of her head.

Mandelbrot stood quietly, apparently reviewing and rejecting possibilities.

"We can't find him by staying here in this room, can we?" Derec spoke softly, admitting what none of them wanted to say.

"The principle of identifying useful questions and seeking their answers through the central computer is sound," said Mandelbrot. "Theoretically, the search could be narrowed a great deal in this manner if we ask the right questions."

"And if we *can't?*" Derec demanded irritably. "What then? Maybe we don't have enough information to figure out the right questions, no matter how long we sit here."

"Leaving this office to explore the planet greatly increases the danger to you," said Mandelbrot.

"Now don't you start more First Law objections. Sitting here doing nothing will eventually harm us the most."

"I am not arguing against leaving itself," said Mandelbrot calmly. "I do recommend a specific plan of action."

Derec shrugged in agreement. "Like what?"

"That has yet to be identified."

"We're going around in circles!" Derec threw up his arms in frustration. He banged one hand against the desk when he lowered it and grabbed it in surprise.

Wolruf was watching him again.

"I suggest that Wolruf and I go out first," said Mandelbrot.

"How so?" Derec rubbed his hand surreptitiously, pointedly ignoring Wolruf.

"Consider this. As a robot, I do not attract undue attention here. On our first sojourn through Robot City, Wolruf was of no particular interest to the robots of this community. We have the best chance of gathering information and returning here safely to report it."

Derec thought a moment. "The terminal here confirmed your report that no special alerts are out. So the robots aren't on the lookout for humans, particularly."

"The presence of humans, however, will at the very least trigger the applicability of the Laws of Robotics. If their behavior is changed because of the Laws, even in small ways, the shifts may be noted by the central computer and attract the notice of Dr. Avery."

"You mean if I instruct a robot to tell me something, he might be late fulfilling his duties or something." Derec nodded slowly. "With someone as paranoid as Dr. Avery, I guess maybe those small variations might cause a review ... if he noticed them."

"I am calculating probabilities only, of course," said Mandelbrot. "I am balancing potential benefit against possible danger."

Derec realized, suddenly, that he welcomed the chance to rest. He didn't think of himself as a coward, or feel afraid.

In fact, the Robot City he remembered had not been nearly as dangerous as Aranimas, the pirate. Still, he just didn't feel right. Maybe he should lie down.

"All right, Mandelbrot," he said. "You two go. We'll stay here."

CHAPTER 4

PRIORITY 4 REGIONAL CONTINGENCY POWER STATION

Mandelbrot climbed up the ladder from the office to the top of the Compass Tower with Wolruf clinging to his back. They got through the trapdoor without incident. Then the robot began the long but simple task of descending the narrow line of footholds down the steep front face of the pyramid.

He almost certainly could have found his way down the labyrinth within the Compass Tower to the main entrance. However, he did not want to be questioned by security robots about his presence if he was found there. Derec had pointed out that if he was questioned about climbing down the outside of the Compass Tower, he would not have to reveal his knowledge of a secret entrance.

Derec had also told him of how he and Ariel had painstakingly climbed down these small hand and footholds when they had first arrived on the planet. They were only as large as a hand or foot might require, and the severe angle of the pyramid face offered little margin for error. For a robot, of course, the descent presented no significant challenge.

Mandelbrot spent the time of the descent considering how best to proceed. When they reached the ground, Wolruf let out a long sigh and collapsed in relief to the ground.

"Are you harmed?" Mandelbrot asked her.

"No." The little alien shook her caninoid head back and forth. "Don't like rride."

Mandelbrot looked around. A number of humanoid robots were walking briskly on their way; among them, a much larger number of function robots, of all sizes and varied shapes, pursued their own duties. In spite of the unfamiliar architecture, this was basically the Robot City he remembered from his other visit here.

"What arr 'u going to do now?" Wolruf inquired.

"I must take a calculated risk," said Mandelbrot. In a space of time too quick for the alien even to notice, he made contact with the central computer and said, "I am a humanoid robot requesting duty assignment in the city matrix."

"WHAT IS YOUR PRESENT ASSIGNMENT?"

"None."

"WHAT WAS YOUR PREVIOUS ASSIGNMENT?"

"None."

"YOU ARE IN ERROR. ALL ROBOTS IN ROBOT CITY HAVE BEEN ASSIGNED DUTIES. IF YOU HAVE RECENTLY BEEN RELEASED FROM A REPAIR FACILITY, YOU SHOULD GO THROUGH NORMAL REASSIGNMENT CHANNELS AT THAT FACILITY."

"I have not been recently released from a repair facility. I am prepared to undertake duty assignment."

"WHAT IS YOUR SERIAL NUMBER?"

Mandelbrot invented one that fit the pattern of other serial numbers he had noticed on his last visit.

"IT IS NOT ON FILE. ARE YOU A VISITOR TO ROBOT CITY?"

That was the question for which Mandelbrot was waiting. The way the computer responded to his answer might determine whether or not he would become a fugitive. "You should have me on record. I have past history on Robot City." It was not a falsehood, but it was deliberately misleading. He didn't add that he was on record by the names Alpha and Mandelbrot, not by the number he had just made up. The need to protect himself and his human companions allowed him to feel comfortable with the misdirection.

"YOUR NUMBER IS NOW ON FILE. YOU ARE NOW INCORPORATED INTO THE CITY MATRIX. YOU ARE ASSIGNED TO DUTY AT THE PRIORITY 4 REGIONAL CONTINGENCY POWER STATION. REPORT IMMEDIATELY." The computer proceeded to give city coordinates for its location.

Mandelbrot waited to see if the computer would attempt a shift in his programming, but it did not. No matter how paranoid Avery was, he had not programmed suspicion of unemployed robots into the central computer. Now Mandelbrot was relieved.

"I have been assigned a duty in the city matrix," he said to Wolruf. "This will aid me in gathering information." He was aware that the little alien had hardly had time to blink while he had conducted his exchange with the central computer.

"Wherr do we go?" She asked.

"We are going to Priority 4 Regional Contingency Power Station. This way."

"What is it?" Wolruf asked as she ambled along beside him, gazing around at the sights.

"I surmise from its name that it supplies power to a limited portion of the city in the event of a failure in the main system. Priority 4 suggests a relatively important part of the city."

"Long walk?"

"It is a greater distance than you would care to walk. However, I believe we will find a tunnel stop shortly along this street. Certainly one will be near the Compass Tower."

Mandelbrot did not want to consult the central computer again so soon for anything he could learn himself. The current location of tunnel stops was an example. Every time he asked a question that a Robot City robot should already know, he would increase the chances of being investigated or even forcibly repaired.

They located a tunnel stop promptly, and rode down the moving ramp into the tunnel itself. Mandelbrot again placed Wolruf on his back, before stepping into the cramped platform booth. There was just enough room for both of them. He gave his destination to the console and let it figure out the nearest tunnel stop. Then they were off, riding the upright booth as it slid forward on the siding.

A moment later, the booth swung into one of the trunk lines with the other moving platforms. Humanoid robots rode with them on all sides, as motionless as Mandelbrot within their booths. The computer sped them up, slowed them down, and changed them from one parallel trunk line to another as the traffic flow changed as a result of some booths entering from sidings and others exiting onto them.

The booth they rode slowed smoothly, swung onto a siding, and glided to a stop. Mandelbrot stepped out and rode the ramp up to the street before setting Wolruf down again.

This area of the city was not noticeably different from the one they had just left. The city was too new to have old and new neighborhoods as such. It was highly organized, of course, but much of the pattern was not readily visible, such as the power grid or the tunnel system.

Mandelbrot oriented himself and led Wolruf to the power station. It was hardly more than a door in a very tall, narrow building wedged between others on three sides. Just as he entered, he used his comlink to report his assumed serial number, his name, and a request that communication be spoken aloud. In work stations of this kind, robots in Robot City often used their comlinks exclusively.

"I am the Station Supervisor," said a humanoid robot inside the door. "My name is Tamserole. I was told to expect you, Mandelbrot. Why do you wish to speak aloud?"

"I have a personal preference for this." Mandelbrot did not draw attention to Wolruf by looking at her or mentioning her. He knew she would listen carefully to any conversation. "What are my duties here?" He waited to see if Tamserole would require the use of comlinks.

"Come with me." Tamserole had glanced at Wolruf, but apparently had no interest in her.

Mandelbrot and Wolruf followed Tamserole into the building. The inside was quite narrow and its single impressive feature was a pillar of shiny metal alloy, one meter thick, rising into the ceiling. A console of some kind was set into its base.

"Our task," said Tamserole, "is to make this unit fully automated so that I—and now you, of course—may discontinue our duties here and accept our migration programming."

Mandelbrot had no idea what migration programming was, but Tamserole obviously assumed he knew. At the moment, Mandelbrot did not dare reveal his ignorance.

"I do not understand why I have been given an assistant by the central computer, when I have been told to reduce staff here to zero, not to increase it," said Tamserole. "Do you know why?"

"I believe so," said Mandelbrot. "The central computer could not locate any past duty file on me. I think it decided to give me a redundant position until I prove my efficiency."

"That is logical enough," said Tamserole. "I wish I had been informed, however."

"What is my duty?" Mandelbrot asked again.

"I have been changing the procedure since learning you would join me," said Tamserole. "Until now, I have been programming the local memory of the central computer terminal in this console to make the judgements I have previously made myself. I will now leave you here to familiarize yourself with what I have done. Improve on it if you can."

"What is your new duty?"

"I located areas in the power system that can be streamlined. I have already instructed function robots assigned to this station to meet me at certain areas of the city. I will supervise their improvements and attempt to identify other potential ones on the spot."

"Very well." Mandelbrot moved to the console and began studying the various readouts. Wolruf followed him unobtrusively.

Tamserole left the station without further discussion.

Mandelbrot first looked quickly through the information that told him the range and system that the station governed. As he had surmised, this was a backup facility that only went on line when and if the main power system failed. Once he had learned some basic information about his new duty, he ignored his work in order to call up the central computer through the console.

Questions posed through the console would initially be interpreted by the central computer as normal activity at the power station. If they aroused enough suspicion, of course, the central computer would realize that they were irrelevant to station duty and might be coming from the same humanoid robot who could not explain his recent past. Mandelbrot could not, however, pass up this opportunity.

Since the central computer had already refused to admit that Dr. Avery was on the planet, he would have to begin with indirect approaches. At least he had more information to work with than he had had in Avery's office.

"What is migration programming?" He asked.

"PROGRAMMING THAT INSTRUCTS EACH HUMANOID ROBOT TO REPORT TO ITS ASSIGNED ASSEMBLY POINT."

"What is the purpose of this programming?"

"TO INSURE THAT EACH ROBOT ARRIVES ON SCHED-ULE AT ITS ASSIGNED ASSEMBLY POINT."

That was no help.

"What is the purpose of the assembly point?"

"IT IS A RENDEZVOUS SITE FOR MIGRATING RO-BOTS."

"What will the robots do at their assembly points?"

"THEY WILL FOLLOW THEIR PROGRAMMING."

"What will their programming be at that time?"

"IT WILL VARY WITH EACH ROBOT."

Mandelbrot was about to ask for an example when the computer returned with its own question.

"WHAT IS THE PURPOSE OF YOUR QUESTIONS?"

Mandelbrot considered aborting the dialogue, but did

ROBOT CITY

not want to raise any further questions about his behavior. He answered cautiously. "To learn why robots are migrating and what they will do at the assembly points."

"YOUR MIGRATION PROGRAMMING IS SUFFICIENT INFORMATION FOR YOU AT THIS TIME."

Mandelbrot did not dare reveal that he had not received such programming. If the city realized that, it would almost certainly try to program him. He might lose his independence in that event, and become an integral part of the city matrix. He looked down at Wolruf, who was waiting patiently.

"I will fulfill my duties here for a time and try to gather more information," said Mandelbrot. "Do you feel safe in moving around on your own?"

"Yess," said Wolruf. "Will walk around. Come back herr to meet u'. Okay?"

Mandelbrot considered the central computer. If he inadvertantly alerted it in some way and triggered an investigation, he would not want to remain here. "I prefer a neutral site. Can you get back to that tunnel stop we used to get here?"

"Yess," Wolruf hissed with her version of a grin. She obviously thought it a silly question. " 'U say when."

Derec was lying on the couch with his eyes closed, tossing fitfully. He had eaten as much as he wanted, though he had had to force down enough to constitute even a small meal. Before, he had felt too weak to sit up; now, he was too restless to relax.

"Turn over," Ariel said gently.

"Huh?" Derec started to look up at her, but he felt her hands slide under his shoulders and push him carefully onto his other side.

246

"Lie face down," she said.

He welcomed the chance to follow directions instead of make decisions. When he tried to push himself to roll over all the way, though, his hands kept slipping on the fabric. Both his arms flailed weakly, accomplishing nothing. Finally, her slender fingers groped under his arms for a moment and gripped him just enough to help him onto his front.

Derec let out a long sigh and closed his eyes. Her fingertips began massaging the muscles of his upper back. Instantly, the tension began to break a little at a time.

As he relaxed, he concentrated more on the relief in his muscles that her massaging brought about. He could feel tiny vibrations each time she pushed, as though very slight kinks were snapping. It was like loosening any ordinary adhesion that might build up, such as a crick in one's back, only they were very small.

"Is this helping?" She asked.

"Yes," he whispered, not wanting to put out the energy to speak aloud. "It's wonderful."

She gradually worked her way downward. He could feel her breaking these kinks all the while. As more of his muscles were freed of them, he was able to relax a little more, and he became drowsy.

She continued for a time without speaking.

"You really feel bad?" Ariel spoke softly after a while. "I mean, you haven't been awake that long."

"Sleepy," he whispered faintly. Her fingertips were a persistent, rhythmic source of pleasure. They moved back up to his shoulder muscles again and broke more of the adhesions.

He stopped relaxing. After a moment, he noticed it himself. As he started to wake up again, he opened his eyes, wondering what had happened.

"Feeling better?" She asked cheerfully.

"No. Not exactly."

"What is it? Should I stop?"

"Could you—I mean, would you mind doing my upper back again? Right away?"

"Sure." She returned her hands to the area where she had started, and where she had just kneaded a second time already.

"Thanks." Derec paid close attention this time. The same kinks were loosened as before. He felt the same vibrations, the little snappings that relieved him of tension in the muscle.

Only those kinks had returned almost instantly. Not as many were back, at least not yet. He felt fewer this time than either time before. Still, the pattern was clear. The massages would have to be constant to do him any good.

"Is that better?"

"Uh—it's fine. Look, I don't want you to tire yourself out. Thank you. It does help." That was true, but he couldn't have her do so much work indefinitely for relief that lasted only a matter of seconds, or perhaps a few minutes.

"I'm glad." Ariel quit, but remained sitting next to him, flexing her fingers.

"Could you help me turn over?"

"Of course."

Again, his arms were weak and rubbery when he tried to push himself onto one side. She took his shoulders and brought him around in a kind of twist, where his pelvis and legs lay prone, but his upper body lay on one side. Then she moved to his legs and, with considerable effort, pulled him entirely onto his side.

"There." She let out a breath and smiled.

He looked up to study her face. His secret hadn't lasted very long. He was clearly in serious trouble and worsening rapidly.

"Derec? What is it?"

"I don't see how I'm going to make it."

"What? What do you mean?"

"I'm so tired. And weak. You can see for yourself. Avery could be anywhere on the planet, and I don't think I have much time." Even his tongue was slurring a little.

"You shouldn't talk like that." Her voice was sharp with some of her old spirit. "Mandelbrot can do anything a robot can do, plus some extras. And hasn't Wolruf proven herself many times over?"

"The time," said Derec. His anger flared, giving him energy. "We just don't have much time. Sure, I think we—or they, anyhow—can find Avery sooner or later. But it may be too late for me."

"After everything that's happened to us? You're going to give up *now?* Come on!"

"Well, what can I do? Just lie here?"

"Maybe we can still think of something. We got away from Aranimas, didn't we? We got out of Rockliffe Station, and we solved the shapechanging and the murder mystery— or I should say, you did. . . ." Her voice trailed off.

He waited a moment, expecting her to continue. When she didn't, he looked up at her.

She was staring at him with horror on her face. Startled, he raised up enough to look himself over, but saw nothing unusual. He passed his hand in front of her face but she did not react.

"Ariel," he said firmly.

"It's Derec," she whispered. "He looks just like Derec. It's impossible." Suddenly she turned and leaped off the bed,

only to run into the desk almost immediately. Her legs buck-
led and she thumped hard on the floor, blinking rapidly.

Derec forced himself up on one elbow and reached down
to grip her arm. "Ariel. Can you hear me?"

She was looking around the room very slowly. At first
she didn't seem to hear him, but then she nodded, almost
imperceptibly. "You're up," she said, surprised.

"Not very far."

She reached back with her hand and slapped him across
the face hard, leaving his cheek stinging from the blow.

Derec sat up straight, swinging his legs over the side of
the bed. "Are you *crazy?* What—"

"Look at yourself!"

"Myself? What are you talking about?"

"You're sitting up. Derec, you have to stay alert. I don't
know if it's the adrenaline or the fear or the, the . . . I don't
know what. But when I went into a fugue state again, the
emergency started bringing you back to normal."

"And then you hit me . . . and I sat up." Derec nodded
slowly. "I'm hardly back to normal, but I see what you
mean."

"Don't give in to it, Derec. You have to fight it."

"All right. I get it. It's like cold when you're in danger
of freezing. You have to move around and keep the blood
circulating. Something like that." He stood up, and winced
at the stiffness in his joints. "I still hurt all over."

Ariel rolled the desk chair into position for him. "Come
on. Back to the terminal. The work will keep your mind
busy, and maybe we'll think of something useful."

CHAPTER 5

EULER

Mandelbrot realized the time had come for him to rendezvous with Wolruf. Since he might still benefit later from acting within the city matrix, he did not want simply to abandon his duty. Tamserole had not returned, so he took the greater risk again of reporting to the central computer.

"This is the Priority 4 Regional Contingency Power Station. I am reporting a leave of duty because my supervisor is not present to receive it."

"WHERE IS YOUR SUPERVISOR?"

"I do not know. He is fulfilling his duty elsewhere."

"WHY ARE YOU LEAVING YOUR DUTY?"

"I have an emergency."

"EXPLAIN IT."

"I do not have time." Mandelbrot broke the connection, hoping that he would be able to return to duty here later if it would be useful. He did not have an explanation yet. Attempting to create one could wait until it was necessary.

Considering the immense size of the central computer and its total data, the oddities of his behavior might still escape the notice of Dr. Avery.

Mandelbrot had spent his relatively brief time at the station actually performing his duty. He had made some progress in creating an autonomous system that would free Tamserole to activate migration programming, but he had not quite finished it. If he had, he might have been able to leave without suspicion. He was not certain.

One problem Mandelbrot faced was that he was intellectually distinctive from the robots of Robot City and at any time might reveal his differences by the questions he asked or the actions he took.

Mandelbrot rode down the ramp of the tunnel stop and saw the little alien sitting calmly to one side of the loading area. She was in a slight shadow, out of the way of robots getting on and off the platform booths. When she saw him, she stood up impatiently.

Mandelbrot did not speak right away. Instead, he lifted her onto his back and stepped into one of the booths, where they would not be overheard by accident. The booth would not start until it had a destination, so he entered the one for the Compass Tower. They could change their minds later if necessary.

"Have you learned something?" he asked once the booth was on its way.

"Yess," Wolruf hissed eagerly. "Robots moving everywherr. Change city so that fewer robots arr needed at each place. Then they leave theirr dutiess."

"The migration programming. Do you have any clues about what that means?"

"No."

"I don't want to take the risk of asking the central computer myself or asking through the station terminal, for fear of attracting too much attention. We'll have to return to the office."

"Good," said Wolruf, with her caninoid grin. "Getting hungry now, anyway."

Derec was forcing himself to sit up at the terminal despite the painful stiffness in his back. He had been asking the central computer all kinds of questions, anything either he or Ariel could think of, shooting wildly in the dark. So far, they had not discovered anything that led them anywhere.

The blank screen shone patiently in his face. "Any more ideas?" he asked her.

"What about those robots at the Key Center? If my memory serves—" She smiled at the irony. "*If* it serves, they seemed to be chosen for their high quality. What are they doing now?"

"Good idea. Let's see." Derec asked, "What activities are underway at the Key Center?"

"NONE."

Derec straightened in surprise. "Where is Keymo and the team of robots assigned to him?"

"KEYMO IS AT THESE COORDINATES." The central computer gave some numbers. "NO TEAM IS CURRENTLY ASSIGNED TO HIM."

"What is he doing?"

"HE IS FOLLOWING HIS MIGRATION PROGRAMMING."

"What are the other robots doing?"

"THEY ARE FOLLOWING THEIR MIGRATION PROGRAMMING."

"Where are they?"

The computer responded with a long list of coordinates.

They represented a very wide range of locations. Most of them were on parts of the planet far from here at the heart of Robot City. These locations had not even existed as part of the city when Ariel and he had first arrived. Some co-ordinates, however, were listed more than once. Keymo's location was included.

"What pattern of significance do these coordinates represent?" Derec asked.

"THEY ARE PRECISELY 987.31 KILOMETERS APART. THE PATTERN COVERS ALL THE LAND SURFACE OF THE PLANET."

"Why?"

"THIS DISTANCE RESULTS IN EXACTLY THE NUMBER OF ASSEMBLY POINTS DESIRED."

Derec felt a surge of excitement. "Desired by whom?"

"DESIRED BY THE PROGRAM."

"What is the purpose of the program?"

"ACCESS DENIED."

Derec slapped his hand on the desk. He was too weak to hit it very hard. "So this terminal is blocked now, after all. We just didn't ask it the right questions before to turn up the blocks."

Behind him, Ariel said nothing.

"I wonder. If Avery put some blocks on this terminal as a precaution before we got here ... why didn't he put the standard blocks in? Why did he ignore most of the blocks the other terminals have but leave some of them?"

On the screen, the words "ACCESS DENIED" taunted him silently On the walls all around them, Robot City bustled in the shining day. The room was silent.

"All right," Derec said to himself. "Maybe the block really isn't on this terminal. He's set himself up somewhere else, of course, and he's simply blocked whatever he's done at that terminal. That must be it. He hasn't thought to block this one. Makes sense, doesn't it?"

When Ariel didn't answer, he painfully looked back over his shoulder at her. "Ariel?"

She was standing motionless with her eyes open. They seemed to be aimed at the floor just past the desk, but she was not blinking. When he put his hand in front of her, she did not react. He gently reached up to close her eyes with his fingertips. They remained closed.

"We can't wait," he said quietly to himself as much as to her. "We can't just sit here and try to think our way out of this. We don't have the time."

He stood up and carefully put one arm around her shoulders. With gentle pressure, he was able to guide her to the couch. She walked stiffly and slowly, with her eyes still closed. He could not get her to sit until he sat down first and pulled her down into a sitting position next to him.

"Ariel?"

He could see her eyes moving beneath her closed lids. After the last few episodes he had seen like this, he didn't dare try to bring her out of it himself. He would probably just make her worse.

After a few minutes, he moved away from her a little bit and watched her. She was sitting straight, rather primly, with her head up. Maybe she was reliving a trip in the seat of a spacecraft or something. She offered no clues.

Finally she inhaled sharply and blinked a couple of times.

"Ariel?"

She looked at him and then at one of the viewscreens.

"Ariel, are you . . . with me again?"

"I did it again, didn't I?" She reached for one of his hands.

"It was different this time. You weren't shouting or any-thing." He held her hand and put his other arm around her.

"I was watching the play," she said softly. "It was real, wasn't it? You know the one I mean? I don't know what I'm doing. I can't even be sure where I am, or *when* I am."

"Slow down," he said patiently. "One question at a time. You said the play. You mean *Hamlet?*"

She nodded. "When we did it here."

"Did it come out any better this time?" He forced a smile, hoping to lighten her mood.

She shook her head, not responding to his humor.

"All right. Look, I've decided something. Let's go see Avernus. Or Euler. Or any of the Supervisors. They're prob-ably right here in the Compass Tower."

"Are you sure?"

"We've been stuck in here long enough. Come on." He got up, wincing at the shooting pains in his legs.

She stood up reluctantly. He pushed a button on the control panel on the desk, and a doorway opened in one of the viewscreens. It was a black maw in the center of down-town Robot City.

"Come on." He edged carefully out the doorway, looking around. All he saw was the short spiral staircase, maybe three meters or a little more, that he had come up when he had first found the office. From here it led down to a closed door. "We won't find any robots near here. We'll at least be safe until we get out of the taboo area."

"All right." She hadn't moved from the couch. "But what if I . . . you know. What if I go into one of my states right in the middle of everything?"

"We'll just have to chance it." He looked back and saw

the reluctance on her face. "We've tried being cautious and we haven't gotten anywhere. We have to go."

"I might foul you up, Derec. Not knowing what's going on and all. If you want me to stay. . . ."

"I may need you to save me, too." He smiled wistfully. "We're still a team, no matter what."

She relented, then. "No matter what." She followed him to the door and gave his arm an affectionate squeeze.

Derec clung to the rail of the spiral staircase all the way down. His knees burned at every step. He took a deep breath at the bottom, thankful for the rest as she came down behind him. Then he opened the door.

A short hallway extended ahead of them. He recognized it and the gently glowing wall panels that provided light. The end of this hallway marked the nearest limit to the office that robots were allowed to come. Past that point, he and Ariel could encounter robots on their normal duties at any time.

He walked forward slowly, watching for shadows and listening for any sound that would mean unwanted company. If they could get down to the meeting room of the Supervisors, on a lower level, the robots might assume that they had entered from the street level. He did not want them to suspect any other possibility.

Ariel followed closely as he moved through the hallways. These halls were narrow, but this level of the pyramid had very little floor surface. In just a few moments, they came to an elevator.

He took a deep breath and pressed the single button on the wall panel. "About six floors down, if I remember right," he said quietly. "Do you remember any of this?"

She nodded.

They waited in a tense silence. When the door began to open, he drew in a sharp breath and felt her grab a fistful of the back of his shirt. It was empty, however, and they entered with embarrassed smiles of relief for each other.

He pressed the button for six levels down. The elevator dropped precipitously, but slowed gently enough and came to a smooth stop. Again, they stood completely still while the door opened.

No robots were waiting outside the elevator, but for the first time they could hear sounds of activity. The noises were not specific; perhaps they were no more than a variety of hums created by function robots cleaning the rooms and halls. Still, this level was clearly occupied.

"We're okay now," he said quietly. "In fact, we may want to meet a robot who can act as a guide. Just remember. If a robot asks how we got in here, our story is that we came in the front door."

"And got lost." She grinned.

"Uh, yeah."

The halls were wider here, and the ceilings higher; to make the trip worse, the maze was far more intricate. Intersecting halls crossed the main hallways more and more frequently, and they could look down any of them to see further expansions of the labyrinth. Long ago, he had guessed that this level was roughly halfway up the pyramid. The floor surface of this level was very large.

"I just can't remember," said Derec, stopping at an intersection of halls. He leaned against one of the glowing panels for support. "We could wander indefinitely. I've been taking all the largest halls, but they still haven't led anywhere."

Ariel studied his face. "You're in pain, aren't you?"

"I can't let that stop me, or we won't get anywhere."

"Then quit dawdling and come on!" Ariel pushed past him and started down the wider of the two hallways.

He smiled weakly as he followed her. She was being brusque in the hope of angering him, and causing another brief remission of his condition. It didn't work because he recognized the effort, but he appreciated it as he forced his burning legs to follow her.

Suddenly a rhythmic beeping sound echoed down the hall toward them. A small function robot, only a meter high, rolled toward them with a blue light on its front. A small scoop front functioned as a vacuum, and brushes on retracted entacles betrayed its second duty as a sweeper. Its beeping recognition of strangers in the halls was probably a third function, nearly an afterthought.

Derec and Ariel stopped, watching it hurry forward. It skidded to a halt in front of them, still beeping.

He laughed. "I guess that's our alert. I thought we'd rate a siren or two, at least."

"It's kind of cute. I suppose it's sending out another signal as well, huh?"

"I'm sure it is. Hey, there's a familiar face—if you want to call that a face." Derec grinned. "Euler!"

The humanoid robot striding down the hall toward them was one of the first they had met on the planet. Euler was one of the seven Supervisor robots whose brains together constituted one of the complex master computers of the city. His head was molded to the human model, and he had glowing photocells for eyes. To complete the pattern, he had a small round mesh screen in place of a mouth.

"Hey, Euler!" Derec repeated. "Why isn't he answering? What's wrong with him?"

Euler walked right up in front of them and stopped. The little function robot whirred and rolled away, apparently in response to a comlink order.

"Greetings, Derec. You are not allowed here. Come with me." Euler stepped aside to let them go first.

"What kind of a welcome is that?" Derec demanded, walking forward reluctantly. "Euler, it's *us*. We're back. And we need help and information."

"I recognize you, Derec and Ariel." The robot was walking just behind them both.

Derec had the uneasy feeling that they were being guarded rather than accompanied in a friendly fashion. "You used to call me Friend Derec," he pointed out.

"We are conducting urgent and important business," said Euler. "You are acquainted with Robot City and you know you will be safe here. You must leave the Compass Tower."

"I told you we need help!" Derec shouted angrily. "The First Law! Have you forgotten all about it—"

Ariel tugged hard on his sleeve, slowing him down. He shook her off, turning to stop and face Euler eye to eye.

"No," Ariel insisted. "Don't give anything away. Something's gone wrong."

Derec froze in his angry posture, glaring at the impassive face of the Supervisor. He hesitated, absorbing the unexpected behavior of Euler. She was right.

"What's happened?" Ariel asked Euler. "Why are you acting different now?"

"You are not allowed in the Compass Tower."

"Wait a minute," said Derec. "What about your study of the Laws of Humanics? Remember those? You need humans for that."

"Please continue forward. You will be removed by unharmful force if necessary."

"Ha! 'Unharmful force'? You don't know how fragile we are, do you?" Derec laughed derisively.

"What's happened since we were here last?" Ariel asked. "Have you changed your plans for the city?"

"Come with me." Euler reached out with each pincer and took their arms.

Even the gentle pressure caused a snapping of adhesions in Derec's arm. He winced in surprise, though the feeling was partly one of relief. The pincer immediately withdrew.

"You hurt me!" Derec shouted. "Ariel, come on!" He grabbed her arm and started to run.

CHAPTER 6

ON THE RUN

His legs burned painfully and his back felt oddly stiff as he tried to hurry down the hallway. She was already ahead of him now and pulling him, rather than the reverse. Behind them, Euler was hesitating, his decision-making slowed by Derec's accusation.

Ariel pulled Derec around a corner and down another hallway. "They've been reprogrammed," Derec called to her, panting. "They must have been. If the robots had evolved new priorities themselves, they would still have the same personalities."

"Shut up and come on!" She turned another corner.

Derec stumbled after her, forcing his legs to stretch out. "Look for an elevator!"

They skidded around another corner, trying to gain traction on the clean, polished floor. Her grip had slid to his hand, and their arms were fully outstretched as she pulled him along after her. She turned another corner, continuing a zigzag pattern.

"Do you know where you're going?" Derec asked, as quietly as he could.

Ariel slowed to a halt at another intersection of hallways. No pursuit was evident yet, but in a building this size, the Supervisors could certainly marshall a large number of function robots to detect their presence. Some humanoid robots would undoubtedly be around to join the chase, also.

"No, I don't know where I'm going," she said.

Derec looked behind them and down the four halls that met where they were standing. "Where is everybody?" He gritted his teeth against the pains shooting through his legs and his back.

"Come on." Ariel started again, then noticed he was still looking down the other hallways. She leaned back to grab his hand and pull him after her.

They turned several more corners, always looking for doorways or main hallways.

"There!" Ariel shouted, as they rounded one corner. "Isn't that an elevator?"

"Worth a try," he gasped, wheezing as his chest heaved for air. "Hit the button. I think we're in real trouble."

They waited anxiously, looking behind them as they waited. At last the door opened, and again the elevator was empty. They got inside and Ariel hit the bottom button.

Derec fell back against the wall for support and closed his eyes. "I hope nobody's waiting for us when the door opens."

"What did you mean, we're in real trouble?"

"Two things. The way Euler acted, I think Avery reprogrammed all the Supervisors while we were gone. That means the whole city is operating under different rules. I'm also guessing that as soon as our presence was reported in

Euler's positronic brain, the central computer reported right to Avery, wherever he is."

"Then why isn't anyone chasing us?"

"I'm afraid . . . he's ordered Hunter robots after us. And the others are simply staying at their regular duties."

The elevator door opened into dim light. No one was waiting for them, however. Derec stepped out first, looking around.

They appeared to be in a small tunnel stop. In most of the others, the multiple tracks were visible from the loading area. Here, a wall isolated the siding, keeping it out of the sight of travelers passing on the main trunk.

Derec edged toward the siding and looked around. He could feel the rush of air moving past him from one side to the other as it blew in from the main tunnel. Ariel followed him.

"I pushed the 'wait' button," she said. "They won't be able to call this elevator back up."

He nodded approval. "Come on."

They crowded into the single platform booth waiting on the siding. He started to punch a code into the console, then hesitated.

"What's wrong? We have to get away from here as fast as we can." She tugged on his arm.

He entered a code for a tunnel stop just a short distance away and the booth started to move. "The tunnel computer is a branch of the central computer. As soon as someone asks, it will report our destination."

"What?"

"That's right." He nodded grimly. "We have to get away from here and get out quick. If we ride too long, we'll have a welcoming committee by the time we stop."

The transparent booth followed the siding around a

curve and onto one of the parallel tracks in the main tunnel. Derec looked around anxiously at the stolid robots riding nearby booths, but none showed any interest in them. On the other hand, the robots presented their customary expressionless aspects while riding the booths, and if one was scared enough—as Derec was now—they seemed stern.

A paranoid might easily imagine that they were secret escorts, not incidental travelers.

He shook his head angrily. That line of thought would make him as crazy as Avery.

Suddenly the booth slowed and swung into another siding. This was an ordinary stop, with a loading area fully visible from the main tunnel. That stop under the Compass Tower was the only disguised one Derec had ever seen.

"Nobody's waiting for us," said Ariel as the booth came to its carefully calculated stop. She stepped out onto the empty loading platform.

He came out behind her. "If Hunter robots are on the way, they may just be getting the coordinates now. They can pick up our trail here, though, without going to the Compass Tower at all. I—hey!"

"Derec, what is it *now?*" She wailed.

He whirled and leaned back into the platform booth. After a quick glance down the way they had come, he entered a series of further coordinates, punching codes as fast as he could remember them.

"Derec, let's *go.*" She looked down the main tunnel anxiously herself. "What are you doing?"

"That'll help." He stepped out of the booth and it immediately took off down the siding.

"What did you do?" She asked as they stepped onto the moving ascent ramp.

"They'll have to check all the destinations I entered." He

grinned, then winced at the pain in his legs. "Maybe we got off here; maybe we rode on. They can't know."

"Do you think it'll matter? Won't they just call out more Hunters to cover every stop?"

"Maybe." He shrugged. "If nothing else, it'll spread out their resources some."

They rode up into the sunlight and stepped out onto the street. He looked around, feeling totally exposed. As the only I humans on the planet except for Avery, they could be spotted instantly virtually anywhere they were.

"Our only chance is if the Hunters are the only ones alerted to the chase," he said, eyeing an approaching humanoid robot suspiciously. It was alone, with a number of varied function robots moving about on the street near it.

Ariel followed his gaze and lowered her voice. "When we were looking for Jeff, the whole planet cooperated in the alert, didn't they?"

"They had the First Law giving them an extra push in that case," said Derec. "In this case, I don't know what they'll do. If even the Supervisors have been reprogrammed, then new priorities may be in effect for the entire population."

The humanoid robot walked past them without interest. Down the block, a couple of others were crossing the street away from them. They just didn't react to Derec and Ariel's presence.

"Shouldn't we get out of here?" Ariel looked back down the tunnel stop. "We're just standing around."

"I'm thinking!" Derec whispered hoarsely. His legs were throbbing painfully. "We have to know where we're going. We can't just run down the sidewalk. I won't last."

"I've got it. Come on!" She grabbed his hand and started pulling him again.

He clenched his teeth at the shooting pains in his back and his legs as he hurried after her.

Mandelbrot was walking briskly down the sidewalk toward the Compass Tower with Wolruf trotting alongside. They were coming from the regular tunnel stop closest to the pyramid. Suddenly, ahead, the distinctive forms of two tall, powerful humanoid robots with multiple sensory apparati crossed an intersection in the distance on their way toward the Compass Tower. They were Hunter robots, programmed with a particularly high sensitivity to pattern recognition and detail.

Mandelbrot stopped abruptly.

"What iss the matter?" Wolruf asked as she came to a belated halt and looked up at him.

"Hunters," said Mandelbrot. "Unless other intruders are present, our group is certainly their quarry. And they are going right to the Compass Tower." He accessed the central computer. "Please inform me of any general alert that has been issued."

"NONE," said the central computer. "PLEASE IDENTIFY YOURSELF AND YOUR DUTY TASK."

"What is the current assignment of active Hunter robots?" Mandelbrot guessed that he could risk one suspicious question before the central computer would start a trace on his transmission.

"IDENTIFY YOURSELF AND YOUR DUTY TASK," the central computer repeated.

Mandelbrot broke the link. "I can't get any significant information without endangering our position," he said to Wolruf. "Since no general alert has been made, only the Hunters are a danger to us."

"To uss?" Wolruf asked. "Or only to the 'umanss?" She

looked back toward the Compass Tower. "Ssee Hunterss now. Going away from uss to Tower."

"We'll have to assume that the alert is for our entire group. If Derec and Ariel have been identified, then we certainly were included. If they have only been identified as intruders, we may not have been." Mandelbrot picked up Wolruf and placed her on his back, where she clung by herself.

"Now what?" Wolruf asked.

"I must take one more risk," said Mandelbrot. He attempted to reach the terminal in the Compass Tower office. No response came back of any kind. "Puzzling," said Mandelbrot.

"What?"

"I think Derec and Ariel must have left the office Even so, I would normally receive an acknowledgement of contact from the terminal and a request for a message."

"Perrhaps the offiss is different," said Wolruf. "Special arrangement forr Averry."

"That is probable," said Mandelbrot. "In any case, they are not answering. They have probably fled, which is fortunate. We have no way to reach them through my comlink, however, and no way of knowing where they are."

"Follow Hunterss," Wolruf said softly. "Iss only way."

Mandelbrot nodded agreement. "As long as they do not become aware of us."

Mandelbrot took Wolruf to a slidewalk and they rode up to an overpass near the Compass Tower. It gave them a view of the front of the Compass Tower and several of its many sides. They could not watch every side, but this was a reasonable start.

Before long, five Hunter robots appeared from the front entrance of the Compass Tower. Two of them immediately headed for the tunnel stop that Mandelbrot and Wolruf had just used. Another pair mounted a sidewalk and took a path roughly at a right angle to the previous pair. The last Hunter remained on the stationary sidewalk, within the right angle formed by the routes of the two pairs.

"Good news," said Mandelbrot. "They have not caught their quarry, nor are they confident of doing so immediately."

"Bad newss," hissed Wolruf. "They know what direction to look in. We musst 'urry, or will lose them."

"Granted." Mandelbrot was already back on the moving slidewalk, keeping as many of the Hunters in sight as long as he could. The first pair was soon out of sight, down the tunnel stop. The second pair was moving quickly on the slidewalk and was intermittently visible between various buildings. Mandelbrot and Wolruf had now descended the overpass and were coming around a curve. Not too far ahead, the last Hunter was just mounting the same segment of slidewalk.

" 'Ope 'e doessn't come thiss way," said Wolruf.

The Hunter did not. It was going away from them and was clearly in a hurry. Instead of just standing, it was walking forward even as it rode and Mandelbrot had to keep pace.

"Not too close," Wolruf said.

"Nor can we afford to lose it. Further, I speculate that other Hunters may have left the Compass Tower from exits out of our sight. We must remain on the alert for others. As we approach the humans, the Hunters will all begin to converge."

"Then what do we do?" Wolruf asked.

"I don't know."

CHAPTER 7

THE HUNTERS

Derec was hobbling painfully, slowed to a walk, as Ariel finally dragged him to her destination. It was a depot of the vacuum tube cargo transportation system. He stopped when he saw it, pulling back on her arm.

"Wait a minute," he said. "They had humanoid robots staffing these depots. They'll report where we've gone."

"Not if no one asks. Come on." She pulled harder than he had, and he allowed himself to follow.

As they came up on the loading dock, he saw that he was wrong. A small function robot was alone here now, loading cargo without supervision.

"What if it doesn't let us get in?" He asked.

"Ignore it." Ariel pushed a small container aside, out of the reach of the function robot's extended pincers.

The robot itself was a small ovoid shape with six tentacles ending in various gripping tools. Without a positronic brain, it would not interfere deliberately, or respond to the Laws of Robotics, either. As it rolled forward after the small box, Ariel climbed into the open, transparent capsule and reached out to help Derec climb in.

Reluctantly, he stepped over the side of the capsule, in extreme pain, and slowly stretched out inside it.

"We have to go somewhere," he said. "This thing doesn't have a console inside it. It has to be programmed on the dock console, over there." He pointed.

Ariel hesitated while the function robot placed the small box inside the capsule between her feet and Derec's head. She squatted down quickly and stretched out just as the function robot closed the trapdoor.

"We're going wherever this box is," she said. "The good thing is, we haven't left any kind of trail. That programming is completely independent of us."

"Yeah—"

His comment was cut short by the sudden acceleration of the capsule. It moved forward on rollers to push through a door that gave under the pressure. Then they were in the vacuum tube itself, and the capsule really picked up speed.

As before, the momentum pushed both of them back against the rear of the capsule. Derec was too sore to brace himself with his arms, so his head and shoulder were jammed against the back surface. They were rushing through darkness, blasted by the air that swept over them from unseen vents.

Before, the flight from their pursuers had kept his adrenaline flowing, and he had experienced some remission of his stiffness. Now even the excitement of riding the vacuum tube was not enough to keep the symptoms from recurring. His legs continued to throb painfully, and the shooting pains in his back seemed to settle in with the increasing stiffness he felt.

His one relief was that she was right. They had not left a trail.

The tube curved upward. He closed his eyes in anticipation of light, and brilliant sunlight flooded the capsule. Opening his eyes slowly so they could adjust, he took in the new scene around them.

This section of the transparent vacuum tube rose high above the ground and used the existing supports of various buildings to wind over the city. At this altitude—and it was still rising—it would not interfere with earthbound priorities. Their capsule was shooting along the tube at high speed over what should have been a spectacular view. He was in too much pain to enjoy it.

Suddenly a thought struck him.

"Ariel," he said, with effort. "That entire staff at the Key Center has been reassigned. But it was the Key Center that provided the vacuum to run this vacuum tube system. That means the Key Center itself is still working. What's going on around here, anyway?"

She didn't answer.

"Ariel?" He called louder over the rushing air, but he knew what her silence meant. With a sinking feeling, he turned his head to look at her, feeling more snappings in his neck.

She lay on her back, holding herself in position by pushing against the rear of the capsule with both hands. Her face, turned to the side, showed exhilaration and excitement as she gazed at the panorama of the city. She did not seem to see him at all.

Derec guessed that she was reliving their first wild ride in the vacuum tube, long ago. It was a happier period in some ways, though they had felt burdens at the time. At least he had been healthy, and she had been functionally so before her disease had really struck.

He turned his face away from her. If she was reexperiencing those memories, she was probably more comfortable at the moment. He could let her have that. Then, once they were safely out of this capsule, they could get their bearings.

The tube did not always go straight. Its various straight-aways were broken with curves, loops, and changes in altitude. These most often simply accommodated architecture that must have been already in place. Sometimes they brought the capsule to an intersection of tubes, where curves allowed it to change direction with minimal loss of speed. Occasionally the shifts in direction led by depot sidings that their capsule shot past. Every so often the tunnel dipped underground, and once it ran along the ceiling of the platform booth tunnel system for an extended period.

Finally the capsule leveled off near the ground and decelerated sharply into a siding. It stopped abruptly, sliding them both to the front of the tube with the small package. Derec lay panting on his back, looking up through the transparent capsule and tube at the impassive face of a Hunter robot.

The slidewalk was the slowest of Robot City's powered transportation systems. Mandelbrot and Wolruf followed the single Hunter on it with increasing boldness. The various Hunters had obviously taken different assignments and they had no way of knowing what role this Hunter actually had.

"Not too close," hissed Wolruf softly over Mandelbrot's shoulder. " 'U will get itss attention, I tell 'u."

"I doubt it," said Mandelbrot. "I now think it, as a Hunter, maintains an awareness of everything around it. It must have scanned us and rejected us as its quarry."

"That iss sstupid," said Wolruf.

"Eh?" Mandelbrot said stiffly.

"Not 'u. 'Im," she said patiently. "Why would theirr order include Derec and Ariel but not us?"

"It does seem to be poor programming," said Mandelbrot. "However, I do not judge it as stupidity."

"Then what?"

Up ahead, the Hunter still advanced along the moving slidewalk. It seemed to know where it was going.

"Derec often spoke of the single-mindedness of Avery robots," Mandelbrot explained. "Their task orientation is narrow. If the central computer or the Supervisors, or even Avery himself, learned of the presence of Derec and Ariel, perhaps the order to the Hunters specifically named them and did not extend to anyone else."

Wolruf shook her head at the Hunter ahead of them. "Iss stupid. Good for us, but still stupid."

Ahead of them, the Hunter moved on. Mandelbrot strode tirelessly after it.

Derec and Ariel were in no shape to protest as two Hunter robots lifted them out of the capsule door. The function robot on the dock waited until the humans were out before grabbing the small package that had been scheduled for the trip. Derec hurt all over and was simply too weak to struggle.

One Hunter held him by the arm, and he actually leaned against the robot for support. Ariel was just now blinking at the Hunter holding her. He recognized that as one of the signs that she was coming back out of her latest memory fugue.

"Ariel," he said quietly.

She turned at the sound of his voice, then started at the sight of the Hunters. "Derec—"

"They've got us," he muttered wearily. He shook his head as the Hunters turned and started for the nearest slidewalk, pulling them along in their inflexible grips.

Derec still tried to think of a way out of this. They were positronic robots and would respond to protests based on the Laws. From past experience, however, he also knew that they had been programmed to detain and arrest humans without harming them. He could argue, but he didn't know how to win.

Besides, he was just too tired.

Derec stumbled several times, forcing himself to keep up with the Hunter. Finally the Hunter lifted him bodily and carried him, not out of concern but for efficiency of travel. The other Hunter lifted Ariel at the same time.

The Hunters turned to ride the slidewalks and Derec found himself facing Ariel.

"How did they get us?" She mouthed the words silently, with a quick glance at her captor's head.

"I don't think they care if we talk," he said aloud. "I'm guessing now that some other Hunters started by questioning the tunnel-system computer. That gave them the coordinates of the tunnel stop where we got off the platform booth, as I was afraid might happen. From there they must have used heat sensors to track us along the street to the vacuum tube depot."

"But the capsule in the vacuum tube goes so fast. How did they get in front of us?"

"They must have found out which depot that package was going to and called ahead to have these guys waiting for us."

"After that long ride," said Ariel. "You make catching us sound so simple."

"Apparently it was," he said ruefully.

"They've *got* us," she said, in a voice that cracked. "Derec, look out! They're right behind us in the conduit—"

Derec stared at her in a kind of resigned worry as she entered another displaced memory episode. This one must be from the last time Hunters had tracked them down and captured them, when they had tried to run away through the maze of underground conduits in the city. The vacuum tube hadn't worked any better.

He ached all over. Having the Hunter carry him was almost a relief after the effort to escape. Ariel was squirming and protesting in the grasp of the other Hunter, but she had no idea of where she was or what was happening now. He closed his eyes and tried to relax.

The Hunters only rode the slidewalks a short distance. They were soon intercepted by a large function robot in the shape of a transport truck. The Hunters mounted the open back of the truck, still carrying Derec and Ariel.

The switch to the truck woke Derec up, and he watched the city pass by as they rode. Ariel was now silent, her eyes closed. The city streets seemed depopulated to him, at least compared to what he remembered from their previous visit to Robot City. Maybe, he thought, the city had expanded faster than the robot population, causing the robots to spread themselves thinner over the whole planet.

He glanced at Ariel periodically with growing concern. Her episodes seemed to occur more frequently under stress. That might mean she was getting worse, not better.

The truck stopped several times to pick up other Hunters from the slidewalks. Now that the search was over, they would probably be taken to a storage area or something.

They were all unusually tall for humanoid robots, with expansive torsos. Narrow benches molded from the truck bed itself provided seats for all of them along the side walls. They sat with their knees drawn up and their waists level with the top of the walls, watching Derec and Ariel without a word spoken.

The truck slowed down as it approached one more lone Hunter on a slidewalk. Two familiar shapes caught Derec's eye in the distance, and he stiffened.

"Ariel," he said quietly.

She didn't answer.

He glanced over his shoulder at Mandelbrot, who was standing on the stationary shoulder of the slidewalk just a few meters away. Wolruf had been with him a moment ago, but was now out of sight. The Hunter was climbing into the back of the truck, making a total of six. Derec reached over and shook Ariel's limp arm.

"Ariel."

She opened her eyes and looked at him, still partly disoriented. "What? Derec, where are we?"

It was too late to get off the truck, even if the Hunters could be distracted somehow. The last Hunter was on board and the truck started up. Then the engine began a high, irregular whine and the truck coasted back to a stop.

The Hunters remained motionless for a short time. Then Mandelbrot stepped forward. Derec was certain that they were all communicating through their comlinks.

"What's going on?" Ariel whispered.

"I'm not sure."

Mandelbrot suddenly climbed onto the front of the truck and sat down. Derec had trouble seeing what he was doing, but a minute later the truck began to move forward, Hunters and all. Apparently Wolruf had sabotaged the function-robot brain and Mandelbrot had successfully volunteered to operate a manual override. Derec hoped Wolruf was safe, wherever she was—most likely under the truck and hanging on precariously.

By now, Ariel had also recognized Mandelbrot. She and Derec exchanged puzzled glances, still in the firm grip of the silent Hunters who had taken custody of them. They watched the Hunters carefully as the truck picked up speed and rolled along, but the robots seemed perfectly content with the situation.

Soon Mandelbrot had the truck up to a considerable velocity, much faster than the truck had driven itself. The Hunters gripped the sides of the truck to stabilize themselves. Derec did not feel any loosening of the hold on him, however.

Mandelbrot was going to try something to free them. Derec tensed himself in anticipation.

He was not too surprised when the truck suddenly took a sharp left that sent everyone in the back sprawling. With a hard, painful yank, he wrenched himself free of the Hunter holding him, knelt on the bed of the truck, and got leverage under the robot. He gave a heave and flipped the Hunter clean out of the truck.

Next to him, Ariel had almost pulled free of the Hunter holding her before it regained its balance. All of them leaped to their feet to restore order, but Derec shouldered another Hunter into the one grappling with Ariel. The truck took another sharp turn and all the Hunters stumbled again. Derec watched for anyone to become overbalanced toward the edge of the truck bed and managed to shove another one out of the truck.

Their massive size and great strength had become a liability on the unstable truck bed.

The vehicle came to a sudden, screeching, careening halt that threw everyone in the back forward. Mandelbrot, who had been braced for the stop, leaped into the back of the truck and hoisted out another Hunter who was still in the act of standing up again. Mandelbrot rolled one more out on top of that one and then pulled Derec free of the one grappling with him.

Mandelbrot's great advantage became clear to Derec. The first priority programmed into the Hunters was to find and detain the two humans. The First Law's demand that they not harm the humans overrode the Third Law's requirement that they protect themselves.

While the remaining two Hunters grappled with Derec and Ariel, Mandelbrot was able to get the right leverage under each Hunter and lift them out of the truck.

"Hang on," Mandelbrot called out in a remarkably calm voice. He jumped back to the manual console in the front and drove off.

Derec fell back on the bed of the truck, gritting his teeth in pain but relieved that they had escaped. Ariel scooted over to him and sat down, her hair blowing in the breeze.

She smiled faintly. "That was close. How did they—"

"Look out!" He shouted.

Behind her, over her head, one of the Hunters was climbing up the side of the moving truck, where it had gotten hold before the truck had started again. Derec tried to stand, but the pain in his legs was too great. His feet slipped and he fell back again.

The Hunter was just climbing over the side when it suddenly vanished from sight and hit the street with a crash.

Then Wolruf's head appeared over the side with her caninoid grin. "Hunterr poorly balanced," she said, climbing over the side.

Ariel jumped up to help her over.

Mandelbrot turned another corner on the city street, then another. After speeding quickly down another block and taking one more turn, he came to a stop, a smooth one this time.

"What is it?" Derec called, but he was too uncomfortable to get up. "Ariel, find out what's going on."

"Mandelbrot?" Ariel said, standing.

Derec could hear both their voices.

"This vehicle has a comlink that must be fully disconnected," said Mandelbrot. "Wolruf successfully disconnected the function-robot brain from the truck controls, but it still works, and the central computer may be able to locate our position through it. However, as soon as I finish disabling it. . . . There."

Derec heard a heavy object hit the pavement alongside the truck.

"The truck is now comlink invisible," said Mandelbrot. "We cannot be tracked through it. We are free to move about." He sat down at the console again and drove off.

Derec let out a long sigh.

CHAPTER 8

HIDEOUT

Derec stared up at the bright sky overhead as the truck moved along. Now that the danger of the Hunters was over for the moment, Mandelbrot proved to be an efficient driver. He took a number of turns, Derec guessed to complicate the reports of robots who witnessed their passing.

The Hunters would not have taken long to resume their single-minded pursuit. However, they would now have to follow the truck's path. They had no way of learning its destination and instructing others to lie in wait for it.

As far as Derec knew, Mandelbrot didn't even have a destination.

Ariel and Wolruf sat quietly with Derec, all three slumped so that they were not visible from the street, though any robot observing from the buildings above had a clear view of them if it looked.

"That seemed awfully easy," said Ariel. "I don't understand how those big, strong robots with their positronic brains could let themselves be thrown overboard like that."

Derec laughed in spite of the pain it caused in his ribs.

"Surprise, mostly. Robot drivers are always very careful. Those Avery robots have never experienced a human driver speeding along recklessly."

"But Mandelbrot's a robot."

"Yeah, but he was in the rescue business. He must have weighed the relative danger to us from an accident against the certainty of danger if we were taken to Avery, and decided to throw them off balance—literally."

"That sounds like a touch of creative thinking, too," said Ariel. "Lucius, the Cracked Cheeks, all the other robots who were showing signs of 'contagious' robot creativity. Poor Lucius. I wonder where the rest of them are now."

"Come back to prresent," said Wolruf. "Hunterrs won't give up. Robotss learn fasst. Won't fool them the same way again."

Eventually, Derec closed his eyes against the light. They were safe for the moment and could relax. He dozed, still vaguely aware of the stiffness in his legs and back and of the rhythmic motion of the truck.

He woke up in subdued light to the wonderful sensation of Ariel massaging his back. They were on a clean floor inside a large building. The truck was nearby, also inside. A large door, big enough to accommodate the truck, was in the front wall of the building.

"What is this place?" He asked softly.

"You're awake. How are you feeling?" She paused to ruffle his hair affectionately.

"A little better. Sort of. Where are we?"

"I'm not sure. Mandelbrot can tell you." She turned. "Mandelbrot, he's awake."

"Greetings, Derec." Mandelbrot walked over and looked down at him. "We are temporarily safe. The Hunters will have to locate us by questioning witnesses along our route, and they became quite sparse after a time. I used an evasive pattern that included doubling back and crisscrossing at random. I cannot calculate how long we have."

Wolruf joined them and sat down quietly.

"You're quite a truck driver, Mandelbrot." Derec forced a smile. "Thanks."

"I had the vehicle under control at all times," said the robot. "The First Law—"

"I never doubted it, Mandelbrot. Time to reconnoiter, though, I suppose. What do we do now?" He tried to raise up on one elbow, but winced and lay down again.

"I will bring you up-to-date," said Mandelbrot. "This building houses fully automated, non-positronic equipment that cannot identify and report us to the central computer."

"You mean something actually happens here? I thought it was a warehouse or something." Derec looked around at all the empty space. "Avery robots don't waste facilities like this."

"The only functioning equipment is in the far corner from here. It sends vibrations into the ground that report the firmness of pavement and building foundations within a certain radius."

"That's all?" Derec laughed. "All this space for a systems-maintenance sensor?"

Ariel shrugged. "You can see for yourself. Nothing else is here. Four walls, a ceiling, and a floor."

"It follows some information Wolruf and I were able to gather before the Hunters prevented us from returning to the Compass Tower," said Mandelbrot. "The robots here are under migration programming of some kind."

"Yes! Did you find out what that is?"

"Not precisely," said Mandelbrot. "It has caused a general instruction, however, to reduce the staffs all over Robot City to skeleton level."

"That's something," said Derec thoughtfully.

"As an example," said Mandelbrot, "the size of this building implies equipment no longer present. I surmise that the original functions taking place here were either discontinued or improved technologically to the point where humanoid robots became unnecessary. At that point, the staff followed its migration programming and departed."

Derec nodded. "Without eliminating or modifying the building for greater efficiency. This migration must have an extremely high priority."

"And he told me that no general alert has gone out for us, as you guessed," said Ariel. "That's still the case, isn't it?"

"Yes," said Mandelbrot.

"Something big has been going on here for a long time," said Derec. "Think about it. This must be the Robot City that Dr. Avery actually envisioned."

"What do you mean?" Ariel asked.

"When we first arrived, that wild shapechanging dominated the city. The Supervisors befriended us because they needed help and they wanted to serve humans."

Ariel nodded cautiously. "And solve the mystery of that murder. We never did figure out who the victim was." She closed her eyes and shuddered. "Who just happened to look exactly like you."

Derec chose not to discuss that. He was afraid of sending her into another displaced memory episode. "Then, while the Key Center was in operation, the city was in a lull while a huge number of Keys were being duplicated and stored. We were treated with a kind of benign neglect, wouldn't you say?"

"I guess you could call it that," she said. "But they were very cooperative in finding Jeff Leong, the cyborg."

He nodded. "Temporarily a cyborg. The Laws of Robotics required that. Now, though, everything seems to be changed. And it happened after we left for Earth and Dr. Avery remained here."

"So every robot here has been reprogrammed?"

"I think so. The city has that same sense of obsessive purpose that I first saw on that asteroid. And I haven't seen any sign of the robot creativity we saw before we left here."

Ariel tensed. "Oh, no. You mean you think it was programmed out of them?"

"It looks that way to me. Right now, Mandelbrot may be the only robot on the planet who can think independently enough to do things like rescue us by driving crazily."

"You said the local robots are now acting like the ones on the asteroid. You mean the asteroid you were on right after you first woke up with amnesia, before we met?"

"Yeah."

"I agree," said Mandelbrot. "The narrow focus of the Hunters supports your conclusion, though now Wolruf and I must have been added to the list of quarry."

"We need a new plan of action," said Derec. "And I'm getting sicker all the time."

"At the moment, I suggest that you three remain here," said Mandelbrot. "I must find a new food source for you. Also, while the Hunters must now be looking for me also, I still blend the most with the native population."

" 'U 'ave no wherr to go," said Wolruf.

"Good point," said Derec. "Maybe you can get a lead on that from the central computer without giving yourself away. Go ahead."

"I can try. And I still have the use of the truck." Mandelbrot walked to the far corner of the building and pushed a button to open the big door that led to the street.

"Does the equipment here include a terminal?" Derec asked.

"No. I will have no way to contact you." Mandelbrot mounted the front of the truck and looked down at them. "We have been out of sight here for a while. If the Hunters have widened the radius of their search by this time, I may be able to avoid them."

"Good luck, Mandelbrot," said Ariel. "Don't take too many chances, all right?"

Mandelbrot drove out into the sunlight and turned onto the street. Someone closed the big door behind him. As he drove, he kept watch for Hunters, aware that they would recognize a function truck being driven by a humanoid robot before they would recognize him in particular. He accessed the central computer.

"Transmit a topographical map of this planet with land use identified," he said.

"WHAT IS YOUR IDENTITY AND YOUR DUTY TASK?" The central computer asked.

He broke the link. The central computer had not always required that information during every communication, but now it was asking him every time. Perhaps it was part of the new security system. He accessed again, just to make sure.

"Give me the location of agricultural developments on this planet," he said.

"WHAT IS YOUR IDENTITY AND YOUR DUTY TASK?"

He broke contact again. Identifying himself was too risky, and doing so still might not get him the information. He would have to think of something else.

In the meantime, he drove. He kept watch for any break in the grid of city streets and buildings that might indicate a change of land use, but that would only work if Avery was growing food in the open . . . and doing it nearby. Mandelbrot also turned his attention to smells, in the hope of detecting chemical processing of edible substances.

Far above the planet, a small spacecraft was just entering the atmosphere, still too distant to be visible from the ground. It carried only one passenger.

His name was Jeff Leong, and he had come to repay a debt of gratitude.

Jeff was entering the atmosphere of Robot City in a Hayashi-Smith, which was a small, discontinued model with facilities for ten people. It bore the exotic name of *Minneapolis*. The ship computer was doing the flying. Jeff had managed to rent it with his father's credit after persuading him that no one else could be trusted with the task of making this trip.

"Status report," Jeff said to the computer, watching the screen that showed him white clouds ahead and the glittering pattern far below of urban development.

"EXCELLENT," said the computer. "SYSTEMS ARE OPERATING EFFICIENTLY AND WEATHER IS OPTIMAL. SELECT LANDING SITE."

"I don't know where to land yet," said Jeff. "I never really knew the geography of this place. Uh, scan for a big pyramid with a flat top, okay? And I mean a *big* pyramid."

"SCANNING. THIS MAY REQUIRE A PROLONGED PERIOD IN VERY LOW ORBIT, DEPENDING ON CLOUD COVER."

"Whatever it takes." Jeff leaned back and relaxed.

This was much better than his last arrival on this planet. That had been an emergency crash-landing that had killed everyone else on board. He shook his head to avoid the memories of that frantic descent.

"Computer," he said aloud. "While you're scanning, keep watch for humans. I'm looking for a couple of them. And as far as I know, they're the only humans here."

"SCANNING MODIFIED."

The ship computer was not fully positronic, but it was efficient enough to accept Jeff's orders and translate them into ship controls.

He hoped that finding Derec, Ariel, Mandelbrot, and Wolruf would not take too long. When he had left the planet in the only functioning spacecraft it had—a modified lifepod that supported only one passenger—he had promised to send help back if he could. The craft had taken him to a space lane, and had remained there, sending out a distress signal while keeping him alive.

The ship that had rescued him had been jumping from star to star back to Aurora, and he had yet to reach Nexon, where he hoped to start college. This rescue mission was an important matter of pride to him, since Derec and Ariel and the robot medical team had saved his life. Then Derec and Ariel had sent him away when each of them would have liked to use that ship personally.

He sighed and watched the screen. He expected most of the problem to be in locating them. The *Minneapolis* was outfitted to take them all back to Aurora together.

"PYRAMID LOCATED," said the computer. "CLOSE-UP ON SCREEN. PLEASE IDENTIFY."

On the viewscreen, the Compass Tower shone in the sunlight. The angle was from above, of course, and a little to one side. At this distance, it looked like a flawless model on a design display.

"That's it," said Jeff excitedly, sitting forward to look.

"Can you land near it somewhere without smashing up anything?"

"SCANNING FOR A LOW-RISK LANDING SITE IN THE AREA," said the computer. "TO AVOID ALL CHANCE OF DAMAGE TO MANUFACTURED AND CONSTRUCTED PROPERTY, THIS CRAFT REQUIRES MORE LANDING SPACE THAN THE AREA HAS SO FAR OFFERED."

"Show me the area as you scan it," said Jeff. "Just try to land as close as you can."

"DISPLAYING."

Jeff watched the screen closely as the view pulled back to a greater height and began to move quickly across the landscape. At first he tried to recognize other places, such as a city plaza he remembered and the distinctive bronze dome of the Key Center. He couldn't find them. Then, as the camera continued to scan, he realized that they were covering a lot of area very quickly.

"Look for an open grassy region," he said. "It was just outside the city. I'm sure it wasn't more than a few kilometers from that tower."

"PERIMETER OF URBAN DEVELOPMENT NOT LOCATED. SCANNING CONTINUES."

He watched as block after block of city passed beneath them. The robots had continued building, much faster than he had ever imagined. He couldn't afford to land on the other side of the planet. Derec and Ariel had lived close to the tower.

"Listen," he said. "Most of this population is robots. If they're damaged, they can be repaired. Just don't hit the buildings, 'cause we won't survive, either." He grinned at his own humor.

"CLARIFY."

"We have to land around here somewhere. Try to avoid

the robots, but give us priority. Watch out for humans; other than that, find a place in the city near that tower where we can land. A park, a plaza, a big intersection. Something like that."

"SCANNING MODIFIED FOR MODERATE-RISK LANDING SITE. SITE SELECTED."

"Good," said Jeff. "That was quick. See if you can reach the city's central computer. Give it fair warning of our landing site so it can tell everybody to get out of the way."

"LINK ESTABLISHED. WARNING SENT AND ACKNOWLEDGED. CURRENT SPEED REQUIRES WIDE TURN. PREPARE FOR LANDING IN APPROXIMATELY TWELVE MINUTES."

Jeff grinned. "Good job."

Eleven and a half minutes later, Jeff stared in tense fascination at the screen as the small ship sliced through the atmosphere at a low angle and came shooting straight toward the skyline. The *Minneapolis* was versatile enough to act as both a shuttle and starship, which was why he had chosen it. He trusted the computer, which would not allow him to come to harm if it could help it, despite being non-positronic ... and yet even the computer couldn't prevent every malfunction. After all, he had just barely survived one crash here.

He was gripping the sides of the chair and sweating freely as the screen showed a broad boulevard stretching straight ahead. The ship was going to land along the pavement—did this thing have wheels? In a panic, he couldn't remember.

It must have; the computer wasn't stupid.

The streetfronts of a thousand buildings shot by in a blur, first below and then on both sides. The ship touched down and streaked along the empty street, suddenly decelerating sharply.

Everyone was out of the way; the city's central computer had done its part. The boulevard was as flat and straight as only a city of robots would construct. The ship came to a halt.

CHAPTER 9

WELCOME BACK

Jeff lay back in the chair panting heavily, with sweat running down his face and arms. That was a lot more frightening than he had expected ... but a lot better than last time. The ship computer had been flawless.

Next time, he'd shut off that stupid viewscreen. Who needed to see that, anyhow?

"LANDING COMPLETED," said the computer cheerfully.

"Shut up," Jeff muttered.

He didn't want to stay in this can. Shakily, he got up and moved to the door. "Exit access," he instructed.

The door unlatched and opened. A flexible ladder extended from it. Jeff held the sides of the ladder firmly, turned, and climbed down.

On the street, he drew in a deep breath and looked around. It was Robot City, all right; it had the slidewalks, the tunnel stops, the clean, organized buildings and streets. On the other hand, it was totally unfamiliar.

A couple of humanoid robots were just now coming into view ahead. The central computer would have removed the alert, of course. He turned and looked behind him. A few more robots appeared, riding the slidewalks along the side of the boulevard.

The nearest robot approaching him was remarkably tall and full-chested.

"Excuse me," said Jeff. "I'm in need of assistance."

The Hunter robot took him firmly by the upper arm.

"Hey! Wait a minute. What are you doing?" He pulled back, but the robot didn't let go.

"I am detaining you," said the Hunter. "You are in custody and will remain so at least until you have been positively identified." It turned and began to walk.

"I'm Jeff Leong. That's no mystery." He hurried alongside, walking awkwardly, almost sideways.

"I am programmed to locate and detain two humans among the four intruders known to be in Robot City. You will not be harmed. However, you must come with me."

"And if I don't?" He demanded, looking up at the robot's expressionless face.

"You will come willingly or unwillingly. You will not be harmed. I prefer that you not resist."

The robot continued walking, dragging Jeff along with it. They stepped onto a slidewalk and went on walking.

"Who are you looking for?"

"The two humans named Derec and Ariel," said the Hunter. "Also an alien robot named Mandelbrot and a small living creature of undetermined type."

"Hold it. You think I'm Derec? Is that it?" Jeff tried to pull back again, to no avail.

"I am instructed to take you into custody pending identification," said the Hunter impassively.

"It's not necessary." Jeff managed to turn enough so he could walk straight ahead, at least. "Look, other robots know me. Contact the medical team. What was their name? Some kind of hospital. A Human Medical Center, or something like that. They can tell you who I am. Call them through the central computer."

The robot did not respond.

"Are you calling them?"

It still did not respond.

"Not programmed for that, I suppose," said Jeff. He sighed. "Welcome back to Robot City, Jeff."

They walked along the moving slidewalk for quite some time. Jeff's belongings were still stashed in the ship, of course; he had intended to grab his personal luggage after getting directions to Derec and Ariel. Resigned to a long and probably frustrating interrogation by more robots, he marched along in step.

A certain amount of foot traffic and vehicular traffic went by, but Jeff was sure that it was less than he remembered from his previous visit. Somewhat belatedly, he was recalling just how many unexplained oddities this city had had. Then, lost in thought, he was not paying particular attention to the details around him until he heard a screech of tires coming up right behind him.

Jeff flinched and whirled around. The Hunter holding him turned its head but did not break stride.

A humanoid robot was just leaping out of the cab of a large, halted vehicle.

"Mandelbrot!" Jeff shouted. "Tell this robot who I am, will you? It thinks—"

He was interrupted as the Hunter spun completely around, at the same time yanking him to the side away from Mandelbrot. The robot's hold on him did not loosen even for a moment.

"You are harming the human," said Mandelbrot to the

Hunter, in a remarkably unemotional voice. He stepped onto the slidewalk and approached them.

"I am not harming him." The Hunter's voice was equally calm. It stood still.

Jeff understood that Mandelbrot had spoken aloud so that he could hear. Apparently Mandelbrot intended to rescue him—and that implied changes here in the city that were completely beyond Jeff's expectations.

Jeff let out as loud and intense a scream as he could and dropped to his knees on the slidewalk, which was still moving.

The Hunter still had him by the arm.

"Release him!" Mandelbrot shouted, striding forward and lifting Jeff in his own arms. "Hunter, you are inefficient! You are violating the First Law!"

"You ... are ... Mandelbrot ... the fugitive robot," the Hunter said slowly. It was quivering slightly, its functioning impaired by the uncertainty that it might have harmed Jeff. Yet it had not let go.

Mandelbrot gripped the wrist of the Hunter and gently held Jeff's captive arm, as well. "Release him," he ordered again. "I will take him into custody."

"You ... are ... not ... fooling me," said the Hunter. "Step ... away."

Jeff could see that. The Hunter knew that Mandelbrot himself was a fugitive from the central computer, so his words were all suspect. However, the combination of his accusation and Jeff's play-acting was enough to raise a reasonable doubt in its mind, and the force of the First Law was so great that it was now hesitant to act.

"Mandelbrot, carry me," he pleaded, in as anxious a voice as he could muster. "He's hurt me."

The Hunter was in trouble, but not fully convinced.

Mandelbrot did manage to force its grip open, however, and remove Jeff's arm. Then he picked up Jeff around the waist, jumped off the slidewalk onto the stationary shoulder, and ran for his truck.

"Stop!" The Hunter moved to action the moment Jeff was free, though it was still not at full capacity.

Jeff was facing backward as Mandelbrot ran with him, and could see the Hunter gradually entering a slow run after them. The Hunter's instructions were still in effect.

"It's already sent out a call for other Hunters," said Mandelbrot, still running. "You will get an explanation at a safer time. For now, when I hoist you into the back of this vehicle, lie down and hang on. You will be safest that way."

"Uh—okay—" Jeff complied as Mandelbrot jumped into the cab and drove off fast.

Derec was awakened from a deep sleep by the sound of the big door opening. Light hit his closed eyelids and he reluctantly opened them with a squint. So Mandelbrot was back. He took in a deep breath, hoping to wake up completely and find food being offered.

The vehicle entered the building and then Ariel was already closing the door again.

Mandelbrot turned in the cab and helped another figure in the back to his feet.

"Say!" Ariel cried excitedly. "Is that . . . that's Jeff!"

Amazed, Derec forced himself up on one elbow. His back and shoulders ached painfully.

"Hi, gang," said Jeff. He stood looking around at them all from the back of the truck. Then Mandelbrot lifted him down.

"Jeff," said Derec. He grimaced as he sat up all the way. "What the . . . what are you doing here?"

He gave an embarrassed shrug. "I came to get you. To rescue you from Robot City."

Derec felt his jaw drop open.

Ariel clapped both hands over her mouth.

"Ooooo," said Wolruf.

"Oh, no." Derec rubbed his forehead, stifling an embarrassed smile of his own.

"What is it?" Jeff asked, looking at them all one after another. "What's wrong? Don't you want to leave any more?"

"Jeff." Ariel went over to him and gave him a hug. "You actually came back for us. That's wonderful. Please don't misunderstand. It really means a great deal. Thank you."

Jeff hugged her back lightly, clearly uncomfortable. "I don't get it. What's going on?"

"Jeff," said Derec. "We can get off the planet now if we want. In fact, we can travel pretty far—as far as Earth and back. We . . . I . . . have a different problem now."

"You can travel now?"

"I'm afraid so," said Derec.

Jeff looked at Ariel, who shrugged. Then he gave a short laugh, shaking his head. "Mind if I sit down?" He collapsed on the floor where he was, not too far from Derec.

"I thought you were going to send someone else back," said Derec. "I had no idea you'd come yourself."

"How did you find it?" Mandelbrot asked. "If you remember, I had no navigational data to give you."

"I had a computer cross-reference the Aurora—Nexus route with what little I knew. It worked." Jeff ran a hand through his black hair, staring at the floor. "I'm a little shocked. But I'm glad you haven't been stranded."

"How *did* you get here?" Derec asked.

"I was picked up by a ship headed back to Aurora. Once

I got back there, I put together the location where I was picked up, the length of time it took me to get there, and the nearest stars. A computer gave me the likely directions, but I had to try several before I got the right one." He shrugged. "The hard part was getting my father to spring for the rental of a ship. And now I have to tell him it was unnecessary."

"Well. . . ." Ariel started.

Jeff turned to look at her.

"We could still use some help," she said. "We have to find Dr. Avery before his robots get ahold of us."

"Avery! Did you say Dr. Avery?" Jeff sat up straight.

"You've heard of him?" Ariel said, dropping down to sit next to him. "Where?"

"Mandelbrot, Wolruf," said Derec. "Come closer and follow this. It may turn out to be important."

"Well," said Jeff. "I tried to explain to my father what I needed the ship for and he reminded me that this weird guy named Avery once had some wild plans about a planet with a planned community sort of like this one."

"Wait a minute! This was supposed to be a secret," said Ariel. "My mother funded it. How does your father know about it?"

"He doesn't, really. It's just that Dr. Avery gave away some hints when we met him."

"Met him?" Derec and Ariel cried in unison.

"Look, I don't remember it very well—"

"We've all had a few memory problems," Ariel said with annoyance. "Come on, this is important to us."

"When?" Derec demanded. "Recently? Back on Aurora?"

"No, no, no. A long time ago. A couple of years ago."

Derec settled back. "What happened?"

"He was still planning then, I bet," said Ariel. "Considering how fast these robots work, that's plenty of time."

"He came to consult with my father," said Jeff. "My father is a professor of Spacer cultural studies. His specialty is tracing the development and evolution of the various Spacer communities."

"What does that mean?" Derec asked.

"They're comparative studies," said Jeff. "What planets have in common and what they don't. How they're organized. How their values differ. Stuff like that."

"Your father must be an expert in that, huh?" Ariel said. "That's why Avery sought him out."

"I guess." Jeff shrugged. "Anyhow, a couple of years ago, this Dr. Avery asked to consult informally with him. My father was real impressed with the guy. He said Avery was an eccentric genius, and made me tag along to meet him."

"What did he want to talk about?" Derec asked.

"He was asking about social matrices," said Jeff. "In particular, how my father would set up a utopia, if he could."

"Utopia." Derec exchanged a glance with Ariel. "That's how he viewed this experiment, isn't it?"

She nodded. "Jeff. We can use any clues you have to Avery's personality."

"I can tell you what I remember. Why do you have to find him, anyway?"

"He implanted a kind of . . . well, sort of a disease in Derec that only he can remove. We have to figure out where he is on the planet. Can you tell us what he's like?"

"I hate to tell you this, but I don't remember him very well." Jeff looked at all of them apologetically. "I wasn't that old, and I didn't really care about seeing him. I went because my father wanted me to meet this genius. He said it would be a good experience for me. The truth is, I didn't get much out of it."

"Anything," said Ariel. "Just start talking. Maybe things will come back to you."

"Well . . . my father had a very high regard for him. More than usual. I mean, he's surrounded by very capable people all the time. They were pretty friendly for a while."

"Then what?" Derec asked. "Dr. Avery left Aurora, I suppose?"

Jeff shook his head. "Not right away. That is, he came and went for a time. My father had some sort of falling out with him, I think, but I never bothered to ask about it."

"Are you sure you don't know why they stopped being friends?" Ariel asked. "It might turn out to be important."

"I think he was pretty egotistical. I got that impression right away. And he was definitely eccentric. I guess my father just got tired of listening to him."

"That fits my mother's description," Ariel said to Derec. "Can we use that somehow?"

"I don't know. We've all found dealing with him unpleasant." Derec shrugged. "Mandelbrot, you can correlate data the best of us all. What do you think?"

"We have information about Robot City," said Mandelbrot. "And we have information about Dr. Avery. However, we don't have the necessary correlations to narrow the scope of his whereabouts."

"What about our staying here?" Derec asked. "Are we safer staying here longer, or should we move?"

"I only have a guess," said the robot. "I again used an evasive route in returning here, but the fact that the truck vanished from sight in the same general area as last time will narrow the Hunters' scope considerably. On the other hand, traveling somewhere else clearly provides more data to the central computer of our whereabouts every time we are witnessed by any robot in the city."

Derec sighed and rubbed the stiff muscles in his legs. "Thank you for the lecture. What's your conclusion?"

"We are better off remaining here for the remainder of the day. At nightfall, travel will be safer than staying here. These are both calculated risks, not cert—"

"I understand," said Derec. He gritted his teeth and lay down again. Normally he wanted to know how Mandelbrot formed his judgements because the robot's consistent logic could be informative. Now he was just too tired and in too much pain for that.

"Maybe we should all rest," said Ariel. "If we're going to go somewhere else after dark."

"Good idea," said Wolruf.

Derec closed his eyes. He heard Wolruf pad away, presumably to relax in a spot of her choosing.

"I was planning to go out again to seek a food source," said Mandelbrot, "but I now consider it too risky. All of you can remain healthy through the day without sustenance. When we travel at night, we may find food in some way. Is this acceptable?"

"Sure," Derec muttered, without opening his eyes.

"All right," said Ariel.

"You know," Jeff said slowly, "I have plenty of supplies on board the *Minneapolis*. I didn't realize food was a problem for you. The only question is how to get it."

"I doubt it's a simple question," said Ariel. "It must be well guarded by now."

They could have dismantled it by now, Derec thought, but he was too exhausted to speak up.

"Perhaps we can look into this," said Mandelbrot. "Though the risk is very high."

"How about a review of the whole situation?" Jeff asked. "I never did know the origin of this place. Would you mind giving me the entire story? We apparently have the rest of the day."

"You know, Jeff," said Ariel, "you really don't have to get mixed up in this. If we can get you back on board your ship, you can get out of here again."

"I'm ready to help."

"I don't think we can ask you to do that." She lowered her voice. "You haven't heard what Dr. Avery has done to Derec."

"I'm staying," Jeff said firmly. "I came here to repay a debt. Since you don't need help getting off the planet anymore, I'll repay it with help you do need."

"Maybe you should know what you're getting involved in before you decide."

"Go ahead," said Jeff. "But I'm staying, period."

Derec drifted off to sleep to the sound of Ariel's voice recounting their story.

CHAPTER 10

THE *MINNEAPOLIS*

He awoke again, much later, as strong arms slid under him and lifted him. "What's happening?" His throat was rough and dry. He cleared it, opening his eyes.

Mandelbrot was carrying him to the back of the truck.

"Time to go, huh?" Derec smiled weakly as he settled onto the truck bed.

"We're all here," said Ariel, next to him. "Mandelbrot's in charge so far. Ready?"

"Sure. Where are we going?"

"We're going after my supplies," said Jeff.

"What?" Derec struggled to sit up, looking at them in surprise. "That's a perfect trap. What's the plan?"

"We don't have one yet," said Ariel. "Mandelbrot couldn't get any information about the ship through the central computer without giving himself away, so we don't know what kind of security it has around it or anything."

"I don't like this at all," said Derec. He turned to Mandelbrot, who was pushing the button on the wall to open the door. "Mandelbrot, this sounds like walking into a trap to me. Have you considered that?"

"Yes." Mandelbrot hurried back to the cab of the truck as the door began to open into a Robot City twilight.

"You have? Then why are we doing this?"

"The plan is flexible. All I intend to do now is take an evasive route back to the landing site for observation. We will not take unnecessary risks."

"Well . . . okay." Derec sat back against the wall of the truck. If he could just feel better, he could be more persuasive. Or help make plans. It was just so hard to concentrate.

The truck rolled out onto the empty street. The robot population seemed to be getting thinner all the time. That was good for his purposes, Derec thought, but the mysteries remained. What was the purpose of the robot assembly points . . . and where was Dr. Avery?

Robot City had street lights, but they were not as bright or as frequent as in other cities. The robots' superior vision made more light unnecessary. The entire planet was a city of technological marvels and striking robotic capabilities.

"What did Avery get from your father?" Derec asked suddenly. "He's called Professor Leong? What have we seen in this city that Professor Leong provided?"

"I haven't seen anything like that," said Jeff. "He was talking about culture. I've seen science, technology, and architecture taken to new heights, but that's all."

"The play," said Ariel. "We had the robots do *Hamlet* here after you left. That is, Derec chose it but the robots were ready for it. Some of them were involved with robot creativity."

"The arts," said Derec. "Of course. And maybe a system of ethics beyond the Laws of Robotics—"

"The Laws of Humanics they used to talk about," Ariel

said excitedly. "Some of this crazy stuff is starting to make sense now."

"Instead of being just oddities." Derec nodded. "Robots are too logical to leave a lot of loose ends."

"Rrobot creativity," said Wolruf. "Came at ssame time Dr. Averry returrned to Robot City."

"That's right," said Ariel. "And now, after he's apparently reprogrammed all the robots, there's no sign of it."

"The creative impulse caused too much trouble," said Derec. "But originally, he programmed some artistic abilities into his robots. Jeff, does this fit what you remember?"

"That's along the right line, yeah. And I remember now that he had one interest in particular."

"Really? What was it?"

"Cultures that could endure."

"Endure," said Derec. "You mean like republics and empires and so on? Dynasties and stuff like that?"

Jeff shook his head in the darkening light as the truck slowed for an intersection, then speeded up again. "Cultures. They generally outlast politics. They evolve in response to politics and economics and technology, but they have lives of their own. My father called them the sum of all the disciplines."

The truck came to a halt, drawing their attention. Derec looked out and saw that they had stopped on an overpass. The bright twinkling lights of Robot City stretched in all directions, implying the shapes of buildings and streets by their patterns in swooping curves and mighty blocks and spiraling towers and a fully reliable grid on the ground.

"Down there," said Jeff. "That's the boulevard I landed on, running parallel with this one. See between those buildings there?"

"I see it," said Ariel. "Just barely."

"I dare not take the truck any closer," said Mandelbrot, standing in the open cab to face them. "I can approach it on foot and survey the security measures."

"Hold it," said Derec. "If they left it just sitting there, it has to be a trap. Mandelbrot, that means they're ready for you, too, in some way. They wouldn't leave bait like that just waiting to be flown away."

"Too bad we can't move it," said Jeff.

"Wait a minute," said Ariel. "Maybe Mandelbrot can communicate with its computer."

"I doubt they left the ship operational," said Derec. "That doesn't make sense, either."

"Unless they're overconfident of their security measures," said Jeff. "Mandelbrot, if you want to try, it's a ten-passenger Hayashi-Smith named *Minneapolis*. It's nonpositronic but it's smart enough to handle the flight instructions I give it, which are pretty general. That's about all I know about it."

"I am currently trying standard frequencies," said Mandelbrot. "The customary range is small. No response."

"Good," said Derec.

"*What?*" Ariel demanded.

"Maybe we have a chance after all."

"What do you mean?" Jeff asked.

"If we're lucky, the only way they disabled the ship was to disconnect the computer. Mandelbrot, your comlink can send out the same impulses it did."

"I might be able to start the ship," said Mandelbrot, "but I can't fly it from here. The boulevard is too narrow and I'm not familiar with the ship itself."

"I can't 'elp 'u, eitherr," said Wolruf apologetically. "Can navigate, but giving orrders to Mandelbrot takess too long for shuttle takeoff. And 'ave no line of sight from herr, eitherr."

"We don't have to fly it," said Derec. "The boulevard goes straight. All we have to do is get it away from their security long enough to get inside and grab the supplies."

"The robots would know that," said Jeff. "Don't you think they must have accounted for that somehow?"

"Maybe," said Derec. "But remember how logical this place is. The Hunters don't have much experience with devious thinking."

"They were programmed by a paranoid," Ariel pointed out.

"It's worth a shot," said Derec.

"I believe I can make it go straight," said Mandelbrot. "I suggest, however, that we first take the truck to the rendezvous site so that we are waiting when it arrives. It will not take the Hunters long to catch up with it."

Derec's heart was pounding with excitement, and the adrenaline seemed to be loosening up his muscles. He grinned. "Let's go!"

Mandelbrot drove the truck a much longer time than Derec had expected, but the distance he covered made sense. The fifteen kilometers the ship would travel down the boulevard to reach them was virtually nothing to it, even in its shuttle mode. Mandelbrot pulled the truck into a side street and brought it close to the intersection with the boulevard. Then he stopped the truck and sat motionless.

"I guess he's concentrating," said Ariel.

"They ought to rename this street Minneapolis Boulevard," said Jeff, grinning. "If this works, anyhow."

Derec was tingling with excitement. "Wolruf, when you and Mandelbrot are both inside, you can fly this thing, right?"

"Rright." A slash of street light cut across her face as she gave a nod and a caninoid grin.

"Here it comes," said Jeff.

A high, even whine was coming toward them in the distance, growing louder as Derec listened. They sat motionless, unable to see around the corner of the nearest building. Only Mandelbrot was visible, and Derec watched his dark, motionless profile as the sound grew louder.

Soon the sound was almost deafening. The ship pulled into view in the intersection, seeming to loom over them in the garish light and deep shadows, both huge and wonderful. Then it stopped.

Mandelbrot stood up and turned to help Derec out of the truck. The others took it as a signal to climb out themselves and run for the waiting ship.

Mandelbrot picked up Derec under one arm to save time by carrying him. At the robot's command, the door opened ahead of them and the ladder slid to the ground. Derec looked down the boulevard as Mandelbrot ran with him.

A crowd of robots was rushing toward them in the far distance. Hunters were running along the moving slidewalks. Function robots of various sizes and shapes were rolling and driving down the boulevard. They constituted the surprise element of the trap, now neutralized by the stealing of the bait.

The function robots did not have positronic brains to think with, but they could follow orders from the Hunters to move in paths that would block or even ram the ship and the truck. The fastest of them were coming on rapidly.

Mandelbrot set Derec down on the highest rung of the ladder that he could reach. Derec's foot slipped on the ladder. As he clung to the ladder with another nervous glance at the oncoming rush, he felt Mandelbrot take him under his arms and lift him. Mandelbrot climbed the ladder, holding Derec up until he could deposit him inside the ship. Jeff and Ariel pulled him to one side as the robot entered last.

Wolruf was already in the navigator's seat looking at the override controls. The ladder retracted and the door closed as Mandelbrot took the pilot's seat.

"Straight on down boulevarrd," said Wolruf. "Space is enough forr takeoff."

Mandelbrot was reaching for the manual controls. "These will be safer than risking comlink control. Everyone, please strap in."

"We're all strapped into seats," said Jeff. "I'm sure glad you can do this. All I can do is tell the computer what I want."

Just as the ship began to move forward, a heavy thump struck the rear of the ship. The impact was faint but clearly noticeable.

"Damage insignificant," said Wolruf.

The ship was picking up speed. Another crash against the rear of the ship swayed it crookedly for a moment before Mandelbrot brought it back into line. A horrible screeching sound raked along the left side.

"They can't do much," said Derec. "The First Law won't let the Hunters order anything that might cause a crash. They must know by now they can't stop the ship without knocking us out of control."

"Hope you're right," Jeff said grimly, as another thump shook the rear of the ship.

That was the last one, however. The ship had left the last of the function robots behind and was angling steeply into the air.

CHAPTER 11

IN ORBIT

"I have chosen to go into a low orbit," said Mandelbrot. "This ship does not carry large amounts of fuel for shuttle mode and it will be needed for landing here and also for Jeff's eventual trip away from the planet. However, as long as we are off the surface of the planet, we are safe from the robots of Robot City."

"That's a relief," said Derec. "Unless they've developed a space program we don't know about."

"The navigational sensorrs indicate no ssign of that," said Wolruf. "Suggesst I take manual controls. Mandelbrot can reconnect ship computerr."

"Agreed," said Mandelbrot.

"The First Law won't let them shoot us down or anything like that," said Ariel. "But they can monitor us, can't they? And have a welcoming committee anywhere we land?"

Mandelbrot now had a panel open by the controls and was studying the interior. "This craft is small and its shuttle mode offers high maneuverability. We should be able to land with an evasive pattern that will make our site unpredictable until the last few seconds."

"I'm glad to hear it," said Jeff. "This planet is never dull, is it?"

"No," said Derec, "but it hasn't always been this dangerous, either. One time we had to solve a human murder, and another time we had to solve the apparent murder of a robot. But it's only recently that we've been anyone's target."

Jeff laughed. "Last time I was here, they took my brain out of my head and stuck it in a robot. That struck *me* as dangerous."

Ariel laughed. Derec grinned in spite of the pain in his ribs when he started to laugh. Even Wolruf glanced back over her shoulder with an amused look.

"I'm glad you're okay," said Ariel. "And thanks again for coming back, even if it was under mistaken assumptions."

Derec felt a twinge of jealousy but said nothing. Now that the crisis was over, his body was stiffening up rapidly again. He reclined in his seat and felt the adhesions snapping in his back.

"I believe this connection is now sufficient," said Mandelbrot. "Jeff, will you test the VoiceCommand?"

"Hayashi-Smith *Minneapolis* ship computer," said Jeff. "Please acknowledge."

"STANDING BY," said the computer.

"Can you assume flight duties?"

"AFFIRMATIVE."

"Do so, maintaining status quo."

"FLIGHT DUTY ASSUMED."

"Also record the following voices into your Voice-Command and prepare to follow any of them." Jeff nodded to the others.

Each of them spoke in turn to the computer.

"What's our next move?" Derec asked. "We're safe for the moment, but we aren't any closer to Dr. Avery, are we?"

"We know a little more about his aims for Robot City," said Ariel. "Based on Professor Leong's knowledge of him."

"But we haven't turned that into a clue to his location," said Derec. "Mandelbrot, any ideas?"

"One, Derec," said the robot. "Computer. Scan for any sign of large-scale crop growth or organic chemical stores."

"SCANNING," said the computer.

"Dr. Avery's food source may not be in a quantity or storage facility that we can locate from here," said Mandelbrot, with a humanlike shrug. "It is only a possibility."

"Are carbon compounds used for anything else here?" Jeff asked, looking around at everyone. "Besides that hospital place I was in, or whatever you called it."

"I'm not sure," said Derec.

"We are safe in saying that the amounts are quite small," said Mandelbrot. "In addition, the amount of food required for a single human is small, as well. Our best hope of finding a source in quantity is the chance that Dr. Avery may wish to extend his interest in culture to the art of cuisine."

"Or at least, maybe he wants better food than those chemical processors give you," said Ariel. "Fresh produce, maybe."

"Hey! Speaking of which," said Jeff, "what did we grab this ship for in the first place? Come on, let's eat. Ariel, the compartment's next to you."

Jeff distributed rations to everyone but Mandelbrot, even locating some items Wolruf could tolerate.

"EXTENSIVE AGRICULTURAL GROWTH LOCATED," said the computer. "COMING ON SCREEN."

"Close-up," ordered Mandelbrot. "Identify if possible."

Everyone watched the screen. A tiny dark spot rapidly grew into a green rectangle. That rectangle, a moment later, was clearly a quilt of many different shades of green. On extreme close-up, the shapes of the plants came clear.

"MANY CROPS ARE PRESENT. THEY INCLUDE CORN, SORGHUM, WHEAT, AND BEETS. AT FIRST SCAN, AURORAN STRAINS OF EARTH-NATIVE PLANTS PREDOMINATE. MANY CROPS ARE UNIDENTIFIABLE AT THIS HEIGHT AND ANGLE."

"Maybe the robots bred some of them themselves," said Ariel. "Or they're native here."

"Pull back the view," said Mandelbrot. "Show the surrounding geography."

The view drew back to show the spine of a mountain range. It was geologically old, exhibiting the gentle edges and curves of long erosion. The range was fully forested but occasionally dotted with buildings. The agricultural park was nestled in a high-altitude valley within the mountain range itself.

"It's not city," said Jeff. "It's the first place I've seen since coming back that isn't all built up."

"Us, too," said Ariel.

"The robots are probably using the forests for lumber and the slopes for industrial power or something," said Derec. "They don't generally let anything go to waste. But those crops are all food. I think this is it. Mandelbrot?"

"The probability is extremely high that this is a human

food source. We must investigate it. I remind everyone that Dr. Avery himself is not necessarily present."

"It's a start," said Jeff. "Now what?"

"First we must find a place to land," said Mandelbrot. "These mountains are unsuitable. Second, I suggest that Wolruf and I scout the location alone. Third, the safest place for the rest of you to wait is in the air."

"Makes sense to me," said Jeff. "You can use your comlink to reach us when necessary, and we can fly this thing ourselves again now."

"Derec?" Ariel asked.

"Yeah, okay." He shifted uncomfortably, angry that he couldn't participate more. Still, this plan was simple enough.

"Computer," said Mandelbrot. "Scan for landing sites as close to the crop field as possible."

"CURRENTLY OUT OF VISUAL RANGE," said the computer. "SCANNING WILL BEGIN WITH THE NEXT ORBITAL PASS."

"We'll need multiple sites," said Mandelbrot. "The Hunters will undoubtedly secure the first one after we've used it."

"Computer," said Derec, with effort. "Don't allow our orbital route to give away our interest in that area."

"ACKNOWLEDGED."

Derec collapsed again. He wasn't sleepy, but he was worn out. The short period of excitement had revitalized him, but now he was paying the price.

Everyone seemed to be unwinding from their escape in the ship. Derec lay with his eyes closed and he heard someone switch out the light directly over him. The darkness on his lids was a relief.

No one spoke for some time. Then, quietly, he heard the computer again.

"NEAREST LANDING SITES TO AGRICULTURAL PARK

COMING ON SCREEN AS FOLLOWS: FIVE WITHIN FIVE-KILOMETER RADIUS; TWO MORE WITHIN TEN KILOMETERS; THREE MORE WITHIN TWENTY KILOMETERS."

"Are any of them in relatively uninhabited areas? Especially away from urban streets?" Mandelbrot asked.

"DISPLAYING THE FIVE CLOSEST SITES. THESE ARE THE ONLY SITES NOT USING CITY PAVEMENT."

Derec forced his eyes open. He hated feeling left out.

"It's an ocean," said Jeff, in surprise.

"A stretch of beach," said Ariel.

As they watched, five separate areas of beach on the screen were colored lightly by the computer.

"THESE SITES REPRESENT STRETCHES OF SAND LONG ENOUGH AND FIRM ENOUGH FOR A SAFE LANDING," said the computer.

"For the purpose of evading the Hunters, this might as well be one landing site," said Mandelbrot. "When they see the first, they will find the others."

"We'll have to take the chance," said Derec. "We'll drop off you and Wolruf as fast as we can and take off again. Then we'll go back into orbit until we hear from you."

"Or until your fuel level reaches minimum," said Mandelbrot. "I will alert the computer to warn you when you must land."

Derec closed his eyes again.

"All right," said Jeff.

"Computer," said Mandelbrot. "On the next orbit, take an evasive route down to the first of the landing sites. Avoid revealing our destination as long as you can."

"ACKNOWLEDGED."

Most of the next orbit was uneventful, but Derec found the evasive maneuvers extremely unpleasant. The ship descended, turned as sharply as it could, ascended again, turned again. Each change shifted his weight and pressed his aching muscles. None of the others seemed to notice.

The changes began to include speed as the ship worked its crooked way down toward the planet. Derec gripped the strap holding him in both hands and clenched his teeth against the pain shooting through his back. Finally the descent smoothed out and he realized they were about to land.

The ship landed on a surface that listed somewhat to the left and halted so suddenly that everyone was thrown forward against their restraining straps. The door opened automatically and the ladder extended. Mandelbrot and Wolruf were ready to go. Moments later, the door closed again and the ship waited briefly for them to get a safe distance from the ship.

"PREPARED FOR LIFT-OFF AS ORDERED," said the computer. "PLEASE INSTRUCT."

"Return to the same altitude we just left," said Jeff. "Uh, use evasive pattern and take a different orbit when we get there."

"ACKNOWLEDGED."

The acceleration pressed Derec back against his seat again. He closed his eyes, resigned to the ride, and lay still.

CHAPTER 12

DESERTED STREETS

Mandelbrot and Wolruf ran straight up the beach. The sand was pale blue and packed hard all the way to the line where the ground cover began. There they climbed up the dip between two high, rounded, grassy dunes.

"Careful," said Mandelbrot. "The Hunters will be on their way here already."

Wolruf nodded.

They moved cautiously over the next rise and Mandelbrot found the edge of the urban area. The dunes were bordered by a curving boulevard. Ahead of them, a smaller street stretched away from them, lined with buildings on both sides.

"No one is 'err," said Wolruf.

The streets were deserted in all directions.

"We will be very easy to spot here," said Mandelbrot. "I have no crowd to get lost in and you are now on the Hunters' list."

"Should move."

Mandelbrot looked toward the mountains that loomed

over them slightly to the left. "The valley itself is no farther than five kilometers, but the mountains begin much closer. The greatest danger to us is crossing the city to reach them."

"Greatest danger to us iss waiting 'err," said Wolruf.

"Agreed. Let's go." Mandelbrot started across the boulevard, striding at a pace that was fast but dignified.

No robots were visible in either direction. On the first city block, they stayed near the edges of the buildings themselves and glanced inside any doorways or windows that offered a view. The city was functioning here without humanoid robots.

"Assembly points," said Wolruf. "Robots 'err have already lefft." She glanced behind them, over her shoulder. " 'Unterss could come from any direction."

"A tunnel stop would help us considerably," said Mandelbrot. "If we stay on this street we will encounter one, if they were built with the same frequency in this area as in the area we are familiar with." He paused to look inside a window. Inside, function robots were scuttling about on their duties.

"Maybe they didn't build any 'err at all," said Wolruf as she trotted alongside to keep up.

"That is possible. If this portion of the city is built on sand, then tunneling is more difficult. However, these robots do not seem to factor difficulty into their considerations."

"Therr," Wolruf said emphatically, pointing ahead.

A humanoid robot was just disappearing from sight around a corner ahead of them.

Mandelbrot reached down to lift Wolruf, and began to run—not at full speed, but quickly enough to make up some ground.

"Careful," said Wolruf, clutching him around the neck.

"I believe that a Hunter this close to us would have

come in this direction," said Mandelbrot. "However, I do not want to contact any robot without the chance to observe the situation first. Pursuit is the only recourse."

A moment later, they turned the corner after the other robot. He was now riding a slidewalk, standing still as it carried him parallel to the mountain range. Mandelbrot hurried to the slidewalk and then walked slowly after him once they were on it.

"I think I understand," he said quietly. "Either this humanoid cannot be replaced here by function robots, or else he is one of the last, possibly the very last, in this area to follow his migration programming."

"If that iss the case, we should forget about 'im," said Wolruf. "Go to the mountains and 'ide from 'unters. Find Avery."

"We will be safer taking evasive action than simply racing the Hunters to the mountains. In fact, we should avoid indicating to them what our destination is, if possible. I am hoping to find a group of humanoid robots to observe so that we can imitate their actions without being witnessed by them."

"Too late," said Wolruf, looking back over his shoulder. " 'Err come 'unters."

Mandelbrot turned to look. One humanoid, clearly a Hunter by his size and sensors, was riding a distant slidewalk toward the landing site.

"Good. They intend to pick up our trail at the beach. That gives us a little more time." Mandelbrot set Wolruf on her feet. "I will try to manage among the robots. See if you can reach the agricultural park. I will attempt to meet you there."

Wolruf hissed a kind of agreement and hopped off the slidewalk. Then she darted away.

Mandelbrot considered a number of options for himself instantly and chose one. He sent a distress alert to the robot ahead of him through his comlink.

"I am in need of assistance," he said.

The other robot turned to face him, then stepped onto the stationary shoulder to wait for Mandelbrot. "What is wrong?"

"I am on the verge of physically shutting down." That was true; Mandelbrot neglected to say that it was voluntary. "Please take me to the nearest repair facility. Report me as a malfunctioned robot, failure unknown."

"Agreed."

Mandelbrot froze in place but kept his positronic brain functioning. He had deliberately avoided identifying himself.

This robot was complying with Mandelbrot's request under a subtle but real compulsion. The Third Law of Robotics required robots to avoid harm to themselves through action or inaction but did not specifically require them to keep other robots from harm. However, in the robot society of Robot City, Mandelbrot had observed that such cooperation was common. Perhaps it was even programmed. In any case, he knew he could count on another robot's help, at least in the absence of more pressing problems.

The robot stepped back onto the slidewalk next to him. Apparently the nearest repair facility was in this direction. At least it would offer a kind of camouflage from the Hunters since he would not just be wandering around by himself or, worse, with a highly recognizable caninoid alien.

He hoped Wolruf could make it to the mountains. She was still of no interest to most robots, though they could act as witnesses to her presence and her direction for the

Hunters. In the forested mountains she would have a better chance.

At present, the Hunters would almost certainly be tracking them by infrared heat sensors. When they had followed Mandelbrot and Wolruf to the point where they had mounted the slidewalk, they would ride it while scanning the shoulder for the spot or spots where their quarry had gotten off again. He rode on.

Finally the other robot lifted him and stepped off the slidewalk. This kept Mandelbrot's robot body heat off the ground; the Hunters would not be able to detect where he had left the slidewalk. However, they would be on Wolruf's trail without a problem.

Wolruf trotted down the empty sidewalk, alert on all sides for the sight, sound, or scent of humanoid robots. The city here was as striking as ever; she passed a gigantic, many-faceted dome glittering in the sunshine, a spiraling jade-green skyscraper that resembled loosely twisted ribbons frozen in midfall, and a multitude of combined pyramidal, hexagonal, and conical shapes. The quiet hum of machinery and the occasional function robots moving about told her that the city was still active here.

The absence of humanoids was eerie. The city was just too big and elaborate to seem normal with deserted streets and nearly vacant buildings. She felt exposed.

Wolruf grinned to herself as she turned corners, circled blocks, doubled back, and then moved on, always working her way closer to the mountains that were so invitingly close. As a navigator, she was no stranger to evasive maneuvers. She had not usually conducted them on foot, however, or been limited to one plane.

She was not certain how successful these maneuvers would be. If the Hunters possessed heat sensors that could consistently choose the warmest trail, then she was not going to confuse them by crisscrossing her path. Instead, she was just wasting time and letting them get closer. After she had done a little more of that, she resorted to a zigzag pattern that angled her toward the mountains more quickly.

When she reached the edge of the city, she stopped to consider her next move. A long boulevard lined the base of the first foothill; beyond it, the forest began. If she could disguise her point of entry into the mountains, it would help her a great deal.

She hopped onto the slidewalk that ran down the side of the boulevard, looking around. The Hunters could be right behind her or a long way back; she had no way of knowing without risking them seeing her. She could be sure, however, that they were coming with that inexorable robot logic and single-mindedness.

Nor could she ride here indefinitely; she could be seen easily by anyone looking down the straightaway. She jumped off again.

What she needed was a mobile function robot she could ride across the boulevard, or anything else that would keep moving after she left it, so that the traces of her body heat would be carried away. With an anxious glance behind her, she turned a corner and looked down the street.

It was empty.

Time was growing short. She would either have to find a way to break her trail, or else leave a track into the mountains that any Hunter could follow.

She started down the street, peering inside any windows she could reach.

• • •

"ORBIT ATTAINED," said the ship computer. "PLEASE INSTRUCT."

"Maintain altitude," said Jeff. "Vary the route at random."

"ACKNOWLEDGED."

Jeff turned to look at Derec. He was reclining in his seat, eyes closed, jaw clenched. Jeff unstrapped and moved over to him.

"What is it?" Ariel asked.

"These seats convert into berths. If you'll unstrap him, I'll get the seat all the way down flat. Then flexible privacy walls pull down from the ceiling."

"I see."

They worked in silence, watching Derec. He was clearly awake, but in no mood to converse. When he was lying down comfortably, Jeff pulled down the walls, leaving one open just enough for him to see out if he wished.

Jeff and Ariel sat down in the two control seats in the front.

"Can we do anything for him?" Jeff asked.

"No," Ariel whispered.

He looked at her in surprise.

Her eyes were wide and staring at the blank viewscreen on the console.

"Ariel? What's wrong?"

She didn't respond.

He took hold of her arm, gently, and moved his face in front of her unwavering gaze. "Ariel. Can you see me?"

Her eyes were steady, open, and beginning to water.

Jeff felt a tickle of fear along the back of his neck. Ariel had told him something of the chemfets in Derec and her memory loss and regrowth. However, he had had the impression that she was getting much better. Now he was alone in orbit with both of them and didn't know if he should try to help or what he could do.

"Computer," he said. "Review landing sites. Skip the ones on the beach. They'll be guarded."

"LANDING SITES COMING ON SCREEN."

"Which one is the closest to the crops now?"

"IT IS MARKED IN BLUE."

"Can you describe it?"

"IT IS A MAIN THOROUGHFARE IN THIS PART OF THE CITY, STRAIGHT AND OF SUFFICIENT SIZE FOR A SAFE LANDING. THE SHIP WILL HALT APPROXIMATELY 6.4 KILOMETERS FROM THE AGRICULTURAL FIELD."

"What are the chances that Hunters will be waiting for us when we get there?"

"UNKNOWN, BUT VERY HIGH. THEY ARE CERTAINLY IN THE AREA AND WILL SEE AND HEAR THE SHIP ON ITS FINAL APPROACH. IF THEY ARE NOT WAITING, THEY WILL CONVERGE QUICKLY."

"Faster than last time?"

"DEFINITELY."

Jeff looked at Ariel again. She hadn't moved. Behind them, Derec seemed to be asleep. Neither of them would run very far.

CHAPTER 13

INTO THE MOUNTAINS

Wolruf had been trotting up and down the blocks, growing more frantic in her search for a moving vehicle of some kind. Inside the buildings, most machinery ran smoothly without even the presence of function robots. Finally she spotted a small wheeled function robot rolling at a good clip along a side street.

She took off at a dead run for it. Oblivious to her, it turned a corner and disappeared from sight. By the time she got there, it had gained more distance on her and was angling across a wide street. None of the slidewalks would take her that way.

She was slowing down, about to give up, when it abruptly changed direction toward a doorway. The door opened automatically, timed so that the function robot did not have to slow down at all. She forced herself to hurry on.

Wolruf was not in particularly good condition. Since joining Derec, she had been starved on several occasions, overfed on others, injured, and—like all of them except

Mandelbrot—sometimes overworked and stressed to her limit. She was now basically healthy, but she had not had exercise like this for a long time.

Then she saw the function robot emerge from the doorway and zip across the boulevard again. It mounted a slidewalk this time and actually came back toward her. Panting heavily, she turned and ran for the slidewalk, angling toward a likely intersection point with it as it rolled along the moving slidewalk.

She got a better look at it as she converged on it. It was only about a meter square and two meters high. The wheels, as she had first identified them, proved to be a bed of spheres that gave it the capacity to alter direction without turning its body.

The body of the little robot was smooth and featureless. Wolruf had no chance of catching it if it passed her again, considering how exhausted she was. As she closed with it, she leaped, scrabbled for a hold, and managed to hang on.

The robot immediately slowed down. It did not stop, however, so she clung to its body and rode. At least her body heat had left the stationary surfaces on the ground. Now she had to catch her breath and hope this thing didn't carry her right into the view of a Hunter.

She realized that she had no idea what this was programmed to do. From its size and what she had seen, she guessed it was a courier of some sort, perhaps for small parts and tools. That might account for its slowing down in response to her weight, but not otherwise reacting. Right now, though, it was taking her away from the mountains that she desperately wanted to enter.

Suddenly it moved onto the stationary shoulder, slowed down, and came to a halt. She looked around, puzzled, and saw nothing. Then it started across the street.

She raised up and looked off to her side, which was now the way they were going. A large Hunter robot was striding down another slidewalk toward them. When it had seen her, it had obviously instructed the function robot to move toward it.

Wolruf jumped off the function robot and ran the other way, turning the first corner she reached. A slidewalk here would carry her in the direction she wanted, so she mounted it and went into a trot. At the next corner, she jumped off and turned another corner. The Hunter could move faster than she could, and she was tiring rapidly even after her brief rest riding the courier, or whatever that thing had been.

She had only moments left to think of something.

With no other recourse, she headed straight for the mountains, only a few blocks away. Another slidewalk would help, though of course the Hunter could ride it, too. As the boulevard bordering the foothills came into view, she looked behind her.

The Hunter was in full view and running down the moving slidewalk toward her.

She glanced quickly in both directions as she crossed the boulevard. The street was empty as far as she could see on both sides. Then she was across it, darting among the trunks of tall trees.

She climbed the slope as fast as she could, ducking under branches and dodging bushes. The forest showed signs of the careful Robot City planning: The types of trees and bushes varied with a certain regularity, as did their sizes. Planting had been done with the long view in mind, both of harvesting and of soil usage.

As she bent low to pass under the arching branches of a large bush shaped something like a simple water fountain, she realized that she just might gain some ground here. Her size was a considerable advantage in the close maze of growth. As far as she had seen, the Hunters were uniformly among the tallest and bulkiest of the humanoid robots.

If only she could gain enough time to rest.

Derec awakened in the berth, at first puzzled by his surroundings. Then he remembered, vaguely, that Jeff and Ariel had somehow reclined his seat into an entirely flat position so that he could rest more comfortably. He lay quietly for a while, staring at the ceiling.

Thankfully, he had not experienced any of those wild dreams in some time. Their weirdness was frightening. Yet he felt worn out, even after sleeping.

Maybe he had been having those nightmares and not remembering them. The chemfets were growing inside him like an organic parasite. Their symptoms also evolved, like those of a disease. Not having those dreams, or at least not remembering them, was yet another sign of how far beyond the early stages his condition had advanced.

He reached over to one of the screens and sent it back up into the ceiling. When he rose up on one shoulder to look around, he saw the silhouettes of Jeff and Ariel in the front of the ship. They were turning around at the sound of the wall screens moving.

"Derec?" Ariel said softly. "How are you feeling?"

He cleared his throat and swung his legs over the side of the bed, hiding the pains in all his muscles.

"Derec?" She repeated, moving to him.

"A little better," said Derec. He started to stand, then decided not to take the risk of falling.

"I had one of my . . . memory fugues again."

"Really? How bad was it?" He looked up at her in surprise. "You haven't had one for some time."

"I don't know how bad it was."

"What?"

"Jeff told me I was just staring at nothing. And I don't remember it at all."

"Maybe you phased back to the time before I had your new memory developing again. Right into that empty period. Anyhow, it's over." He sighed. "As for me, my symptoms have been . . . changing."

She looked at him without speaking.

Derec knew she understood that meant he was getting worse.

"We have to land," said Jeff, joining them. "I can't do anything for either one of you if . . . if something happens again."

"Then you've heard from Mandelbrot?" Derec asked.

"No. We haven't. But our fuel is running low."

"All we're using here is enough for life support," said Ariel.

"And for evasive changes in direction. Landing and takeoff will also use a lot." Derec nodded. "All right. Do you have any plan of action?"

"Yeah, but it's not very good. Basically, we land on one of the big boulevards the ship computer has identified as a site and drive this thing to the edge of the mountains. Then we run for it."

"I'm . . . not going to be running very fast."

Jeff nodded.

"And the central computer can study our final approach and tell the Hunters where we're likely to land."

"The Hunters will be waiting at the landing site," Ariel agreed. "But we can gain some ground on them by taxiing in the ship right to the foothills."

"And then?" Derec said pointedly.

Jeff and Ariel just looked at each other.

"All right," said Derec. "We can't stay up here. We'll have to take our chances."

Wolruf darted under another of those thick, fountain-shaped bushes and paused to rest. She had had two glimpses of her pursuit down the slope; at least two Hunters were now behind her. Though her crooked path had made calculating distance difficult, she did not think they had gained ground on her.

She continued to study the ground around her, as she did when fleeing. Finally, here, she located what she had expected to find all along. The robots were too efficient and well-organized to cultivate a forest without them.

A small metal stud protruded from the ground in front of her. She studied it carefully, poking at it with her stubby, sausage-like fingers. Then she began to look around in the dirt again.

A high-pitched whine caught her attention. It was faint at first, but growing louder quickly, turning into a wail from the sky. Human ears could not have heard it at this distance, but she could, and that meant the robots easily could. She could not see upward clearly from the forest floor, but the sound of the *Minneapolis* in shuttle mode was unmistakable to her sensitive ears.

She waited, quivering with tension. As she listened, the ship obviously came to land safely somewhere in the urban area. Then it grew so faint that she wasn't sure if it had stopped or not. After a moment, it began to grow louder again.

She understood that the humans had decided to risk getting to the crop field however they could. That meant she could help them, if the Hunters did not come upon her too soon. She finally located a small rock in the dirt around her and began striking it against the little metal post with glancing blows.

At first she couldn't hit it at the right angle. Then, even after she had produced a few sparks, she found all of them flying away from the metal. Eventually, however, one of the sparks fell back onto the small metal post itself.

Instantly, one of the highly sensitive Robot City sensors responded to the heat by producing a fine spray of water, no more than a meter high. Greater heat would undoubtedly have triggered a stronger spray; however, this would be good enough for her purposes. The sprinklers would dampen the ground behind her, eliminating the body heat that the Hunters had been tracking.

She looked around, blinking against the spray. Other sprinklers near her had also been triggered, as far as she could see. As always, these robots had designed their system efficiently.

The *Minneapolis* had come to a halt some distance to her left, according to the sound, at the bottom of the foothills. She wanted to join the humans again, but did not dare. They could lose their pursuit now in the sprinkled area, but the Hunters behind her were too close. She might just lead them right to the others.

She took a deep breath and darted away from the bush, looking for rocks, roots, and other hard surfaces to step on. The Hunters could no longer follow her heat, but they could see footprints. She ran on up the slope, away from the crop field.

As Wolruf had surmised, the *Minneapolis* had landed safely at a site surrounded by Hunter robots and had successfully driven through the crowd down the boulevard straight to the base of the mountains. As soon as it had stopped, the door had opened and the ladder had extended. Jeff and Ariel were helping Derec out the door when he stopped on the top rung of the ladder.

"Hold it," said Derec. "Ship computer!"

"STANDING BY."

"You have a record of all the Hunters who were waiting for us at the landing site just a minute ago?"

"AFFIRMATIVE. ALL ROBOTS PRESENT AT THE SITE WERE RECORDED ON THE VIEWSCREEN TAPES."

"Chase them," said Derec. "As long as you can do so without endangering the ship. Pursue them up and down any boulevards big enough for you."

"CLARIFY."

"Make them think you're going to run them down—in fact, do so if you can. The Third Law requires them to take care of themselves, so keep as many of them distracted and out of the mountains as you can. Got it?" Derec indulged in a grin.

"ACKNOWLEDGED."

"Let's go."

Jeff and Ariel walked on each side of him, holding his arms draped over their shoulders as they hurried awkwardly to the edge of the forested hills. All three of them had to watch the ground right in front of them and each other's feet just to keep from stumbling.

"This is insane," Derec said through his teeth. "We can't even outrun an Auroran striped hastifer. How are we going to get away from the Hunters this way?"

"Better than a crash landing with no fuel for shuttle mode," panted Jeff.

"It's getting worse," said Ariel. "Yuck. I'm getting wet. It must be raining."

Derec jerked his head up and looked at the brush and

trees around them. "Really? No, it's not raining. . . . Look—sprinklers!" He grinned. *"Sprinklers!"*

"What—" Ariel paused to edge around the trunk of a tree, as she was still tangled in Derec's arm. "What are you so happy about?"

"The Hunters have been using heat sensors to track us. We have a chance now."

"Mud," said Jeff. He turned his head to one side and ducked under a branch. "That's our next problem. We have to watch our footsteps or they'll just follow those."

Derec pulled his arm free from Ariel. "And I've got some adrenaline flowing again. I'm loosening up. Come on—as long as I'm really worked up, I can move." He pulled away from Jeff, too, trying to hide the extreme pains he still felt.

Jeff studied his face. "Whatever you say. But if you really need help, say so, all right?"

"Yeah, yeah. Come on."

Jeff led the way up the slope. The forest grew thicker very quickly and then remained almost uniformly the same, probably the result of precise robot planting. Derec followed him, straining not to show how much difficulty he was having. Still, Jeff tended to gain on him, while Ariel was always moving up right behind him.

As Derec struggled on, one fact kept returning to his thoughts. Dr. Avery had done this to him—and Derec had never done anything to him. His anger served to fire him, to keep him moving, to force him onward. Dr. Avery would not escape.

Jeff stepped onto a ridge of white rock and stopped, breathing hard. Derec came up and joined him, but collapsed into a sitting position. Ariel stood next to him.

"That agricultural park, or whatever you want to call it, is that way," said Jeff, nodding at an angle over the mountains. "According to the viewscreen, there are passes on each side of us."

Derec looked up at him, but was too out of breath to speak. He just nodded.

"It looks like these rocks extend across this foothill for some distance," Jeff went on. "They'll take us toward either pass. I think we should stay on this ridge for as long as we can to avoid leaving footprints."

"Maybe the ship really slowed down a few Hunters," Ariel said when she had the breath.

"We can hope so," said Jeff. "But we'd better get going."

Derec struggled to get up. "Okay," he said huskily.

They started again, more slowly this time.

CHAPTER 14

THE AGRICULTURAL PARK

Twilight had fallen on the mountain pass by the time Derec plodded after Jeff and Ariel to its far side. They waited for him to catch up and he leaned an arm across Ariel's shoulders when he arrived. Together, the three of them looked out over the green valley below.

The valley was divided into many different fields, all of them tended by function robots. The hoes were easily identified, even at this great distance. There were others moving about, some clipping and spraying. The lower slopes leading into the valley were terraced and cultivated, also.

"This has to be the place," said Derec. "Robots just don't need this stuff."

"I agree," said Jeff. "This is Avery's grocery store. Or at least, his produce market. If he has livestock, they must be somewhere else."

"They would require different care and processing." Derec nodded. "And these robots are too efficient to put this here and Avery a thousand kilometers away. I'm betting he's in the neighborhood, someplace."

"And we made it," said Ariel. "This far, anyway."

"We couldn't help leaving a few footprints here and there," said Jeff. "And those Hunter robots may have sensors I can't even imagine. They don't have to stop for the night, either."

"They'll spot all kinds of details we left behind," said Derec. "Broken branches and things like that. As much as I hate to say this . . . we'd better move on."

"Some of them probably went to the other pass," Ariel pointed out. "There won't be as many behind us."

"That pass leads to this valley, too," said Jeff. "We might just meet them coming the other way."

Ariel shook her head. "You're so optimistic. Come on."

They started down the slope and soon entered the cultivated rows of some plant that none of them could identify. It grew in a straight stalk with stiff, narrow leaves angling sharply upward, roughly three meters high. The stalks were planted close together, forcing them to walk in single file between the rows.

Jeff looked back over his shoulder nervously. "We're leaving a track even I could follow. Look down."

Derec looked. The soil was freshly turned and damp. Their footprints were clear and deep. "These robots must hoe and water constantly."

"It hasn't gotten any darker," said Ariel. She looked up at the sky. "It should have by now."

"Lights must have come on," Derec said. "I can't tell from where, though. The function robots here may need some to work at night. Or else this is growth light of some kind for the crops."

Jeff was pushing experimentally between two stalks in one of the rows. "Come on. We can squeeze between these. We have to break up our trail a little."

The others followed him through. The next row was identical to the previous one as far as Derec could see. They walked down it for a while, then found another spot where they could push through into the next row down into the valley.

"Up there," said Derec, pointing. "We have to catch it. Come on!"

Some distance ahead, a function robot was moving away from them at a moderate speed. The body of this robot was roughly a cube two meters on a side. It seemed to advance on a bed of vertical spikes that chewed into the ground as it walked forward, thereby hoeing the soil it covered. At intervals, it stopped and sent tentacles out to each side that stabbed into the earth in the rows of crops and pulled out small plants into its own body.

Jeff ran for it. As Ariel tried to help Derec along, he glanced at the rows of crops as they passed. Apparently that stabbing motion cut the roots of unwanted plants that had grown up between the desired crops. The weeds were drawn into the function robot, ground up, and deposited through the bottom to be left behind as instant compost. He could see the tiny bits here and there in the soil now that he was looking.

"I got it but I don't see any way to stop it," Jeff called. He was now sitting on the body of the hoer, facing backward.

"Stupid thing," said Ariel. "I wish it had a positronic brain so we could order it around."

"No," said Derec, struggling after her. "It could also report to the Hunters, in that case."

The hoer would not wait for them, but every time it stopped to weed they gained on it a little. At last they were able to climb on board with Jeff, where they sat awkwardly on its crowded top.

"Now we just need some luck," said Jeff. "If this thing stays out of the sight of the Hunters until it takes a few turns here and there, they won't be able to track us easily after all. All the rows have the same appearance after these things go through them."

"I can use the rest," said Derec. "But we have to figure out where Avery is while we can. I didn't see any buildings in this valley when we came in."

"I didn't either," said Jeff, shaking his head.

"Then what else do you remember?" Ariel asked. "From your father? Anything."

"I thought about it while we were climbing up the mountain," said Jeff. "But I didn't have breath to talk. You remember how I told you that Avery wanted to know about cultures that could endure?"

Ariel nodded. Derec was alert but too tired to respond.

"My father told him that two groups exist even now, in space, that are descended in a straight line from ancient Earth. Both of them have continued to evolve in Spacer communities, but their longevity really got Avery's attention."

"What were they?" Ariel asked.

"One is the Spacer minority culture descended from China through a couple of migrations on Earth. The other is the Spacer Jewish communities."

"What did he want to know about them?" Ariel made a face. "I don't see how this is going to help us find him here."

Jeff shrugged. "I do recall that he didn't care about their details. My father tried to tell him that both these cultures had continued to evolve in space. He even said that in many ways they were totally unrecognizable from their ancestral Earth cultures. But all Avery wanted to know was how they had survived as specific entities."

That was consistent, Derec thought to himself. The guy only cared about his own project and what he could do to improve it.

"He was looking for clues for Robot City," Ariel said. "To make it endure across the centuries. That's what he was researching with Professor Leong. He needed to program cultural values into the city. But we haven't really seen very much of that."

Derec forced himself to speak. "I'm sure that he reprogrammed the city while we were on Earth. I think after the incidents surrounding the performance of *Hamlet*, the robot creativity scared him. He couldn't have his robots committing crimes against each other."

"The arts aren't the only part of culture," said Jeff.

"What do you mean?" Ariel asked.

Derec shifted slightly so that he could hear Jeff better. The hoer moved right along, still hoeing and weeding. The sky above them now looked dark, but a soft glow of light from somewhere illuminated the rows of crops.

"My father gave Avery two reasons for the cultural survival of those groups while they were on Earth. One is that the original cultures had very strong family units that passed values on. The other is that, outside of their native countries, both groups on Earth experienced limited assimilation as minorities and often faced prejudice from the majority culture."

"But only on Earth?" Ariel said.

"That's right. Modern Spacer families aren't personally close the way families used to be, I guess. And now the ethnicities are from one planet to another, or Spacer versus Earth."

"My mother didn't like Solarians," said Ariel. "They program their robots funny or something." She smiled. "She told me a joke once that went—"

"How could Avery have used that information?" Derec asked firmly, stopping her with a hand on her arm.

"Come to think of it," said Ariel, "how can these minorities still exist if the original reasons for their endurance no longer do? That doesn't make sense."

"I'm not sure," said Jeff. "But on Aurora, I still look different. That always kept me distinct. And, you know, my father took more interest in me than my friends' fathers. That's why he dragged me out to meet Avery, remember?"

"I think I see," said Ariel. "Maybe some of these tendencies still exist to a degree."

"At least in comparison to the majority cultures on the planet." Jeff nodded.

They all clutched for a hold on the hoer as it reached a perpendicular row and made a right-angle turn without slowing down. It made another right turn at the next row and started down the direction it had just come on the previous one. They could see a long way ahead of them.

So could the Hunters, if they looked down the right row.

Derec was uncomfortable with this talk of families and fathers and sons. He hadn't had any family to speak of since he had awakened with amnesia.

"We still have to find Avery in this valley or this mountain range or somewhere," said Derec with annoyance. "What are we going to do about that?"

"Just one more thing," said Jeff. "My father told Avery that two major events changed both these cultures in ancient times. One was moving from the so-called Old World of Earth to the United States."

"What difference would that make?" Ariel asked. "They were still on Earth."

"He said that while prejudice didn't vanish there, these

two cultures were part of a nation of immigrants and their descendants for the first time. They were a fundamental part of these societies even while maintaining their identities."

"What was the other event?" She asked.

"Going into space. The same situation occurred again with the settling of Spacer worlds. Being an Auroran, say, is now more important than one's Earth ancestors. As demonstrated by your mother's attitude toward Solarians."

Ariel nodded thoughtfully.

"So what does all this get us?" Derec demanded. "Robots never did have this kind of identity, anyhow. What does this have to do with Robot City? And finding Dr. Avery?"

"Now, look!" Jeff whirled on him. "You're the one who started asking me what I remembered. I'm just telling you. If you don't want to hear it, don't ask me."

Ariel grabbed both their arms. *"Robots,"* she whispered.

Far in the distance ahead of them, the silhouettes of human-oid robots were moving from right to left, down the valley slope, across their open row.

Wolruf gathered her legs under her and leaped from a small rock to a fallen branch large enough to hold her. She landed on it on all fours and hung on till she got her balance. This forest had very few fallen branches, or loose matter of any kind.

The robots obviously cleared the forest floor frequently. She had seen a few function robots in the distance but had kept clear of them. She didn't want the Hunters sending any more orders to function robots that would help them capture her.

Still, she had managed to minimize the footprints she left behind. A fairly small area had been sprinkled by the sensor she had triggered and she had left it before the sprin-klers quit operating. She wondered how long they had con-tinued to run.

She hoped they had remained on for some time. If they had sprayed long enough, then the water eventually would not only have eliminated the body heat of her footprints on the ground, but also would have washed away the visual traces.

That and the difficulty the big Hunters would have in moving through the crowded forest might account for their falling behind. When they had lost her trail, they probably would have had to resort to a pattern search to pick it up again, and that would cost them time.

She stayed on the branch to catch her breath. Her mem-ory of the terrain on the ship viewscreen was clear enough, but she wasn't sure exactly where she was. Nor was she sure of what to do.

So far, she had been angling up the slope and away from the pass that the humans had been near, certain that they were heading there. Anything she could do to draw Hunters away from them would be a contribution. She also remembered that another pass led into the valley somewhere in this direction.

She was torn between two impulses, with no way to know which would better serve the cause of Derec's getting to Avery before Avery's robots got to him. If she got to the pass and joined the humans, they could work together as a team again and perhaps accomplish more. However, that would mean leading the Hunters following her right back toward them again.

This was not getting her anywhere.

She could not afford to rest anywhere too long, even now. After balancing along the fallen branch as far as she could, she jumped off to a patch of ground that looked firm. From there, she stepped on the top of an exposed tree root, grabbed a low-hanging branch, and swung over to a small rock.

Then she paused to look back, wondering if this was worth the effort. If the Hunters came up quickly, their heat sensors would tell them where she had been. Now, however, she was hoping that they were too far behind to use those sensors effectively. If the traces of her body heat subsided before they arrived, minimizing her visual track could be critical.

She continued to move along this way. It was a gamble, but probably worth it. If she could actually lose the Hunters, then she could look for the humans in the valley without endangering them further. In order to know, however, she would have to double back at some point and actually watch the Hunters in action.

That might be too risky. Still undecided, she fled on up the slope, still moving roughly in the direction of the pass. Once she got there, she could make her final decision on whether to enter it or not.

CHAPTER 15

MUGGINGS

Since the hoer was moving down the row toward the humanoid robots, its passengers had no choice but to get off
and go the other way. Derec was surprised that the robots
had not looked down the row already and spotted them, but
apparently they had not. As before, he followed Jeff and
preceded Ariel, all three of them now crawling along the
damp earth so that the body of the hoer would block them
from view.

Before long, they reached the perpendicular row they
had seen a short time before. It ran parallel with the one
the humanoid robots were taking in single file to go farther
down into the valley. Derec stopped there, breathing hard,
unable to go on.

"Derec?" Ariel crawled up beside him. "Jeff, wait."

Jeff looked back over his shoulder and then came back.
He watched Derec for a minute and shook his head. "I don't
know what to do. We can't just stop."

Derec coughed and shook his head in frustration. He
wanted to speak and didn't have the breath for it yet.

Quickly, he pointed in a stabbing motion in the direction of the humanoids.

Ariel turned to look. "They aren't coming yet. At least, I don't see anybody."

"No," Derec wheezed. "That's not what I mean." He paused again, still breathing hard. His head was spinning dizzily.

"We could try supporting you between us again," said Jeff. "But we can only do that by standing up and walking."

"Wait, wait." Derec inhaled deeply and looked up at both of them. "Those aren't Hunters. I'm sure of it."

"Really?" Ariel scooted closer to him. "Derec, are you sure? You're not exactly in the best condition."

"Hunters wouldn't just pass by like that without even looking down the row. They can't be Hunters."

"Makes sense to me," said Jeff slowly. "So who are they, then? And what are they doing in this valley?"

"I was thinking about that, too," said Derec. "I think they're migrating. They're following that mysterious migration programming we told you we heard about."

"So the only danger from them," said Jeff, "is that if they notice us, the Hunters can ask them where we were. Otherwise they won't bother us?"

"That's right," said Derec. "But we can also find out where they're going—where their assembly point is. And what this whole operation is for."

"*Now?*" Ariel said, making a face. "Derec, we don't have much time left to find Avery. We can't just go wandering off—"

"No! Don't you understand? This migration thing is Avery's doing. If we can figure it out, maybe we'll find him. He's behind it all, and it's obviously very important to him."

"That sounds awfully risky," said Jeff.

"Look at me! Risky? I don't have much time left!" Derec spoke forcefully, but was too weak to speak loudly now. "I think we've talked long enough. What are we going to *do?*"

"That row is full of robot footsteps, too," said Ariel. "Ours would be camouflaged some."

"It is something to go on," Jeff said slowly.

"I wish Mandelbrot was here," said Ariel. "And poor Wolruf, running around in Robot City with him. I wonder where they are. I hope they're all right."

"We can't worry about them," said Derec. "We can't help them directly now, anyway. If we get to Avery, we can make him ease up on them, too. We have to concentrate on Avery."

"That's right," said Jeff. "The truth is, they can probably take care of themselves better then we can, especially Mandelbrot. And Derec seems to be the one Dr. Avery is after."

"I've been putting some ideas together," said Derec. "While we were crawling in the mud back there, just now."

"All right," said Jeff, "let's hear 'em. If they aren't going to come after us, we have a few minutes."

"Unless the Hunters get here too," added Ariel.

"Listen," said Derec. "Avery learned from Professor Leong that the two most important forces behind cultural longevity are passing on values and maintaining a distinct identity. Right?"

"Sure," said Jeff.

"So passing values down is not a problem with robots; they're just programmed. They can process information much faster and keep more of it accessible than humans."

"No argument there," said Jeff.

Ariel nodded. "And all along, we've seen that these Avery robots are different from any other sort. They behave in a different way. Their programming must have been special from the beginning."

"Exactly," said Derec. "Both of those facts fit perfectly. And the isolation of Robot City prevents it from being altered by cultures from the outside."

Jeff nodded. "Its location is still a secret."

"So Avery really took those two lessons to heart and used them to form Robot City," said Ariel.

"One big question remains," said Derec. "What values did he program into them?"

"Efficiency," said Jeff.

"Harmony," said Ariel. "Both of those. A kind of idealism. Remember when they gave us their provisional Laws of Humanics, for ideal human behavior? Robot City was supposed to be a kind of utopia. We already knew that."

"But now we know what kind—on what basis." Derec nodded with excitement. He now felt a surge of energy again that animated him once more.

"I'm starting to get the idea," said Jeff. "What do you want to do about it?"

"Challenge the system," said Derec. "Force it to malfunction, or at least make it look like it is."

"To make Avery show himself," Ariel said. "All right. I get it. But . . . how?"

"We have to present the system—that is, the central computer—with irrational events," said Derec. "Look—the Supervisors originally needed us to solve a crime against a human when we first arrived. The system here has that weak point."

"And we never did figure out who the victim was, either," said Ariel. She shivered. "He looked just like you. That still gives me the creeps, even now."

Derec said nothing. When he had first entered Avery's

office he had come across some mysterious information about the dead man that he had never shared with Ariel. This was no time to launch into that topic.

Jeff looked at her in surprise. They had never told him that part of their story.

"Well, for the moment, forget it," said Derec sharply. "One crisis at a time. The reason we arranged the *Hamlet* performance was also to accomplish something that the robots weren't ready to handle."

"I see what you're getting at," said Jeff. "That's a weak point in the system. A utopia isn't supposed to have crimes and these Avery robots can't really handle them."

"Exactly," said Derec. "I think we have to commit a few crimes against humanoid robots. We aren't bound by the Laws of Robotics and Mandelbrot isn't around to interfere if a situation arose that involved the Laws."

Jeff grinned wryly. "Okay...let's become criminals. What'll we do first, boss?"

Derec grinned himself, despite his discomfort. "We have to incapacitate a robot."

"Murder one?" Ariel shook her head. "I don't see how. Those heads of theirs are as hard as a ship's hull. We could bonk them on the head and not even get their attention."

All three of them giggled nervously. The tension was broken a little by the hope of taking aggressive action.

"We can't unfasten their bodies, either," said Jeff, still grinning. "No tools. Otherwise, we could just sneak up behind them, power up the tools, and leave a little junkpile behind."

"We could go into business later with used parts," said Ariel. "Discounted Avery robot parts, cheap."

"All right, all right." Derec shook his head. "We don't

actually need any physical violence. The first thing we have to do is get over to that other row, so we can look for one robot walking alone. Let's crawl back over there."

It was a very long crawl. Derec had to stop several times on the way to rest. Each time, he worried that the Hunters were going to catch up to them before they could accomplish anything.

Finally they reached the last few tall, leafy stalks before the break in the rows. The three of them huddled at the corner of the row, where Derec could lean forward and look up the slope. Jeff and Ariel sat on his other side, both of them looking around anxiously for Hunters coming from other directions.

"Nothing yet," said Derec. "That gives me time to explain what I have in mind."

"I hope more are coming this way," said Ariel. "What if the bunch going to that assembly point is all there?"

"Good point," said Derec. "Maybe we should follow them. Just keep a look-out behind us—"

"No good," said Jeff. "These rows are absolutely straight. If the Hunters come along, they can look straight down the slope and spot us instantly even from the very opening of the pass."

"We'd better stay here." Ariel settled into a comfortable position. "Derec, tell us what you're planning while we have a chance to talk it over."

"You mentioned their Laws of Humanics." Derec nodded at Ariel.

"I don't remember the exact wording, but their provisional First Law of Humanics was to the effect that humans wouldn't injure another human or let one come to harm through inaction."

"They just rewrote the First Law of Robotics." Jeff shrugged.

"The Second Law of Humanics might help us," said Derec. "It says that humans must only give reasonable orders to a robot and not require anything that would distress it. Their Third Law of Humanics is the best one for us, though. It says that we must not harm a robot or let one come to harm through inaction, unless such harm is needed to help a human or allow a vital order to be carried out."

"How do you want to use them?" Ariel asked.

"We need to violate the Third Law of Humanics and maybe the Second to prove that this isn't a utopia even for robots." Derec looked at them both. "You follow me?"

"So far," said Jeff.

"How do we do that?" Ariel asked.

"Basically, we have to convince our victim that my physical condition is his fault."

"All right." Jeff nodded. "In other words, force it into shutting itself down because it thinks it has violated the First Law. That makes sense to me. We have a better chance of that than of wrestling it to the ground."

"How?" Ariel demanded. "They aren't exactly stupid. They'll know if they've harmed you or not."

"We'll have to play-act a scene," said Derec. "I haven't really figured out the details. Maybe if it thinks it caused you two to attack me, or something like that."

"I hear footsteps," said Jeff.

Derec got down low and carefully looked around the nearest plant, up the slope. A lone humanoid robot was coming down the row. Derec gathered his feet under him and waited.

"What are we supposed to do?" Ariel whispered.

"We'll all have to improvise," he whispered back, gesturing with his hand. "Quiet."

Just as the robot reached him, Derec threw himself forward to clutch at the robot's legs.

"Stop!" Derec called hoarsely, looking up at the robot's face. He didn't have to fake his pain any, but he gave vent to it in his facial expression. "You hurt me."

The robot stopped, looking down at him. "If I did so, it was inadvertant. I apologize." The robot reached down to take Derec under its arms and lift him.

At the contact, Derec let out a scream and went limp. He slid out of the robot's grasp to lie on the ground face up.

"You've killed him!" Ariel screamed, jumping up. "You murderer, you've killed him!"

Derec struggled not to smile at her vehemence. He lay with his eyes open, so he could follow what was happening.

"Looks that way," said Jeff. "Maybe you ought to shut down, pal. You can't go around violating the First Law like that."

The robot was visibly quivering. "I did not harm him. Our contact was minimal and of very low impact. This is a misunderstanding. I will help him find care."

"No! Don't you touch him!" Ariel shouted, waving her arms wildly. "You'll do it again."

"Humans cannot die more than once," said the robot. "Besides, he is not dead."

"He's in very bad shape," said Jeff. "It's your fault. Do you understand that?"

Derec started grimacing and writhing in pain, with relatively little play-acting required.

"I ... could ... not have harmed him," the robot insisted. "My contact . . . with him . . . would not damage him."

The robot's hesitation revealed his doubt. Derec was encouraged. They just had to keep at it.

"And no reporting to the central computer," Jeff said suddenly. "I almost forgot. You haven't done that, have you?"

"No . . . I was . . . distracted."

"Well, don't. That's an order. Second Law. Got it?" Jeff demanded, pointing a finger at him.

"Yes. . . ."

"Don't you think you ought to shut down?" Ariel said forcefully, her hands on her hips. "After doing this to him?"

"I am . . . not . . . convinced."

"If you won't shut down," said Jeff, "then we'll have beat him up ourselves. And that will definitely be your fault."

"That . . . is illogical."

"Are you going to shut down or not?" Ariel demanded.

"No . . . I will not. . . ."

"Wait a minute," Derec wheezed, trying to sound as injured as he could. "Do you admit that you are in doubt about this?"

"Yes."

"Then you should at least agree to come with us where we can discuss it further."

"That's right," said Jeff. "You can't argue that, can you?"

"Good idea," said Ariel, looking up the slope. "We, uh, don't want to be interrupted."

"Carry me," Derec said to the robot. "Who are you, anyway? And what do you do?"

"I . . . am Pei," said the robot, with somewhat less hesitation. "My task is Architectural Designer." He bent down and gently picked up Derec. "Where . . . shall we go?"

"We want to be out of sight of this row," said Jeff. "But not too far. Uh, let's cross that row and go to the other side."

"Very well," said Pei. "However, we cannot go out of sight of this row unless we go some distance. I see a slight dip in the row ahead that may suffice if we all sit on the ground."

"Perfect," said Ariel. "C'mon, let's hurry."

With Pei carrying Derec, the group moved quickly for the first time since they had left the *Minneapolis*. As they walked, Derec relaxed a little and closed his eyes. It was a relief to rest again, even for a few moments before they stopped.

Pei set him down with extreme care. Then the others sat down around him on the damp, soft soil.

"Explain . . . my transgression . . . of the First Law," said Pei. He began quivering a little more again.

Derec, lying with eyes closed, felt guilty about distressing the robot this way. He reminded himself, however, that the same robot was under Avery programming. He would turn them all in if the central computer or the Hunters knew he was with them and instructed him to do so.

Besides, he could be repaired or reprogrammed later with no lasting damage. I *can't,* Derec thought. He opened his eyes.

"You harmed me," Derec asserted as firmly as he could. "Shut yourself down."

"At least for a while, you know, until you can be checked," said Ariel. "That's standard procedure, isn't it?"

Her phrasing sounded lame to Derec. He realized that she felt guilty about this, too.

"I . . . must be . . . convinced," said Pei.

CHAPTER 16

TO CHALLENGE UTOPIA

Derec suddenly acted on another impulse. With effort, he rolled onto his side and got his aching legs under him. Then he launched himself at Jeff without warning, reaching for Jeff throat as if he wanted to strangle him.

Just as he got his hands around Jeff's neck, Pei gently grasped his wrists. Even at the slight pressure, Derec screamed and fell back, drawing his arms away with his hands limp. Then he collapsed to the ground with his eyes closed.

"You did it again!" Jeff cried, not too loudly.

"You've really hurt him this time," said Ariel.

"This is an acceptable move," said Pei. "I have prevented greater harm to this human by making a less harmful move to the one attacking him. No violation of the First Law has been made." His confidence was returning.

Derec opened his eyes, not otherwise moving.

"Uh. . . ." Jeff looked helplessly at Ariel.

"You overdid it," said Ariel excitedly. "Look at him. That's not called for!"

"That's right," Jeff declared. "Stopping him with reasonable force is all right, but this is something else!"

Pei looked down at Derec. "I . . . could not . . . have hurt him. I . . . was . . . gentle."

"Not gentle enough," Ariel wailed. "That's twice you've hurt him. You just don't understand how fragile humans are."

"That's right," said Jeff eagerly. "That's the problem. If you've never had contact with humans before, that explains it. Suppose you shut down till your judgement is fixed up. Or something." He shrugged lamely at Ariel.

"It's your judgement," Ariel agreed, "that must be faulty at the core, so to speak. You can't risk harming a human because of that, can you?"

"Perhaps . . . you have . . . a point." Pei's voice grew faint and he froze in place.

"Pei, are you awake?" Ariel asked cautiously.

"Pei, if you can hear me, I order you to say so," said Jeff.

When Derec didn't hear anything, he forced himself up on one elbow. "Hey, it finally worked."

"I guess it did," said Ariel.

"Then it should work again," said Jeff. "And now that we know what it takes, we can refine our scenario."

"Let's get back over to that row they're taking," said Derec. "Can you help me up?"

Yet again, Jeff and Ariel helped him to his feet and supported his arms over their shoulders. The trio shuffled back to the one row that these humanoid robots were using for their trip down into the valley. There Derec once more sank to the ground.

Jeff and Ariel this time paced nervously between the high stalks on each side of the furrow.

"Maybe we ought to move on," said Ariel. "Isn't one

ROBOT CITY

mugged robot enough? I mean, one murdered human and one murdered robot caused major crises in Robot City before."

"That's a good point," said Jeff. "Maybe we could drag him over here where the next migrating robot will be sure to find him. But we could move on, keep ahead of the Hunters."

"I can't help you drag him," said Derec. "And he's pretty big. I doubt the two of you could get him all the way over here."

Jeff ran a hand through his straight black hair and sighed. "You're right. It's been a rough day already, and we may have a lot more running ahead."

"One more robot," said Derec. "That's all we need."

"What are you talking about?" Ariel demanded. "If we just stand here and wait for the Hunters, all this has been for nothing anyway. We have to get out of here."

"Just one more robot. Instead of mugging it, we'll just make sure it sees Pei, back there. Then we'll move on."

"Well . . . all right," said Ariel. "We'll wait a little while. But if nothing comes before long, we're leaving anyway. Agreed?"

"Fair enough," said Derec. "But remember, it has to be one robot walking alone. I'm pretty sure that trying to fool more than one would be tougher because the others will observe and may spot the fraud. Let's not chance that."

More robots did walk down the row before much time had passed, and all of them seemed to be migrating alone in the sense that they were not part of a crew or a team. However, they often came down the row in sight of one or more robots behind them, and Derec did not dare attempt their charade under those circumstances.

"Remember," said Derec, "not that much time has really passed for the Hunters to get here. It just seems longer to us than it has been because we're scared."

"Here comes another one," said Ariel, peeking around the leafy stalk on the corner of the row. "It looks good. I don't see anyone behind him yet."

Jeff moved next to her to look. "Hey, Derec. I think this is it. We've got another one."

"Finally. All right. Just before he gets here, I'll throw myself on the ground and you jump on me." He smiled wryly. "Not too hard, okay? I'm half dead already."

"Derec, don't talk that way—" Ariel began.

"Hey—wait a minute," said Jeff. "I know that robot. It's . . . what did I name him? Oh, yeah. Hey, Can Head!" Jeff stepped out in front of the robot.

The robot stopped suddenly, looking at him in some surprise. "Are you addressing me?"

"Identify yourself," said Jeff.

"I am Energy Pack Maintenance Foreman 3928," said the robot. "I am following migration programming. Please allow me to pass."

"That sounds right. I'm sure it's you." Jeff nodded, studying the robot's eyeslit and general shape.

"Jeff, what are you doing?" Derec asked.

"I knew this character," said Jeff. "I even gave him a second name. He was very cooperative."

"They've all been reprogrammed," Ariel said urgently. "We're sure of it, remember? He won't retain anything from when you were here before. Let's get on with it."

"C'mon, pal, remember?" Jeff grinned. "You will also answer to Can Head, won't you?"

"Yes. I also answer to Can Head."

Ariel laughed in surprise, stifling it with a hand over her mouth.

"There!" Jeff grinned at her and Derec.

Derec shrugged at Ariel.

"I'm the human who was in a robot body before," said Jeff to Can Head. "I gave you that name and now I have further instructions. First, don't contact the central computer with any of this. Got it?" He winked down at Derec. "I used to say that on my last trip here, too."

"Understood," said Can Head.

"Do you remember me?" Jeff asked.

"No."

"You don't?" Jeff started. "Then why do you still answer to Can Head?"

"I've got it," said Derec. "All the robots of Robot City were reprogrammed through the central core, but their identities and designations were not changed. That would be counterproductive for Avery because the central computer still has to be able to contact and recognize all the different robots."

"I guess," said Jeff. "I'm disappointed. I thought I had an old friend, here."

"That's nothing," said Derec. "You should have seen the greeting we got from Euler, an old friend of ours. He's the one who sent the Hunters after us."

"Anyhow, he's being cooperative," said Jeff. "Maybe we don't need our scenario." He turned to Can Head. "We must show you something. However, before we do, we request your help—no, we *require* your help under the First Law."

"How may I help?" Can Head asked.

"This human is Derec and he is extremely ill. We—"

"He looks it," said Can Head.

"A comedian," Derec muttered.

"We need you to carry him for us for a while," said Jeff.

"Why?"

"We . . . are being followed by those who would do further harm," said Ariel, speaking slowly to get the right phrases.

"Exactly," said Derec.

"Who are they?" Can Head asked.

"We can't say," said Jeff. "But it doesn't matter, does it? Harm is harm under the First Law."

"I am under high-priority programming to migrate," said Can Head. "To violate it, I must understand the urgency of the potential harm."

"Hold it," said Derec. "Let's combine the two. Look—you see where the ground dips over there?"

"Yes."

"An inactive humanoid robot is lying there. After you take us to safety, we want you to report it to the central computer, but not before. You understand?"

"So far," said Can Head.

"Before you do that, carry me and lead them on an evasive pattern toward your assembly point. That will combine your programming with our needs under the First Law. Can you do that?"

"My programming requires that I migrate directly," said Can Head. He turned to look at the dip in the ground. "A humanoid robot has malfunctioned here?"

"Sort of," said Derec. "It's more like he was mugged."

"Mugged? In the sense of criminal violence?"

"That's what I mean, yeah."

Can Head turned his eyeslit directly down at Derec. "Is this development directly related to the danger you are in?"

"Uh—yes! It is directly related," said Derec. "But we don't need to discuss how. Will you help us or not?"

"I believe this is sufficient reason to take you on an evasive pattern toward my assembly point." Can Head leaned down and picked up Derec with surprising gentleness, even for a robot. "Follow me," he said to Jeff and Ariel.

Derec let out a sigh of relief. As long as they were moving ahead of the Hunters, they had a chance, and an evasive pattern taken by a robot might at least be the equal of the Hunters' ability to solve it. It would be better than their own, at any rate.

He would instruct Can Head to drop them off before he reached his assembly point and to keep his contact with them secret. At that time, he thought sleepily, he could cajole an explanation of the migration programming out of him. Right now, he was just so tired. . . .

He was comforted by the strong, rhythmic stride of Can Head and by the sound of the footsteps of Jeff and Ariel right behind them. News of the mugging of their victim was certain to reach Dr. Avery. What Derec needed now was Mandelbrot. Mandelbrot could contact the central computer and, unlike Can Head and the other Avery robots, he could he trusted to help without these convoluted discussions of the Laws.

Mandelbrot . . . and Wolruf. He drifted off to sleep wondering what had happened to them.

Mandelbrot was standing motionless in a repair facility. The trip here had been a long one, covering a surprisingly long distance. He had been deposited here just a moment before by the helpful robot.

He had successfully evaded the Hunters behind him by dual moves. The first was having that other robot carry him to eliminate his heat trail, and the second was being identified as a malfunctioning robot. Apparently the Hunters, with no reason to believe he was in need of repair, were acting under the assumption that he was still in full flight. He would have to move on before they thought of checking here.

Mandelbrot also had to get out before the repair robots required his identification, and that would be any time now.

At first he had been surprised by being set down and left to wait. The efficiency of the Avery robots had led him to expect immediate handling. As he observed the workings in the repair facility, however, he concluded that Robot City was, as usual, functioning under its own distinctive style of efficiency.

The repair facility was processing a large number of damaged or malfunctioning robots. Mandelbrot guessed from the conversations he overheard through his comlink that migration programming had largely been completed. Apparently only skeleton staffs remained anywhere in Robot City now.

For that reason, most repair facilities had also been shut down. The robots being repaired here were either already assigned to those skeleton staffs or they were being reprogrammed. Those that entered with migration orders had them purged and were placed in a pool to act as reserves for the skeleton staffs instead.

So Robot City intended to function without the migrating robots for an extended period. Further, any robot that did not reach its assembly point within a short time would be reassigned. Mandelbrot concluded that he could not afford to wait here longer at all, or he would risk being reprogrammed and so lost to the humans as a source of help.

Mandelbrot was standing by four other robots. Two were sitting because of mechanical failures that impaired standing or walking. The other two were standing, the extent of their malfunctions not visible. All of them had managed to reach the repair facility alert and functioning just short of one hundred percent.

Mandelbrot observed the entire room for a moment. A couple of humanoid robots assigned to the facility supervised a large number of function robots doing the actual repair work. One function robot was rolling down the row of waiting robots that Mandelbrot was in, observing serial numbers or something with an eye on a long, flexible tentacle.

Mandelbrot turned and walked quickly out of the building. Outside, he mounted a slidewalk and began to run on it toward the mountains, now invisible in the distance. He knew their direction but had to follow his memory of the ship viewscreen for the best route.

"Stop," called a robot on his comlink. "You are malfunctioning and therefore endanger yourself by risking greater malfunctions. This is a Third Law violation that requires you to shut down—"

Mandelbrot broke his reception. Since he was in fine condition, none of that applied. He had known they would see him take off, and he was gambling that they would not place as high a priority on catching him as the Hunters had. At worst, they would assign a Hunter to catch him as a malfunctioned rogue instead of as an intruder involved with Derec.

Ahead, he saw a tunnel stop. Without looking back, he leaped off the slidewalk and ran down the moving ramp to the loading dock. Then he was inside a platform booth and had programmed it to go as close to the mountains as it could take him.

The trip would take some time. He opened his comlink again to reconnoiter.

Two general alerts were coming from the central computer with high priority codes.

One was that Hunters were now seeking a malfunctioning robot who had apparently violated the Third Law by running away from a repair facility. Because the force of the Laws was involved, all humanoid robots were ordered to watch for him. His physical description was given. Since he had escaped from the repair facility before any scanning was done, they had no more to go on than that, but he was distinctive from the Avery robots even by sight.

The second alert was that a mysteriously shut-down humanoid robot had been found in the agricultural park. Nothing was known about the cause. The Supervisors entered an urgent order that any robots with information about this development report it immediately.

Total malfunctions of this kind were extremely rare in Robot City. Mandelbrot was sure that this one called up memories in the minds of the Supervisors, and probably in Avery himself, of the robot murder that Derec had solved here.

Mandelbrot, of course, was not bound by the instruction. He was sure that his human friends were somehow responsible and he was also certain that the Hunters would guess this, as well. Nevertheless, none of them had proof.

Mandelbrot also figured that the Hunters would guess that the rogue robot was the same one they were hunting. It made no difference, since he had to avoid them either way. He now felt the First Law impetus pushing him on, since the Hunters were likely to be closer to the humans than he was.

The platform booth continued to shoot down the tunnel toward the mountains. It was the fastest transportation he had, and it seemed painfully slow.

CHAPTER 17

JEFF'S FAVOR

Derec heard Ariel calling his name. It came out of darkness, out of fog, out of chilly air . . . until he finally opened his eyes and found himself looking up at her with some thick, tall grass waving behind her in the dim glow suffusing the entire valley. He said nothing at first, trying to remember where they were. The surroundings were totally unfamiliar to him.

"Derec, *please* wake up. We have to move again." Her voice was pleading.

"Come on. I'll help you." Jeff got an arm under Derec and pulled him into a sitting position.

"Where are we?" Derec asked, looking around. His voice was dry and hoarse. "What's happened?"

"You fell asleep while Can Head was carrying you," said Ariel. "He's gone now."

"You've been asleep for some time," said Jeff. "It must be the middle of the night by now. It's getting colder."

Derec nodded, folding his arms and rubbing them. "But

Can Head must have reported the mugged robot to the central computer, probably right after he left us."

"As to where we are," said Ariel, "Can Head let us down through the valley floor, kind of zigzagging, and partway up the far slope. I think we're in a wheat field."

Derec reluctantly let Jeff pull him to his feet. His whole body seemed to ache. He leaned against Jeff's shoulder, breathing hard, trying to gain his balance.

"We woke you up because we have to keep going," said Ariel. "The Hunters aren't going to stop for the night."

"Have you got any more ideas, Derec?" Jeff asked. "Avery should have heard about the mugging by now."

Derec shook his head, still trying to wake up. "I don't know what to expect. I don't know how long that news will take to have an effect, either." He straightened up. "I meant to ask Can Head about the migration. Do you know where his assembly point is?"

"Not really," said Jeff. "He went sideways across the slope when he left, but I imagine he was heading back to that one thoroughfare they were all using."

"We don't dare try that," Derec muttered to himself.

Ariel suddenly clutched his arm. She nodded toward something over his shoulder without speaking.

Derec and Jeff turned to look. Far across the same slope, a humanoid figure was just barely distinguishable in the distance, coming toward them.

"Let's go," Derec said, feeling a faint surge of excitement. "It's not on the migration route, so it must be a Hunter, and it's sure to have seen us. I'm afraid it won't be long now."

The three of them started along the row in the opposite direction, but Derec was just barely stumbling along. As before, the others each supported one of his arms across their shoulders. Derec realized with frustration that he was now too far gone for even the adrenaline in his system to make much difference.

When they reached an intersecting row between the wheat field and a field of some low, bushy plants he could not recognize, Jeff stopped and lowered Derec's arm.

"Look, we'll have to split up." He looked back at the Hunter, which was still distant but visibly closer.

"Why bother?" Derec said wearily.

"Maybe I can divert it somehow. And if they get me first, I'm probably in the least danger from Avery. He doesn't have any business with me."

"He's crazy," Ariel said sharply. "You can't expect rational behavior from him."

"Well, maybe not. But splitting up is the best chance to keep Derec away from him a little longer. Maybe Avery will show himself in that extra time."

Derec looked up to study his face. "You sure you want to take this much risk?"

Jeff grinned at him and shrugged. "Hey, I said I owed you a favor, didn't I?"

Derec gripped his arm for a moment in thanks, then turned and started up the slope. Ariel threw her arms around Jeff in a brief hug and then hurried after Derec. Jeff moved a few meters down the slope and then got down on all fours to crawl through the low bushes of the adjacent crop field.

Derec leaned on Ariel for support as they plodded slowly up the furrow between the fields. In a moment, the tall green Auroran-bred wheat had hidden them from immediate view of the Hunter, but it would have noted the trio's movements and communicated them to the other Hunters, wherever they were.

• • •

Mandelbrot stood at the opening of one of the passes into the valley, looking out over the agricultural park. It was dimly lit and he could just barely see, with his superior robot vision, tiny figures moving in the distance. He paused to study the entire valley.

Some of the taller and thicker crops blocked his sight, but he could see a couple of humanoid robots moving straight up a row on the far slope. They were not behaving like Hunters, and he suspected that they were migrating. Down in the valley floor, he saw two large robots moving systematically among the rows of the crops and was sure that they were Hunters.

Then, at another spot on the opposite slope, he saw a human figure crawling through one of the fields. As he watched helplessly, a lone Hunter ran up behind him and lifted the human off the ground. From the lively struggle he saw he knew the human was not Derec and he judged that Ariel was smaller.

Above the struggle a short distance, he located Derec and Ariel moving painfully and slowly as they wove their way among some short trees.

Mandelbrot's programming and his understanding of the dangers posed by Dr. Avery placed Derec at the highest of his priorities. While the Hunters were programmed with a narrow definition of duty that allowed them to detain humans without harming them, Mandelbrot had a larger perspective and saw detention by the Hunters as a first step toward virtually certain harm. At the moment, he would have to ignore Jeff's capture and help Derec and Ariel if he could. He noted the positions and current movements of the Hunters he could see, and started quickly down the slope.

Derec and Ariel stumbled out of the far side of the fruit orchard onto a well-traveled footpath headed straight up and down the slope.

"I'm totally lost," Derec wheezed. He stopped, bending forward to lean on his knees. "But this must be the migration route again. Look at all the robot footprints. This valley can't have very much foot traffic. And if it did, they would have paved this."

Ariel nodded and prodded him up the slope, where the soft mud had been churned unevenly with the heavy use. The irrigation was obviously turned on at regular intervals. "C'mon," she muttered breathlessly.

They had just started up the incline when a large figure stepped out of the crops above them. It threw a massive shadow as it started down the slope toward them. Derec looked up at the great bulk of a Hunter as it moved toward them carefully, watching its precarious balance on the poor footing.

"Come on!" Ariel yanked him sideways back into the fruit orchard. "Hurry."

"I can't," he whispered apologetically. "I'm too weak to hurry." He followed her, though, until she halted abruptly a moment later.

Another Hunter was waiting for them in the trees ahead, a dark silhouette against the glow of light behind him.

They turned again and found two more Hunters pushing through the trees, breaking branches and shaking leaves as they did so, coming right up the slope without bothering to follow any rows and furrows. Their very silence and dispassionate demeanor discouraged rebellion.

Derec leaned wearily on Ariel's shoulders, unable to struggle. She wrapped her arms around him, more for his sake, he guessed, than because she was scared. He glared helplessly at the nearest Hunter.

As he watched the Hunter reaching for them he saw a weirdly flexible robot arm curl around the Hunter's neck from behind. It made a couple of quick motions and the Hunter froze, completely shut down.

Derec blinked at it, too surprised to react.

"Run!" Mandelbrot shouted, emerging from behind the Hunter. His cellular arm, which Derec had long ago installed and ordered him to disguise as a normal robotic arm of the time, was just now stiffening back to normal.

"Come on!" Ariel shoved Derec past Mandelbrot to put their protector between them and the Hunters.

They began stumbling through the trees again, their hope renewed by Mandelbrot. Ariel led him through a crooked trail, turning and twisting through the fruit trees in a clumsy, crashing route that ignored stealth entirely. At one point Derec got caught in a leafy branch and had to pause to get out. He took the moment to peer back at Mandelbrot.

Four Hunters had originally closed in on them. Mandelbrot had apparently pushed the controls on that first one to neutralize it and then had attacked the other three. By attacking them, he brought the Third Law into effect, forcing the Hunters to protect themselves. This imperative overrode even the strongest programming, so that they could not continue their pursuit until they had subdued Mandelbrot.

Mandelbrot was outnumbered, but had the advantage of instructions to use his cellular arm. Further, in the close quarters among the trees, the greater size of the Hunters impeded them. The struggle continued, buying Derec and Ariel more time as they hurried on.

Ariel led the way until finally he reached out and grabbed her, too out of breath to speak up. She waited anxiously until he could, looking around fearfully.

"Where are we going?" He panted.

"I don't know. Anywhere. Just away."

"Mandelbrot can't win that fight. He can only slow them down. Then it'll start all over again the same way."

"Have you got a better idea?" She demanded.

He nodded and got down on the ground among the trees. "I've been thinking about this park. The way that robot path is chewed up by the footprints and all. It means this park normally doesn't have an erosion problem."

"Yeah, so?"

"So these crops still need water, and it's obviously managed with their usual efficiency. If this valley is irrigated by under-ground pipes or something, we've had it. But I don't think the robots would do that, because leaves need external moisture, too."

"Get to the point, will you? Or let's go."

"Irrigation outlets. This valley has to have them in some form. If we turn them on, they'll eliminate our heat trail."

"Well. . . ." She knelt down beside him. "They could be anywhere. And it's dark. Besides, Derec, this is a high-altitude valley. Maybe the natural fog and rain take care of all that."

"That would be leaving too much to chance. We have to figure this out."

"How?"

He sat back and looked at her. His legs no longer hurt; they were nearly numb. "All right. Instead of looking at random, we have to work it out logically, like the robots would. Where would you place irrigation outlets for the greatest efficiency?"

"How do I know?"

"Well, I can hardly think at all!"

"All right, all right. Concentrate. We're on a slope. . . . Derec, come on. This way."

He nodded and forced himself after her, stumbling on feet he could hardly feel.

After a walk that seemed much longer than it could possibly have been, they stopped along a row between the trees that ran horizontally along the slope. Now Derec was the one looking all around for Hunters that could come from any direction.

"They must use these furrows as a kind of terracing," said Ariel. "I think we're right in the middle of the vertical rows. If they put the irrigation spigots near here, they would lose the least amount to runoff down the slope. The same with fire control."

"It sounds good to me," said Derec, collapsing to the ground again. "Let's find it."

"If it's here," she added, joining him on the ground.

"I got something." Derec's hand had come across a small cylinder sticking up perhaps fifteen centimeters from the surface of the ground. He got down low to look at it in the faint light.

"Now what?" Ariel whispered, moving next to him. "It doesn't have any controls or anything. What if the sensors are somewhere else?"

"It's possible," said Derec slowly. "But look how high it is. Why would they do that? They don't do anything sloppily here, or without a reason. They don't waste material, either."

"Derec, we can't just sit here and try to outguess them. Who knows?" She shook her head. "Maybe we should just keep running, huh?"

He shook his head. "This is the only real chance we have left. Come on, help me bury it."

"What?"

"Hurry! Why else would it be so tall? This whole thing is its own sensor. It probably judges air moisture and precipitation and who knows what."

"How do you know?"

"I think they designed it at this height so it wouldn't be covered by minor shifts in the soil during hoeing and other care. If we cover it with dirt, it'll stop sensing. Come on!" He was already scraping up the soft black soil, which the function robots seemed to keep turned constantly, and began packing it around the cylinder.

She joined him without further argument. They found the soil damp enough to stick to the cylinder if they packed it hard, and before long it was covered. Derec wiped the dirt off his hands on some leaves.

"Now what?" She asked, wiping off her own hands. "Nothing's happening."

CHAPTER 18

DOWN A HOLE

At the far end of the valley, Wolruf sat quivering in the chilly air. She was huddled high in the mountains in a vertical crevice of rock. This was the compromise she had reached for her conundrum: she was in the valley where she could try to observe the humans or even Mandelbrot if they were here when day broke. At the same time, she would not lead the Hunters following her directly to them.

Now she could not see any of them in the faint light down in the valley. In the nearer regions below her, function robots were visible doing their regular chores among the crops. Her physiology kept her just warm enough at this altitude to remain for a while, but she was not comfortable. Nor did she have the energy left to run farther.

She waited patiently, reviewing the moves she had made to break her trail. None of them could avoid a systematic search by the Hunters if they were close enough to detect her heat. Also, the Hunters probably had checked the pass at some point, because it was a bottleneck that could quickly tell them if she was inside the valley or out.

If her heat trail had faded before they had reached it, they still had physical signs to rely on. She had been as careful as possible, but the robotic vision of the Hunters could detect extreme detail. The rest was up to them.

Her ears perked up at the sound of footsteps on the rock fall below her. With no more energy left for fleeing, she waited patiently. The giant shape of a Hunter emerged from the darkness, thrown into silhouette by the distant glow emanating from the crops below. She knew it would not harm her, but it would take her prisoner and possibly deliver her to Dr. Avery, who could certainly harm her if he wished. She shivered as the Hunter reached down to pick her up.

Derec was staring disconsolately at the dirt-covered sensor when it suddenly erupted in an uneven spray, knocking loose some of the dirt. Ariel and he both flinched. All around them, other spigots were also spraying jets of fine mist into the air.

"That's it!" Derec lifted his arms toward her. "Let's go. Can you help me up?"

Ariel took his arms and pulled. His legs gave out under him. She wasn't strong enough to lift him.

She started to pull again.

"I can't walk any more." His lower legs and feet had lost all feeling.

"You can't walk at all?" Her shoulders slumped.

"But I can crawl. Let's go."

"Derec . . . ?"

"Come on!" He started crawling through the soft earth, which was quickly turning to mud.

She stood and walked alongside him. "This is crazy. We're hardly getting anywhere."

"We have a lot more time now. The Hunters can't follow our heat trail so they'll have to start a pattern search. And at least one of them will have to carry Mandelbrot after they've shut him down."

"Derec, you've only gone two meters!"

He stopped, sighing, and looked ahead. She was right. He could barely move. "Hey—what's that thing?"

"What?" She looked, too.

Some kind of large rectangular shape, at least a cubic meter in size, was emerging from the ground below the trees.

"That . . . thing, there. We haven't seen one of those before." He started crawling again.

"There's one behind us, too," she said. "And beyond that one. They're coming up all over. They were completely hidden before."

"We must have triggered them along with the irrigation. Go see what it is."

She hurried ahead and stopped in front of the object, bending low in front of it. After a moment, she came back and knelt down. "I think we can get inside it. It looks like a ventilation duct or something."

Derec nodded. He had stopped crawling to get his breath again. His head was spinning dizzily.

When she got down on all fours and moved under him, he let her. She gathered his arms around her neck and maneuvered under him. Then, supporting his weight, she began to crawl much faster than he had, carrying as much of his weight as she could.

He hung on with his arms and closed his eyes against the spray of water.

"Here," she said, after a few moments.

He opened his eyes into a gaping black opening with no other features. As she eased out from under him, he reached inside and felt for the shape of the object.

"It's not a straight drop." She helped him climb inside. "You can feel a gradual incline."

Derec hesitated, too disoriented to speak but still reluctant to throw himself into an unknown hole.

"Go on, get in before the Hunters see us."

He was losing all sense of his surroundings. Following directions was easier than arguing. He worked his way inside the opening and then suddenly was sliding downward and accelerating.

All was in darkness. He felt a rushing of air, the smooth pressure of the surface against his back as he slid, and Ariel bumping against him from above as she slid with him. Vaguely, he realized he was too exhausted to feel any fear.

He should have been terrified of winding up in a moving fan blade, for instance, or in the workings of some mysterious robot creation that would convert them both to fertilizer. Apparently he had been on Robot City too long for that. The robots couldn't allow that much danger to a human to exist here.

No, that wasn't it, either. The reason was even simpler. Nothing on this planet was more frightening than the chemfets destroying his body from the inside at this very moment.

The sensation of falling continued as they entered some turns, gradual curves, and finally reached a sudden upturn.

In the short ascent, gravity broke their momentum and then they slid backward again. Derec lay motionless, aware that they had stopped in the bottom of this thing, whatever it was. No light reached them at all.

He felt Ariel move a little, probably getting her bearings.

"Derec?" She said softly. "Are you hurt?"

A moment passed before he had the breath to answer. "No," he whispered. "But I've had it."

"We're safe now," she said, feeling for him and stroking his hair. "At least from the Hunters. I'm sure of it. They'll have to search the entire valley, and every one of these things. And these were popping up every few meters, it looked like. . . . well, every fifty or sixty, anyhow. Without a heat trail to follow, it'll take them forever."

"I can't do it."

"But we're onto him! Avery, I mean. I'm sure of it." She shuffled around and seemed to stand. "You know that upward curve at the end of our . . . little ride? It's here and not very high. The duct continues on a level from here. Say, you know what else? There are handholds of some kind on the side opposite the one we slid down."

"Maybe for service robots to make repairs down here." He thought a moment. The temptation to go on was strong. Confronting the crazy doctor after all the suffering he had endured . . . but he couldn't move. All he wanted to do was sleep.

"I think you're right," he said finally. "This is a ventilation duct. From the size and number of them, it must lead to an immense living space."

"Avery's home. Robots wouldn't need it or the produce in the valley. Come on, let's go. I'll help you up."

"You'll have to go on alone. I honestly can't move."

She was quiet a moment. "Do you really want me to go on without you?"

"Yes."

"All right," she said slowly. She waited, perhaps trying to think of something else to say. Then she got her arms around him and embraced him very hard, and held on.

He was too weak to respond. After a moment, he felt her let go and stand up. Then she was climbing, and he heard her moving down the ventilation duct away from him.

He closed his eyes and slept.

Ariel felt her way forward slowly with her hands as she crawled, not making any move until she knew what was ahead of her. She was still in absolute darkness in some kind of giant tube that was so far stretching straight ahead on a level course. With Derec unable to move, she was painfully aware that she was the last of their group to have a chance at finding Dr. Avery.

She was not exactly in top condition herself. Her hands and feet were painfully cold and she was drenched from the sprinklers. She was worn out, too, though not sick like Derec was. The climb up the mountainside and down into the valley had taken a lot of energy out of her.

She hoped, with guarded optimism, that her memory was growing stronger. Those weird memory fugues had grown less frequent and she wished fervently that none would strike while she was alone in this thing, whatever it was.

She began to find branches and intersections in the passageway. Without any way to pick one direction over another, she attempted to go as straight as she could. Going in roughly one direction would at least prevent her from wandering hopelessly in circles. She suspected that the intersecting tunnels represented those other openings on the surface they had seen.

After a while, she thought she had picked out a pattern. From what she could feel, smaller tunnels seemed to converge more often and become larger ones consistently to her left. She began to move leftward and discovered that the tunnels were now high enough for her to stand if she bent over.

Now that she was moving in this direction, more tunnels converged around her all the time. Then they started branching out again, some of them splitting off above her. Finally she realized that she could see hints of shapes: dark spaces that represented openings one way, a faint reflection of an inner surface another way.

The traces of a light source shone from just one direction.

She dropped to all fours again to pursue the light source, now more concerned with making noise than with the height of the tunnel.

Around a curve, she reached something recognizable: a covered opening into a room. Barely daring to breathe, she moved as quietly as she could toward it until she could peek through the opening.

It was nearly opaque.

The room was lit, but she couldn't see much. It was carpeted in brown. Nor could she hear anything.

After the silence had continued, she decided that she would have to risk entering the room. She began studying the edge of the covering to see if she could get it loose. In a moment, she found that pressure on the covering itself caused a hole to appear in the middle. The substance, whatever it was, receded from the hole to fade outward into the surrounding wall until the vent was entirely open.

She let out a sigh of relief that the room was deserted. It was still silent, as well. After shifting around to get her feet out first, she dropped to the floor of the room and looked around.

It was a small room, perhaps only three meters cubed. The brown carpeting went all the way up the walls and covered the ceiling as well. The light came from a globe floating just under the center of the ceiling.

She looked again at the ceiling, then at the walls. The room was not built on right angles. The corners were slightly askew.

A couple of computer tapes were piled on the floor. In one corner, a small stuffed animal of unrecognizable type lay on its side. The room was not being used for anything that she could see.

This was not what Ariel had expected from Dr. Avery.

The door was closed. She held her breath and pushed the stud on the wall next to it. It slid open silently.

She remained where she was, waiting. When nothing happened, she stuck her head out slowly. She found a hallway extending maybe six meters one way and four the other. The hallway itself was oddly shaped, but familiar—then she recognized it. It was a hollow three-dimensional rendition of the Key to Perihelion.

She stepped into the hallway. The closed doors at each end of it were also shaped like the Keys. She chose one and walked toward it.

This one opened as she reached it. She hesitated, then edged through. Her mouth dropped open in surprise.

This room reminded her of some ancient historical paintings she had seen. The high vaulted ceiling was at least two stories high and hung with curtains of burgundy velvet. Imitation Renaissance paintings in garish gold frames seemed to fit what she remembered of that period . . . or did they? Yet that furniture . . . was classic Auroran design, developed many centuries later. She looked up again, trying to orient herself . . . and shuffled quickly to one side to catch her balance.

This room was also askew. Worse than that, she guessed,

it was not built on angles at all. Though the corners of the ceiling and walls were partly hidden by curtains, the whole room seemed oddly rounded, even twisted out of shape, as though the room had begun as a rectangle, had started to melt, and then had frozen again.

She started across the room to look more closely at the furniture. After four steps, the floor gave out beneath her and she fell, sliding this time down a short, twisting chute. She heard the trapdoor above her hiss closed again as she landed somewhere else with a thump.

This room was tiny, with just barely enough room for her to stand up. It, too, was in the shape of the Keys. There was a door in each wall that was big enough, and nothing else. The walls glowed with light, as in the Compass Tower. She pressed a stud by one of the doors.

The door slid open to reveal a solid glowing wall. She opened another one. This door opened to reveal a dark, narrow hallway. Before trying it, she pushed another stud.

A weirdly sculptured face stared at her from an archaic red brick wall. It had pointed ears, a long pointed face, and was laughing. Grimacing, she closed that one and tried another.

Another dark hallway stretched in front of her.

She had to go somewhere. With a glance at the other open doorway, she edged inside. The walls here didn't glow, and she slid her feet carefully along the floor before committing her weight forward. After a few steps, the corridor began to curve.

A moment later, she had followed it right back to the same little room again.

CHAPTER 19

THE CORPSE

Ariel closed the doors to the circular hallway and stood inside the room. It might not have an exit, of course; this was the work of a paranoid whose tendencies had been openly revealed. The room could just be a prison.

"Well, now what?" She said aloud.

A muffled response sounded behind one of the doors. She pressed the stud and found herself looking at the grotesque sculptured face again. All its features were exaggerated.

"What did you say?" She demanded.

"Pull my nose," it said.

"Who are you?"

"Pull my nose."

"What happens when I do?"

"Pull my nose."

"Is that all you can say?"

"Pull my nose."

She watched it for a moment. "One, two, three."

"Pull my nose."

She figured it out, then. This was a function robot without a positronic brain. It had one line to say, triggered by any sound of human speech.

Holding her breath, she pulled its nose.

The long, narrow nose stretched toward her and then suddenly snapped back, out of her grasp. On impact, the entire sculpture collapsed into itself, inverted, and pushed itself out the other way. Then the brick wall broke into quarters and each piece receded sideways, carrying the inverted face with it.

She was looking down a short ramp into another corridor, this one lined with glowing stones cut in the shape of the Keys but not in a smooth surface. Their corners protruded irregularly out of the wall to create a jagged, textured wall. The entire shape of the corridor as she faced the opening was in the shape of the Keys, as well.

Still stepping carefully, she ventured down the ramp. After a moment, she realized that she was chillier than before ... air was moving against her soaked clothing. Puzzled, she turned around—and found the walls, ceiling, and floor behind her converging to pinch off the corridor after she had passed.

She hurried forward a little, despite her caution, and came up against a stone wall at the end. Starting to panic, she ran her hands across the stones, feeling for a control of some kind. She felt nothing and whirled around to look at the shrinking corridor.

Suddenly something dropped from the ceiling in front of her and she flattened against the end wall, trying to see the object as it swayed before her face. She recognized it as Wolruf's head, dangling on a long piece of rope tied into an ancient noose.

As she stared at it in horror, she realized that it was only a function robot rendered in realistic detail.

"Why arr 'u 'err?" The robot asked, in Wolruf's voice.

Ariel spine prickled at the sound. She glanced behind the hanging head. The corridor had stopped closing behind her and now had left her in a very small dungeonlike space.

"Wrong answer," said the robot, though she hadn't spoken.

Suddenly the floor rose under Ariel's feet, pushing her up toward the ceiling. The rope retracted with her, keeping the Wolruf head level with her as she rose. The ceiling opened and then the section of floor stopped, now flush with the floor just above the stone corridor.

The abrupt halt threw her off balance and she fell on a rich, gold carpet. Above her, five elaborate chandeliers sparkled and shone from a surprisingly low beamed ceiling. She rose up on her elbows, looking around fearfully.

She was in a library. Shelves of antique books, not computer tapes, stretched around all the walls and were protected by a transparent barrier of some kind. Turning, she stepped off the lift platform away from the Wolruf head.

A candelabra of some sort was on a shelf outside the transparent barrier that protected the books. It stood inside a blue and white bowl, leaning to one side. The candelabra was on a round base, with one central stem holding one candle and four branches arching upward on each side to total nine. She had never seen one before, whatever it was, and thought it seemed out of place here, as though someone had set it down and forgotten it.

She stepped back and looked at the bowl. It was large enough to serve four or five people plenty of food. Light blue designs danced around the white background on the outside. It had never been meant to hold a candelabra, though. Someone had left these here carelessly.

"What iss it?" The Wolruf head asked.

Ariel flinched at the sound and looked at the head. "A candleholder of some kind, obviously."

"Wrong again."

One of the shelved walls glided away soundlessly. She stood where she was, eyeing the dark opening that appeared. An animal—no, a function robot, almost certainly—stepped into a space where light fell on it. It had Wolruf's caninoid body and Ariel's own face.

"If you're standing on the surface of the planet Earth in Webster Groves, Missouri," said the robot-Ariel, "which way is Robot City?"

She stared at it hopelessly. "I'm no navigator. Not without some kind of information to use, anyway."

Robot-Ariel cocked her head, turned, and trotted away.

The wall of shelves slid back into place.

Ariel sank to the floor in a mixture of relief and despair. She couldn't just go on wandering aimlessly in the real-life manifestation of one man's insanity. If this place offered a way out, she could figure it out. If it didn't, she might as well stay in this room instead of going forward into some dungeon cell or something worse.

As before, her knowledge of Dr. Avery was the only source of clues she had, and she no longer had Jeff's memories or Derec's facility with robots to help. All right. Basically, what did she know?

She knew he was a genius, that he was paranoid, that he wanted to create a perfect society. But what did this crazy place have to do with order and rationality?

What was it doing on Robot City?

Everything she knew about Robot City said that this place just didn't belong here at all. The more she thought about it, the more she realized that every line of thought brought her back to that one conclusion. "That's it," she whispered to herself suddenly. "He's gone over the edge. He's even crazier than before."

In the heart of a planet-wide city based on logic and efficiency, its creator had lost his mind.

She smiled at the irony. It wasn't funny, exactly, but it was . . . funny. Somehow.

Exhaustion and fear made her giddy. She began to giggle. The more she thought about this—about all their discussions of the Laws of Robotics and all their convoluted efforts to reason with the positronic brains of the robots—and how it had led to *this*. . . . She really began to laugh. She fell onto the floor on her back, laughing in the little room by herself.

The wall of shelves slid open again, apparently triggered by the sound of her laughter.

Suddenly on guard again, she sat up and looked around. The function robot with her face was back.

"If you're standing on the surface of the planet Earth in Webster Groves, Missouri," said the robot-Ariel again, "which way is Robot City?"

Ariel giggled again. "Up, of course." She laughed—and the floor gave way beneath her.

She was in one more chute, twisting in a tight downward spiral. Just as it began to level off, the dark space ahead of her irised open into light. She spilled out onto a polished hardwood floor.

Shaken by the ride, she lay still for a moment gazing at a very high beamed ceiling that was nearly lost in shadows. She turned her head to the side and found walls of gray stone, precisely chiseled and fit again in the modular shape of the Key to Perihelion. The room was huge, stretching meters on each side of her.

She raised onto her elbow, still getting her bearings. The

end of a large, intricately carved table was in front of her. Its legs and feet were sculpted in the shape of some furry, clawed animal she did not recognize. It was made of a dark, deeply polished wood.

Struggling to rise, she reached up and grabbed the edge of the table. She pulled herself up to lean on it and then froze in surprise. At the far end of the table, many meters away, a man sat in a high, straight-backed chair with a gigantic fire blazing behind him in a stone fireplace twice her height.

"Welcome, Ariel. I am Dr. Avery."

She stared at him with nothing to say. After all the effort to find him, landing here like this was so unexpected that she hadn't formed any plan of attack, any arguments to use with him. She wasn't ready to talk to him.

"You are welcome to warm yourself by the fire," said her host.

She was willing to stay chilly to keep away from him, but she wanted to stall a little if she could, without getting too close. Slowly, she moved around the corner of the table and began to walk down the side of it. Dr. Avery seemed relaxed, even unconcerned, as he fingered some small object in front of him on the table.

The long, narrow table had all kinds of articles on it: flowers, dishes, trinkets, small sculptures. She didn't dare take the time to look. Her eyes remained on Dr. Avery.

He was short, looking especially so in the high-backed chair. His build was stocky. Wavy white hair framed his face, which was also adorned with a bushy mustache. He looked friendly and benign.

His coat was too big, as she remembered from the other times she had seen him, and he still wore a white shirt with a ruffled collar.

He didn't look crazy.

Ariel stopped a good four meters away, still watching him. What was a crazy man supposed to look like?

"I was not expecting visitors, Ariel," said Dr. Avery. He was still studying the object in front of him. "Though I had warning that oddities, shall we say, were occurring in this vicinity."

He didn't sound crazy, either.

"Ariel, you don't remember me, do you?" His gaze remained on the table.

"Yes," she said timidly.

"No, not really. You remember me after the performance of *Hamlet* and when the Hunter robots located all of you in the passageways beneath the city and you remember me from when they brought you to me. That's all."

"That's when we met."

He smiled and picked up the little object. "Automatic alarms were triggered tonight. A couple of them, in fact. When a man who enjoys his privacy feels it may be disturbed, he likes to have alarms installed. Did you trigger them, Ariel?"

She watched him silently, surprised by his changing subjects so quickly.

"A humanoid robot mysteriously shut down completely just a short distance from here. Then a shift in the soil was reported. Did you do those, Ariel?"

"Kind of. I guess."

"You guess. I guess, too. Violations of the provisional Laws of Humanics? Perhaps. I haven't yet investigated the details. But how did you enter my abode?"

Derec was lying helpless along her route. She didn't dare answer that question.

"One of the few weaknesses in my security here is in

my emergency ventilation system. It opens when unexplained malfunctions occur in this valley." He sighed. "I could have had the robots make it entry-proof, but it happens to represent my escape routes, as well. If no one could get in that way, then I couldn't get out that way, could I?"

"What do you want?" she demanded, hoping to get him off that subject. "What is all this about, anyway?"

"Of course, I do have a maze that one must negotiate. It acts as a buffer zone. Perhaps you managed that."

She was shaking with tension, unable to get a handle on a conversation that kept jumping topics.

"By the way, I've misplaced a couple of items. Have you seen them? One is an antique menorah crafted in the ancient Earth empire of the czars. The other is a Ming Dynasty bowl."

She stared at him, vaguely remembering a fancy bowl.

"You really don't remember me, do you, Ariel?"

"Why do you keep saying that?"

"You have new memories now, clearly. You are not the Ariel I last saw. You are again the real Ariel, if you only knew it. A few more accurate memories will trigger the rest, I believe."

"What are you talking about?"

"Your memories now are accurate. It is the real you. The one you thought was you . . . no. You never knew a Spacer who contaminated you. You never had a disease. You will, I sadly suppose, recall the name . . . David Avery." For the first time, then, he looked up and met her eyes.

David Avery. David. Derec . . . ?

Suddenly memories did come flooding back. "David! Derec is David! And you hated me!"

"Oh, now, now. What I attempted with you failed. Bygones are bygones, eh?"

"You . . . what have you done?" She was horrified, yet fascinated. Finally, after such a long time, the mysteries were being answered. "Oh, no. Wait a minute. Is Derec really David . . . or what about the corpse? Was that David? Did you kill him?" She was nearly hysterical, partly from the shock of understanding.

"No, no, of course not." He waved a hand in dismissal. "The corpse, as you call it, was merely a synthetic physical imitation of David. A good one, of course, that used genuine human blood. I used him in a dry-run test of David's encounter with Robot City."

Ariel, still quivering with tension but now composed again, leaned against the table for support. "So you planted memory chemfets and disease in me a long time ago to give me a false memory. Memories of events that never existed to replace my memories of real life. And . . . Derec is David."

"And you were his lover. Oh, by the way, didn't you ever wonder what happened to the corpse? The cleaning robots recognized it as nothing more than waste material and hauled it away."

"You destroyed my memory," she said again, slowly. "And his. The amnemonic plague was artificial, created by chemfets. It was you. To separate David and me. You must have given him his amnesia for the same reason."

"I always knew you had intelligence. My son's taste was always exceptional."

"And ever since my memory returned on Earth, I withheld telling Derec the truth because I was afraid these memories might not be correct. All this time, I could have put his mind at ease if I had only trusted my memories."

"A compliment. Consider my actions a compliment. Breaking your hold on my son's will required extreme measures. Judge it as the extent to which he cares about you."

He leaned back in his chair, holding the little item he had been playing with. "Cared, I should say. He doesn't remember even now, of course . . . but he does seem to have formed an affection for you all over again, seen by the way you two have remained a team."

"You practically destroyed two people just to keep them apart." Her anger was mixed with sheer astonishment.

"Ah, no. Sorry. You are not so important as you think. My other motive was to test my son's resourcefulness. You see, if he succeeded in manipulating and controlling Robot City, then he was truly worthy of my final plan for him."

"Final plan . . . ? Do you mean to say," she said slowly, "that you wiped his memory and placed him on that asteroid as a *test?*"

"It is what I mean to say and what I have said." He sat up and for the first time his face reflected enthusiasm. "You see, Robot City has been finished. Now each of the humanoid robots here has had implanted in his body . . . one or two duplicate Keys to Perihelion. Even now, they are marching to predetermined sites around this planet from which they will launch themselves to different galaxies. In each galaxy, they will begin replication of themselves and construction of more Robot Cities. And David, my son who has now earned the right to act as my son, will control each and every robot in every Robot City . . . making him the most powerful man in the universe!"

"He *what? How?*"

"The chemfets, my dear. The memory chemfets in his body. You see, a tiny Robot City is growing inside him . . . and when it matures, his mere thoughts will control every Avery robot in the universe."

"Oh, no . . . you *are* insane. You don't know what's happened to him!"

"Of course I do. The chemfets develop slowly and cause certain physical disabilities. I know that. They behave like a disease and can even cause the formation of antibodies in the bloodstream."

"You're murdering him! He's almost dead now!"

"Oh, nonsense. The chemfets didn't kill you, did they? I wouldn't kill him, would I? After all this? Why would I throw away all this effort?"

"But you're wrong! Your chemfets for me were much simpler. He's *dying!*"

"Where is he?"

She paused, suddenly realizing the dilemma that Derec and she had never solved. They could not force Dr. Avery to cooperate. He had to be convinced.

"The central computer is calling. For several moments now, I have ignored a little light on my table here. I have done so because I know what it signifies, I believe. Excuse me, will you?"

Ariel stared at him, amazed at his composure and his refusal to believe her.

A small section of the table in front of Dr. Avery swiveled to reveal a computer console on what had been the underside of the table. "Would you like to hear?" He pushed a button. "I'll set it on voice, which I usually find intrusive. Report," he said into the console.

"HUNTERS REPORT APPREHENSION OF HUMAN NAMED DEREC."

"Thought so," said Dr. Avery pleasantly. "Report status of Hunter project."

"THE FOLLOWING HAVE BEEN APPREHENDED AND ARE HELD ON THE NORTH SLOPE OF THE VALLEY: DEREC, JEFF LEONG, MANDELBROT, WOLRUF. STILL MISSING: ARIEL WELSH."

Dr. Avery laughed casually. "Now, who would have thought I could outperform my own team of Hunter robots?"

Ariel's heart was pounding with tension. If Derec was already in Avery's control, very little risk was left. "Dr. Avery. Will you agree to a test?"

"Eh? What kind of test? Haven't we had enough testing around here for a while?"

"Have the robots check David and see if he is in danger from the chemfets. They'll tell you."

"A party," said Dr. Avery. "An excellent idea. I'll have the Hunters bring everyone. We'll have a party." He tossed the object in his hand over his shoulder into the fire.

Ariel saw it clearly for the first time. It was a small model of a humanoid robot.

CHAPTER 20

TO RULE IN ROBOT CITY

Ariel watched the gray stones, or whatever they were, in the wall dissolve into air for a moment and the Hunters brought in their captives through the opening. The first one carried Derec gently in his arms as though he were a giant baby, but limp and unconscious. The second entered holding Jeff Leong firmly by one upper arm as they walked. The third held Wolruf cradled on one elbow and the fourth marched in with Mandelbrot lying over his shoulder, completely shut down.

The stone wall reformed behind them.

"Clear the table," said Dr. Avery. "Don't worry about where the stuff goes."

The Hunter carrying Mandelbrot laid him down on the floor and then extended his arm along the full width of the table at the far end. He then walked down the length of the table as his arm knocked everything it struck onto the floor. By the time he had reached the near end, Dr. Avery had himself swept aside the items within his own reach.

Ariel watched in horror. She had never seen a humanoid

robot act so messily, even destructively, on a casual instruction. This one must have known that Dr. Avery wanted to be taken literally and did not want him to remove the items on the table with any care.

"Put him down." Dr. Avery nodded to the Hunter holding Derec. Then he waved at the one carrying Mandelbrot. "And turn him on, will you? This won't be much of a party with so many people feeling unsociable."

Ariel felt some relief as the Hunter located Mandelbrot's controls and activated him again. "Mandelbrot, tell him. Tell Dr. Avery what's happening to Derec."

Mandelbrot scanned the room quickly. His observation probably told him as much about the current situation as Ariel already knew. "Dr. Avery," he said clearly. "Derec has undergone extreme physical debilitation that continues to increase. He believes that the chemfets you placed in his body are killing him. My observation of his symptoms confirms that likelihood."

"Doesn't anybody here want to have a party?" Dr. Avery sighed. "Everyone is so morbid. Say, Mr. Leong. Haven't we met before? Not lately and not on this planet, however."

"That's right," Jeff said sullenly. "You were more sociable in those days, yourself."

Dr. Avery pushed back his chair and stood up. Trailing the fingers of one hand along the table, he walked down its length looking at the motionless figure of Derec. "He has done very well. I have not given him any challenge he cannot surmount."

"Till *now*," Ariel insisted. "How can you take a risk like this? Even your own robots wouldn't risk his life for a test."

Jeff, Wolruf, and Mandelbrot all looked at her in surprise.

"Oh, I don't think he'll have any trouble. He'll be fine."
Dr. Avery nodded to himself.

"Aren't you even going to test him? Check him out in
your laboratory?" She cried.

"He'll be fine. Let's have a party." Dr. Avery turned to
the Hunter who had brought Derec in. "Take him to one of
the guest rooms, though. We can't have a party with a guest
lying motionless on the dining table, can we?"

"Hold it!" Ariel got between Derec and that Hunter.
"Can't you understand that he's dying?"

"Pick him up," Dr. Avery ordered.

The Hunter gently but firmly moved Ariel aside and
lifted Derec. She threw her arms around Derec's shoulders
and hung on. "Wait! Mandelbrot, they're letting him die!"

Mandelbrot was standing by the Hunter who had
brought him in. That Hunter, however, had one hand resting
on Mandelbrot's open control panel. At the slightest resis-
tance from Mandelbrot, the Hunter would shut him down
again.

The next sequence of events took place very quickly,
some of it timed by the speed of positronic brains.

Suddenly Jeff, who was still held by one Hunter,
reached over and started grabbing Mandelbrot's Hunter by
the neck, feeling around quickly for his controls. The Hunter, required by the Third Law to protect himself, grasped
Jeff's arm in his other hand. In the tiny fraction of a second
that the Third Law imperative was foremost in the Hunter's
mind, Mandelbrot stepped away and closed his own control
panel with his flexible cellular arm.

From the moment Mandelbrot was free, the battle was
on. His belief that Derec's life was in danger forced him
under the First Law to take Ariel's anxiety seriously. At the

same time, the Hunters believed Dr. Avery's declaration that Derec was not in danger, so under the Second Law they followed their orders from him to detain and control the others.

Mandelbrot also shot out an array of information through his comlink to the Hunters. He told them of Derec's delicate condition, of Ariel's memory failures, of their physical hardships. In the tiny instant it required, he demanded that they back away from Derec and Ariel immediately or risk major violations of the First Law.

He did not know if it would work, but even the slightest hesitation and doubt on their part would help.

Even as Mandelbrot sent these signals, he moved toward Derec. Ariel let go of Derec to grab the Hunter holding him, knowing that the Hunter would be impeded by the necessity of not harming Derec or her. In a couple of quick moves, Mandelbrot's flexible arm had shut down this Hunter in a motionless standing position, still holding Derec. Mandelbrot and Ariel lifted Derec and placed him back on the table.

One Hunter had now taken Wolruf and Jeff under each arm and had lifted them into the air where they squirmed helplessly.

"You're hurting me!" Jeff shouted. "First Law violation!"

The Hunter was not convinced.

"Stop them!" Dr. Avery screamed. "Don't hurt them, but stop them! And don't collide with David! His condition is too fragile!"

"You've got to believe us!" Ariel shouted, turning to plead with him. "You don't want him hurt, either! Just test him!"

They stood face-to-face now and Ariel saw a strangely twisted expression on his face. It was an angry smile of triumph. For the first time since meeting him, she understood that he truly was crazy—and beyond persuasion by reason.

"You did this!" Dr. Avery hissed in her face. "Without you, these extremes would not have been necessary. Leave him alone!"

"How *dare* you blame this on me?" She screamed, and in a mixture of frustration, rage, and exhaustion she lost her temper completely. Unbound by any Laws except her conscience, she launched herself at him angrily, grabbing his sideburns in both hands.

One of the four Hunters had been shut down. Another was holding Jeff and Wolruf away from Mandelbrot. Mandelbrot was trying to reach the unguarded control panel of this one with his flexible arm while using his other arm to grapple with the other two Hunters. With all the robots' attention focused on each other across the room, they did not notice or respond to the potential harm Ariel and Dr. Avery might do to each other.

Dr. Avery grimaced in pain and growled at her as they shuffled around in a tight struggle.

Deep in the darkness of Derec's mind, robots marched. He was lying on his back in darkness as robots stepped in rhythmic time with a precision only robots could maintain. They strode by him in files that split at his feet and tramped past him on either side, their heavy feet pounding by his head. He was ignored, insignificant, not even present in their positronic awareness.

Out of darkness, the robots marched. A slight glow of skyline shone behind them but mostly he could see only a bloodred sky above, one that had never really existed, where space stretched endlessly beyond the planet. Still the robots

WILLIAM F. WU

streamed past, intent on their destination with that single-mindedness so evident in the Avery creations.

Avery. Avery. Avery. The beat of pounding feet seemed to take on the name. It was name of his enemy, the name of . . . of . . .

His dream shifted. Even as the robots continued to march, he watched strange green shapes, some cubic and some pyramidal, rising in the air around him. When he reached for them, missing, he floated up after them. They turned, light shining off their different facets as they rose. He snagged one and it became a computer console under his hands.

He was floating higher in the air now. The blood night of Robot City threw its myriad streets into a golden glow without logic or explanation, and still the robots marched. His fingers seemed to type without thought from his mind: "Stop them."

"NO," answered the central computer.

"Stop the city."

"NO."

"Why not?"

"WHO ARE YOU?"

"I am I am I am . . . who am I?"

"WHERE ARE YOU?"

"I am . . . Robot City."

"ERROR. I AM ROBOT CITY," said the central computer. "WHO ARE YOU?"

"Who am I?"

"YOU ARE DAVID AVERY."

"I am David Avery?" Derec stared at the name on the dream console. The dream console was green, made of a floating pyramid like a tiny Compass Tower . . . made of a chemfet.

399

He looked around. This wasn't the real central computer. The blood-red sky told him how small he was. He was floating in his own bloodstream, watching chemfets and Robot City grow inside him . . .

"I am David Avery," he typed. "I am David Avery. This is my bloodstream, my body, my . . . Robot City."

"ACKNOWLEDGED," said the central computer.

The robots stopped marching. He floated in the air high above them now and looked down on the endless rows of robots. Every single Avery robot on the planet raised its head to await Derec's commands.

He raised his head and shouted, "Robot City is mine! I am David Avery and I am Robot City!"

At his shout, the sky split. The scene dissipated. He blinked and gradually heard more yells and scraping sounds around him. A chandelier was blazing over him. He took in a deep breath—and realized that, for the first time in a very long time, his body felt normal.

His mind was clearing slowly as he came awake. His body was tired, and cold with dampness, but the weird stiffness was gone. He was no longer in physical danger.

"Derec!" Ariel yelled. "You're awake? Tell him! Tell Avery what's happening to you."

Avery? With a surge of fear and anger, Derec sat up and found himself on a long table. He turned. Ariel and—his father, Dr. Avery, were scuffling around in a circle.

"I'm all right," Derec said hoarsely.

"What?" Ariel looked at him in surprise. "Then help me!"

"No!" Dr. Avery roared. "No! This is not right! You must help me!"

"Help you?" Derec shouted angrily. "You're crazy!"

"Kill them!" Dr. Avery screamed at the Hunters. "Kill them! You must kill them or everything will be for naught!"

Ariel pulled free of him and turned toward the two Hunters who were still functioning; Mandelbrot had succeeded in shutting down a second one. "Dr. Avery is mad. You understand? He's ... he's malfunctioned. You remember the Laws of Humanics that the Supervisors were trying to devise?"

Dr. Avery had backed away toward the fireplace. "You must save us!" he shouted at the Hunters. "Kill them!"

"Listen to him," Ariel called out, now more in control. "His orders violate the First Law. You can't trust his orders any more. Orders that violate the Laws of Robotics also violate the Second Law of Humanics, which says humans will not give robots unreasonable orders. Listen to him, and you'll understand that he can't be followed anymore." If the Hunters had learned how she and Jeff and Derec had shut down Pei, they wouldn't listen to her, either.

The remaining Hunters had not moved. One held Jeff and Wolruf. The other was in a stand-off with Mandelbrot, as each tried to reach the manual controls of the other to shut him down.

"Acknowledged," said the Hunter holding Jeff and Wolruf. "Dr. Avery's instructions cannot be followed. However, the central computer also directs us. We are still under orders to detain the members of your group without harming them."

Dr. Avery had cowered into a corner, still shouting.

"I am Robot City now," said Derec. "The chemfets in my body have matured and I have reprogrammed them." He visualized the computer console in his mind. Maybe he wouldn't always have to do that, but right now it made the task easier. "Central computer," he thought. "Eliminate the orders to the Hunter robots regarding Derec or David Avery, Ariel Welsh, the robot Mandelbrot, and the caninoid alien Wolruf. Then notify all pertinent robots of the change." Then aloud he said, "Hunters. A new order should come through to you—"

"Acknowledged," said the Hunter in front of Mandelbrot. He straightened, dropping his guard.

"Acknowledged," echoed the other Hunter, releasing Jeff and Wolruf.

"I received it also," said Mandelbrot.

"Now, then," said Derec, turning to Dr. Avery.

Dr. Avery was standing in the corner of the room to one side of the giant fireplace. As the others turned to watch him, he drew himself up. "Consider what you have accomplished, my son," he said. "Think of it. Everything I envisioned to this point has come to pass as I intended. Well, almost—never mind this young woman. You rule in Robot City. Soon you will rule in every Robot City, in thousands of them throughout all the galaxies."

A stinging sadness came over Derec, draining his anger. "You're . . . not right. Not right in the head. You started out seeking a utopia and instead you've gotten sidetracked. This has become a springboard for power, not for good. Maybe if you took it easy for a while, got some professional advice . . ."

"You dare to order *me?*" Dr. Avery yelled. "No! You join me! I order it!"

"I'm not a robot. You can't order me." Derec turned to the Hunters. "Please detain my . . . detain Dr. Avery without harming him."

The two Hunters started forward.

With a twisted sneer, Dr. Avery lifted a small object in one hand: a Key to Perihelion. He laughed derisively and then vanished.

Derec walked slowly to the head of the table, still looking at the space where Dr. Avery had stood. His relief was tinged with melancholy at understanding his father's condition.

Everyone was watching him.

He turned at his father's chair, resting one hand on the back of it. "Mandelbrot, please put those items on the floor back on the table. Hunters, your task is over. Please return to your holding area, or wherever you normally reside."

The robots obeyed.

"Are you really okay?" Ariel asked, moving toward him. "David?"

He grinned and put his arm around her. "I guess so. David seems to be okay, and so is Derec."

"I seem to be okay, too." She put her arms around him and they embraced.

None of them wanted to split up for the night or go exploring for bedrooms in the Avery estate. As tired as they were, Derec, Ariel, Jeff, and Wolruf were able to sleep by the fire even on the hard floor. Derec knew that Dr. Avery might have transported elsewhere on the planet and could still pose a danger, but he doubted any threat would be immediate. Just before going to sleep, he gave a general order throughout Robot City that all robots were to remain where they were until further notice, except for minimal activities to keep the city operating. That way he would have time later to figure out exactly what status the city was in and how to return the robots from their assembly points to normal duties. With Mandelbrot standing by and Robot City under his own mental control, he fell into a genuine sleep.

The next morning, Ariel pointed out the table console to Derec in case he had a use for it. He really didn't, finding that he was able to contact any branch of the computer system on the planet with his mind. This morning he started with the one in Dr. Avery's kitchen.

The entire group, including Mandelbrot, sat at the long table with a real breakfast served by two kitchen robots. It included fresh produce and dishes processed from produce instead of from limited nutrient tanks. Derec and Ariel shared their separate adventures with everyone, then Wolruf and Jeff gave their stories. Since Mandelbrot had been shut down for much of the time they had been separated, he had little to tell.

When the anecdotes had ended, Derec sat at the head of the table in an upbeat mood, thinking over his new responsibilities.

"I guess I can have the central computer worry about the particulars of what I have to do," he mused. "If I instruct the central computer to return all the robots to their normal duties, it will do all the organization itself."

"But you can really control it with your mind?" Ariel asked. "And you can program robots mentally, too?"

"Apparently I can. I'm still getting used to the idea myself."

"To all your human attributes," said Mandelbrot, "you have now added some of the advantages of a robot."

Jeff laughed. "Without the liabilities, if you know what I mean." He winked.

While the others laughed, Derec was aware of a message

in his mind from the central computer, answering a question he had posed.

"NO EVIDENCE OF DR. AVERY ON THE PLANET HAS BEEN REPORTED," said the central computer.

If Dr. Avery was here at all, Derec realized, he now had all the disadvantages they had had while on the run from him. They now had all the resources he had used. Even more, considering that they were not burdened by insanity.

Considering Dr. Avery's paranoia, Derec felt certain that he had left the planet. Maybe he had gone home to Aurora. Perhaps he had returned to his apartment on Earth, or had other hideaways in reserve, as well.

"Thank 'u," said Wolruf. "Good brreakfasst. Could sleep morr now."

"I believe we can locate comfortable sleeping rooms here," said Mandelbrot. "The luxury of this room and this meal imply similar luxury elsewhere in this residence."

"I'll find a way to shut down the booby-traps and riddles," said Derec, grinning at Ariel.

She laughed. "It's hard to believe. For the first time, Robot City will beat peace, running smoothly, and no longer full of mystery."

"And you have plenty of Keys to Perihelion with which to travel," said Mandelbrot. "Perhaps Wolruf can be sent home."

She shrugged her caninoid shoulders. "Resst first."

"I wonder what kind of shape the ship is in," said Jeff. "I only rented it."

"Don't worry," said Derec. "I'll have the *Minneapolis* fully repaired, cleaned, polished, and outfitted for you. We're more than square for any debt you felt you owed us. But you're welcome to stay as long as you want."

"Thanks," said Jeff. He shook his head, grinning. "Robot City. It's never been a dull town."

When everyone had finished breakfast, Jeff and Wolruf excused themselves to accompany Mandelbrot in further exploration of Dr. Avery's immense quarters.

Later, after function robots had cleared the table and Derec and Ariel were alone in the great hall, he stood gazing into the fire that continued to blaze. He still felt melancholy.

"Is something wrong?" Ariel asked quietly.

"Oh . . . I was just thinking about Dr. Avery. How his wonderful plans got all twisted. And how after researching cultures with Professor Leong and all, he just seemed to drop that subject after a certain point. He is obviously a brilliant man, yet he threw so much away." He looked up at her. "I found out something, too."

"What?"

"I'm not sure we stopped him in time after all. From what I can get out of the central computer, I think some of the robots may have launched themselves from their assembly points before I cancelled that instruction."

Ariel drew in a quick breath. "If that's true, then they will be building more Robot Cities, just as Dr. Avery wanted. And who knows what precise orders he gave them?"

"I may be able to find that out in the computer," said Derec. "Maybe I can even call them back somehow; I won't know till I spend some time on it. But there's something else."

"What? What's wrong?"

"I have my identity back, but . . . I still have amnesia. I don't have all my memory back." He turned to look at her. "Finding my father wasn't exactly constructive."

"Maybe you could . . . oh, I don't know. Perhaps locating your mother would help. Or some of the Avery robots might know of a way to help. Just think how much help you might get from Robot City and even the robots that may have left."

Derec nodded. "I haven't given up. Don't worry about that." He grinned. "That isn't me. And from what I've seen, it isn't you, either."

"It certainly isn't . . . David."

Ariel laughed, looked into his eyes, and tossed her hair back. On an impulse, he slid his arms around her waist and drew her close. Then he kissed her waiting lips and felt her arms tighten around his neck.